DIVISION OF CHAOS

THE BOOKS OF THE CUARI
BOOK 2

MARIE ANDREAS

OTHER BOOKS BY MARIE ANDREAS

The Lost Ancients
Book One: The Glass Gargoyle
Book Two: The Obsidian Chimera
Book Three: The Emerald Dragon
Book Four: The Sapphire Manticore
Book Five: The Golden Basilisk
Book Six: The Diamond Sphinx

The Lost Ancients: Dragon's Blood
Book One: The Seeker's Chest

The Asarlaí Wars Trilogy
Book One: Warrior Wench
Book Two: Victorious Dead
Book Three: Defiant Ruin

The Code of the Keeper
Book One: Traitor's Folly

The Adventures of Smith and Jones
A Curious Invasion
The Mayhem of Mermaids

Broken Veil
Book One: The Girl with the Iron Wing
Book Two: An Uncommon Truth of Dying
Book Three: Through a Veil Darkly

Books of the Cuari
Book One: Essence of Chaos
Book Two: Division of Chaos
Book Three: Destruction of Chaos

ACKNOWLEDGMENTS

Writing is easy—take a bunch of weird ideas and mush them together. And then lie about how easy it is. Writing is hard, I love it, but it's hard. It would be impossible without a lot of other folks.

I'd like to thank everyone who has ever supported me, read chapters, edited, let me cry on their shoulder, read my books, given nice reviews, and/or bought me soothing beverages. I could never have done this without ALL of you. I can't list you all here, but you mean the world to me.

My awesome editor- Jessa Slade—thank you for keeping the mayhem under control. Lisa Andreas for beta reading and proofreading above and beyond the call of duty. Thanks to the naming of the boat- Jeff Neinast. Any errors or mistakes are completely mine.

And to the two extremely talented artists of Joolz & Jarling (Julie Nicolls and Uwe Jarling) thank you for a gorgeous cover! And thank you to The Kim Killion Group for the interior formatting.

To all my readers—thank you for coming along for the ride!

CHAPTER ONE

———◆———

JENNA WAS LYING on her back across the huge bed, her long dark hair dangling almost to the floor as she contemplated life as she knew it. So much for coming back as heroes. This wasn't what she'd expected would happen when they returned to Lithunane. They'd won the battle in the Markare, but lost the king. Ghortin was sure King Daylin, his long-time friend and Storm's father, had been killed and replaced not long after he'd been taken. Three months before they rescued what they thought was the king.

Spending those months looking for him, then finding out he'd been murdered and replaced by a demonspawn long before, hadn't been horrific for everyone. And they'd lost many good people trying to get him back.

As soul weary and physically exhausted as they were when they returned, being locked up the moment they walked into the city of Lithunane had been a cruel blow. And a confusing one.

Storm's brother Resstlin, the current heir to the throne, had been in disagreement with the actions of both Storm and Ghortin long before the battle. But this was too much. Jenna had stayed back, ready to throw whatever spell might help as all three started yelling at each other.

Storm and Ghortin backed down and went to speak to the heir in private. The moment they left, the returning fighters had been locked in their barracks. Including Crell's rangers. That hadn't gone over well, but Jenna was escorted away before she could find out more.

Those who had housing in the palace, such as Jenna,

Keanin, and Edgar, were locked in their rooms. They'd
been set up with food, water, and no idea when they'd
be released. Jenna had enough magic and training that
she could blow the door apart if needed. But Ghortin's
last words, before he stalked off to go smash some heads
together, had been to stay put and no magic.

That had been six hours ago.

Napping hadn't worked, her mind wouldn't slow down
enough for that. So, she waited.

She almost didn't hear the soft knock and the unlock-
ing of the door that followed.

From her position she had a good view of the doorway
when it opened, so there wasn't a reason to sit up.

Storm, also known as Prince Corin, cautiously stuck
his head in. Long deep brown hair, sharp wide blue eyes,
pointed ears, and an inhuman beauty. He was a kelar,
an elven-like species. Coming to this world from Earth
almost a year ago had been painful for her in many ways,
but being around him was not one of them. Even if she
wasn't completely sure what was going on between them
or if a prince could be involved with a commoner. Even
better, one who wasn't from this world. Yeah, things were
too complicated right now to contemplate relationships.

She still didn't sit up but nodded for him to come in.
"About time. I was getting very tired of trying to see pic-
tures in the beams." She pointed to the dark wood beams
crossing the light ceiling.

Storm looked up. "I only see wood."

"You have to look very, very carefully and be very, very
bored." Jenna stretched and rolled herself to her stomach,
finally crawling off the bed. "Ouch, I hadn't realized I'd
been in one position that long. Now, what the hell has
been going on? Ghortin took off, you took off, and we
get locked up? I heard yelling a few hours ago, but no
one came to tell us anything."

"I'm sorry. I didn't know he'd locked everyone up until

a few minutes ago. The yelling, which I also didn't know about, was Crell and her people taking exception to being locked up." He frowned. "She's in the dungeon now, and the rest of her rangers are locked in the barracks. Things are more complicated than Ghortin or I thought, and my brother is being an ass." He sighed. "Let's get the others out of their rooms."

"They locked up Crell in the dungeon? What is wrong with these people?" Jenna wanted to go break her friend out now. Storm looked like he felt the same, yet wasn't moving for the door. He must have a good reason for waiting, one he'd better share soon.

"As I said, it's very complicated and Resstlin is an ass. I didn't see what happened, but I do know Crell was pissed. I have a feeling that derawri temper of hers got the best of her when they tried to put all of her people in locked barracks. We'll get her out, don't worry."

Jenna debated adding a knife to her ensemble. Just in case. "I still don't get why we were all locked up. Or treated so badly the minute we arrived." She tucked one of her smaller blades into the top of her boot when Storm was looking elsewhere. Openly carrying weapons was frowned upon within the palace, but it never hurt to have something. Edgar had taught her that.

Storm glanced at the guards at the end of the hall as they left her room. He kept his voice low. "I have some theories based on my yelling match with Resstlin, but I'd rather wait until we get the others. We can talk more freely in my room."

Jenna nodded and dropped her voice as they walked. "Is your brother sending troops to the Markare? There could still be demonspawn there. What about Raven-hearst?" They hadn't found Ravenhearst with the demonspawn encampment after the battle, but she knew he was involved. Even before one of the enemy soldiers had called out for him as he died.

"Resstlin doesn't believe us, he's not sending anyone." The not-being-armed caveat didn't hold for the royal family, and Storm's hand tightened on the hilt of his sword. His jaw also looked tight enough to snap.

"What? Is he that clueless?" She glanced around the hall. Luckily no one was around. "Sorry. You don't think he's working with Ravenhearst, do you?" Ravenhearst had been an ambassador from the human kingdom of Strann. And apparently a traitor who might or might not have been working with the demonspawn that had crossed into this world. There was no doubt in Jenna's mind that he was involved. She just hadn't been able to prove it. Yet.

Storm shook his head sharply. "No, of course not. Resstlin may be a lot of things, but he's loyal to Traana-faeren." He stopped in front of the next hallway. "Our people should all be in their own rooms, but they might not know they're free yet. You take this side; I'll take the other."

"Aren't the doors locked? I heard a distinct locking going on when I was put in mine."

"They were magically locked. But the guards and I had a discussion and once they released the locking spell on your door, the others would have dropped as well." Storm looked like he should have magic, with his elven-looking ears and grace—but he was magic numb. He couldn't use it, nor in most cases, sense it. Sometimes his annoyance at that fact came out in his voice—like now.

"I'll start with Keanin." Jenna knew her friend would be relieved to be free. The flashy kelar wasn't fond of being locked up alone. She knocked on the door first, then stuck her head in.

"Come on, Keanin, you're free." Not a bit of rich auburn hair was in sight. Only a massive pile of blankets in the middle of his bed.

"I don't care what you say," Keanin's muffled voice

came from under the mound of covers. "I'm not coming out; in fact, I may not come out until sometime next seedtide. Come back then." The mound curled in tighter.

Jenna gave a sharp jerk on the outer blanket, succeeding in loosening the main layer from Keanin's grip. "It's okay now, Keanin. Honest. Storm needs us all together to sort things out, that's all."

He raised his head out of the covers enough so his tawny golden eyes were visible. However, he still had a death-grip on the remaining blanket. "How do you know? Things aren't normal. Home should be normal."

Jenna gave him a sad smile. The kelar noble didn't ask for much in life, just to be left alone in his status as adopted kin to the royal family. And for life to stay the same. In the last year, he'd witnessed a brutal massacre during what should have been a joyous ball, been dragged across the length of this land against his will, lost friends, been kidnapped by the demonspawn replica of a king who treated him like a son, and seen that replica destroyed to save his life.

All in all, she couldn't blame him for thinking that hiding under a bunch of covers in his room seemed like a proper action. Jenna almost wanted to join him.

"I'm sure everything is fine here. People were surprised to see us, that's all." At a slight narrowing of his elegant almond-shaped eyes, she hastily added. "Do you want me to poke everyone I see to make sure they aren't demonspawn?" Demonspawn were monsters out of a twisted nightmare, but they could take over the form of people they murdered. Only when they were wounded and their blood ran green was it clear what they were.

Keanin let the blanket fall from around his face. "Could you?"

Jenna seized the chance, and the blanket, and pulled the rest of it off. "Keanin, get out of bed. We have to find the others." A thought hit her. Not nice to threaten him, but they didn't have time for him to wallow all day. "If you don't come right now I'll remind Ghortin about your magic lessons. I think he's almost forgotten by now." Keanin's mage gifts had come as a shock to everyone, and while his innate Power was amazing, his control over it was abysmal. Ghortin had been trying to drill him on the basics since his gifts came to light. And Keanin had fought him every bit of the way.

The lean and graceful kelar noble leaped to his feet so quickly that Jenna stumbled to keep her balance. "No need. I am up and ready to face the current disasters." Amazingly, after all his lurking under mounds of covers, not a single strand of long auburn hair was out of place and not a single wrinkle dared to appear in his deep green tunic. Jenna sighed. Only Keanin could constantly look so perfect. The man would make the fabled elves of Middle Earth green with envy.

With another sigh, she led him out into the hall. In the time it had taken her to get Keanin out of bed, Storm had liberated two more of their companions. Sir Edgar and Armsmaster Garlen both looked seriously pissed at having been locked in their rooms. She was surprised either of them had let it happen, as both could easily have fought their way out. Like Storm, they both must have decided to give the heir a chance to sort things out. From the looks on both their faces, that chance was over now.

With a nod to Keanin, Storm motioned down the corridor. "I thought we could talk in private. We can't do anything until Ghortin returns, but I refuse to not be prepared."

Keanin's eyes got wider. Storm patted his friend's shoulder. "No, I won't ask you to fight with us if we have to fight our way out of here."

"Fight? In the palace?" Keanin's wide eyes were focused on Jenna now. "You said things were normal."

Jenna took his arm and propelled him toward Storm's

room. "I lied."

Keanin was silent as Armsmaster Garlan walked alongside them. Jenna noticed far more lines than she remembered on his weathered face. His lips were lined and pale.

"Are you all right, Garlan?"

The stocky half-human/half-kelar shook his head. "Sixty years I've trained royal guards. Over sixty years I have been the trusted man-at-arms of this kingdom, confidante to the king himself. And now I am called a traitor." The venom in his voice was tinged with deep grief, but his face was carved in stone.

"No one has called you a traitor."

"Corin's brother did one and the same when he locked us up. I can't believe that simpleton is going to be king." It was good he didn't have anything in his hands, they were clenched so tightly they looked ready to snap something.

CHAPTER TWO

———◆———

IN ANOTHER PART of the palace, Ghortin fought to keep his temper under control. He'd been sent in circles for hours, trying to find out what was going on and how to get Crell out of the dungeon before someone got mad enough to break her out. He'd let Storm and Resstlin deal with the issues on their own at first and as far as he could tell, nothing had changed.

But by damn, he was cornering Resstlin now. The last three months had been too hellish for the heir to do something this foolish. Ghortin himself had been seriously shaken by the recent disaster. Twice this mysterious enemy had reached out and overpowered *him*. Other mages often gossiped of Ghortin's quite healthy ego, but it was based on fact. The way with which he was pushed aside by this unnamed enemy was truly terrifying.

And not something he intended to admit to anyone.

A guardsman stepped in front of Ghortin as he neared the King's chambers. "I am sorry, mastermage, but His Highness isn't…"

Ghortin glared at the man until his babbling stopped. "I have no care what His Highness is, or is not, doing." He stepped in closer toward the guard but kept his voice low. "I do care about what *I* am about to do, which is talk to him. You can either step aside like a life-loving young man, or you can spend the rest of your short existence wishing you'd taken up farming."

To his credit, the guardsman didn't flinch. His skin faded a few shades and his eyes became unnaturally round. Wiping away the growing beads of sweat on his upper lip, the guardsman stepped clear of the doorway.

"Wise boy." Ghortin's smile was almost real as he patted the guard's arm. Without waiting for more guards to arrive, he shoved open the two heavy ornate doors.

"I said I was not to be disturbed." Resstlin's dark head shot up from the pile of papers he'd been reading. "Good day, Master Ghortin. I should have been expecting this visit. Please, have a seat."

Ghortin ignored Resstlin's outstretched hand and stomped past the offered chair. "Thank you, no. This needs to be dealt with standing."

He was rewarded by a tic that appeared in Resstlin's check. Let him be nervous. He should be. Resstlin had always been a pompous blowhard even as a child. But there was more to it now; a level of superiority over even the mastermage.

That would not do.

"I am so sorry; I did not mean for them to keep *you* under guard. I was simply assuring that any potential traitors to the crown were secured." His eyes drifted back to the pile of papers on his desk.

"They didn't keep me under guard. They managed to send me to every single room in this palace looking for you." There was no way Resstlin didn't know what had been done. Ghortin leaned close. "And none of those people are traitors. Nor are the ones who gave their lives out there." He stared into Resstlin's eyes until the prince pulled back.

"Now, now." Resstlin coughed in an attempt to pull further away without looking like he was. "Corin's report claimed that traitors were found in the ranks. I was merely being cautious."

"Demonspawn. Not traitors. Vast difference. Good people, *our people*, were murdered so that those creatures could take their places." Ghortin gave Resstlin some breathing space and began pacing.

Resstlin pulled himself up. "See here, couldn't some of the others who returned be demonspawn as well? We have no proof of any of it."

Ghortin whirled on him. "Do you take your brother and me for fools? We checked *everyone* after the battle." He forced Resstlin to meet his eyes. "If you want a trai- tor, look to your friend Ravenhearst."

Resstlin had drawn back during Ghortin's tirade, but the mention of Ravenhearst drew him back up to full height. "How can you possibly accuse Lord Ravenhearst, while no one will admit who killed my father?"

"The creature who took him from the ball four months ago killed him. The same one who took and tried to kill *me*, killed him." Ghortin took a deep breath. He and Corin had discussed this, and Corin had finally agreed to let Ghortin tell Resstlin. The two brothers had never gotten along, and this information was going to hit hard. "Corin killed the demonspawn who was pretending to be Daylin. He did it to save all of us. My magic was nothing compared to what that monster could pull in. We were overwhelmed."

That was an admission that would take a few decades to process, providing he lived that long. "Trust me, I knew your father long before you were born, the creature who died *was not him*. And yes, I meant what I said, Raven- hearst is a traitor to Traanafaeren. I'd give him the benefit of being a demonspawn himself except that he's always been so slimy I think the mage council itself would be hard-pressed to tell the difference." He leaned even closer to the prince. "And one of the traitors pleaded for Raven- hearst to come to rescue him right before he died."

Resstlin took a step back, his face darkening with

anger. "I do not doubt that all of you, particularly you, have been through a horrible ordeal—which is why I forbade Corin from the journey in the first place—however, I will not sit by and let you slander an honest man in my presence!"

Ghortin held back the angry retort he was thinking and studied the young man-who-would-be-king. Resstlin was so unlike Corin, it was hard to believe they were brothers unless they got angry. He took a deep breath and lowered his voice. "It's good that you question my attack on Lord Ravenhearst. As heir to the throne, you must take all aspects of a situation into mind before action is ordered. I wish you had held the same regard for the people who fought that monster and the creatures it brought with it in the Markare." He picked up a gloriously hued wine glass and slowly twirled it in his fingers. It was a simple calming spell but one both he and Resstlin needed right now. "I can show you where Ravenhearst's true loyalty lies." He spoke softly, making Resstlin lean forward to hear him. "But you must bring him here."

Resstlin's eyes darkened with a brief flicker of doubt, then he turned to look out the large window. After a few moments, he finally went to the chamber doors and spoke to a guard. He kept his voice low so Ghortin couldn't hear the exact words, but Resstlin was more subdued when he returned. "I have sent for him. But you must understand, Lord Ravenhearst has been a solid supporter during the recent tragedy. I'm sure he's innocent; obviously, the traitor who called for him was simply trying to stir mischief."

Something Jenna and he had seen in Irundail came to mind. "Was he here the entire time we were gone? He wasn't called back to Strann?" After the attack at the ball, all of the royal family except Resstlin had been magically transported to the far north city of Irundail. It was the former capital for Traanafaeren and a secure location for the royal family.

Storm had been gravely wounded during the attack, but hung onto Jenna as the spell hit, so she went up as well. Ghortin's body had been taken by the rogue mage who also captured King Daylin, but he'd transferred the essence of himself into Jenna's mind during the attack. Since he'd been residing in Jenna's head at the time when she swore she saw Ravenhearst in Irundail, he believed what she'd seen. But better to find out what had gone on at this end.

"Of course, he was here." Resstlin paused. "Well, he did have to leave at one point and later said he'd been called back to Strann. However, he convinced the empress that Strann's interests would be best served by helping us cope with our losses."

"I see." Ghortin softened his voice. Ravenhearst was either a hidden mage or had one backing him. If a mage had tampered with Resstlin's memories, the wrong word from Ghortin could trigger a spelled response. And probably a nasty one. "However, immediately after the attack, when we'd all been taken to Irundail—he was here then?" Only the rest of the royal family, and Jenna, had been pulled through to Irundail. Ravenhearst would not have been drawn in by the family spell. That didn't mean he didn't have a pet mage ready to send him there though.

Resstlin looked disgusted. "Of course he was here, he was at the ball." An odd look crept across his face and he shook his head. "Now that you mention it, where was he? No, he must have been there, where else would he have gone? But when did I see him next? He had to have been there, you're trying to confuse me. I'm sure he was there." His forehead was still wrinkled in confusion.

The huge doors swung open as Resstlin finished his interesting conversation with himself. "You sent for me, my prince?"

Ghortin kept his gut in check at the florid and overly solicitous bow the pampered blond ambassador flung at Resstlin. The blond human looked better groomed than the prince himself.

Resstlin narrowed his eyes, then shook it off and smiled at Ravenhearst.

"Thank you for being prompt, Ambassador. Please be seated." Resstlin turned his back to them, but not before Ghortin saw a worried frown cross his broad face. Ravenhearst saw it as well.

"My prince! What has happened to displease you? Please tell me and I'll—"

Resstlin cut him off with a flick of his wrist. "No. Please excuse this intrusion, but mastermage Ghortin has a few questions he wishes to ask you."

The look on the thin ambassador's face as he turned toward Ghortin was predatory and not altogether human. Ghortin briefly wondered if they had misjudged and the demonspawn had gotten more of their own into the palace citizens. His earlier comment aside, it *was* difficult to tell Ravenhearst from a demonspawn.

With care for any imaginary dirt lurking on the offered chair, Ravenhearst lowered himself and carefully crossed his legs. "Ask what you will. I have nothing to hide from the prince."

"Very well, *Ambassador* Ravenhearst." Ghortin resumed his pacing. "How long have you been a follower of Qhazborh?" Qhazborh was the single embodiment of a group of gods and goddesses on the side of evil. Their followers had been fading up until a few years ago. But the resurgence had been subtle enough that it had gone unnoticed. Until they started attacking villages and towns.

"What?" Resstlin spun around. "Now see here, I agreed to questions, but not heresy!"

Because his eyes were on Ghortin, Resstlin missed the

brief change that over took Ravenhearst's face. Something dark and mocking lingered there for a few seconds before it vanished.

Ghortin said nothing but continued to watch Ravenhearst. He knew the man wouldn't answer such a question, but he hoped his sudden leap might make Ravenhearst give something away. Their fears had been correct, Ravenhearst was on the other side and might have been changed into demonspawn.

Ravenhearst rose from his seat, waving down Resstlin's protestations with a negligent hand. "I have no fear of answering such a blatant attempt at rumor-mongering."

His next words were swallowed by the clang of weapons and armor in the courtyard below the wide windows in Resstlin's chamber and the slamming open of the doors. A thick-necked guard nodded as he saw the prince. "Forgive me, my lord, we're under attack and I must secure this area."

Resstlin covered the entire length of the chamber in three long strides. "Attack? How? From whom?"

The guard faltered at Resstlin's intensity, then finally shook it off. "The derawri, your highness. The palace is under attack from a group of heavily armed derawri."

CHAPTER THREE

GHORTIN TOOK ONE look out a window above the courtyard and then grabbed a guard on their way toward the dungeons. It took a few tense moments, but he convinced the guard to find Storm and tell him what happened. Those weren't just a group of annoyed derawri down there, that was a band of derawri deathsworn. This situation could fall apart in minutes.

Resstlin had been leading the way down the outer stairs but turned around as the guard Ghortin borrowed went the opposite direction. "Now see here, Ghortin, you can't dwindle our defenses—there's no reason for my brother to come down here."

"One guard, *Prince* Resstlin, is not going to make much of a difference in any defense we may or may not have to exercise." Ghortin nodded to the scene in the courtyard at the base of the stairs. "Not to mention the palace isn't under attack, only the dungeon is currently being invaded. Or should I say, a falsely imprisoned warrior is being liberated." Derawri were a fierce race, short in stature but massive in heart and fighting skills. The derawri deathsworn were an exclusive group of derawri fighters who mostly defended against direct attacks on their homeland, Derawri. Crell was more a member of Traana-faeren than her own, but her high-ranking status as Ki', a term only given to a relatively few fighters, meant she would always be defended by the deathsworn. Whether she wanted it or not. Ghortin knew she wouldn't want the deathsworn to attack the palace on her behalf.

Resstlin shook his head but didn't descend any further. "Come, come, you don't mean to say a group of warriors would risk certain death against overwhelming odds because I temporarily placed Ki' Crell under guard? She did threaten my people after all."

"Your people threatened her rangers and she defended them, from what I heard. And I mean to say that very thing." Ghortin turned Resstlin around so he got a clear look at the bristling force surrounded by palace guards below them. "In case you missed it, those people are derawri deathsworn. That means to *their* death. Odds are they would decimate most of the palace guard before your people took them down. Your lack of respect for all of us certainly hasn't made you a welcome face down here. I would tread lightly with these derawri."

The only reaction at first was a flush to the tips of Resstlin's pointed ears and a slight darkening of his eyes. Ghortin's guess had been correct. Resstlin hadn't bothered to look at them before now. Even Resstlin wouldn't be so foolish as to challenge deathsworn protecting their leader.

"I will not be intimidated—"

"You'd best act quickly, because here comes the second in command." Ghortin cut off Resstlin's blustering.

Resstlin whirled around and adopted the proper serious mien.

A leathery-looking male derawri approached and gave a small bow. "We come to speak to he who leads." He was only half as tall as Resstlin, but that didn't appear to bother him.

Resstlin copied the man's bow exactly. "I am he; I act for my father who is absent."

The grizzled warrior stared up in Resstlin's eyes with an intensity that belied his advanced age. "We have heard. Your father is among the ancestors now. He can have no say among the living. You will do. We come to let you know that Ki' Crell will be freed or we will die in the attempt." He said it with the same intonation one would order a bowl of stew. It was a fact.

"No." The single word echoed through the room. Crell stepped forward, free of the dungeon, and surrounded by the rest of the deathsworn. "I will not go against the laws of this land. And neither will those who fight for me." Like all derawris, Crell was shorter than a human. But even at less than four feet high, no sane person would take her on in a fight. Her long red hair made her look almost sweet until someone saw her with a blade of any kind.

Ghortin saw the conflict crossing Resstlin's face. The more he saw, the less he thought that Resstlin had gone to the side of evil like Ravenhearst. It was appearing that he had been confused and misled by the ambassador. Probably a spell or two were also used.

Something made Resstlin pause and look behind them with a scowl. "Where's Lord Ravenhearst?"

Resstlin continued to look around, but Ghortin grabbed a guard immediately. "Go bring Lord Raven-hearst back, immediately."

———◆———

Jenna picked at the remains of her meal, noticing the others were lingering as well. Storm ordered food to be sent up as they got to his room. There was little to talk about aside from the locked-up Crell and her rangers. At least until Ghortin came back. She was sitting near the door when a barrage of knocks hit it.

"We might as well answer it, but I'd doubt even Resstlin would be so stubborn as to try and lock every-one up again." Storm was reaching for the door when it slammed open of its own accord. The kelar's amazing reflexes saved him from a nasty collision.

"Your Highness!" The guard pulled back instantly. "I feared you had left your rooms."

Storm folded his arms and looked down at the human guard. "As you can see, we're all here. What of it?"

"I am sorry." The guard blanched. Jenna could tell that even though he didn't look young, he wasn't used to being around the royal family. "I was sent to get you, we're under attack." Jenna, Edgar, and Garlan all leaped to their feet; Keanin carefully dusted his clothing off before joining them.

Storm spun around and grabbed his sword from the bed. "Who is attacking us? Why hasn't an alarm been sounded?"

"The deathsworn derawri are attacking, your highness, and I guess no one thought to call a general alarm. They're only in the dungeon levels."

Storm shook his head and sheathed his blade as Jenna watched his battle stance vanish. "The deathsworn?"

The guardsman paled further as he nodded. "I believe they came to rescue Ki' Crell. However, they are heavily armed, and it was Ghortin who asked for your presence, not Prince Resstlin."

Storm's eyebrow rose at that. "The dungeons you say?" He turned to the rest of the group with a grin. "Come my friends, it looks like we get to break Crell out after all."

The guard blinked rapidly as he processed the comment. Jenna could tell this was not what he'd expected. "You're joking, aren't you, Prince Corin? I mean, you aren't really trai…." The guard let the words trail off as he got a good look at Storm's intense blue eyes.

"Traitors? Was that the word? No. I am not. We are not, and more importantly, that woman locked in Resstlin's dungeon is not. One way or another, Crell is going free." He buckled on his sword belt.

The guard dropped his eyes, standing motionless as the rest of them funneled past. Jenna gave him a sympathetic pat on the shoulder. It wasn't his fault he didn't understand what was going on.

Edgar and Storm kept to the front, with Jenna and Keanin close behind and Garlan bringing up the rear. Jenna had no question as to the placement; without the stout Armsmaster behind him, Keanin probably would have conveniently fallen behind and vanished back into his room. This was what he wanted to avoid, more unnatural behavior in the palace.

Edgar tried to slow Storm down. "Don't you think that for once we might want to wait until we can get some more fighters? I've no lack of faith in any derawris' fighting skills, especially those of the deathsworn, but I also am painfully aware of how many guards this palace can muster."

Jenna knew Edgar had probably trained many of those guards in various forms of sneakier fighting. Edgar was the spymaster, but also a knight. He could fight extremely well in many disciplines.

Storm flashed a bright grin. "I don't think we'll need them, even my brother isn't thoughtless enough to try and fight the deathsworn." He slowed their pace as they rounded the last curve of stairs.

The tableau before them was odd, to say the least. Twenty derawri deathsworn warriors stood in tight formation around the dungeon entrance, weapons bristling outward. Fifty royal guards stood gathered around them, trying to look both threatening and unconcerned at the same time.

If the numbers remained the same Jenna had no question who would win that battle. Crell had told her of the deathsworn, and it would take a number far larger than the palace guards currently had out there to even slow them down. By the lack of pressure from the royal guards, she guessed they didn't wonder who would win either. The derawri would slaughter them. Ghortin and Resstlin were locked in a fierce discussion but turned at the sound of Storm's group.

Ghortin stepped forward with a nod. "I see my message made it through."

"Yes, although," Storm gave his brother a pointed look, "the guard had some qualms about dealing with a *traitor.*"

Resstlin flushed. "This is getting completely out of hand. Half of your original forces come back from the abyss knows where, telling the most outrageous stories, and claiming our father was murdered months ago by demonspawn. And you take offense at my questioning the pattern of events?" He waved a hand around the courtyard below them. "How am I not to think that something else happened when you're all acting like this?" He narrowed his eyes and waggled a thick finger at Storm. "I was warned this would happen."

"Warned of what?" Storm asked, but Ghortin nodded.

Resstlin's face gave away far more emotions than Storm's usually did. Jenna didn't even know the man, and she could tell he felt he'd said far too much.

"What did Ravenhearst tell you, *brother*? Did he tell you that he tried to have me killed?" Storm stood nose to nose with Resstlin.

"Killed?" Resstlin's voice rose. "Why would he possibly want you killed? You're seeing things that don't exist."

Ghortin took advantage of their fight and leaned over to Edgar. "Try to find Ravenhearst. Resstlin sent a guard, but she should have been back by now."

He nodded once, then disappeared up the stairs. Jenna was in constant awe of his ability to vanish into shadows. With a sigh of envy, she turned back to the fighting royals.

"He tried to kill your brother because of me." Jenna stepped forward, batting away Keanin's hands as he tried to hold her back. "Lord Ravenhearst is working for people who want me. I think they'd prefer me alive, but dead would be better than alive and free."

Resstlin pulled back. It was obvious he didn't know who she was, although as Ghortin's apprentice she had been introduced to him at the ill-fated ball. He looked perplexed as he shook himself out of his fight with his brother. His look became condescending a second later.

"I'm sorry, my dear. But whoever you are, I'm certain no one is after you. You are Ghortin's apprentice, are you not? Well, I'm sure you might have thought someone was after you, but I would think your master would be a far greater target. The idea of anyone, let alone Lord Ravenhearst, wanting to murder an apprentice is ridiculous."

Both Ghortin and Storm looked ready to defend her worth, but a rustle from the stairwell broke the issue. Edgar, making more noise than Jenna had ever heard from the man, burst out of the hall behind them sorely out of breath. "The bigger question is where Ravenhearst went and why did he murder your guard?"

"What do you mean?" Resstlin paled. "If Lord Ravenhearst is missing and a guard sent to him has been murdered we must assume whoever killed the guard also kidnapped Lord Ravenhearst!"

Edgar's large black eyes were bright. "And they kidnapped his entire entourage as well? And left behind one of Ravenhearst's personal blades stuck in the guard's back? I seriously doubt that, *Your Highness.*"

Storm grabbed Resstlin's velvet-clad arm. "You have got to believe us. You need to send guards after Ravenhearst now."

"I doubt it will do any good." Ghortin shook his head. "There's only one way that Ravenhearst could have gotten everyone out so fast. They've got a very powerful mage, or mages, on their side."

Resstlin looked from one to the other, still ready to argue. Then his posturing fell. With lowered eyes, he turned toward the derawris in the courtyard. "I have made an incorrect assessment of a situation based on someone I thought was a good man. I have misjudged what actually occurred." He waved at the guards. "Ki' Crell is free, as are all of the rangers and fighters locked in the barracks. Send out guards to look for Ravenhearst or any of his people." He watched as the guards moved away from the deathsworn. "I would like to say that I believed Ravenhearst out of grief over the kidnapping of our father, but the fact is, it never should have happened. Forgive me, Ki' Crell." He gave a deep bow.

Crell came up the steps and nodded, her tiny face still lined with sorrow. "We've all been through much more than anyone should have to bear. And I fear there is more to come. I can't give you forgiveness for what needs no forgiving." She turned toward the derawri warriors. No words were spoken, but silent nods were made. With a final nod, she turned back to Prince Resstlin. "I will go out of the city, and spend time with my people. I need to decide on my next action. My rangers will come with me." Crell's family had sworn allegiance to the royal family of Traanafaeren decades ago. From the look on her face, she was contemplating if that arrangement should stand.

Resstlin's brown eyes widened, but Jenna gave him credit for not pushing the issue. He recovered quickly and then nodded once. "So be it. But know that the royal house of Traanafaeren is forever in debt to you and your people. Please take what time you need."

Crell bowed to Resstlin, then nodded to Storm, Ghortin, and Jenna. Without looking at anyone else, she led the derawri deathsworn and her band of thirty or so rangers beyond the palace walls in silence.

Muttering and rustling reminded them that Resstlin's personal guards were still in place, although the prince appeared too distracted to notice. Ghortin took care of the situation and looked around. "I do believe *all* of you have other duties. Elsewhere."

It only took that comment followed by a glare and the small area was cleared of everyone except Resstlin and themselves.

Armsmaster Garlan stepped forward stiffly. "I ask leave to go question the upper-level guards. There is a chance that some might have heard of Ravenhearst's plans."

Resstlin had still been lost in his thoughts when Garlan spoke and failed to notice what Jenna saw. Garlan was barely keeping his fury in check. "What? Oh yes, that is a valid plan."

Garlan left immediately.

The group stood in silence for a few more minutes, waiting to see if Resstlin had other plans. But the tall prince simply stood there scowling. Ghortin coughed and stepped forward.

"I think this development would best be discussed in Prince Resstlin's chambers." As they followed Resstlin and Storm up the stairs, Jenna saw Ghortin take Edgar aside. "Could you go find out if Tor Ranshal has arrived yet?" Edgar arched one black eyebrow; Ghortin laughed and patted him on the arm. "No fear, I haven't taken over your area of expertise. The seneschal had simply said he would come south as soon as he was able. I have a feeling he should be here by now."

Edgar grinned and gave an elegant bow. "I live but to serve." With a quick wink and nod to Jenna, the black-haired kelar was gone.

"What now?" Jenna walked up the steps with Ghortin; it seemed like in the year she'd known him he'd aged ten years. At this rate, he'd be showing his three-thousand-year-old age soon.

"I've no idea what we'll do now. That, I think, is part of the problem. I am glad Resstlin followed Ravenhearst out of ignorance and not intent." He slowed his steps. "But still, I've never seen him so unnerved. He's always been the cocky royal, far too sure of himself for most to

stand. Seeing him like this is disturbing. He will have to
be watched carefully."

"There you two are." A long shadow that had lain
against a wall freed itself and became Keanin. "I'd thought
you two had found a secret way out and abandoned me.
I'm afraid the brothers royal aren't good company right
now. Couldn't we deal with this later?"

Jenna almost smiled. Keanin's pathetic whine was close
to the old Keanin, but the way he panicked if she or
Ghortin were out of sight for too long wasn't. Even
Ghortin's constant reassurances that their enemy was too
far away to get to him didn't work. He was terrified that
the enemy would find a way to work through him again,
to somehow take him over to who knew what end. He
was certain only Jenna or Ghortin could protect him. He
very carefully avoided remembering that both of them
had been almost as helpless as he had been at the end of
the last battle.

Ghortin studied Keanin before speaking. Jenna had
noticed Ghortin's uncommon gentleness with Keanin
on the way back from the Markare. But it now looked
like that time was gone. "We can't wait, Keanin, any
more than our enemy will. They chose the time of the
first attack, and all of the ones since then. Our world is
changing out of control, and if we don't find a way to
stop them we'll be crushed by it."

Keanin's handsome face fell in on itself. "But we're not
ready. We're all going to die. Just like Kern and all those
soldiers did. We're going to—"

Jenna reached up with a single finger and laid it across
his lips, cutting off the panicked refrain. "No. We're not
going to die." She pulled Keanin's chin down so his eyes
were forced to meet hers. The terror in those glorious
golden eyes was chilling. "I won't let you die. You're an
important part of this, even Ghortin isn't sure how, but
you are. And more importantly, you're my friend." She

shook his chin. "You believe me, don't you?" Jenna made him focus on her but didn't cast a spell on him. It was vital that Keanin get ahold of himself, and he needed to do it on his own.

Keanin shut his eyes and let his chin slip lower. Finally, he opened his eyes and smiled. "How could I doubt such a beautiful lady?" He bent his head down to kiss her hand as he whispered, "Thank you." When he raised his head, the abject terror was gone from his face.

"Shall we go save the brothers royal from each other?"

CHAPTER FOUR

———◆———

GHORTIN HAD PICKED up speed as he walked down the main corridor and was already at the royal chambers by the time Jenna and Keanin caught up to him. Raised male voices echoed into the hallway through the closed doors.

"I thought that if he agreed Ravenhearst might be involved, it meant he agreed with Storm in terms of what happened? What are they still fighting about?" Jenna was beginning to agree with Keanin about waiting back a bit. Constant fighting wasn't going to resolve anything.

Keanin rolled his eyes. "Anything and everything. They always find something to battle about."

"I'm afraid he's right. Those two have never gotten along, but usually the rest of the family could keep them in line. And they still aren't down from Irundail yet." Ghortin frowned as he studied the door but didn't open it.

Jenna nodded at his trepidation. "We'll have to do that for them, won't we?"

Ghortin flashed her a smile. "That's the spirit, lass. Shall we?" At her nod, he swung open the doors.

Jenna dragged Keanin behind her into the room. Both kelar princes were locked in a staring contest. Neither spoke, nor looked at the new arrivals, but the animosity between them crackled in the air.

"Mastermage Ghortin, perhaps you can reason with my younger brother." Resstlin kept his eyes on Storm. "I apparently can't."

Ghortin stood in front of both of them and faced

Storm. "Oh? And what is the issue?"

"He *still* doesn't think we should take action." Like Resstlin, Storm kept his eyes on his brother. By the way his jaw was working Jenna could tell he was fighting to speak slowly and not yell. "*He* thinks we should wait and see if they still will attack. *He* wants to stay here until they slaughter more of our people."

Resstlin broke the stare-off and spun away toward his desk. "I never said that, and well you know it. Damn it, Corin; listen to yourself. They? We don't know who they are! Would you have us take apart the Markare pebble by pebble? And what do you think our neighboring kingdoms would think? Strann has always been wary of their desert border, and Derawri and Khelaran are no better. Am I to tell them I've moved armed troops into the borderlands to look for an enemy we can't confirm?"

"Resstlin is right." Ghortin held up a hand at Storm's glare. "Easy there. He is correct about the futility of hunting them down in the desert. We have no idea where they went. If they stayed in the Markare, I'd bet they're deep within the desert by now."

The Markare was a brutally uninhabitable desert that bordered three of the four kingdoms in this part of the world. What most people didn't realize was that it had been created by the gods and goddesses themselves when they fought back against the cuari uprising thousands of years ago. Strange monsters had come out of it since then, including a deadly and destructive one barely fought off by Ghortin and a group of adventures over a thousand years ago.

"What do you mean? Where else could they possibly be?" Resstlin turned with a frown. "I doubt any land would hide a group of demonspawn."

Ghortin frowned. "I'm not sure. But if you hadn't been so quick to lock us up, and if you," he turned to Storm, "hadn't been so busy picking fights with your brother, you both might have heard my theory much earlier. I have a feeling that our friends have strongholds in many places, including one deep in the Markare. However, I do think we need to consider the state of our neighbors. Ravenhearst probably acted with at least some knowledge from the Strann government. And we haven't had solid communications with Khelaran or Derawri in years. Our next move will have to be sure and strong. To do that we need to make certain we know who our enemies are. And who will stand with us."

Jenna kept quiet as the two princes processed Ghortin's information. Storm wouldn't be a problem; his flexibility regarding new ideas was far more advanced than his brother's. It was terrifying that these demonspawn had breached the portal between worlds to invade this land, and Resstlin still looked like he had to think about things.

Ghortin watched Resstlin for a few moments, then changed topics. "But first we should work on Resstlin's coronation. Most of Traanafaeren doesn't have the least idea of what has happened recently. Once they know their king has been murdered, they will be at a loss. It would be best if the transition of Daylin to Resstlin takes place quickly and smoothly. We can't afford to have the land divided."

Jenna opened her mouth to object. Saving this world, and possibly her own, was more important than putting a crown on Resstlin's head. Ghortin silenced her with a quick shake of his head.

Resstlin's face went blank for a moment. Fortunately, decades of being groomed for this day took over and he responded with a somber bow. "I am ready. I had hoped it would be many more years before my time came, but I am ready. And I agree, the transition should be quick and smooth. With enough time for proper grieving, of course."

Jenna could see what Ghortin was doing, but she had

to say something. "But what about that monster out there? He, it, whatever that is, may not be in the desert right now, but he's still out there." A horrific feeling hit the back of her mind, a connection of some sort. "I don't know how, but I can feel it."

It was true; it was like a faint ichor creeping down the back of her skull. The only reason she hadn't noticed it before must be because she wasn't thinking about it. She shuddered again. Whatever the connection was between herself and that monster was, she needed to find a way to break it. She'd come into this world by being slammed into the body of a mindslave, a woman whose mind had been sacrificed to Qhazborh by his followers. Sometimes remnants of the lost woman rose in her mind. Then there was another odd presence, one not tangible enough to mentally grab, but had helped her in times of danger. If this feeling was because of either essence in her head, she wished they'd be clearer about it.

A long arm draped over her shoulder. Keanin didn't say anything, but the look in his eyes told her he knew what she felt. That demonspawn king had wanted to bring both of them to his master's side. It had been in the process of doing so when Storm broke free of the spell engulfing all of them and fired an arrow into the creature, killing it.

"All the more reason to proceed with caution." Resstlin glanced briefly to Jenna but then turned to Ghortin. "We have no idea what is awaiting us."

Storm let loose a few choice swear words at the ceiling. "We can't wait. Jenna's right; whoever they are, wherever they are, they are still gathering. They are breaking through into our world. Ghortin stopped them from bringing more over during the fight, but we've no idea if that held. We may have slowed down their plan, but I can promise you, we didn't stop it. We need to strike before they regain their power."

Ghortin let the two brothers glower at each other for a few moments. "Again, strike where?" He put a hand on both princes' shoulders. "This round and round arguing is getting us nowhere. We can't go after anyone until we have an idea where they are. Even with Edgar's spies, it will take time to find out where to attack."

"I have to say I agree with the mastermage. My people will do what they can, but they were caught unawares this time. That won't happen again." Edgar came into the room escorting a tall, thin, white-haired old man. He was human but almost as tall as the kelar. Jenna felt calmer the moment he came into the room.

Ghortin wordlessly engulfed the new man in a hug. "Damn good timing, old man." Tor Ranshal, the palace seneschal, returned the hug and smiled at the others.

"It is wonderful to see you all as well." His eyes were bright as they rested on the two princes. "Greetings, my princes. Please accept my condolences at the loss of your father. King Daylin was a fine man and a good friend."

Resstlin and Storm nodded in unison. Resstlin stepped forward and laid a hand on the seneschal's thin shoulders.

"I am most glad at your return. Lithunane suffers when you are absent, Seneschal Tor Ranshal."

Tor Ranshal smiled warmly and motioned to a semi-circle of seats. "May I suggest we sit? I am not a young man, and while my journey wasn't as dangerous as yours, it was quite long."

Jenna smiled at Tor Ranshal. In seconds, he had managed to reduce two battling princes to meek schoolboys. Pulling the still silent Keanin in tow behind her, Jenna joined the group around the fireplace.

Edgar turned toward Resstlin as he took a seat. "I have other important news beyond the seneschal's arrival." The dark man shot a quick look at Storm. "The Lady Mikasa vanished along with Lord Ravenhearst's entourage."

Storm's face was unreadable as everyone looked toward

him. Even Resstlin appeared sympathetic.

"I am truly sorry, brother. Perhaps your betrothed went without knowledge of Ravenhearst's true nature, or mayhap she was taken against her will."

"She wasn't my fiancée anymore." Storm looked away briefly, and Jenna felt a faint stab of jealousy. That he may have had feelings for Mikasa, the woman his mother had betrothed him to as a child, was something she had discounted long ago. Had she been wrong? He was doing his stoic bit, so telling what was going on behind those blue eyes was impossible.

Resstlin straightened his doublet with practiced nonchalance. "She mentioned that perhaps she had been too hasty in what she had written to you. She indicated she was looking forward to your return." His almost condescending smile told Jenna that he thought Storm was heartbroken, and that he didn't think he deserved Mikasa.

"I really don't care." Storm shook his head and gave a small sigh. "You don't get it, do you? She was working for Ravenhearst, she was a spy."

Resstlin pulled back as if struck. "That's preposterous, she couldn't be a spy, she was from a noble house."

Jenna had to choke back a laugh at that comment, and at the reaction of amused pity reflected on most of the other faces in the room.

Edgar, however, ignored Resstlin's comment completely. "I can't believe I didn't think of it sooner. She arrived not too long after Ravenhearst replaced the old Strann ambassador."

"But what about the arrangement our mother made? You two were to be wed and that was set long ago. Our mother grew up with Mikasa's mother, her family is nobility." Resstlin looked far more like he had been the one taken advantage of by Mikasa, not Storm. The concept of someone of noble lineage being anything of ill-repute was so foreign to him he was completely at a loss.

Storm turned to him. "Think about it, Resstlin, think hard. How difficult would it have been to groom her for the part? Nothing was heard from her concerning our betrothal until the same week Ravenhearst arrived?" He shook his head and gave a self-deprecating laugh. "I know you always thought her reaction to me was a bit overdone; let's face it, we all did. I'm too difficult to get along with for someone of her nature; my status as a prince wears off pretty fast."

Keanin finally pulled back out of the corner he'd been lurking in. "I, for one, want to know why she, or they, thought that latching onto Corin would do any good at all. Everyone knows how little time he spends in the palace."

From the look on his face, Jenna could tell he was both feeling better and was quite smug that his hatred of the missing Mikasa was so well supported.

Something clicked into place as Jenna looked at the arguing royals. "No, Storm doesn't spend much time in the palace, but look where he does spend time, and with whom." She pointedly looked at Ghortin.

"She couldn't have thought of getting anything from me." Ghortin frowned as he folded his arms. "You didn't tell her about Jenna, did you?"

Storm gave him a rude look. "Of course not. Mikasa knows that Jenna is your apprentice, nothing more."

Resstlin looked at Jenna with new interest. "What could be so important about an apprentice that you'd want it a secret?"

Storm and Ghortin both winced. Jenna knew they were trying to limit who knew about her abilities and where she was really from, but that neither of them trusted Resstlin with it was worrying.

Ghortin relaxed his shoulders and tried to look unconcerned. "It's simply that she has a few skills that are unusual in the mage community. Purely stuff of interest to academics, mind you. But the less the enemy knows about it the better. You never know what we might need."

Resstlin nodded, but his eyes narrowed slightly and he watched her more carefully than before.

"What have we settled and where do we go from here?" Edgar flashed Jenna a quick wink, he was trying to keep Resstlin's focus away from her.

"That's an excellent question." Storm folded his arms and glared at his brother.

"As I was saying before." Ghortin raised his hands to ward off another round of princely verbal sparring. "The first thing we must do is hold a formal service for Daylin. The rest of the family will have to be transported down from Irundail, of course. Then have the coronation as quickly as possible." He nodded to Tor Ranshal. "The rest of the family should be sent back to Irundail immediately after the coronation; it's too dangerous down here."

Tor Ranshal took over at that point, mostly making Resstlin focus on all of the formal obligations that would be handled in a short time. Ghortin took advantage of the situation to herd the others out of the room.

Resstlin didn't look up at their leaving.

CHAPTER FIVE

———◆———

IT TOOK A few days for Crell to get the deathsworn to return home without her. They had already been en route to join the battle in the Markare when their far-seeing mages notified them that Crell had returned to Lithunane—and was in trouble.

They came to provide aid, but also to request that she come immediately back to Derawri. There wasn't a solid reason given, and from what Jenna had seen on Crell and the leader of the deathsworn's faces as they left the court-yard, the leader couldn't tell her why either. Both looked seriously pissed as they left—and not only at Resstlin.

After much debate, some of which Crell shared with Jenna while drinking in the pub, Crell convinced them to go back without her. There was a looming danger to all of the lands and they needed to be back to defend it. But she needed to stay here whether the deathsworn agreed or not.

A small group had gathered in the inner bailey to watch the derawri contingent officially depart. Most were simply curious observers taking advantage of a rare sighting of the derawri deathsworn.

Crell said her official farewell, then gave a wrapped gift of parting to the leader, Tigan, and the group marched out of the palace gates.

She came back to where Jenna and Edgar stood. "I snuck the taran wand in his gift of parting, along with instructions. I hope you're wrong about keeping it a secret from Resstlin."

Edgar watched the people gathered around the courtyard as they went about their business. "I'm more concerned that he would try and take the wands, than him knowing about them. They were hard to find and little more than a myth these days. I hope I am wrong as well."

Edgar and Jenna had a late night helping Crell get past her guilt for not going back with her people. She knew staying here with her obligation to Traanafaeren was right, but it hurt her heart. That was when Edgar brought up the taran wands. They looked like hollow sticks to Jenna's eyes, but supposedly they could communicate between them without other magical assistance. It was a way for the deathsworn and Crell to keep in touch without needing the use of a farspeaking mage.

Crell and Edgar went inside to discuss utilizing her rangers within the protection of the palace. Normally, they roamed the land, coming to check in regularly. She'd gathered them when they left Irundail months ago and felt it prudent to keep them nearby now.

Jenna enjoyed the sunshine for a bit longer. She'd spent the past few days locked up in her room working on spells. It was nice to be outside. She finally turned to go back into the palace, when Storm caught her arm.

"Where's Ghortin?" He wasn't smiling, but then he hadn't smiled much for the past few days. He'd also appeared to be deliberately avoiding her.

She returned his glare. This attitude was getting old and annoying. "I have no idea. He was up here with us during the leave-taking, didn't you see him go?"

Storm's frown went into a full scowl. "I'll find him myself." He stomped off before Jenna could respond.

"Of all the rude…"

"Now, my lady, swearing to yourself is one step closer to madness." As usual, Edgar slid up next to her without a sound until he spoke. His conversation with Crell had been short, or someone came to speak to her. "Might

I guess that the current object of your ire is our young Corin?" The grin on his dark face was innocent, but his sharp black eyes were lively.

"I don't understand what's happened to him. He was fine when we got here, but now he's becoming nastier; especially to me."

"He's been rude to me as well." He shrugged. "Perhaps it's that Mikasa issue. Any man would be in a foul mood to find out his fiancée was a spy for people trying to destroy the world—even if they disliked the fiancée." He smiled broadly. "But I'm sure his surliness is general and not directed at any of us specifically. Now, might I change the subject? Do you happen to know where I can find our dear Ghortin?"

Jenna sighed and pointed over her shoulder. "No idea. Follow the royal brooding prince; he's looking for Ghortin as well."

Edgar bowed over her hand, giving a rare glimpse of his other persona as a knight. "Thank you most kindly." With a wink, he followed the path Storm had taken.

Jenna had no idea what to feel or think about Storm. She thought a relationship had been growing between them, but once he found out about Mikasa's betrayal, he'd withdrawn and totally ignored her. Crell said it would pass; she'd known Storm since he had been a child and under her care as royal guardian. Sadly, that didn't cut down on the annoyance level much.

Jenna continued to stew in her thoughts as she wandered around the gardens outside the bailey. Consequently, she was not in a good mood when she tripped over her mentor.

Ghortin was sitting on some garden stairs reading his gray book when she bumped into him. It was all she could do not to swear at him and she knew she didn't hide it well.

"Here now!" He got to his feet. "As I see it, you're the

one who stumbled into me."

Jenna shook her head with a sigh. "I'm sorry, it was my fault. I'm not mad at you, it's just been a lousy morning." She looked at her three-thousand-plus-year-old mentor and tried to think of how to explain what she was feeling without sounding like a total ass. She couldn't think of a way. "Let's say things are messed up right now and leave it at that."

The frown on Ghortin's face told her he was going to launch an interrogation.

But she spoke before he could. "Oh, and both Edgar and Storm are looking for you. I have no idea why."

"They'll find me, they always do." Ghortin closed his book and peered at Jenna. Her attempt at distraction didn't work. Jenna took another tactic before he started asking questions she wasn't sure how to answer.

She gave a pointed look at the book in his hands. "Have you remembered it yet?" The small gray book was one of a set of three, the Books of the Cuari. They supposedly held secrets passed down over thousands of years that *might* have a way to stop whatever was currently happening. Except they only had two of the books, with this one being extremely difficult to work through. Ghortin had been working on it when she first came to this world. Unfortunately, after spending a few months floating around in Jenna's head—he'd completely forgotten it. The relearning was slow. The book wouldn't let the user progress to the next page until it felt the user understood the one they were working on.

Ghortin turned it over a few times. "I still don't remember having read it before, but I've managed to get through the first fifteen pages. It's being stubborn about letting me go further. You wouldn't happen to know how long it took me last time would you?"

"I'm afraid not." Jenna didn't believe he'd taken the diversion, but judging by his face, he was going to let her keep her secrets for now. "You were already well into it when I arrived here." A movement on the grass below them caught her eye. Two figures strode toward them, one tall, the other shorter. She nodded toward them. "You might ask his cranky highness, he might remember. I'll be in my room working on spells if you need me." Jenna marched off before he could respond.

———◆———

Ghortin sighed as he watched his apprentice vanish. At least he knew for certain where *that* problem lay.

"Ghortin, we've got to deal with my brother." Storm launched into his tirade as he leaped up the stairs taking two at a time. "He has now decided that I need to be sent to Khelaran as some royal ambassador."

Ghortin shook his head. He agreed that sending someone, preferably of high political stature, to the ancient Kelar homeland was a good idea. It would be foolish to think the demonspawn and the followers of Qhazborh were only going after Traanafaeren. They needed to reestablish communications with the other kingdoms and work together to stop this. Preferably before the next attack.

He couldn't believe Resstlin would pick his stubborn and very uncourtly little brother to be that someone. However, that could be Resstlin's hidden agenda. He'd never given up on trying to make Corin more like himself; perhaps he felt that if he exposed him to enough court situations something would rub off. Before Ghortin could venture his opinion, however, Edgar joined them and jumped in.

"That might be a good idea. And it lends itself to what I came to talk to you about." Edgar was so wrapped up in whatever scheme he had that he didn't see the annoyed look Storm was sending his way. Or he did but didn't care. Ghortin doubted that Edgar missed much.

"Ahem, well I'd advise you to speak quickly or Storm here might throttle you before you can get the words out." Ghortin gave Storm a reassuring smile; something had gotten his young friend very annoyed.

Edgar didn't look at Storm, but he did take a step away. "There's more than only Traanafaeren involved in this, you know that, Ghortin. I've asked the leader of the deathsworn, Tigen, to report back if he notices any odd situations in their homeland. Or rather, report them to Crell." His sharp face frowned. "As of this morning, I received indications that my spy network may be compromised. It might have happened while we were traveling, but it could have occurred before that. The point is, we need information, and we can't trust my usual sources."

"You mean when Resstlin stuck his nose in." Storm's annoyance changed focus. "He tried to run the spy network while you were gone, and you're right, he may have let Ravenhearst have access. But I don't see how my being paraded about as the royal fool of Traanafaeren is going to help the situation."

"Actually, Resstlin has a good idea. Think about it." Ghortin nodded. "Our quarry has gone aground. Now as I see it, we are most likely facing two factions that may or may not still be working together. Ravenhearst is obviously with the Qhazborh priests, but as much as they wish, they would never have enough Power to bring over all those demonspawn we faced. Nor would any of them have been as strong as that mage in the ballroom last year. Although the two groups have overlapped, I'd wager Ravenhearst and his priests have no idea what that rogue mage's plan is. The deities who gather under the name Qhazborh wouldn't want the destruction of this world—there would be no followers. Not to mention all of the deities are terrified of the portal and what it could do if fully open, at least according to Rachael and Tor Ranshal."

Ghortin looked at his young friends and suddenly felt his full age. He shook it off. "But gloom aside, my point is, and what I believe our erstwhile spymaster was suggesting, is that a royal visit to Khelaran, with full entourage, would be a perfect way to find out what is really going on there."

Storm tilted back his head and shut his eyes, a trick Ghortin had taught him long ago as a calming and focusing technique when his temper was more of a problem. With a sigh, he opened his eyes. "Fine, I'll tell my brother to set up his plans. But you're all going with me."

Edgar nodded in agreement, and then left on more of his errands.

Ghortin waited until Edgar was out of earshot before he brought up another issue. "You've done a very good job of alienating her, you know." He fixed what he hoped was an appropriately stern look upon his friend. He couldn't afford to have the two annoyed at each other the entire trip. He'd kill them both long before they got near their enemies.

"Alienated? Who have I upset? And whoever it was, I'm sure I didn't intend to." Storm's face was matching his nickname and getting worse.

Ghortin would have none of it. "You know very well who, and I'd wager it was completely deliberate." Storm looked more obstinate than he had when he arrived. "Jenna, you dolt. You've said naught but short words to her the last few days. I can't have you two sniping at each other while I'm trying to figure out who is trying to destroy the world."

A look of surprise crossed Storm's face, but he schooled it quickly. "I have no idea what you're talking about." He looked out across the gardens.

Ghortin turned Storm to face him. "What is wrong?" He relaxed his grip at the look in his friend's eyes. "This isn't only because of Mikasa is it?"

"No, yes, I'm not sure." Storm let out a long sigh. "Mikasa being a spy shook me. Not that I cared about her, you of all people know I didn't. One way or another, that marriage was never going through. Still, to have that level of betrayal take place that close to me." He shook his head. "I might have lashed out at Jenna simply because she was here. I certainly didn't mean to, but it happened."

Ghortin nodded and patted his friend's shoulder. "I understand. But that is all? No other reasons?"

The frown came back at the word 'reasons'. "Nothing else. Whatever happens between Jenna and Edgar is between them, I won't stand in their way. I'm glad they're spending so much time together." The frown now deepened into a scowl. "Now, if you don't mind, I'm going to go apologize to your apprentice for my behavior and get ready for this hellish voyage."

Ghortin started at the comment about Jenna and Edgar—there was nothing romantic going on with them. But best for Storm to find that out himself or he wouldn't believe it. He patted Storm on the shoulder again but kept quiet. He'd planted the seed, but only talking between the two would resolve the issue. One way or another.

Storm tried to clear his head as he walked down the corridor. Surely he hadn't been that bad? He certainly didn't object to Edgar courting Jenna. She was a beautiful, intelligent woman, with a great sense of humor and spirit. Edgar was one of his closest friends and an excellent man, even if he was only second to Keanin in the number of female conquests. Maybe the spymaster had finally decided to settle down.

At first, Storm hadn't noticed how much time the two had been spending together. It had started on the way back from the Markare, but Storm was grieving and trying to keep his battered troops together. He hadn't had time to deal with anything else. Here in the palace, they had spent far more time together, both disappearing for hours. He'd noticed it this time.

Still lost in thought, Storm rounded a corner and stopped. Jenna was not ten feet in front of him. She was leaning in a doorway talking to someone, so he turned to go. Unfortunately, the person she was speaking to was Edgar and he hadn't become the youngest spymaster in the history of Traanafaeren by being unobservant.

"Corin! Just the man I was looking for." Edgar's voice rang out, dashing any hope Storm had of pretending not to hear him.

With a wince, Storm slowly turned to face them. He was surprised to see his own annoyance reflected on Jenna's face.

Edgar however, ignored both of them. "Come, come. You know, I was saying to Jenna here that you don't mean to be rude, it's that—"

"Rude?" Storm cut him off and looked at both of them. "When have I been rude?"

Jenna looked ready to retort, but Edgar literally jumped between them. "You see? I told you he simply didn't realize what he'd been doing. I'm sure he's upset about women in general and—"

"I have not been rude and I'm not upset about Mikasa. Or women in general."

Jenna pushed Edgar aside. "I don't care. You've been a rude pig to everyone. Edgar's trying to defend you. You have no reason to yell at him."

"Actually, he wasn't yelling that loud—"

"Shut up!" Both Jenna and Storm yelled at the same time, but neither looked at Edgar.

"Shutting up." He started to back down the hall. "And all I ask is that any bloodshed is cleaned up before the maids see it." An instant later Jenna and Storm were alone.

"I cannot believe what you just did." Jenna leaned forward, poking Storm in the chest to emphasize her words. "He was taking your side, you cold, inconsiderate, pig-headed, stubborn pointy-eared hobgoblin."

Storm had been backing up under her barrage and ended up taking an awkward backward step down the stairwell. Unfortunately, Jenna was leaning further into him as he did it and tumbled into him, crashing both of them down the five steps to the landing.

CHAPTER SIX

FORTUNATELY FOR BOTH of them, the fall was short. Still, Jenna landed on Storm with enough force that she heard the air escape out of his lungs. She also managed to pull a plant down with them as she attempted to stop the fall.

Storm gave a half-cough, half-laugh as he got a good look at Jenna with a plant headdress.

Jenna started laughing as well, the tension between them of the last few days finally broke. Still laughing, Jenna leaned further down and brushed off some dirt that had fallen on his face. It wasn't fair. Not only was he gorgeous, she honestly liked him. Hell, she may have been falling in love with him. At least until all the drama with Mikasa surfaced and he became the world's biggest jerk.

"What are you thinking?" Storm's voice was soft as he interrupted her thoughts.

"Nothing." Jenna noticed her hand was still brushing away dirt from the side of his face that had been gone for a while. She stopped but couldn't make herself move off of him. "Um, what are you thinking about?" She tried to sound casual.

Storm reached up to gently pull her head down. "I was thinking about this."

The kiss started soft, but quickly grew as a different type of tension filled the room. Jenna couldn't think beyond the parts of her body that were touching him. After a far too short amount of time, he pulled away.

He looked awkward and Jenna wondered if her weight

was too much lying on him with a plant like she was. Maybe they should go to one of their rooms and discuss this situation.

Storm's train of thought, however, was completely different.

"I shouldn't have done that. I don't want to get between you and Edgar."

Jenna gaped at him for a few seconds as her mind tried to follow. "Edgar and me—what?"

"You and Edgar; that's what I was coming out here for. I'll understand if the two of you are involved. I don't want to interfere."

Jenna put a hand to his mouth as her slightly kiss-besotted mind made the connection. "Wait. You thought that Edgar and I were sleeping together? And that's why you've been so nasty?" She thunked him on the chest. "Why didn't you ask?"

Storm winced, but she was sure it wasn't from the thunk. "I wasn't that bad, was I?" She gave him a look. His wince grew into a grimace. "Okay, I might have been. It's nothing against Edgar."

Jenna leaned forward and made him stop talking by kissing him. When she let him go her voice was soft. "There's nothing between Edgar and me; he's been teaching me those martial arts of his. So I can defend myself if my magic winks out again."

He smiled. "There's no one to be upset about me wanting to—"

"Ahem."

Both Jenna and Storm jumped as a cough cut Storm off.

"Not to worry, you two, it's just me." Ghortin chuckled as he peered down the short stairwell. "I wanted to make sure you hadn't damaged my apprentice. I must say, I've never seen her wear a plant before, but she does seem happy."

Jenna buried her face into Storm's chest to hide her reddening face. Nothing like being caught making out like in high school to bring one back to reality.

Ghortin continued as if there everything was normal. "Although you might want to move your…discussion somewhere less public. You know how folks like to spread royal gossip."

Jenna turned toward Ghortin, but he was already gone.

She felt Storm's laugh an instant before she heard it. "I felt like a schoolboy!"

Jenna looked down at him. "He did seem to take it rather well. I suppose you aren't too bad of a choice. Although I think he's holding you responsible for this plant."

Storm stopped laughing as he slowly and very deliberately began brushing plant debris and dirt off Jenna. "He is right. We should probably move somewhere else. I have ideas that really shouldn't be shared with the public."

Jenna laughed. "I think I may like to hear those ideas, and I think I need to hear them as soon as possible." With a quick kiss, she rolled off of him and finished dusting herself off.

"We can take care of that." He smiled as he got to his feet. "And as for my previous surly behavior, I promise to be good on this trip."

"Trip? What trip?" Jenna froze as she started to go up the stairs. She had been looking forward to at least a few more weeks of staying in an actual bed and not being on the road.

Storm winced. "Sorry. Resstlin has decided that I need to go to Khelaran to see if Mikasa was working alone, or if we have the entire country to worry about. He wants me to go play courtier, but Ghortin and Edgar believe we can gather important information." He kissed her briefly. "And I have no intention of suffering alone."

They'd left the stairwell when a sapphire and emerald-clad messenger slammed into them. Literally. Fortunately, no one went back down the stairs this time.

"Prince Corin, thank the stars I found you! They need you at once!" The young boy tried to pull on Storm's arm.

"Easy there." Storm gently but firmly disengaged the messenger's hand from his arm. "Now slow down, who needs me? Are we under attack?"

The boy shook his head frantically, but Jenna could tell he was trying to stay calm. "We're not in trouble; Khelaran is. They've closed their borders! Prince Resstlin said you need to go to him immediately." The boy was practically dancing in his urgency to get them moving. "They are in the royal hall, but I have to find Sir Edgar as well, and he's vanished."

Storm had already grabbed Jenna's hand and started down the hall.

Jenna turned to the frenzied messenger. "I think Edgar went toward Keanin's rooms; you might start there."

"Thank you, my lady!" The boy was gone an instant later.

Storm was silent as they walked quickly down to the royal hall. Jenna finally broke into his thoughts. "What do you think happened?"

Storm shook his head sharply. "I've no idea, but I'm sure somehow our friends are behind it. I don't know if it's that mage or Ravenhearst and crew."

"Do you think Mikasa is involved?" Jenna had to ask, she needed to know what he was thinking about the kelar noblewoman. And her vanishing from here less than a week before her homeland went into lockdown was a bit suspicious.

Storm didn't slow his pace, but Jenna felt the pressure on her hand increase briefly. "She wouldn't have been the one planning it, that's for certain. But she's most likely involved."

An instant later they were at the royal hall and barging through the doors.

Tor Ranshal, Prince Resstlin, and a handful of gray-haired advisors were gathered around a wide map table and an exhausted Khelaran messenger. That no one looked up at their abrupt entrance spoke volumes of the seriousness of the situation.

"What's happened?" Storm led them into the room.

Resstlin glanced up at Storm's question. "There you are." He belatedly noticed Jenna as well. "Where is Master Ghortin? We really do need mage advice on the situation."

"Ghortin and the others will be here." Storm grabbed his brother's arm. "What has happened?"

Resstlin pointed toward the messenger. "We've received word that the Khelaran capital, Craelyn, fell under attack. It was weakened from the inside, then a band of mercenaries swarmed them from the outside. The mercenaries were led by a mage matching the description of the one who took our father. One of the betrayers on the inside was Lord Ravenhearst; they speculate he used Lady Mikasa to get inside. However, the lady vanished before they were certain." Jenna thought she saw an instant of sympathy cross Resstlin's face as he looked at his brother, but it vanished immediately.

"But how could they have gotten there that quickly? There must be a mistake." One of Resstlin's advisors whined. Jenna looked around the room and realized Resstlin wasn't the only one who had underestimated Ravenhearst, nor the only one to have called him a friend. The flat-faced man was also studiously looking at Storm's hand, the one that was still holding her own.

Still glaring at them, he continued. "It has to be an act by the cuari. No one else could do what has been happening. The cuari have never been trustworthy. And lately, they've not been seen at all. It's them, they're behind all of this."

Jenna spoke up without thinking. "They wouldn't do that." All eyes turned to her as she realized she couldn't explain why to this group. "They have always been neutral, haven't they?"

"Prince Resstlin, who is that woman?" The advisor looked like Storm was holding a spitting snake in his hand. "If Prince Corin wants to bring his doxy around the palace that's one thing. But to bring her into the innermost sanctum of the royal halls?"

Storm cut the man's next comment off with a glare. "First of all, Charloe, this is the Lady Jenna, apprentice to mastermage Ghortin, and by order of my mother, an official friend and advisor to the royal family."

"And secondly, you should never randomly insult people you don't know." Ghortin's voice cut in as he entered the room. "You never know which ones have the ability to blast you into crumbs."

Jenna turned and gave Ghortin a short smile. Turning back, she noticed the other advisors had all stepped away from the obnoxious Charloe.

"Mastermage Ghortin, you humor us." Charloe bowed, but his voice held a quiver now.

"I never make light of someone's abilities, Charloe; you should know that by now. My apprentice has more Power than anyone I've ever met. Except for my mother, who, if my old ears heard correctly, you also insulted mere moments ago."

Charloe looked ready to be sick or pass out. The other advisors took another step away. Charloe finally nodded and took a seat.

Resstlin nodded toward Ghortin. "Thank you for clearing that up. Lady Jenna, I apologize on behalf of my advisors. Some of them speak long before they have formed a coherent thought."

"Thank you." She vowed to keep as quiet as possible

with this group. She'd almost let slip the secret about the cuari; who knew what else she might say.

Ghortin marched over to the map table and bullied a few of the advisors out of the way. This also put him close to the exhausted Khelaran messenger; the man noticeably cringed when Ghortin stood near him.

"Here now, what mischief is this? I've always had excellent relations with Khelaran."

The blond messenger flushed slightly in embarrassment. "I apologize. Please forgive me, but the atrocities I have seen of late have made me hesitant toward the other races." He stole a glance at Jenna and the other non-kelar people in the room, then quickly turned back. "And I do hate to say this, but Advisor Charloe was not the first to voice distrust of the cuari, neither here nor at home. I don't think anyone truly believes it, but the city fell so quickly…we're not sure who else could do it." He shook his head to himself. "Although they gave it back quick enough."

Ghortin nodded and smiled briefly. "It is completely understandable, I assure you." He turned toward the rest of the assemblage. "Could someone please bring us up to date on what has happened? And clarify that they stormed the city, then *gave it back*?" As Ghortin spoke, Jenna felt a subtle spell flow out from him into the exhausted messenger. The man revived noticeably.

"I should be the one if His Highness agrees." The Khelaran messenger looked to Resstlin for approval. At the prince's nod, he continued, "Very well. Is everyone here?"

Resstlin looked around at the assembled advisors. "Not yet. I would like to wait until Sir Edgar and Armsmaster Garlan are here as well."

"We can't speak for the Armsmaster, but Keanin and I are here." Edgar's voice came from where he had silently appeared in the back of the room. Jenna was disturbed again at how silent the man was; and that he was rubbing off on Keanin.

Resstlin had an odd look at the appearance of Keanin, but Jenna noticed he subtly looked to Ghortin for guidance. When Ghortin gave him the tiniest of nods, he welcomed both men to step closer. Before he could speak, however, the door swung open again and the stocky Armsmaster entered the room. "I believe we are all here. Serik, would you please repeat what you told me earlier?"

The messenger was beginning his tale when the huge windows behind the group swung open and a gust of wind filled the room.

"Mind if I join you on this?" The disembodied voice was followed an instant later by a tall, dramatically beautiful woman as she appeared to step out of the window. It was impossible to tell her race except that she didn't look to be of any of them. Her long black hair lifted lightly in the breeze she was creating to hold herself afloat. She gazed around with sharp green eyes that were almost the same shape as of the kelars', but different enough to point out she wasn't one of them. Her ear tips were longer and thinner than those of the kelar. She stopped her study of the room at Ghortin with a grin. "Hello, boy. Haven't mucked things up too much, have we?"

CHAPTER SEVEN

GHORTIN TURNED PALE and grabbed the edge of the map table.

It took only a second to put two and two together. "Is that Carabella?" Jenna barely whispered into Storm's ear, but the woman heard her anyway.

According to Storm, Carabella had been hiding from Ghortin, her son, for roughly a thousand years. Ghortin would hear rumors of her being seen, but she'd always be gone when he got to where she'd been sighted. Storm told her Carabella thought it was a great game—Ghortin wasn't amused.

The smile she flashed Jenna and Storm was nothing short of blinding. "In the flesh." She let her feet touch the floor and looked down at her body. "Well, what passes for flesh these days." She gave Jenna a wink. "You must be Jenna. I do hope you've had better luck with him than I have."

"Ghortin's been great, really," Jenna stammered. She wasn't sure how to treat this immortal, almost mythical, woman. It didn't help that nearly everyone in the room looked as poleaxed as Ghortin.

Carabella took a step forward and tweaked Ghortin's nose. "Snap out of it; there's too much work to do." A brief flicker of doubt crossed her inhuman features. "At least I think so; events have been hazy as of late."

"What..." Ghortin took a deep breath and shook his head to clear it. Jenna didn't blame him; seeing your mother after a thousand years was bound to cause issues. He tried again. "What are you doing here, Carabella?"

Carabella splayed her long-fingered hands on her hips as she surveyed the room. "I'm trying to figure that out myself." She peered down at the map before them. "Important events are taking place, correct?" As she peered around the room Jenna noticed that her pupils weren't completely round, but slightly elongated like a cat. She didn't look like any of the other three species, but the differences were subtle. Cuari were the first species until they mucked things up by trying to overthrow the gods and goddesses.

Resstlin regained his composure first, his royal diplomatic training kicking in. "Please sit, my lady. While we are humbled by your visit, you are correct; dire occurrences are happening even as we speak."

The advisors all appeared on the edge of a collective collapse. The battered Khelaran messenger looked about to crawl out of his skin. "Is she really who she says?" His voice was a few octaves higher than previously.

Before the words finished leaving his lips, Carabella had the man in the air and lounging on pillows. Unlike when others used magic, Jenna didn't sense anything.

"I'm Carabella, my boy. If I'm not me, you could be in some serious trouble right now." With no effort, she lowered the man, pillows and all, back to his chair. With a studied look at the room, she whirled and settled down on an ornate chair that hadn't been there a moment before. "Now that we've all established who I am, can I please find out why I'm here?"

Serik recovered from his trip into the air with surprising grace. "Gladly, my lady. As I told Prince Resstlin, Craelyn was attacked from within and without. The villains came to our land via Lithunane and my king sent me to ask King Daylin to fall back and explain his intentions. Once they captured the city, the miscreants left suddenly but it was still an affront." He gave a small bow to Resstlin. "When I arrived, I was told of what havoc these same villains practiced upon Traanafaeren and the loss of a good king."

Carabella's emerald eyes narrowed and the cat-like pupils were more noticeable. She looked around the room quickly. "Daylin is dead? I should have felt that." She glanced quickly to Ghortin. "I see there is much I have missed." She nodded for Serik to continue but the worry was clear on her face.

"I have told them some of it already, my lady." The messenger's face grew grim. "We had no idea who he was, this cloaked attacker who came with Lord Ravenhearst and Lady Mikasa of Khelaran; the king feared that King Daylin was launching an attack and the mage came from him. But now that I have heard what has taken place here the last few months, I fear it was the same mage who killed King Daylin. He briefly managed to make his way deep into the palace before we could throw him back; he wanted us to know his name though. He said he was called Sacaranz."

Carabella blinked rapidly a few times and then crumpled out of her chair and began a muted keening. She clutched her ears and rocked back and forth as if in horrific pain.

Ghortin and Tor Ranshal both rushed forward, keeping the others from her. "Clear the room. Now. Everyone except Jenna and Tor Ranshal." Ghortin didn't look up as he tried to comfort his mother.

"Do you want to be responsible for the death of a cuari?" Tor Ranshal spoke directly to Resstlin when it looked like no one was going to move.

Prince Resstlin blanched but turned toward the waiting advisors. "Everyone out except Ghortin, his apprentice, and Tor Ranshal."

Jenna shrugged at Storm's unspoken question but went to the side of the fallen cuari.

Tor Ranshal began to help Ghortin move Carabella to

a sofa when he noticed that Resstlin still lingered. "I'm afraid you must go as well, Your Majesty. On your way out could you ask Corin to find Rachael and bring her here? But no one else must come in, or Carabella's life, as well as the lives of many others, may be at risk."

Resstlin clearly wanted to question him, but instead nodded and quietly left. His fear of something bad happening to one of the fabled cuari overrode his need to be involved.

Once he'd finally left, Jenna moved closer to see what she could do to help. Carabella was no longer whimpering, but Jenna couldn't tell if she was conscious or not. Her eyes were tightly closed.

Ghortin looked more scared than she'd ever seen him. "What happened to her?"

Tor Ranshal patted his hand. "I'm not sure, but I'll wager it had to do with that name." Before Jenna or Ghortin could respond he shook his head quickly and held up both hands. "Don't either of you give a thought to that name. I need Rachael here to determine if that name was what caused it. If it caused her collapse, a second exposure this quickly could kill her."

They sat in silence watching the cuari woman fight for breath. Jenna was shocked anew at this world. That Ghortin was over three thousand years old was one thing, but his mother had been around since this world began. She was shaken out of her thoughts as a soft voice came from beside her.

"Oh, dear. I knew she had to come here; I didn't foresee the danger for her."

Jenna was only mildly surprised to see the tiny white-haired Rachael standing next to her. Storm couldn't have possibly left the palace more than a few minutes ago, yet time and space looked to have little concern for the ancient kelar woman. Her lined face crinkled with a friendly smile for Jenna, then Rachael bustled forward and claimed one of Carabella's hands. She looked carefully into the pale face for a few moments before turning to Tor Ranshal with a frown.

"What struck her down? I see no marks."

"I'm afraid any marks are locked within that thick cuari skull." Tor Ranshal sat and took Carabella's other hand. "Craelyn has been attacked by the same individual who led the attack on us during the ball. Only this time he shared his name before he vanished." There was some unspoken communication between the two, and then a slight pause before Tor Ranshal continued. "At the very mention of his name, Carabella fell as if mortally wounded."

Rachael nodded slowly. Her eyes settled on Ghortin. "Did you feel anything at all at the sound of the name? Perhaps a twinge?"

Ghortin started to shake his head, then paused. "Wait, I did feel a slight throb in my temples. It wasn't painful, just odd."

"It is worse than I feared." Rachael's frown deepened. She tightened her grip on Carabella's hand and closed her eyes. When she opened them, her eyes were unfocused. "I am shielding her mind right now. Please tell me what this enemy's name was."

"Sacaranz."

Although Tor Ranshal barely whispered the name, Jenna saw Rachael's hand tighten its hold on Carabella's.

"A cuari. This was not expected." Rachael released Carabella's hand and slowly steadied herself.

Jenna nudged Ghortin and whispered, "Why would another cuari's name do that to her? Can't they associate together?"

Tor Ranshal answered. "The cuari have no problem with each other. Those of the remaining one hundred, that is."

"You mean this cuari isn't one of them? This monster that attacked us and the Khelarans is a cuari from *before?*" There was no way that could be good. Thousands of years ago, the gods and goddesses had destroyed all but one hundred cuari when they'd created the portal to other worlds and tried to remake the world to their liking. The remaining one hundred were supposed to watch over the younger races, but they had no memory of what they'd done before.

Tor Ranshal was grim. "Aye, lass. This monster, as you appropriately called him, is one of the cuari from before. One of the ones who supposedly died at the beginning of our time at the hands of the gods. His existence, including his name, is part of the forbidden knowledge of the cuari." He looked down sadly at the still form before him. "We often speculated what would happen if a cuari came into contact with that forbidden knowledge. Now we know."

Jenna studied the faces around her. She was upset at Carabella's collapse, but they were missing an important piece. "But how can he exist? If all of the remaining cuari except the one hundred were killed eons ago, how could one appear now?"

Rachael gave Jenna a comforting smile but didn't drop Carabella's hand. "I'm sure there's a logical explanation. We have to—"

Rachael's words were cut off as a force outside of Jenna took over—or rather a force from inside. She felt it, a pressure in her head. Her voice was no longer her own. "Nay, my good woman, there is not a simple answer. Long have I watched the Guardians, the Protectors such as this vessel from whom I speak. For centuries, I was unaware of who I was." Jenna thought she should be concerned, but something about this presence was familiar, comforting on a level she'd never experienced before.

The voice continued. "I know more now than before, but that is not enough. I can tell you that all of the forbidden knowledge must be kept from the first race; it will kill them otherwise. And you must find and study those books that were passed down to you. But most important, remember that the three who are one must find the one who is three. Upon loss of all you hold dear, do not forget that your enemy is also aware of this." Jenna dropped to her knees as the presence that had taken her over vanished, but she asked one question before it fled completely, *who are you?* The response was so faint she almost didn't catch it. *I believe I was once called Typhonel.* With that, the presence was gone and Jenna fell back onto her tailbone.

"Typhonel," she repeated it out loud so she wouldn't lose it.

Ghortin helped her up. "What did you say, child? Is the presence gone?"

Jenna shook her head slowly; this certainly answered a few things. "Typhonel. The presence that's been helping me, the one that was more than just the mindslave's echo—it's the lost god Typhonel." The final act of the cuari, the one that prompted the destruction of most of their race, had been to banish the god Typhonel into the portal between worlds. Trapped forever. And he was somehow in her head.

Rachael reached over to steady her as she tried to get to her feet, which was good since Jenna hadn't noticed she was swaying. Maybe she should have stayed on the floor.

"Are you certain?" Then Rachael shook her head at herself. "Of course, you're certain. It's very hard to lie to someone when you're in their head." She looked to Tor Ranshal. "What do you think, old friend? What would a long-lost deity want with us? And how is he in her head?"

"Maybe he wants out." Jenna shrugged as all eyes focused on her. "No really, think about it. He's a god. He was around long before the cuari. Would being trapped beyond the portal have killed him? Couldn't he have the ability to project himself out of that world or whatever lies on the other side?" She nodded to herself and began pacing before she caught what she was doing and stopped. "His presence is probably what differentiated the Protectors from the other Guardians. Only before he was only a vague essence, for some reason he's now becoming aware." Everything snapped into place so quickly, she figured he'd tried to help her sort it out.

"Perhaps." Ghortin was the first to respond, but like the other two, he looked perplexed. "However, we've now more questions instead of answers. I'm still not sure about the ancient prophecy of the three, but that presence being aware of it does have me concerned. Particularly if he is who he said he is." Ghortin began his trademark pacing; Jenna stepped out of his way as he didn't always notice people when he wandered.

"We need to find out how this enemy cuari of ours rose from the dead. Or perhaps he wasn't killed to begin with," Tor Ranshal added.

Rachael held up one small hand. "I know the two of you are terribly interested in putting this puzzle together, and we must do so. But right now, we have other urgent issues that must be attended to." She motioned for the three of them to surround Carabella. "I believe I can bring her safely out of this and make it so it won't happen to her again." Even Tor Ranshal raised an eyebrow at that. "Oh, it will work, but not without a cost. Whenever Carabella hears something that she shouldn't, like that monster's name, or any other knowledge forbidden to the cuari, I can make it so she simply falls asleep. I can set the spell directly in front of the killing mind-block originally lain on all the cuari. We can say there is a rare magical disease affecting the cuari, that she has come seeking help for. However, she will have to stay with you,

Ghortin. I'm not sure how often she sees the other cuari, but running into another one would ruin our story."

Both Ghortin and Tor Ranshal nodded in agreement, but both looked concerned.

Jenna shook her head. "One problem though, others heard that name. The messenger knows the name, and others might remember it." She thought for a moment and an old fairy tale came to mind. "Wait, we could give that monster a new name, maybe shorten it to Ranz. Tell everyone who heard the full name that to use it is a trap and will give our enemy power."

Ghortin frowned. "That won't work; you can't gain power over someone by knowing their name."

"But how many people know that?" Jenna asked. "If you and Tor Ranshal said it was so, wouldn't the magical community at least consider it could be new? There have been many new creatures coming about, strange illnesses, and unexplained disasters, why not this?"

Rachael latched on to the idea first. "Child, that is a wonderful idea. And it will take the strain off my spell if it's not being triggered by that name fifty times a day."

"Very well, you have you a point." Ghortin looked vaguely disapproving. "I do so hate propagating false myths about magic. Just goes against my grain."

CHAPTER EIGHT

———

ONCE THEY MOLLIFIED Ghortin, Rachael linked them together and magically repaired and shielded Carabella's mind. She was starting to wake when Rachael chased them all out from the room. She reasoned that it would be easier for her to convince Carabella of the fabricated situation if no one else was around.

Tor Ranshal and Ghortin went in search of a secure place to continue their discussion about the identity of Jenna's mysterious mental visitor. Jenna found herself wandering around looking for Storm. She still hadn't come to terms with what had happened in the stairwell. She wasn't surprised at her reaction to him; she had figured out a while ago that his ability to push her buttons in a bad way was directly related to how she felt about him. But building a new romance while the world was possibly falling apart didn't seem like the best idea. But she had to admit kissing him was much better than fighting with him. It would definitely make their upcoming trip interesting.

Lost in her thoughts, Jenna didn't see Storm until he ran into her. Literally.

"Watch where you're go—" Storm caught himself mid-snarl as he realized who he had almost knocked down. "I'm sorry."

Jenna frowned. She thought he was past this anger issue. "What's wrong with you?"

Storm ran his fingers through his hair and let out a very long sigh. "Resstlin is at it again." He took her arm and led her down the hallway.

"He's at what again? Is this about the trip to Khelaran? Are we not going now because they've sealed their borders?" There was more than a little hope in her voice, but she didn't think Storm would be this worked up if they *weren't* making the trip.

Storm rubbed her arm where he held it, then stopped walking. He waited until she looked up before speaking. "It's more important now than it was two hours ago that someone officially goes from Traanafaeren. But yes, the borders are closed; to any *non-kelar* peoples."

It took Jenna a full five seconds to get what he was saying. "I can't go with you."

Storm pulled her close and held her. "No. And I have no idea how long we'll be gone. Only Edgar and Keanin will go with me." His grip on her tightened. "And we leave at dawn."

Jenna flinched as if she'd been struck; pulling back, she saw the same loss in Storm's eyes. Not only were they being pulled apart as they were finally figuring how they felt about each other, but he would be riding into danger without her. Jenna was terrified of her friends separating and this announcement was making the hairs on the back of her neck stand up. Part of her knew life would never be the same for any of them once they were parted, and it chilled her soul.

She covered her fear with anger. "He's going to send you off? With no chance for farewells? Keanin can't go, he needs to work on his magic. And—"

Storm pulled her in for a long kiss that completely derailed her thoughts. "I'm going to miss you too," he said softly when they parted.

Jenna thumped him on his chest. Anger was better than fear, but the kiss was damn nice. "It's not fair. You can't go. Things are just starting to get interesting, and now you're going away."

"Nice to know I'm more interesting than what's been

going on in the world lately." He shook his head and looked away briefly. "I don't want to leave you behind either. But it has to be done." He resumed walking and led them out into a small treelined courtyard. "And I'll feel better if you're safe here."

Dusk was falling. Jenna's heart and soul still felt like they had been ripped out and dumped somewhere. It was more than only the new situation with Storm, and that was bad enough.

"I'll be back before you know it." His kiss this time was lighter, but it relaxed her.

She sighed. "It'll be too damn long." Storm gave her a lecherous look that finally made her laugh. "Not because of that, although that's an issue as well. I worry about us all being separated. I think we need to all stay together to get through this." She rubbed her arms as a chill hit her.

"We'll be all right. We *all* will. We're going to make sure everything is okay between our kingdoms. Keanin is a very good courtier and Edgar is also. If things go wrong, he and I can certainly get us out of there." He traced the side of her face. "I'm glad you and Ghortin will be here."

"I hate to interrupt, but I'm afraid that staying here is a luxury we can ill afford." Ghortin stepped from a side corridor. That Storm hadn't noticed his approach told Jenna that he was more upset than he was letting on. Ghortin continued forward and his face was grim. "Rachael and a connection we had, told me the third cuari book has been found—well, rumored to be found at any rate—in Strann. No one had heard a rumor of it for almost five hundred years. Jenna, Carabella, and I will be going to my cottage to help Carabella recover; but we'll be doing it via Strann. I hate to deceive Resstlin, but he can't know where we're going. I've told him Carabella needs rest so he won't be suspicious of the ride to my cottage. I'm afraid hiding out here is out of the question for any of us."

Jenna watched as Storm's face took an interesting turn. "I can't believe you would think about going there without all of us. You know Strann's never been safe, even in good times. We have no idea whether Ravenhearst is working with the knowledge of the empress or not. Carabella's still ill and you're going to drag her across the country? Not to mention what the enemy would do to get ahold of Jenna." His hold on her tightened but Jenna didn't think it was intentional.

"I can fill you in on Carabella later." Ghortin nodded to Jenna. "Or I'm sure my apprentice can. As for Jenna not being safe; my boy, she'll have a full-cuari enchantress and myself by her side. Carabella's issues have been worked around as best we can—she's still one of the most powerful beings in this world. Not to mention Jenna's own formidable abilities. I believe *she* shall be quite safe. It's you three young hooligans I'm worried about." Ghortin waved off Storm's protests, then frowned and looked around the darkening courtyard.

"Hmmm, it is getting late, isn't it? Please do excuse me; I have many items to take care of before we leave. We'll wait until the heroic farewell for you three, then leave when the palace has calmed down." He turned and crushed Storm in an embrace, and a bit of Jenna who happened to still be attached. He pulled back and looked at Storm intently. "Take care of each other out there, and don't go charging forth like you usually do. I can't afford to lose any more friends this year." He gave Jenna a small smile. "Besides, I don't want to deal with a languishing apprentice any longer than absolutely necessary." One more quick hug and the large mage strode back toward the palace.

Jenna waited until he was out of sight before turning to Storm. "You're the son he never had, you know."

"I wouldn't go that far." He shrugged, but Jenna saw

that Ghortin's emotions were echoed by Storm. He'd never felt like he fit in with the rest of the royal family.

"Yes, you are. I realized it the first time you were a day late for one of your regular visits when we were still in the cottage." She wrapped her arm around Storm's waist. "He acted like he wasn't concerned, but he was frantic."

"Maybe you're right. I loved my father dearly, but I don't think he ever understood me. Ghortin has always understood me." He looked down at her with a similar intensity that Ghortin had. "Take care of him for me?"

Jenna laughed. "To paraphrase a certain mastermage, he'll have a full-cuari mother and me at his side." She grew serious. There was too much going on and too much potential for loss. "But he did have a good point. You take too many risks, so does Edgar. Who's going to watch out for you two?"

Storm's expression was serious, but he stayed silent. Finally, after a few moments, he smiled. "You know, this is going to be our last night together for at least a month, and I can think of many things I'd rather be doing with you than debating who needs more protection."

Jenna shook her head. He had a point, whether she liked it or not, they were going to be separated. It would be a shame to waste this night. "I believe you're correct. What shall we do instead?"

Storm's answer was a kiss that drove all thoughts of anything else out of her mind. After a few minutes, they made their way to his chambers to forget it all for the few hours they had.

———◆———

The next morning all of her concerns and fears rushed back as Jenna watched the final preparations for the Khelaran excursion in the palace courtyard. Serik was obviously pleased with the prospect of traveling back in such august company but an irrational part of her wanted to smack him. This wasn't his fault, but he didn't have to look so smug.

Carabella said she felt better, but Ghortin had kept her resting in her rooms until they were ready to leave. She was still out of sorts; although Rachael had told them what ailed her now was psychological rather than physical. Like the rest of the cuari, Carabella was used to being invincible. The idea of a mysterious disease that could render her unconscious without warning was not settling well with her. Ghortin telling her about their secret mission to Strann did perk her up a bit, but she was still peevish.

Jenna shook off all of her misgivings and tried to present a dignified and composed façade. She was fine until Storm, Edgar, and Keanin rode out into the courtyard in their travel finery. Since this was an official visit, all three were dressed in full royal court glory. The rich velvets, capes, and jewels would disappear into specially designed pouches once they were free of the city only to be donned again as they approached Craelyn.

Sharp-faced Edgar was striking in deep burgundy with a short black cape. Keanin was amazing as usual in his trademark emerald; Jenna thought whole flocks of courtiers, both men and women, were going to collapse as he rode by. And then there was Storm. All of Jenna's composure vanished as he approached, looking every inch an elven king out of a fantasy novel. His deep blue velvet garb had to have been dyed specifically to match his eyes. All three men got off their horses in front of the waiting crowd and bowed to the heir. Resstlin said a few pompous words that Jenna forgot the second they were uttered. With a farewell to his brother, Storm came and stood in front of her, Ghortin, and Crell. With a brief nod to Ghortin, Storm enwrapped Jenna in a very public embrace and an extremely non-subtle kiss. Jenna had no idea why he was breaking with established protocol, but she didn't care at that point.

Once they'd finished, Storm stood back a pace and looked carefully at both Ghortin and Jenna. His heart was in those amazing blue eyes as he spoke, "Take care of each other." Without glancing around at the ruckus his actions had caused to the watching court around them, he strode to his horse and led the way through the gates.

Jenna was still trying to regain her bearings when Crell coughed once to get her attention. "Well, this should be interesting." Her voice was low and Jenna looked up as Prince Resstlin and his entourage stopped in front of her. She had no idea what was going on, she didn't think the heir would hold her accountable for Storm's outlandish behavior, but it was hard to tell what the man was thinking.

"My Lady Jenna." Prince Resstlin took her hand graciously. "Please forgive my younger brother's rashness, and forgive my ignorance. I had no idea he had chosen a new fiancée. We will celebrate tonight with a feast; you must dine at the royal table."

If Jenna felt that Storm's kiss had pulled the rug out from under her, Resstlin's words just threw the rug over her head and danced a jig on it. Luckily, Ghortin stepped in, as she was certain her brain was not going to find its way around this one anytime soon.

"Yes, that Corin. Up to his usual tricks again, always trying to keep people guessing. But I do believe my apprentice left a small spell running in her room, one that we need to monitor. If you will please excuse us?" He had a tight hand on her elbow, possibly to make sure she didn't run away. Crell followed after them.

With a royal nod, Resstlin waved them on. "Until this eve then." He walked off, but not before all of his advisors nodded and bowed in her direction.

"Damn that boy." Ghortin's tone was a mix of annoyance and humor. "He's getting trickier with age."

"I think I see where you're going." Crell looked like she was fighting not to laugh. "I take it that you and Storm have not gotten suddenly engaged?"

Jenna followed Ghortin into the palace and toward their rooms. "What do you mean trickier?" Then she turned to Crell. "And what the hell just happened? Why would Prince Resstlin think Storm and I are engaged?"

Ghortin patted her arm. "Easy there. He meant nothing bad. Storm was only trying to protect you."

"Agreed. He may not like royal pomp, but he certainly understands it," Crell said.

Jenna looked back and forth between them. She was seriously missing something. "Protect me from what? He's made me into a royal gossip target. How is that going to protect me?" While that last kiss was a very nice unexpected bonus, the last time she checked, kisses couldn't protect people.

"Now, I know that boy did a fine job of addling your senses, but think; what were we supposed to do later today?"

Jenna scowled. "Leave for…" She paused as a chambermaid walked by. "Leave for your *cottage*."

Ghortin nodded and continued down toward her room. "Exactly. And what's the last thing Resstlin will want the newest royal fiancée to do?"

"Leave." Storm's plan finally got past the mental muddling his kiss had left. "But I'm not Storm's fiancée. It was only a kiss for crying out loud!" Last night had been far more than that, but they were by no means engaged.

"Ah, yes." Crell nodded. "But a kiss delivered in front of a royal audience, with extreme passion, and on the launch of a heroic journey. There's simply no way anyone from this court would have viewed it as anything else. Well, anyone who didn't know you." Her look turned to sympathy and she patted Jenna's arm.

Jenna clenched her fists. As soon as she felt that the relationship was going well with Storm, he went and pulled this stunt. "That lousy, stinking, egocentric bastard!"

Ghortin put up a hand in placation as her string of curses became more creative under her breath. "Now, I agree that it wasn't very nice of him to do, but he did it for good reason. And I'm as inconvenienced by this as you are, you know."

"Good reason? Inconvenienced?" Jenna spat back as yet another pair of giggling maids walked by. She was already getting *those* looks. She didn't like being the center of anything. Both back home and in this world, behind the scenes is where she usually was, and she liked it there. The idea of being on display as a royal fiancée was enough to make her run out into the woods and go find some monsters to play with instead. "I'd be safer wandering the Markare alone than staying here as royal gossip fodder."

"Now, now. No one is leaving you here. I'll simply explain to Resstlin that it is vital for you to continue your studies immediately back at my cottage. And we'll be out of here within a few days." He looked down the hall behind her and tried to suppress a grin. "I know we have much to discuss, but I do believe it can wait until you have resolved the evening's attire with your new ladies. I wouldn't tell them that you aren't Corin's fiancée. They won't believe you and it will make getting away that much more difficult." He bowed, then turned and practically ran in the other direction.

"Sorry, I am horrible with fancy dress. Good luck." Crell ducked down a side corridor.

"Crell! Ghortin!" Jenna looked back and saw three ladies-in-waiting scurrying toward her; all carrying armfuls of rich fabric. Behind them trailed a small army of seamstresses. Storm was going to pay for this and pay for an extremely long time.

She swallowed all of the scathing remarks she wanted to

say and smiled at the approaching women. She couldn't say she wasn't Storm's fiancée, fine, but she wouldn't say she was, either.

CHAPTER NINE

MEANWHILE, THE FOCUS of Jenna's annoyance was riding clear of the city gates. Edgar, Keanin, and Storm had been silent for the most part, letting Serik fill the empty space with local gossip from the Khelaran capital.

Storm knew right now Jenna was probably thinking of fifteen different ways to kill him, but it was worth it. The kiss was a great way to take his leave, and trapping her in Lithunane was worth anything she did to him when they returned. This trip to Craelyn shouldn't take more than a month; when they got back they could all go into Strann. Together. Strategically, Jenna was too valuable to be wandering around; emotionally she was far too precious to be put in that danger without him.

The part of his mind that pointed out she was an extremely powerful mage got smothered.

Keanin finally rode up alongside Storm. "Might I inquire as to what has put such a smirk on your face?"

Edgar had been riding a bit ahead of them but turned around. "I'd wager today's food rations that it's because of a certain black-haired apprentice. I must say, while I'm glad you two have worked things out, I never knew you were one for such a public display in front of the entire court."

Storm's smile got wider.

"That's what you're so smug about, isn't it?" Edgar laughed and shook his head.

Storm nodded. "By now Jenna is mired so deep in royal complications that she won't be going anywhere until we get back."

Keanin's amber eyes grew round. "She's going to kill you."

"Possibly. I'm sure she'll calm down by the time we get back. Besides, royal fiancées get the best treatment around; maybe she'll get used to it and forget to be angry at me."

"Congratulations!" Edgar rode back and pounded Storm on the back. "That was a bit fast wasn't it, though?"

"Fiancée?!" Keanin looked like someone had run up and kicked him. "You two kept it from me?"

Serik drew himself out of his self-absorption for a moment. "Royal fiancée? Oh, that lovely human girl you said goodbye to."

Storm winced; he hadn't thought of the rumor spreading to Khelaran. But in a way, it might help since that country was having issues with all non-kelars. Serik certainly looked more amenable to Jenna now that he thought she was Storm's fiancée.

"Ah well, you know we were keeping it quiet in light of all of the recent tragedies." He looked from Serik to Keanin. Keanin should know the truth, but it would be better if Serik didn't.

Edgar picked up on his distress. "Serik, could you ride ahead with me a bit? I'd like to ask your opinion on some trails. Besides, I believe the prince needs to confer with his advisor."

Serik looked torn between wanting more royal gossip and being loathe at offending royalty to get it. "Of course, Sir Edgar. We can ride ahead and await them."

Keanin didn't look happy as the two left but stayed quiet until they were out of earshot. "Why didn't you tell me? Why didn't Jenna tell me?"

"We're not engaged. I just didn't want her to go off to Strann with Ghortin and Carabella. I planted the idea that she and I were secretly engaged in my brother's head at breakfast. When I gave such a public performance as we left, he would have put two and two together. I'm sure he's got her sitting with him at dinner, planning the wedding."

Keanin's face brightened as he followed the tale. "So, nothing is going on between you two?"

"I wouldn't say that." Storm frowned at the gleam in Keanin's eye. "After yesterday, I'd say something is seriously going on, but we're not at an engaged status yet."

"Yesterday? What happened?" Keanin leaned forward to catch whatever he'd missed.

Storm smiled. "I'm not going to tell you about the details of my love life. Suffice to say that I have feelings for her, she has them for me, and last night we ...discussed them. Although after the way I sold her out to the royal court, her feelings for me might change." He shook his head. More than change. Keanin's original assessment was right; she was going to kill him. "I'm hoping that Resstlin won't let her out of his sight, let alone out of his palace until we return. Either Ghortin will wait for us, or he'll go to Strann without her." He was worried about Ghortin as well, but his real hope was that they wouldn't go without Jenna.

Keanin rocked back on his horse with a laugh. "Which leaves us with her killing you and gossip all over the place. You know, with your problem-solving skills it's amazing you're still in one piece." The laughter was replaced with a fond smile. "But I am glad you two had a *discussion*. You belong together even if it took you forever to see it. I knew it ages ago."

Before Storm could respond, Keanin gave a sharp nudge to his horse's flanks, leaving any comments behind.

———◆———

Jenna was having a much less happy time back in Lithunane.

"Try once more, lass." Ghortin was trying to be supportive as she failed once more to master the spell he'd been teaching her.

Her scowl deepened as she reached deep into the realm of chaos within her for more Power. She could craft the spell perfectly in her head; she saw each piece fall into place. But when she went to cast it the entire spell fizzled and vanished. "Damn it! I can't make it fit together; it won't work. What the hell is wrong with me?" She folded her arms and glared at him. "Are you blocking me? Is this a test?" She couldn't cope with complications right now, and so help her, if Ghortin was deliberately blocking her for some sort of extra lesson, she'd point out what Power she did have.

Ghortin shook his head. "I'm not blocking you." His look was focused, but it took a second for Jenna to catch his meaning.

"You're saying that *I'm* causing this? Trust me, I want to learn this damn spell more than you want me to." The spell was complicated but strong. It would enable the spell caster to return another mage's spells with accuracy and at full strength. She had a bad feeling that it would be needed sooner rather than later.

"Did I say you were doing anything deliberately?" The smile on Ghortin's face made Jenna want to smack it off. It was his official, 'yes, I'm making you figure out something I've already taught you' smiles.

"You implied it. But obviously, that's not what you're getting at. Look, I'm tired, and I'm just not getting this spell. All I'm getting is angry."

"No, you already were angry."

"I was not." Jenna flung herself down on a large, overstuffed chair. "Well, maybe I was. Those women and their chatter were driving me crazy. But I don't see how that matters."

Ghortin pulled up a seat as well, then magicked up a

tea setting. "It matters in every way with magic. I've tried telling you before; strong emotions can have horrendous effects on spells. Particularly new, very powerful, and difficult spells. How do you think our enemy would react if he knew that you could be neutralized by a trio of giggling chambermaids?"

Jenna looked out the window. "I'm sorry. I'm not great at hiding my feelings, and besides, it's never caused problems before. I've been angry, scared, lots of emotions and it's never shut me down like this."

"Perhaps it's not the chambermaids that are affecting you," Ghortin said softly as he handed her a cup of tea.

"Damn it." Jenna took a sip, but it didn't help settle her thoughts. "Why did he do this, Ghortin? It's not only him trapping us here; it's the entire situation with him. I'm not sure what to believe right now."

Ghortin reached over and patted her hand. "I'd believe that he cares about you a lot; he did it, in his misguided mind, to protect you. Believe that." He smiled as she looked up. "And trust me, I intend to get us out of here very soon. All of us."

"Thank goodness. Otherwise, I'll end up damaging more of the royal family than my beloved fiancée. I *am* going to get him back for this; nothing you can say can change that. For that monster dress alone." She flung a dismissive hand toward the open wardrobe. "Can you believe that's what they are making me wear tonight?"

Ghortin dutifully marched over and peeked inside. Jenna knew what he saw; a frothy, lacy, pink ball gown with enough fabric in the skirt to clothe a pink army. His grunt was noncommittal. "Now, that's not bad."

Jenna almost spit out her tea. "Not bad? It's hideous. The waist is too tight, the bodice is way too damn low, and worst of all, I look horrid in pink." The entire situation finally went past the angry stage. It was completely ridiculous: the dress, Storm's stunt at the leave-taking, the gossip already flying in the halls. All one massive mess.

The ridiculousness of the situation finally got her laughing. "He got me good, didn't he?"

"Yes, yes he did. I'm afraid we'll be hard-pressed to repay him properly." A mischievous glint filled Ghortin's dark eyes. "However, I'm sure we'll come up with something suitable." He looked out the window. "But I fear our planning will have to wait, we have a dinner to attend. Keeping Resstlin happy will keep him from figuring out what we are planning, so go along with the situation for now."

She let out a sigh as Ghortin opened the door for the giggling ladies-in-waiting. How he knew they were out there, she had no idea; they didn't start giggling until the door was opened. "Very well, I'll see you at the feast."

Jenna took a quick bath, then let the women help dress her. Mostly she was forced to verbally dodge all of their not-so-subtle questions concerning certain aspects of Storm. She'd managed to be assigned three founding members of the Prince Corin Fan Club as ladies-in-waiting. She smiled noncommittally where she could, hedged where she needed to, and added it to the growing list of paybacks that was awaiting a certain prince when he came back.

Once they had finally gotten her primped within an inch of her life, Ghortin appeared to escort her to the main hall.

Resstlin no longer treated her like a glorified drudge; that was certainly positive, and quite welcome. However, it didn't take her long to realize that in her rise from Ghortin's minion to esteemed royal fiancée, Resstlin believed she'd lost any semblance of intelligence. If he spoke to her like a simpleton one more time she was going to blast him so far into the realm of chaos he'd die of old age before he made it back.

Halfway through the meal, Ghortin finally stopped

talking to a white-haired advisor to his right and came to her rescue…sort of. Jenna wasn't listening but had been trying to get Resstlin's flighty little wife to stop trying to tell her tales of wifely wisdom, so she missed his first part.

"But of course, you realize why we cannot stay at this time." Ghortin's voice was just loud enough to gain Jenna's attention.

"What? Don't be ridiculous, you must stay. You must be here for the formal services for my father, and what about the coronation? Besides, we can't have Corin's bride-to-be out traipsing about the countryside, can we? What would he do if he came back and she wasn't here to greet him?" Resstlin nodded to Jenna with a meaningful smile.

Jenna was thinking that Storm would live much longer and happier if she wasn't here to greet him but refrained from saying so.

Ghortin dropped his voice a notch and didn't appear quite as friendly. "We've paid our respects to Daylin, and hopefully we can return for the coronation. Corin is well aware of the importance of our returning to my cottage. We must protect Carabella and he understands that Jenna's studies are vital."

Resstlin leaned over Jenna and patted her hand. "Now, now. Doesn't the world have enough mages? As a member of the royal family, she'll have more important things to fill her pretty head. Magic would be a distraction."

Jenna clenched her fists and reminded herself that blasting him across the room wouldn't be a good idea. It was truly amazing that this pointy-eared buffoon was related to Storm at all or to any of the royal family, for that matter. She liked the rest of them. She watched as Ghortin opened and closed his mouth a few times before he finally appeared under control. "I believe we need to continue this discussion after the meal. In private." His jaws were so tight the words barely made it past his teeth.

Resstlin was not only a buffoon, he was an oblivious buffoon. Anyone else would have read the warning signs on Ghortin's face. Crown prince or not, getting a master-mage of Ghortin's level that upset was usually fatal.

"Of course, you are right." Resstlin waved a hand to encompass the people around them. "We do need to have a private celebratory toast, although it won't be the same since Corin isn't here. He should have given us time to handle this properly before he left. So like him to be inconsiderate."

"Celebratory what?" Carabella said as she finally appeared and took her seat.

Resstlin gave the cuari enchantress a regal nod and smiled. "Ah, fair Carabella, how gracious of you to join us. We are celebrating the recent betrothal of my brother Prince Corin to your son's former apprentice, Jenna."

Carabella took in the annoyance on both sets of faces before her in an instant. She reached over and took Jenna's hand as she smiled at Resstlin. "Isn't that fasci-nating?" She flashed Jenna an understanding look. "You know I haven't had a chance to congratulate her at all." Carabella helped Jenna to her feet. "If you don't mind, I'm going to steal her for a bit and do it cuari fashion outside." The enchantress hastily pushed Resstlin back into his seat when he made to follow them. "Oh no, Your Highness, this must be kept private. Womanly things you know; magical womanly *things.*" With a nod to the rest of the diners, Carabella hustled Jenna out a pair of ornate glass doors and down a garden path lit with small glows.

Once they were clear of the diners from inside, Jenna turned to Carabella. "I'm sorry to have deceived you; Storm and I aren't engaged. There's nothing to celebrate unless it's his having made my life hell for the moment." Jenna took a deep breath to let out some of the tension she'd been holding during dinner. "But thank you for getting me out of there. I'm afraid Prince Resstlin and I aren't seeing eye to eye on my future."

Carabella nodded. "I gathered something was amiss. Ghortin looked ready to throttle someone; actually, so did you. My son can hold his own, but I figured I could try and save you." She tipped her head as she peered down at Jenna. "But why would young Corin make his brother, and the rest of the court, think you were to be married?"

Jenna wasn't sure what couldn't be said around Carabella yet, but she figured this issue was safe. "He thought that if his brother believed Storm and I were engaged that Resstlin wouldn't let me leave with you and Ghortin. He has a foolish sense of trying to protect me that goes far beyond reason."

Jenna still couldn't believe how he'd taken their newly admitted feelings for each other and twisted it around. She didn't think he was lying about how he felt about her. But if this was how he was going to treat her every time something remotely dangerous came up, they were going to have a very short and volatile relationship.

"Oh my." Carabella's green eyes lit up. "He is a sneaky one, isn't he? Not really very sporting of him, especially since he will have little to do with court life himself." She motioned for them to go back toward the building. "You know, I believe you and I shall become fast friends. And whilst I do admire young Corin's ingenuity, I simply can't let such an act against a friend go unanswered. We shall be avenged, my good girl; your handsome prince won't know what hit him. We'll get you out of here, mark my words on that." Carabella frowned as they approached the glass doors. "Although Ghortin hasn't bothered to tell me where we are going as of yet. I'm sure wherever it is, we'll have plenty of time to come up with a suitable reply for our enterprising young prince."

Jenna smiled for the first time that evening and followed Carabella inside. Between Ghortin, Carabella, and herself, Storm would get his due when the time came.

CHAPTER TEN

NEAR THE EASTERN edge of Traanafaeren, Edgar came slowly riding back to the others. The sun was rapidly on its way down and they still hadn't found a suitable place to camp. He had ridden ahead, trying to find a more protected location, or so he said. Storm figured he'd done it to get away from Serik. The messenger was the biggest gossip Storm had ever seen, and he truly loved the sound of his own voice.

"Find a better spot?" Storm didn't wait for a gap in Serik's blather but talked right over him as Edgar rode back.

"Not really. We'll make do with this for tonight." Edgar swung off his horse and tied it to a quick stake with the others.

"But Sir Edgar, this place is barren. How can a prince be expected to sleep in the wilderness?" Serik's eyes were wide.

Edgar looked ready to laugh or run the man through. "I have asked you not to call me 'sir'; I don't use the title when I'm on the road. Furthermore, the prince does not need to be coddled, and I know he has slept in far worse places than this." His voice dropped to a growl. "As I said, there is nothing suitable further down the trail."

Storm pulled back a bit at Edgar's reaction. His voice had stayed calm during the entire exchange until the end, but there was no missing the annoyance in his manner. Storm could probably count on one hand the number of times that Edgar had lost his temper; Serik was going to be lucky if he made it to Khelaran intact.

"What he means to say," Keanin stepped in smoothly, with the grace only decades of court living could provide, "is that our gallant prince is comfortable wherever he goes. True royalty comes from within." Keanin led the blustering messenger away from the other two and toward where they would be setting up camp.

Edgar rolled his eyes as the two walked away. "How are we going to make it to Khelaran with that man?"

Storm laughed and helped Edgar take off his pack and settle his horse. "Ride very fast?"

Keanin and Serik were still gossiping when Storm called to them, "Keanin, why don't you and Serik set up our stores for the night? Edgar and I will see to the firewood."

The look Keanin gave him told Storm he wasn't happy with being Serik's appointed guardian, but he nodded anyway. "At once, your gallant prince-ness." He dipped into one of his standard elaborate bows.

Edgar and Storm had gathered about half an armful each of small branches when Edgar suddenly froze. Storm came to his side as he heard a thin buzzing sound; it sounded like it came from Edgar himself.

"What's wrong? Have you been spelled?" Storm dropped the branches and reached for his sword.

After a tense moment or two, Edgar burst out laughing; dropped his wood, and then began slapping at his shirt. "No, wait, it's okay." He held up one hand and reached into his tunic with the other. He stopped squirming as he pulled out a small, plain brown-gray tube. "I had no idea it would tickle so much."

Storm frowned and lowered his sword. "What in the seven hells was that, and why is it making that sound?"

"Sorry, it's a taran wand. Well, specifically it's one of a set taran wands. Most likely it's Tigan of the deathsworn trying to reach us." He gave Storm a pointed look. "After that little stunt you pulled this morning, I doubt Ghortin or Crell would take a chance trying to contact us until Jenna has calmed down. And it's too soon for Rachael or Garlan to be reaching out."

Storm ignored the look and the comment. "How did Tigan get one? I didn't think they existed." He crowded Edgar to get a better look at the unimposing little tube. It looked so plain, that Edgar could be pulling his leg. The thin stick was hollow but had no markings that he could see. The taran wands were almost older than Ghortin.

"He got it from me, well, from me via Crell. It was in the package she gave him when the deathsworn left. I thought it might be a good idea to have a better way to communicate without trying to find farspeaking mages. I got the wands through sources you don't need to worry about. And I'd rather your eldest brother doesn't know about them." Edgar's grin told Storm he'd never get an answer on where they came from. "I'd better respond." Holding the stick between both palms, Edgar whispered a magically tinged word and the buzzing sound stopped. "Hello?"

"I am trying to contact Sir Edgar of Lithunane?" Tigan's voice seemed to come from the air directly above the stick itself.

"This is he."

"There was some debate among my people as to whether this was a true taran wand or not. I am pleased that it works. Ki' Crell asked that any information we found concerning the Markare be reported to you first. I am reporting." He paused. "A person is claiming to be a deity."

Edgar arched a black brow as he looked at the wand. "A new deity? I'd say that warrants contacting us."

"All we've heard is rumors so far, nothing substantial at this point. But the rumors are new, there are bound to be more." Tigan's voice cut off so suddenly that Storm feared the wands had broken. A second later he came back. "I have to go. My scouts are coming back. I'll keep you updated if I hear more information as we travel." He cut the call.

Edgar looked at Storm as the wand went silent. "Well, you heard him. New gods of all things."

"I wish we knew more." At Edgar's look, Storm continued. "Think about it, what being is most likely to put himself up as a god?"

Edgar let out a sigh and helped Storm pick up his dropped logs. "That mage, Sacaranz. Which means he's in the Markare."

"Did you say Ghortin has one of these wands as well?" Storm nodded at the wand peeking out of Edgar's tunic.

"Yes he does, and I agree we'd better contact him about this. I'm sure Tigan will update Crell, but if we don't tell Ghortin, he'll get annoyed." Edgar handed the last branches to Storm and secured the wand deeper into his tunic. "Unfortunately, I'll have to try later; it takes the wands a while to recharge." An evil grin appeared on the spy master's face. "Would you like me to pass words along to your *fiancée*?"

Storm tried to glare at his friend, but his heart wasn't in it. This mess was of his own design. "Tell both of them that I'm sorry for what I did. But I still think it's for the best if they wait until we get back." He frowned. "Especially after what we just heard."

Edgar led the way back to their small camp. "I'll tell them the first part, but I'm not risking my life by telling either of them where to stay." He looked back over his shoulder at Storm "Annoying mages, particularly powerful mages, is a very good way to shorten your life. Even a royal life."

Storm snorted in response but kept his thoughts to himself.

Back in Lithunane, Carabella and Jenna settled into a much nicer meal than before. With Carabella's help, Resstlin stopped badgering Jenna. Every time he asked Jenna a question, Carabella would answer. Her cryptic answers, and the fact he couldn't very well ask her to stop, increased Resstlin's frustration.

After twenty minutes, Resstlin bid good evening to the assembled guests and escorted his wife out of the hall.

Carabella watched until the rest of the diners had returned to their own conversations before she relaxed. "Thank the stars he's gone." Her rich voice was pitched low enough for only Jenna and Ghortin to catch it. "Are we certain he wasn't a foundling?"

Ghortin hid his laugh behind a napkin. "Unfortunately, he has Daylin's looks, if nothing else."

Jenna glanced around, but it appeared no one heard them. "He was joking about my giving up magic, wasn't he?"

Ghortin raised an eyebrow at her. "Why should it matter to you? You aren't truly Corin's fiancée after all."

"Of course I'm not," Jenna responded quickly. "But the entire idea is barbaric."

Carabella delicately dabbed at the corners of her mouth with her napkin. "That's a very wise apprentice you have there, Ghortin. However, I do believe it is time to return to my convalescence. You two wouldn't mind escorting a feeble, old woman back to her chambers, would you?" She had subtly pitched her voice so that the last sentence could be heard by the entire hall. The courtiers and patrons all politely chuckled at the stunning enchantress calling herself feeble.

Carabella rose and gave a graceful nod to the room, then held out her arms. Holding back a smirk, Jenna took one arm while Ghortin took the other and the trio swept out of the hall.

As they exited, Jenna realized someone had been missing from the dinner. "Where was Tor Ranshal? Shouldn't he have been here tonight?" She knew Crell had ducked out, claimed to be working with her rangers. And she could easily see Rachael not being included and probably not attending if she had been. The mysterious Guardian seemed to function completely on her own schedule. But as seneschal, Tor Ranshal should have been there.

A sharp look of concern appeared on Ghortin's face. "I'm sure he's having a quiet dinner with Rachael. In fact," he carefully steered his two companions down the side corridor that lead to Tor Ranshal's rooms, "I believe we should drop in on them. After all, we had to sit through that dinner; it's not at all fair that they didn't." Any concern that had crossed his face was gone, but Jenna had a feeling Ghortin was worried about his friend's absence.

Carabella let herself be led along. "Very well, we can go visit your friends. But afterward, I want to hear all there is to tell about this young lady." She patted Jenna fondly on the arm.

Ghortin nodded absently as they turned down the hall for Tor Ranshal's room, "Of course, that would be fine—" His words were cut off as a scream ripped through the air.

One coming from Tor Ranshal's room.

He released Carabella's arm and threw himself against Tor Ranshal's door. Unfortunately, Ghortin's impressive size was not enough to win against the very heavy solid wood door.

He looked at Jenna and Carabella with a chagrined wince. "My body moved before my brain did." Shaking himself off, he drew in Power, then instantly let it go in a simplistic but effective blast to the door. This time it shattered.

Jenna and Carabella joined Ghortin as he shoved past the shattered door frame. Jenna could tell the other two were struggling to pull in their Power, but she couldn't seem to grab it either. It was as if a magic-dampening cloth had been thrown over the entire chamber. She briefly thought about trying to make a quick run into the realm of chaos directly, but one look in the dim room told her there wasn't time.

Tor Ranshal was pressed up against the wall. He was pinned to a shredded tapestry that was covered in his blood, but Jenna couldn't get a good look at what was attacking him. At first, it appeared as if nothing more than a shadow was holding him up. But as they moved further into the chamber, Jenna could see a vague outline within the emptiness. The only way to see the creature was to notice where the room itself wasn't. A faint scraping sound came from that area as well, a dry rasping as if the thing had large wings folded up in the confines of the room.

Ghortin swore and sent a disrupt spell at the space where the creature stood. A burst of sparks lit up the area briefly, then fizzled away. An instant later another shadow peeled itself from the walls and dove down on Ghortin, engaging him completely.

Jenna and Carabella sent spells, although she knew hers didn't have much strength behind it. Both spells dissolved without causing any harm to any of the creatures. Jenna scanned the room trying to see if there were any more of the creatures, gasping when she saw Rachael dropped like a ragdoll in the corner.

Ducking over to her, Jenna sighed as she felt a faint pulse. However, she couldn't get Rachael to wake up, and unfortunately, her movement hadn't gone unnoticed. Another shadow peeled from the wall and dove down at her. Jenna still couldn't pull in any real levels of Power, but she cast a destruct spell at it anyway. A few sparks glanced off the silhouette, and it might have slowed down a bit, but it kept coming. She sent more half-Powered spells at it in hopes of keeping it back.

Carabella was trying to move toward Tor Ranshal, but

the instant she tossed one of her own spells, the creature attacking Jenna broke off and slammed the cuari to the ground. Carabella jumped to her feet, picked up a chair, and swung it, flinging the shadow creature off her and across the room. It gathered itself back up and returned to Jenna.

Jenna tried sending more spells at it, but it continued to slowly move toward her. It was on the ground, and the shape limped as if Carabella might have actually hurt it with the chair, but it was still heading toward her and the unconscious Rachael.

A strange tingling in the far reaches of her mind was extremely welcome. The odd presence—Typhonel, she reminded herself—came forward. He seemed more in control this time, or more like he was letting her be aware this time. He didn't speak to her, but she felt his magic slam through her. All of her senses became brutally sharper at the same instant, especially her eyesight. With an inhuman ability, she could now see every aspect of the creature before her.

She had been right about the wings. Long bat-type wings rustled behind the creature, but they were covered in small, greasy-looking black feathers. The creatures were oddly long-legged, with knees that bent like a human, but that ended in sharp bird talons. Their faces were also long, with a narrow jaw and mouth filled with a horrific number of teeth. The image only lasted an instant before her senses returned to normal, but Jenna knew that nightmares of those things would be around for a long time.

Typhonel recognized it and the name dakair floated into her consciousness. Like before when he had taken over, a pure rage filled her mind, pushing out all other thoughts. A spell unlike any she'd ever heard of or felt built up in her then flew toward the creatures. At first, she thought it would have the same effect the other spells had. But this spell seemed to twist as it hit the creatures, flicking like a thrown knife into each one. An instant later the creatures shattered like shards of a broken mirror and fell to the floor. Within moments the remains vanished.

Jenna found herself on the ground, sapped of strength as she was whenever Typhonel stepped in. Although it seemed better this time, most likely because she knew who was doing it. Try as she might she couldn't remember the spell they'd just cast; it was as if it was vanishing as she shouted the words.

Tor Ranshal's chambers brightened considerably with the demise of the dakair. Carabella looked with shock at Jenna, then around the room. The expression only lasted a minute before she regained her composure and rushed to Tor Ranshal's side. The seneschal was bloody, but he stirred slightly at Carabella's touch.

Ghortin joined Jenna at Rachael's side. His dark eyes held hers for a moment before speaking. "I take it we have our friend to thank for our rescue?"

"Yes, but he's gone again." Jenna took Rachael's hand. Unlike Tor Ranshal, the small kelar woman had no visible trauma but was barely breathing. "What can we do for her?"

He closed his eyes and put his hand over Rachael's forehead. "I think the best thing we can do is let her rest. Those things had gone after her mind, but our appearance broke it off." As he spoke, Jenna could see Rachael was breathing easier. She wasn't waking up though.

Jenna frowned. "Will she be okay?"

Ghortin gave her a quick hug. "I'm sure she will. Whether it's her status as one of these mysterious guardians or just clean living, Rachael has always been remarkably resilient." He glanced to where Carabella was still trying to help Tor Ranshal. "How is he? Whatever those creatures were doing, they certainly were more concerned with physically damaging him."

"That may have been to his advantage actually, although he probably won't agree when he wakes up." Carabella rose to her feet, satisfied that Tor Ranshal was going to be okay. "He's going to be uncomfortable for a while, some of the cuts were very deep. But there's no magical damage done, nothing inside him." The beautiful cuari frowned as she studied Jenna. "Just what did you do to those creatures?"

Jenna hesitated to answer; she wasn't sure what information would trigger a collapse in Carabella.

Ghortin stepped in. "I think that should wait. I'm sure that any moment our fight will have some armored respondents." He looked toward the shattered door where a fully armored guardsman approached. "Right on time."

Ghortin waved the guard and his companions inside. "Come in, come in. The attack is over, and the threat is for the moment gone. However, both Tor Ranshal and Rachael need to be attended to immediately. Call in the healers."

The first guard hesitated, taking in the extreme damage done to the room and the lack of any visible assailants. Ghortin folded his arms and glared at the man. "*Well?*" There was enough emphasis to remind the guardsman who he was dealing with. Within minutes litters and healers were brought in and Tor Ranshal and Rachael were on their way to the lower level where the rooms of healing were.

After making sure that the best healers were dealing with the problem, Ghortin, Jenna, and Carabella went to Ghortin's chambers.

"What were those things?" Carabella asked as she sprawled across Ghortin's best chair. "And what did you do to them, Jenna?"

"My question would be why they went after Tor Ranshal and Rachael. Considering who they are, I doubt it was a random attack." Ghortin sat after Jenna had settled, then took a long sip of wine that had appeared from nowhere. At a pointed look from Carabella, he provided her and Jenna with glasses next to them as well.

"I can't answer why they were after Tor Ranshal and Rachael, but I know what they were. They were called the dakair and—" Jenna froze as Carabella reacted to the name.

Carabella's eyes rolled back into her head and she slid out of her chair. Fortunately, she hadn't picked up the wine yet.

Jenna ran to her. "What happened to her? I deliberately didn't say who told me their name."

Ghortin carried his mother to a sofa. "I think this gives us an answer. The dakair must have originally come from the cuari time as well. I recognized them as something out of myth, but they were called the dakan, obviously a mispronunciation of dakair. The original cuari must have sent them through the portal. From what I saw, they had good reason." He shuddered. "The creatures of myth were magic sinks, that's why none of our spells worked right. I'd say our deity friend has many spells far beyond normal magic, however. But someone must have magically brought the dakair into the chamber; they were too big to have gotten in any other way. Disturbing and curious." He rubbed his chin in thought.

"It's going to be hard to discuss things if I have no idea what words could send her under." Jenna started to say more, but Carabella stirred.

"What happened, and why am I over here? Did you put one of your potions in my wine, Ghortin?" Carabella started to sit up, then noticed the concern on the faces in front of her. "Oh no, the illness. I didn't think it would strike again so soon." She sat fully up and smiled. "Although I feel better than the first time."

Ghortin frowned. He had told Jenna earlier he didn't know how well keeping the illness ruse was going to last.

Even so, she wasn't ready for his next words.

"Carabella, it's not an illness at all. It's closer to a spell."

Carabella's bright green eyes flashed wide. "A spell? On *me*?!" Shock was clear on her face. "Who in their right mind would dare to bespell a cuari?"

Ghortin took a deep breath, and Jenna let herself sink back into her chair and drank her wine. This could resolve some issues, or make them horribly worse.

"The Gods did." He met Carabella's shocked expression. "And we can't take the spell off."

Carabella looked from one face to the other, then she finally shook her head. "I must go find the others. This is an outrage! The other cuari can release me from the spell and we'll have a short chat...with Qhazborh, I presume?"

Ghortin made her scoot over and sat next to her. "It won't do any good; all of the cuari have it. Yours has been modified so you only lose consciousness now."

"What would have happened before?" Before anyone could answer she raised her hands and shook her head. "Never mind, I don't think I want to know. Why did they do this? *When* did they do this?"

"We're not sure the exact reason why." A little fib, but Jenna agreed they had to tread carefully here. "But it was done so long ago, it's lost in the past. Suffice to say, the world was different then; there were items that they felt the cuari needed to forget. If you hear any term from that time, you now lose consciousness."

Carabella digested the information slowly, then she looked at Jenna. "What you did to those things, is that something from the past too?"

Jenna shrugged and looked to Ghortin, at his nod she told what she could. "Sort of. It has to do with my not being entirely of this world as well." Maybe if she put the focus on that, she could keep Carabella from wondering about the displaced deity in Jenna's head.

The one she definitely couldn't know about.

Carabella turned to Ghortin sharply. "Where did you find your apprentice again?"

"Somehow—and we don't know how so don't ask—Jenna's mind and mage gifts were flung into the body of a newly made mindslave." He tugged on his beard and got up to pace. "I thought at first that perhaps her coming here was a side effect of a follower of Qhazborh performing new spells. That while he was destroying a village to gather Power for Qhazborh, he accidentally opened a portal to Jenna's world."

Carabella looked ready to ask more questions when Ghortin's left front vest pocket began to hum and wiggle. He pulled out the slim wand just as Carabella's face gave an involuntary disturbing twitch. Jenna could tell she was fighting losing consciousness. The taran wand in Ghortin's hand must have come from the past as well. With a deep sigh, Carabella nodded at her; she wasn't going to pass out.

Ghortin watched Carabella's reaction, then seemed satisfied. Holding the long gray wand in front of him he spoke at it, "I'm here?"

CHAPTER ELEVEN

—————◆—————

JENNA LEANED FORWARD as Edgar's voice sounded clearly in the air above the wand. "Sorry to be bothering you so soon, Ghortin, but Tigan contacted us with an interesting rumor."

Ghortin glanced to Carabella. "Well yes, do go on. *We're* all ears, you know."

Edgar's tone changed slightly as he caught the emphasis. "It appears that someone is setting himself up as a deity in the Markare."

"Ah, yes. I believe I know who you are speaking of. But please don't say his name. Carabella is here with us."

There was a pause from the other end. "Is everything all right?"

"If you mean, has he told me the truth, then sort of." Carabella snorted.

Ghortin shook his head at his mother. "He can't hear you. You have to be touching the wand." When Carabella made no move toward it, Ghortin continued speaking to Edgar. "We had to tell her the truth. Rachael and Tor Ranshal were attacked in the palace by a pair of creatures whose name put Carabella out cold."

Jostling sounds came out of the wand and Storm's voice took over. "What? What happened? How did they get in? Are they all right?"

"Easy there, boy, we're not sure exactly what happened as it occurred less than an hour ago and both are still unconscious. But I believe they will both make a full recovery." He looked over at Jenna's clenched fist. "Which is more than I can say for a certain prince who's going to be mage dust soon, by the look of my apprentice's face."

There was a significant pause on the other end. "I'm sorry, I really am. I think it's still for the best, but maybe I shouldn't have done what I did."

Jenna unclenched her fist. Storm's prank was nothing compared to what had just happened.

Ghortin nodded, then turned back to the wand. "Yes, well we can talk about it later when we are all back here. Does Tigan have more information about this self-proclaimed deity?"

Jenna thought she heard a tone of relief in Storm's voice, but she hoped he didn't think this meant he was off the hook.

"Not really, all he had were rumors of someone powerful claiming godhood. Crell told him to direct any information about the Markare to Edgar, but he's probably notified her by now as well. I think we can guess who it is."

That the rogue mage who'd captured Ghortin and killed King Daylin now had a name wasn't particularly helpful. Especially since they couldn't say the name around Carabella.

Storm's voice lowered a bit and sounded muffled as if he was talking away from the wand. "Could I talk to Jenna? Alone?"

Ghortin tossed a knowing glance to Carabella. She winked at Jenna then left the room. Ghortin handed the wand to Jenna, placing her hands where they needed to go. "Here she is." He nodded to Jenna once his hands were free of the wand. "Just don't be too harsh with the boy. He meant well; besides he's got at least two weeks of hideous royal obligations awaiting him in Craelyn."

Jenna nodded, but her knuckles were still white as they held the wand. She waited until Ghortin had left the room before she spoke, "I'm here."

Storm hesitated so long Jenna thought that maybe she

was holding the damn wand wrong. "I wanted to say I was sorry for doing what I did; it wasn't fair. I wanted to keep you there until I got back."

"No, it wasn't fair, and you should know by now that I can take care of myself." She felt her throat tighten as an unbidden thought crept to the surface. "I thought you and I had something."

"We do, of course we do. Why would you—?" Storm stopped short as he caught her tone. "Do you honestly think that all of that was only to keep you trapped in Lithunane? Last night, everything?"

"Of course not." Jenna felt her face growing hot and was very glad the others left the room. Logically, she knew that wasn't the case, emotionally was a different matter. As ridiculous as she felt, she had to answer him honestly. "Maybe a little bit. I mean I also believed the farewell kiss was real, and I know it's irrational, but this whole relationship between us is still so new, and I'm babbling."

"When have I ever lied to you?" Jenna practically heard his wince. "Okay, except for me-being-a-prince situation. But that wasn't a lie so much as hiding the truth. And if I recall, the stairwell and the rest of last night were a mutual event. Jenna, I have been interested in you since I met you. Haven't you figured that out yet? That's why I went overboard; I can't stand the idea of you being in danger without me."

Jenna was brought up short by the emotion in his voice. "I feel the same way about you, I really do. But it was still a lousy thing to do. Do you realize this palace is filled with battalions of giggling housemaids who spend their days wondering about your sex life?"

Storm laughed, and the tension went out of Jenna as well. "I didn't know that specific information, but now you understand part of why I avoid the court so much." His tone softened, "I'd better go; Edgar isn't sure the length of contact these wands can handle. But take care of yourself, even if you can't stay there, just don't do anything rash. I need you."

Jenna grinned although she knew he couldn't see it. "I think I can do that. You be careful too."

With that, they both let the link go.

During the three days that followed, Storm was having misgivings about his own trip more so than the one that might be taken by Jenna and Ghortin. It didn't help that a freak sandstorm had rendered the taran wand completely useless. Nor did Keanin's rapidly diminishing temperament. The closer they got to the Markare, the more panicked and irrational the auburn-haired noble became. Unfortunately for him, crossing through the Markare was still the fastest way to get to Khelaran. There was a sea route, but it would require traveling on two ships and add a week or more to the journey.

"I'm telling you; I can't go in there. Not only that I don't want to go in there, I *can't* go in there."

Keanin's rapidly rising voice woke Storm out of a sound sleep. Edgar had been on the last watch, but obviously, Keanin had woken early. And was going to wake the whole camp with him. Edgar's voice was low, and Storm couldn't hear his words since he was trying to let Storm and Serik sleep.

Storm rolled out of his bedroll, and then out of his tent. "Never mind, Edgar. I'm already awake. So is probably everyone back in Lithunane and every town in-between." He fought to get some of the grit that now covered everything out of his eyes. "What is biting at you now, Keanin?"

Keanin looked chagrined, but only for a few moments. "I'm sorry I woke you." There was a nervous twitch in his golden eyes. "But I can't go into that desert again; I can't. Something bad is going to happen to one of us if I do, I know it." The edgy nervousness gave way to terror and Edgar looked at Storm with concern.

Storm was concerned himself; Keanin was closer to him than anyone in his life, had always been more of a brother than either Resstlin or Justlantin. He was often afraid of anything outside the confines of the palace, but Storm had never seen him like this.

"What makes you think that?" Edgar's voice was calm, but Storm noticed that the spymaster was mindlessly handling one of his small black throwing blades. Keanin was a magic user, he could be picking up on danger nearby and not realize it.

Keanin turned red in the early morning light, then looked down. "A dream."

"A what?" Storm stepped forward to make sure he heard correctly. Keanin was about ready to crawl out of his skin because of a dream? He knew his lifelong friend was mage-gifted, but the odds of him having dreamseeing were incredibly rare. Besides, Ghortin had been working very closely with Keanin; he would have noticed a gift like that.

"A dream, all right? I know what you're going to say, but it wasn't only a nightmare. It was a warning. I have to stay out of the Markare." His look turned pleading. "Couldn't we ride down to Shettler's Point and take a river ship to Erlinda instead? Erlinda is lovely this time of year, and getting an ocean voyage to Craelyn from there would just take a day or two." He was close to babbling.

Storm rubbed his face and let out a long sigh. "You know that would add at least a week, possibly two, to our trip." He stepped closer to Keanin to look him clearly in the eye like he would a frightened horse. "We'll only be in the Markare a few days." He held Keanin's shoulder with one hand and added some bravado to his voice. "Besides you've got two of the kingdom's best fighters with you; you'll be safe."

Keanin shook his head. "It's not only me that I'm worried about. That dream was a warning. I'm the target, but any who are with me are in danger as well. We won't make it, not all of us, not safely."

The coldness Storm felt in his soul the past few days flickered and increased. He was used to Keanin being jumpy and his ongoing fear of the Markare, but he'd never seen both issues so out of control.

"Keanin, I believe you. But the situation is getting worse. We have to get the Khelaran kingdom on our side; we can't go up against this Sacaranz and Ravenhearst's Qhazborh priests alone. And we've got to do it quickly; who knows when it's all going to blow up on us again." He waited until Keanin looked him in the eye. "But keep telling us what you sense. Maybe if you have a tie to whatever it is, you can warn us and we can avoid it."

Keanin sighed. "I understand. Just promise me you'll listen to me if I say run." He grimaced. "Even if it means leaving me behind." When Storm started to brush him off, Keanin violently shook his head. "No. Promise me. You will get the hell out of there and take Edgar with you if I say to. I can't explain more, I don't know more. I need you to promise."

It would be best to humor him. "Fine, Edgar and I both promise; if you tell us to get out, we'll leave." At Edgar's sharp look, Storm shrugged. There was no way in this or any other world he would leave anyone behind, especially Keanin. But that wasn't what he needed to hear right now.

Keanin seemed to calm down a bit. "Okay, just don't forget."

They were packed and ready to ride within the hour; but not before Edgar made one more futile attempt to activate the taran wand.

"You don't think it's broken for good, do you?" Storm

asked as Edgar slid the wand into his pack.

With a sigh, Edgar mounted his horse. "I don't think so, but then I didn't know a sandstorm could cause problems with it. We don't know near enough about these artifacts; I have no idea if it will ever come back."

"Well, if anyone can get it working, I'm sure you can." Storm checked to make sure the other two were moving. Serik was trying to regale Keanin with another one of his tales, but Keanin only half-listened from atop his horse. His gaze was focused on the desert shimmer that was visible not too far ahead. At least they were mounted and ready. "Shall we? The sooner we get into this damn desert, the sooner we can get out."

———◆———

A few hundred miles away, Jenna was thinking of getting out as well. As in getting out of Lithunane before she went out of her mind.

Ghortin's promise of them only spending a day or so had yet to come true. Three days had passed, and still no sign of Resstlin letting up. He avoided Jenna more than he initially did, but that was mostly because Carabella always seemed to be with her. For some reason, the cuari woman put him on edge.

The attack on Tor Ranshal and Rachael made their escape more complicated.

Even once the two recovered, they couldn't tell Resstlin exactly what it was that had attacked them as Ghortin still wasn't sure that Resstlin could be trusted. So, Resstlin had barred all entrances and exits from the palace until he was certain there were no more threats within its walls.

Plus, none of them wanted to leave until both Tor Ranshal and Rachael recovered more. Ghortin had been very shaken by the attack on his friends, far more so than he was willing to admit. The information they'd been able to tell Ghortin and Jenna had been minimal. The dakair attacked without warning and had appeared out of the walls themselves.

A day after the attack, Resstlin received an official cuari summons. The cuari held towers in each land so they could speak to the royals in times of need. Not all of the one hundred were as gregarious and social as Carabella. Gathering an entourage around him, along with Carabella, Ghortin, and Jenna, Resstlin made the pilgrimage to an ancient cuari tower built just past Lithunane's southern city limits. The tower was huge and triangular. Not shaped like a pyramid, but with three sides. It had a long narrow walkway where Resstlin presented himself. After an hour of no one coming to meet him, he sent Ghortin and Carabella to investigate. Jenna couldn't join them since only those of cuari blood could enter the tower. After fifteen minutes the two came out looking troubled. It was clear that someone had trigged the call to the palace, but there was no trace of them now. Resstlin had ordered everyone back to the palace and re-bolted all the doors.

Carabella spent that night in her chambers, too upset to speak with anyone. She only told Ghortin and Jenna what she had done in the tower; she had reached out to her cuari brethren—and felt nothing. That had never happened before and it shook her to the core.

That had been a few days ago, and each day Ghortin rallied Resstlin to let them go so they could investigate, and each day the frightened heir turned him down. The palace advisors had gone from veiled comments that perhaps the cuari were behind the attacks on Traanafaeren and Craelyn to agreeing that the cuari themselves were victims. Obviously, as such, Carabella could not be allowed to leave the palace. They didn't want Ghortin or Jenna to leave either, and not only because Jenna was supposedly Prince Corin's fiancée. Ghortin was one of the most powerful mages in the world, and if there was to be another attack they wanted him and his apprentice to defend them. Even though there were dozens of powerful mages who lived in or near the palace. At one point yesterday Jenna thought perhaps Resstlin was going to let them go, but the palace advisors talked him out of it.

Jenna could have fried all of them on the spot.

"Now this is completely out of hand and is going to do nothing but help our enemies," Ghortin growled as he paced around the small solarium waving a royal missive in the air. Jenna, Carabella, Rachael, and Tor Ranshal watched him with various levels of amusement and concern.

"What is his answer now?" Tor Ranshal asked softly as he sipped some tea from his pillow-covered chair. The seneschal still had dark scars from his battle with the dakair, and was generally tired, but aside from that, he was recovered from the attack.

Ghortin paused in his stomping long enough to rattle the parchment at his friend. "Not he, *they*. It is a note from the council asking that we please stop disturbing the heir and causing him stress at this important time." He returned to stomping. "It seems our wanting to leave and possibly find a way to save the kingdom and the world itself is interfering with the coronation plans."

Jenna turned away from the window she'd been staring out of. "I thought the coronation wasn't for another two months?" That had been an issue for a while, but Resstlin had finally decided his youngest brother needed to be there. And it wasn't safe to bring the rest of the family down from Irundail at this time. So he'd agreed to a postponement.

"It isn't!" Ghortin balled up the council's request and threw it across the room. "These…these…" His face was almost purple by the time Rachael cut him off.

"It's okay." The tiny kelar woman looked frailer than

usual since the attack, but she was still a bastion of emotional strength. Jenna could almost see the soothing energy coming from her. "Getting all worked up about it isn't going to change the situation. We will find a way to get you three out and on your way; and without the heir or anyone outside of this room really knowing why you're leaving. Although it is going to be more difficult now that we have misplaced the cuari, but it will be done."

She leaned forward from her sofa perch, looking intently at the three of them who would be traveling. "But I warn you yet again, go warily into Strann. I don't think Ravenhearst's involvement was unknown to them, although the empire hasn't openly admitted it. I also believe those creatures that attacked us originally came from that part of the world. And be wary of Ranz; if he realizes what you're after, and what it could mean, he will hunt you down wherever you go."

Ghortin finally gave up his pacing and settled on a large chair. With a sigh, he magically created a cup of tea and looked expectantly around him. "Well then, what's our plan?"

CHAPTER TWELVE

———➤———

GHORTIN'S WEARY WORDS were echoed far away by Edgar. "What's our plan?"

Storm surveyed the mostly flat land around them. They had officially crossed into the Markare a few hours ago, but aside from less plant life than they'd seen in the last three days, it looked pretty much the same. Here and there small thin dark lizards slumbered on bleached boulders; no other life could be seen. There was a ravine in the distance that held hope for some protection.

And he was sure someone or some*thing*, was following them.

No tracks had been seen, no sounds had been heard, yet all of them, including Storm who had no magesense at all, felt like they were being watched.

"I told you, I shouldn't have come here. I shouldn't have been dragged here by that demonspawn king months ago, and I shouldn't be here now." Keanin's jaw was locked. His body was folded oddly around his bow and quiver as he waited for something to shoot at. His parents had been part of a failed expedition into the Markare. And infant Keanin had been the only survivor. There was a lot of fear of this place in his life.

"We've no idea what's out there if there is anything out there," Storm said. But he kept his right hand resting very solidly on the hilt of his sword as soon as they entered the Markare. "It could be a local predator trying to decide if we're edible; it might leave soon."

From the looks on their faces, Keanin and Edgar believed that about as much as he did. Serik, however, had been raised in a sheltered environment, even more so than Keanin. In Serik's nice orderly world, royalty was always right; especially when one needed them to be.

"Prince Corin is surely correct," the thin messenger said with a forced relaxed air. "We most likely disturbed one of those large lizards that live here; it is watching until we leave the area."

Even Keanin gave Serik a look of disbelief at that. "No, it's me. I'm telling you; something doesn't want me in the Markare."

"I'm sure everything is fine. After all, you destroyed those demonspawn. What else could be out here?" Serik failed at his attempt of a reassuring smile.

Edgar shook his head, then turned away and studied the walls of the ravine they were riding into. Storm came up alongside. The ravine didn't go far back, not more than ten feet or so, but the walls were steep. Storm was tired of being followed; whatever was trailing behind them would most likely wait until dark to attack. He intended to force their follower into action when he and Edgar were ready to defend against them. "I think we should camp here. I'd rather not make it easy for who-ever is after us. If we get separated in the open desert we could all be lost."

"I agree on that." Edgar swung down off his horse. "Come on, you two can help roll boulders over here."

"I still say we should leave, but I suppose stopping is better than going forward," Keanin said as he got off his horse.

Serik, however, refused to get off his horse. "Shouldn't we stay mounted? We can outride whoever it is." It was warm out, but not unbearable, yet Serik had rivulets of sweat pouring down his face; his horse was picking up on Serik's nerves and was starting to fidget.

"Who said anything about running?" Edgar said with a disgusted look. "It's best to have a defensive position when you can, especially when there's a very large desert to deal with. Running hellbent isn't going to help us if we come up against something faster than us, now will it?" Edgar squinted across the way they'd traveled. "If we are even being followed."

"But I don't want to—" Serik's last comment was brutally cut off as a black arrow sliced into his throat. Another hit his chest. He was dead before his body fell to the ground.

"Down!" Edgar yelled as Keanin and Storm ran their horses deeper into the protection of the ravine behind them.

"I told you!" Keanin yelled. "The desert doesn't want me here!"

"The last time I checked, the desert wasn't firing arrows at people. Now stay down!" Storm pushed his friend down. All three held still, weapons at the ready, waiting to see what would happen next.

"We know you're back there, Traanafaeren scum." The voice was harshly accented like a low-born citizen of Strann. "We've killed your prince." Both Keanin and Edgar shared confused looks with Storm. "Return to your king and tell him the Markare is ours now." Another black arrow flew out, landing just past Serik's body. Horses were heard running moments later, then silence.

Edgar motioned for the other two to stay put while he crept forward, then disappeared from view. He appeared a few moments later holding the last arrow their attackers had sent.

"They're gone." He looked down at the glazed eyes and open mouth of Serik. "So's the *prince*." He removed a small spade from his pack. "We'd better bury him quickly; I don't think we have much time with Feriani raiders." Edgar was grim as he handed over the parchment that had been wrapped around the final arrow. It was blank except for a crude drawing of a half-fleshed skull with a sword pierced through it. Feriani raiders were a small fierce band of renegades who roamed the Markare. However, Storm had never heard of them recognizing, nor worrying about, the political boundaries of any kingdom; nor were they ones to establish their own.

Either their methods had changed, or someone wanted them to think the attack was by the Feriani. Someone not bright enough to know who they were supposed to kill. Storm moved closer to Edgar and made a show of examining the slip of paper. "How many are still around?" he whispered without looking at Edgar.

Edgar kept his eyes on his digging but answered him softly. "One. But the rest will come back in an instant if they realize that you were the one they were trying to kill. They left us alive so we could go report this death to Resstlin."

Storm sighed and motioned Keanin to come help with the digging for the *prince*. Serik was a fop and a nuisance but he didn't deserve to die in such a way. Especially since it was a case of mistaken identity.

Keanin got out his small shovel and worked alongside them to dig a shallow hole. Boulders would have to suffice for Serik's tomb; the ground was too hard for a proper burial. "But why did they think Serik was the prince? He doesn't look like Corin." Keanin kept both his voice and head low as he spoke.

Edgar glanced around them quickly. "I'd guess it was because they only knew the prince was in this party, not what he looked like. Perhaps they picked the most foppish-looking one. Corin doesn't look like a prince, Serik did."

Storm saw the flash of fear and guilt on Keanin's face; he looked more like a prince than Storm did as well. He patted Keanin on the shoulder and raised his voice enough to be heard by their spy. "I say we bury our beloved prince here. Then we must ride and take this insult to the king."

Keanin's amber eyes grew dark with worry as he watched the seemingly bare desert around them—all the while trying to appear that he wasn't. "I don't understand, if they knew enough to know where we were, and that a prince of Traanafaeren was with us, shouldn't they have known which one he was?"

Edgar nodded for the other two to help him move their "prince" into the hole. "Offhand I'd say our 'raiders' are working with second-hand information. Most likely they're hired thugs with no vested interest in the situation. Someone hired them to kill a prince, they did so, now they go get their money." Edgar got to his feet. "Either way, you get your wish, Keanin; we'll have to go back and travel out to Shettler's Point and take a ship from there. The Markare is no longer an option."

The boundary between the Markare and Traanafaeren didn't look like much, but the sigh that escaped Keanin's lips as they passed it spoke volumes. Storm was surprised his friend hadn't ridden out at full speed.

"Thank the stars." Keanin raised a hand before the other two could speak. "It's not just because of my dream; there was something wrong. I felt it more so after the fake raiders left." Keanin rubbed his long arms as a shudder overtook him. "It felt different somehow."

Edgar nodded. "I felt it too. And you're right, it wasn't the same. Storm? What about you?"

Although they didn't think the fake raiders were still around, they had decided that his nickname would be safer to use than Corin. Fine by him, he never felt really like Corin fit.

Storm shook his head. "Nothing." Not that surprising since he was magic numb.

Edgar tapped his head. "I felt it up here. Right after we started riding out today, it got worse the closer we came back to the border. Which doesn't make sense, malevolent spirits should be happy we were leaving, this almost wanted us to stay there."

"Which is reason enough not to be in there." Keanin shuddered again.

"Whatever it is, it does tell us the Markare is changing, probably because of a new deity who has taken it as a home." Storm looked at his companions. "When we were here a few weeks ago, none of the mage sensitives felt anything, yet now the two of you are practically crawling out of your skin. Not to mention, you didn't have this kind of reaction going in. Those fake raiders were getting us to turn back, but I'd say something more powerful wants us to go deeper into the Markare." He looked around them but didn't see anyone or anything. "I think we may want to try to contact Ghortin again. Maybe the wand is finally working. There's nothing he can do at this point, but he should know."

Edgar gave a careful glance around the area, then he nodded and pulled out the slender wand. He kept it as close to his body as he could. There weren't shrubs out here, let alone trees, and if someone was watching, even from far away, they might notice him talking to a stick.

He slowed his horse as he called Ghortin's name. Minutes of silence went by. "I guess not yet." Edgar was slipping it back into his vest when a very annoyed voice popped out of the air.

"Well, what is it now?" Ghortin's voice was as clear as if he was standing right in front of them. "Be quick man, I can't talk long—we've got an escape in progress."

Storm leaned over. "Escape? From what? Are they in danger?"

"Hold on!" Edgar batted at Storm's hands. "His edginess wants to know what you're escaping from. Are you in danger?"

There was a sigh from the other end. "Only from Carabella if we don't get out of Lithunane immediately."

A rustling sound was heard, and it sounded like Ghortin was yelling at someone. A minute later he returned. "Well, that clinches it. Carabella's flown the coop, she left the palace. Now, what was it you wanted, Edgar?"

Edgar was blunt. "Serik was killed. We were attacked by Feriani raiders right inside the Markare border. They wanted to send a message to *King* Resstlin to stay out of the Markare, so they killed *Prince Serik*. And something is changing in the Markare. I'm not sure if we felt it going in, but both Keanin and I felt something as we came out. Storm felt nothing. Whatever it is, it's pulling a lot of Power."

Storm nodded at Edgar's inflections on the words king and prince; hopefully, Ghortin wouldn't ask any questions. It seemed like he and his friends were the last people in this part of the world, but he knew looks could be deceiving.

Luckily, Ghortin was good at grasping vocal subtleties. He paused, then answered calmly, "I see, thank you for notifying us. Now, if you three don't mind, we have a mission of our own to complete and a wayward cuari to contain." Ghortin's voice picked up some of its earlier agitation. "Which reminds me, please keep an ear out for any sightings of cuari."

"Certainly, but why?"

"They've disappeared." With that, Ghortin cut off his end of the conversation.

Storm whistled as Edgar put the wand away. "Disappeared? How could ninety-nine of the most powerful beings in the world disappear?"

All three looked at each other as the answer hit them.

"The gods?" Keanin voiced it softly, "But why now?"

Edgar started to resume their normal pace. He'd tied Serik's horse behind his and the animal kept trying to walk faster. Keanin wasn't the only one wanting to get free of the Markare. "I'm not sure, but I'd wager if they were involved it had something to do with Sacaranz. If we know there's a cuari from the before time who's alive and well, the gods and goddesses must know it too. Maybe they're trying to capture him."

Storm shook his head as he took them down a narrow trail that would lead back toward water and Shettler's Point. "I don't think they have him. From your reactions, there seems to be a lot of magic bouncing around the Markare. I'd say whatever happened to the missing cuari, there is at least one more besides Carabella who is still free."

CHAPTER THIRTEEN

———◆———

JENNA PICKED BRAMBLES off her clothing as she followed Ghortin. They left not long after Carabella's vanishing act. She'd used magic to leave the palace, but appeared to be traveling on foot—at least Ghortin claimed to be following her trail. Jenna couldn't see anything as it was nightfall. Ghortin claimed that Resstlin had officially let them go, but the fact they snuck out of a rarely used side gate spoke otherwise. She was too happy to be out of the oppressive place to question it.

Ghortin lit small mage glows to bob along the trail for her, but it was still difficult to see where she was going.

A rustle alongside the path next to her brought her sword out in one hand and a spell ready in the other. Ghortin kept moving ahead, but something was coming up alongside them. "Ghortin." She pitched her voice low, but he had damn good hearing.

A small hooded form dropped in front of her on the trail.

Jenna dropped into a fighting stance. "I'd throw back that hood, friend. I wouldn't want to fry someone without knowing who they are."

The laughter tipped her off before the hood dropped back. Crell. "You two have got to pay better attention out here. I've been right behind you since you left the palace."

Jenna put away her sword and released the spell she'd called up. "I thought you had to stay and watch for your rangers?" Not that she was going to complain if Crell's path crossed theirs for a while. The small derawri was a good friend—not to mention a hell of a fighter.

Crell's mirth dropped. "I do. And I'm afraid I can't do that within Lithunane right now. Resstlin isn't the only one becoming paranoid and too many of his advisors want stricter lockdowns of the palace and the city. The trustworthiness of my rangers was brought into question." She folded her arms and glared. "I told the rangers I would be on the road to Strann and to contact me there if needed. They have one of the taran wands. I have to thank Edgar again for those."

Jenna continued to follow Ghortin's trailing mage glows and Crell dropped in alongside. "That's ridiculous. Your rangers helped turn the tide against that thing in the Markare." She reached over and gave Crell a quick hug. "But I'm glad for the company."

"Aye. Figured might as well adventure with friends."

Ghortin waited around a corner. "Good of you to join us, Crell. I heard you an hour ago."

"I'd been following you for two." She winked. "Still haven't caught up to Carabella?"

"I believe I have." Ghortin dropped his voice and motioned for them to follow him around a bend in the trail.

"Finally. It's not my fault you move slower than an ox with a full load for the market. Very nice of you to join us Crell." Carabella flashed a sincere smile as she sat in repose on a flat boulder, a suspiciously flat boulder. "Ghortin has taken so long, I had to provide entertainment for myself." As she spoke she snapped her fingers and food and drink appeared beside her rock chair. She had positioned herself so the moonlight was directly above her and her throne.

Jenna's laugh turned to a gasp of horror as a second later a huge translucent spell bubble appeared out of the air and encased Carabella. She immediately collapsed and curled into a ball within it.

Jenna, Crell, and Ghortin ran to the stricken woman's side, but they couldn't touch her through the bubble. She lost consciousness after a minute. The magical pull on her essence continued and no spell that either Ghortin or Jenna could do would break it. The bubble didn't react to them or their touch, it also didn't give way. Crell wasn't a magic user, but kept her sword out and watched the woods around them carefully. If the attacker was nearby, she'd see them.

"She could be dying; we have to help her!" Jenna was frantic, but none of her spells made any impact on the bubble than bladed weapons did. The bubble encasing her was murky, but Carabella looked pale and gaunt— like her life was being leached away.

Ghortin tried to grab the bubble with his arms spread wide and was flung back about ten feet. He looked ready to charge forth and try it again when a wave of Power rippled through the bubble and it collapsed. Carabella began to breathe normally the instant it vanished, but she was still unconscious.

"What was that? How did you stop it?" Jenna tried to move the cuari enchantress so that she was at least more comfortable.

Ghortin shook his head. "I didn't do anything. It lost Power on its own. There was some sort of surge of Power from wherever it came from, then it was violently cut off. Something attacked whatever was providing Power for this spell, cut it off at the source." He shook his head in concern as he studied his mother. "I have no idea what that was. I've never heard of anything like that. I don't know that it was trying to kill her though; more it seemed like it was trying to channel her mage ability away toward something else."

"Is she going to be alright? Should we try to set up some sort of camp here?" Jenna gently brushed Carabella's hair out of her face. The terror of the attack was still clear on her unconscious face.

"She will if I have anything to say about it." Ghortin squatted down next to Carabella and tapped her head with a finger and a light spell. Carabella coughed but didn't open her eyes. "Come on, you stubborn old goat," Ghortin repeated the move and this time Carabella turned her head. Her breathing returned to normal and she finally opened her eyes. She tried to sit up but then winced in pain.

"I do not believe this will be acceptable." Her eyes drifted shut.

Jenna looked to Ghortin in panic, but he nodded for her to wait. An instant later she felt healing magic unlike any she'd ever felt before flow through Carabella as Ghortin sent a spell through her.

After a few minutes, Carabella's eyes flew open and she sat up.

"What happened?" Both Carabella and Ghortin asked at the same time.

"How should we know? You were the one inside of the thing." Ghortin was back to his usual gruff self, but Jenna had seen that look of terror when he couldn't get past the bubble to save her.

Carabella made a show of only being concerned about the condition of her clothes as she stood, but Jenna figured that was an act too. "Yes, however, you were the one who cut it off." She turned her beautiful smile on Jenna. "Or do I have our lovely Jenna to thank?"

Jenna shook her head as Ghortin answered. "Neither of us was able to do anything against that thing." He began his pacing, a bit difficult through the brush, but he managed. "I don't know what it was, but it was fast, aggressive, and had a great defense system. Honestly, we probably wouldn't have been able to get to you in time; but whoever cast it had a problem of their own. They had a catastrophic Power crash and lost control over the spell.

Whatever they were drawing the power from stopped suddenly."

Carabella shook off the last bits of dirt. "I'd say you've got the right of it. I couldn't feel anything in there really, but the spell didn't feel like it had been broken, more like it blew apart from lack of Power." She shook her head and gathered her belongings from the ground. "Although a being or beings that could hold that type of Power certainly shouldn't have been easy to cut off." A visible shiver went through her. "Whatever stopped it, that thing almost got me. I couldn't tell if it was going to use me up or take me somewhere. It had the feel of a calling spell, one of the old ones. There was something in the background, something I should—"

She froze and rubbed the heels of her hands against her eyes as if that would clarify whatever stopped her. "The rest of the cuari, I was sensing the rest of the cuari. They were there, past my reach, but they're still alive." She smiled, but then the smile vanished as her mind processed more of the information. "The followers of Qhazborh have them. Somehow those snags managed to capture all of them. I can't sense anything more than that."

A rush of pure terror flashed through Jenna. "But if they can take out cuari magic that easily…"

"The rest of us are nothing," Ghortin grimly finished for her, as he picked up a few small items that had fallen out of Carabella's pack.

She took them from him with a frown. "When did you become so negative?" She waggled a finger under Ghortin's nose. "I thought I raised you better than that."

"Raised me?" Ghortin had started going down the trail again but turned at that comment. "Ha! When did you raise me? And you'll have to forgive me for being negative, but in case you haven't noticed yet, several aligned forces are trying to take this world apart. I don't know about you, but I sort of like it how it is."

Carabella shrugged as she followed him. "Yes, I know things are bad. Well, as much as I can know, obviously." Her long hair rippled as she shook her head sadly. "And I did raise you, who else would have had a son who was foolish enough and powerful enough to master a vortex?"

"You know, it's damn disturbing to have someone who's been gone for a thousand years know everything that's been going on," Ghortin grumbled from the front of the trail.

"It wasn't like anyone could have missed that. Besides, just because we weren't speaking, didn't mean I couldn't keep an eye on you. I am your mother after all. Speaking of which, your mother thinks it would be a good idea to set up camp. Soon. She is old and was recently attacked, after all."

Crell dropped in behind them. "There's a clearing up ahead and off the trail a bit. I don't know how it will protect against magic bubbles, but it is a good place to hide from more normal attackers."

"Always listen to the experts, and Crell's far more of an expert on the woods than any of us." Ghortin reached the clearing and sighed as he put down his pack. "I had hoped to get a bit further out."

They quickly set up a small camp. "Now isn't this better?" Carabella set out her bedroll and sat next to the fire.

Ghortin said nothing to her but handed out food. He turned to Crell. "I heard part of it, but what did Resstlin's cronies do now?"

Crell leaned back against a rock. "More of what they've been doing since we got back. But this time my rangers are under suspicion." She patted her front pocket. "I have a taran wand from Edgar and managed to get an extra for my second in command. The rangers are still doing their job, trying to find out what in the hell is going on out here. But there were noises that they weren't going to be let back into the palace." She bit savagely into her piece of bread.

"I think more than only Ravenhearst was influencing things in the palace. You snuck out, I take it?" Ghortin asked.

"Like you two. I don't know what's going on, but I don't like it. I had toyed with the idea of going back to Derawri with Tigan and the deathsworn, but Resstlin talked me out of it. Then he all but banished my rangers."

Jenna watched Carabella, but she seemed fine despite her attack. "Do you have a clue what grabbed you or why it stopped?" Not knowing how it happened meant they had no way of stopping it from occurring again.

"Not from me. I was sitting there, waiting on you all, when all of a sudden, I wasn't." Carabella closed her eyes briefly. "Nope. I was hoping I could sense something... there was something familiar about it... just on the edge of my thoughts." She opened her eyes with an annoyed grimace. "Not a thing. I'd guess it's a modification of a cage spell, one of the really old ones. They are dangerous to use, and take a lot of Power."

Jenna hadn't heard of cage spells, but Ghortin clearly had.

"Are you sure?"

"Of course, I'm not certain. If I were, I would have said so." Carabella shook her head. "I'm sorry. It's been a very long time since I've been on the victim end of things. The good news is those spells, if that's what it was, are treacherous for the caster and can drain Power if they snap back. I'd say that's what cut it off this time."

Carabella seemed settled with that answer, but Jenna noticed the look of concern that flashed across Ghortin's face. Crell gave a nod, she'd seen it too.

"You can't cast any spells." Ghortin raised his hand before Carabella could jump in. "If that was a cage spell, they most likely tied it to your magic—you were creating food and drink when it appeared. You know that better than I."

"I can fight them off. I am a cuari." The haughty grandeur on her face held a tinge of concern, however.

Jenna watched them both. "And someone has managed to grab the other cuari. All of them. I know nothing about that spell, but it seems to me it would be a great way to grab a bunch of strong magic users. It had you."

Carabella opened her mouth to argue, then gave in. "You're right. Damn it. If they hadn't had a Power issue, I'd be gone now."

"Like I said," Ghortin continued. "No magic. No offense, but you cuari use magic far too freely. Whoever took them knew picking you off would be easy."

Crell watched everyone. "I don't recommend drinking heavily on the trail, but maybe we could all use a tipple of Old Hen?" She held up a large flask. "I carry it for medicinal purposes." She handed it to Carabella first.

———◆———

They decided to take turns on watches. Crell said while she wouldn't normally do so in a safe part of the world, that perception of safety was waning.

Jenna was sound asleep when someone kicked her leg. She opened her eyes to see the tip of a knife inches away from her face.

CHAPTER FOURTEEN

I T WAS A few hours' ride down to the small port town of Shettler's Point. In actuality, the port consisted of one rambling wharf that jutted out into the wide Serathian River; the town itself was made up of a smithy, a baker, a butcher, and a shabby, ill-used two-story inn. Even when relations were stronger between the kingdoms, few travelers took sail from this far south. The ship they would take here would be a river craft. They'd take it to the coastal town of Erlinda and catch a larger sea-going vessel to Craelyn.

No one appeared to notice them as the three rode into the dusty town. That was more than odd; three heavily armed strangers on horses should have raised some interest.

Keanin pulled up and looked around. "Where do we find out about the next ship out?"

Storm nudged his horse alongside Keanin's while Edgar held back, studiously watching the locals with the same intensity that they pretended not to be watching him.

"I think the wharfmaster should be in that small shed near the dock." Storm kept his voice neutral, but he had to fight to keep his hand from drawing his sword. He wasn't sure what Edgar and Keanin had felt coming out of the Markare, but he felt something now. There was an illness in this town. Something was very wrong, but it wasn't tangible. He dropped his voice and appeared to be looking off over Keanin's shoulder. "I'm not sure what's going on, but don't you think it's odd that the locals haven't looked up at us once?"

Keanin made to turn around, then caught himself and slowly turned as if he was adjusting something in his horse's pack. After a few moments, he turned back to Storm with a chagrined look. "Sorry, I didn't notice at first, so what do we do?"

Storm studied the buildings around him but kept his gaze moving. Chances were, whatever was going on, some of the townspeople were watching them unseen. "We continue as we would have. At this point, our options are getting fewer." He nodded at Edgar.

The trio made their way to the small wharf and its equally small waystation. The three-sided building was almost a lean-to addition to the greasy inn behind it and would offer no protection for anyone out there during a storm.

It was also empty.

Storm waited a few minutes, then finally led the others toward the inn. Since the two buildings were only a foot apart, there was a good chance the wharfmaster had gone over for a drink. The ill-used ship that was moored there didn't look prepared to sail anytime soon.

The doors swung loudly as the three walked in, but still, no one looked at them. Sand and filthy straw crunched under their boots. Every other floorboard squealed in protest.

Two weary-looking villagers sat silently in the corner, hunched around two mugs of ale. A hardened-looking barmaid brought them two more beers.

The sense of wrongness grew and Storm's hand automatically went for the hilt of his sword. At a look from Edgar, he removed his hand but didn't let it drift too far away.

For the first time since they'd ridden into the village, a pair of eyes watched them openly. The barmaid had been on her way back to the kitchen when she spied them and changed course.

"What can I help you fine gentlemen with?" She reached out to Edgar and ran her hand up his chest.

Edgar removed her hand gently, but his dark eyes narrowed. "Alas, we're leaving immediately. We're looking for the wharfmaster."

She didn't look upset and pointed behind her with a shrug. "He's the drunkard to the left." Without a further glance at any of them, she made her way back to the kitchen.

Keanin frowned and looked around the inn. "Isn't there another way to get there?"

Edgar shook his head. "Not for us. I'd say someone is trying to change our course back into that desert. If that's the case, taking a ship may be the right idea. While this village isn't as deadly as those fake raiders were, it's doing its job to try and change our direction."

At Keanin's skeptical look the spymaster shrugged. "What do you want to do right now?"

"Run as far from here as my horse will go." Keanin shuddered, but he didn't seem as panicked as he had been in the Markare.

Edgar nodded. "Exactly. If our enemy wants us to leave, then perhaps we need to stay."

Storm looked past his friends to where a rumpled shape staggered toward them. "Looks like someone else has finally noticed us."

Edgar held Storm's eye and nodded. "Let me handle this, I've been around his type more than you have."

Storm spared a glare for his friend. Edgar knew Storm wasn't a fragile royal, but sometimes his alter ego as knight took over and his urge to protect the royals overwhelmed common sense. With an exaggerated sigh, Storm motioned for Edgar to go ahead.

None of them were prepared for the wharfmaster to pull back an unsteady arm and punch Edgar in the face.

Edgar had a small black knife in each hand before he'd

regained his feet. Storm had his sword out an instant later.

Far from being cowed or angry, the wharfmaster let out a toothless chuckle. "At least we all know *them* weapons work; now be yer manhood gone or is my girl not good enough for you?"

Wordlessly, Edgar sheathed his knives almost as quickly as he'd taken them out. He made a show of straightening his shirt then turned back to the man. "You attack every-one who doesn't want your serving woman?"

Edgar's voice was neutral, but his eyes were flat. One wrong answer, or move, from the wharfmaster and Edgar would kill him where he stood.

The grimy man shook out his knobby fist. He'd proba-bly hurt his hand more than he hurt Edgar. "Not always. Just didn't like you three dandies thinking you were bet-ter than us, was all."

Storm raised the tip of his sword under the man's chin. "This pride, is it worth dying over?"

He now had the wharfmaster's attention, or rather his blade did. The bald man watched the sword with an awakening dull fear. Finally, he shook himself as if listen-ing to something they couldn't hear. "It's ain't worth that, that's for certain." He nodded at Edgar with an odd smile. "Didn't mean no harm, and your friend's mighty tough for a little guy." A real look of fear crossed the wharfmas-ter's face, as he looked back to Edgar. "Not that being slight is bad, mind you."

Edgar appeared to relax, but Storm knew it was for show. "Not a problem at all. I haven't suffered for not being as tall as those two lunks." His eyes were intense as he watched the wharfmaster's face.

His throat moved noticeably. "I'd wager it hasn't, at that."

Edgar relaxed his stance and looked around the room as if seeing it for the first time. Storm knew Edgar would have taken in everything the instant they set foot inside.

The spymaster was taking another tact. "How long has your business been gone?"

"Nigh on three weeks." The wharfmaster rose out of his stoop and ran his fingers through a patchy, greasy beard. "Ever since that new priest, or whatever he is, started." The man froze and tightened his look on them. "You're not from the Markare, are you?"

"No!" Keanin's fear-filled yelp cut off whatever Edgar was about to say, and Keanin reddened as everyone turned toward him. "Sorry, had some bad things...I mean to say we've heard bad things happen there."

Storm turned back to the wharfmaster who paled briefly, his eyes grim. "Aye, that they do." He nodded slowly. "We've had our bit of trouble of late, but we'll survive." He swung out a surprisingly steady leg and pulled a chair out. Rocking back in it he waved for them to sit as well. "Now, where might you be going to?"

"Erlinda." Edgar folded into his chair.

That should have been a common enough destination. From that major point, people and goods could travel anywhere. Storm was surprised to see the wharfmaster's face pale still more.

"Let's see, should have a barge going up in a month or so. Could send you all over then."

"We need to get there before that." Edgar was carefully keeping the focus on himself; it was better if people remembered him rather than Storm or Keanin. "What about that ship out there now?"

The serving woman came back out and put down four beers. Storm nodded at her but knew better than to think about touching the ale. The smell alone was making his eyes water.

"Nay, that one can't go. Not enough crew, nor goods, to make it worthwhile."

He took a long pull on the ale. "Could let ya all stay here for ten coppers a week until the barge comes through."

Edgar leaned forward. "I've never known a wharf man who wouldn't set sail for the right price. What will it take?"

"Look, I've told you what's offered." The man's face did an odd contortion as he took another sip of the beer, but after a minute he shook it off. "But who knows, maybe in the morning a different light will shine. Things can change quickly." He nodded toward the stairs. "Tonight, the three of you can bunk for a half a copper each, half a penny more for food."

Storm noticed Keanin looking green at the mention of food; he hoped that Edgar would turn down the offer.

Edgar pressed some coins in the man's hand. "We'll take the room, but we've our own food." He met the wharfmaster's eyes. "I could come up with a very generous offer if you can find a way for us to sail tomorrow."

The bald man took the coins only after making sure the right amount was there. He nodded up the ratty stairs to the second floor. "Take yer pick of rooms. Tomorrow will have to wait until it gets here. We'll see what happens then." With a grunt, he made his way back to the kitchen.

CHAPTER FIFTEEN

———————

JENNA FROZE AS her sleep-filled brain tried to process the knife in her face. The person holding the knife was little more than a dark shape, too vague to tell the species or gender. There were no sounds from the others, and without sitting up, she couldn't tell if they were pinned down like she was. Or worse.

"Good. I wouldn't move if I were you." The voice was low, but genderless, or at least pitched in such a way as to not give anything away. Another voice spoke from out of range of Jenna's sight, but still not clear enough to gather information on who was attacking them.

The person pinning her down took two steps back. "I want you to stand, slowly. But keep your hands where I can see them. The slightest move toward a weapon and I will put this knife between your eyes."

Jenna nodded and slowly got out of her bedroll. The fire was still going but much lower, it was probably a few hours after she went to sleep. She stood and tried to look around without making it seem like she was.

Ghortin was standing, but his feet and hands were tied and there was a gag on his mouth. He looked furious and roughed up. He shifted his stance and arcs of magic came out of the cuffs and he stiffed as if shocked. That's why he wasn't fighting back. Cuffs spelled against magic were rare and hard to come by. Someone spent a lot of money to be sure Ghortin couldn't fight back.

"We only want the magic user, not you, or that woman who vanished. If you don't fight, we'll tie you up loosely and you can work yourself free." Now that he was talking more, Jenna could hear his accent—and that he was a male human. From Strann. She didn't know which woman he spoke of, since neither Crell nor Carabella were in sight. There were four other cloaked shapes in the camp, all of whom were watching the dark woods around them.

She didn't know why they didn't know she was a magic user. She closed her eyes briefly, reaching out through the chaotic plane. Nope, only one person showed a magical signature—Ghortin. Which meant they'd been sent to grab him only, but without a magic user among them, they had no way of knowing she was one.

That was foolish on their part and pointed out that someone sent these people out for them at the last minute, and it hadn't been well planned.

"Don't pass out on me." The attacker nudged her with his foot and kept his blade steady.

"Sorry. I've been ill." Jenna pulled up a lock spell, faked a faint, and came up blanketing the area with her spell. The magic flowed out of her—fear must be good for some spells. All five attackers, including the man with the knife, froze in place, then collapsed. The lock spell kept their limbs immobile but if they were moving at all when it hit, they fell over. Handy benefit of that spell, it probably hurt when they fell. Unfortunately, so did Ghortin. He arched back as the spell hit at the same time his cuffs shocked him as he fell.

"Good job." Crell came out from the trees behind her. She put away her bow as she walked up to the man that had threatened Jenna. "There wasn't anything I could do with this one having that knife in your face." She peered closer at the unmoving form on the ground. "He's still awake. Can you do something about that? Eh, never mind." She brought out the heavy hunting knife she carried and rapped the man in the head.

"Do you want me to take care of the others?" Jenna could put a sleep spell over the lock spell. Both were fairly simple and wouldn't tax her too much if there were more attackers out here.

"Might be cleaner." Crell walked to Ghortin and started picking at his cuffs while Jenna sent her spell. She tried to avoid spelling Ghortin this time, but he jerked right as she released it and got included.

"Damn it, didn't mean to get him again." Jenna shrugged and took the weapons of the attackers and pulled down the masks they wore. All human males. "I think we want to tie them up. Where's Carabella?"

With some swearing, Crell got the gag, cuffs, and ankle locks off Ghortin and positioned him to at least look more comfortable.

"That's a damn good question. I turned away from the fire for a moment, turned back, and she was gone. I was looking for her when our friends arrived."

Ghortin's shirt started vibrating. Jenna was closest so she patted him down. The taran wand. It took a few tries but she finally got her hands in the right position. For something fairly small, it was trickier than it should be. "Hello?"

"Jenna? Sorry if I woke you up. Where's Ghortin?" It was Garlan. "You might have a tail."

Jenna watched as Crell stalked around, tying up the attackers. "Yup. We did. They found us. Ghortin is unconscious but appears okay. Carabella is missing, and Crell is tying up the ones who came after us. How'd you know?"

He let out a long sigh. "Thank the goddess. We had word that there was a cell in the outer part of town. A group of Strann natives with ties to Ravenhearst. We caught most, but not all, and it looked like they were after Ghortin." He paused. "Glad to know Crell is with you, next time she needs to leave a better note."

Crell laughed as she tied the last one up. "Tell him sorry, it was a spur-of-the-moment decision."

Jenna passed that along. "Any idea how many came

after us? We got five, but like I said, Carabella is missing and we don't know if she took off before they showed up."

"We're still working on the ones we captured, but so far they aren't sharing much. I only know they sent some people after you because one of them talked too much. Their leader killed him before he could say more."

Jenna looked out into the dark forest around them. "In other words, plan on not sleeping the rest of the night, and keep weapons and spells at the ready?"

"That would be my suggestion. Carabella missing is troubling, but going out looking for her right now endangers you all. Ghortin will be okay?"

Jenna looked down at her mentor. She and Crell might not get sleep, but he would. There was no way she was explaining to Garlan that she'd knocked Ghortin out. "He will be."

"Good. Keep in touch. I know Crell has a taran wand too, so keep me updated. We have to guess someone in Strann knows you're coming and isn't happy."

"Will do."

Jenna started to put the wand back in Ghortin's shirt, then instead tucked it into her pocket. She'd thrown a harder sleep spell than intended, and she wasn't completely sure about the crossing-over impact of it on top of the lock spell. She pulled a blanket over Ghortin as he started to snore.

"What kind of note did you leave?" Jenna pulled out her sword and dagger and sat them next to her near the fire.

Crell brought out more weapons and joined her. "I might have been a bit short. I wrote that I had to go, would be in contact later." She shrugged. "I didn't want to give away too much if someone else found it before Garlan did."

"I reached out magically and only sensed Ghortin.

That means none of our attackers were mages, but that means I also didn't sense Carabella. Do you think another spell bubble caught her?"

"We don't know that. Cuari are different than the rest of us, even among magic users." Crell's words were sound, but the way she kept looking out into the woods indicated she wanted to go after her as badly as Jenna did. "How long will they stay unconscious?"

"I am not sure. I combined spells, and they seemed stronger than usual."

Crell turned back to her. "I'm not a magic user, but isn't it odd to have Power suddenly become stronger?"

"It is. But my abilities are different than other mages, or so says Ghortin." She looked over to his sleeping form. "I wish I'd been able to pull back those spells from hitting him though."

Crell nodded. "Your actions were still sound. Take out the attackers—always. He'll recover. We can blame any new bruises on the people who grabbed him." She got up and walked to the first attacker. "Speaking of which, since we don't know how long they'll be out, let's see what we can learn about who they are, shall we? You watch the woods, I'll check them."

Jenna nodded and kept her focus out past the fire. Crell was silent as she moved between the bodies, but her muttering grew louder as she looked each over.

"Damn it." She came back to the fire and sat. "They might have been sent out unexpectedly, but they're part of a much bigger group—larger than what Garlan found so far certainly. I'll watch the woods, and you go look at the bottom of the closest one's foot. Tell me if Ghortin ever showed you that mark."

Jenna was surprised to see all of the attackers had their shoes and jackets off. "Their feet?" She got up and looked at the one who had held a knife in her face. Nothing on his arms or face, but there was a deep red mark, more scar than tattoo, on the bottom of each of his feet. The two marks were similar, curved daggers with a letter of some sort in the middle of the curve. But they faced each other. "Those had to have hurt."

"And they still would. You've not seen them before?"

Jenna leaned closer; she still couldn't figure out the letter. Or maybe it was a symbol? "No. Are they all the same?"

"Close, the mark in the center appears to be slightly different on each. Ghortin would know them. Those marks belonged to the ancient followers of Qhazborh." She shook her head. "They're far before my time. I only recognize them because I took religious training before I came south to fulfill my family's vows to the Lithunane royals."

"You were going to follow a religious path?" Jenna tried to keep the shock out of her voice. She didn't want to insult her friend, but that would have been one of the last things she could see her as.

Crell laughed. "Not really. I was a bit of a lost cause and tried several paths before my uncle died and I was selected to come and take his place in Lithunane. Probably the best thing that ever happened to me."

Crell's great-great-great-grandfather had traveled with Ghortin, Carabella, and a few other adventurers centuries years ago across the Markare. There had been rumors of a vicious beast that had appeared out of the cuari portal, destroying caravans between Strann and Khelaran. They felt up to the challenge. They managed to shove the creature back through the portal, and shut it down—but they couldn't close it. Even with the power of both Carabella and Ghortin, it had been a near thing and they'd almost all died. When Storm's grandfather decided to create the land of Traanafaeren, Crell's family pledged to always have someone in the palace to serve and protect his family.

"You don't miss Derawri?"

Crell was silent for a few moments, then smiled. "I do, but that is no longer home. Since Traanafaeren is a kingdom for all the races, I see plenty of my people. It's my home now." The snap of a twig in the forest behind her caused Crell to freeze and her hand dropped to her sword.

Jenna picked up a dagger carefully. She had been training on the sword, but like her magic, she was still working on it. The dagger was easier for her, and if need be, she was good at throwing it.

Nothing came forward.

Crell moved a bit closer to the fire so her face was clear and raised her voice as if she hadn't heard the noise. "Yes, this is the better life for me." Then she mouthed, "Stay here."

Jenna nodded.

Crell leaped to her feet and ran into the woods.

Jenna swore. She couldn't see anything out there. When this was over she needed to ask Ghortin if there was an eyesight spell. Humans had the worst eyesight.

Crell had been silent slipping into the woods, but she wasn't now. Jenna got to her feet but agreed that staying there and protecting Ghortin had to come first.

Crell and a hooded form crashed through the brush below the trees and tumbled into the firelight. "Stop fighting me, damn it!"

The hood fell off the other person. Large green eyes looked around frantically. "Who are you? Where am I?" It was Carabella, but she looked lost. And had no magic.

Chapter Sixteen

"I DON'T LIKE THIS." Storm slid the too thin bolt shut on the door to their room. There was no way it would hold against an angry child let alone an armed man or woman.

"Neither do I. It's filthy." Keanin avoided going anywhere near the lice-infested beds and put his bedroll up against the furthest wall.

Storm rolled his eyes; at least some things about Keanin were never going to change. "Not the room, the situation. What kind of a wharfmaster turns down paying customers? He couldn't possibly think we'd wait a month." Following Keanin's idea, Storm took his bedroll out as well. The floor looked bad; the beds were worse.

Edgar had taken up a section of the wall for himself. He pulled out at least ten knives of various sizes and was quietly sharpening them. "He isn't the wharfmaster, there weren't any calluses on his hands." He finally looked up from his blades. "He was trying to get us to leave at first, hoping his act and delay would chase us off. But something changed his mind." Edgar's thin face drew in as he frowned. "It was as if he saw something, or heard something to completely change his view. Unfortunately, I don't know what it was any more than I know what happened to the real wharfmaster."

"I still say we should leave." Storm held up his hands before his friends could continue their arguments. Edgar felt they should stay to find out why someone was trying to keep them from Khelaran; Keanin wanted to get to a civilized city as soon as possible. "I know what you're both going to say; the fact is, something is very wrong here. I've felt it since we came here, something less tangible than the odd villagers." He looked at the blank expressions on his friends' faces. "Come on, neither of you felt it? The hair on the back of my neck has been on end since we came within sight of this place."

Edgar and Keanin both shook their heads.

"I didn't feel anything. The oddness of the villagers was observed, not felt." Edgar continued sharpening a wicked-looking thin blade as he spoke. "What you're describing almost sounds like what Keanin and I felt when we were leaving the Markare."

"I suppose." How could he feel something when the two magic sensitives couldn't? "Maybe you two can't feel it because of a magic block. Keanin, try to do a simple spell."

Keanin looked up from arranging his bedroll. "I can't. Ghortin made me swear not to do anything spell-related until he was with me. He's afraid that whoever sent that demonspawn king after me still wants me. And using magic will give me away."

"Fine." Edgar put down his stone and knife. "I don't like doing this, but here." He muttered a few words under his breath and after a few seconds, a small flame appeared over his open hand. "That's about it for me; I can do a few more spells, but nothing worth talking about." He closed his hand and the flame winked out of existence. "That is odd though, the spell worked but it was smaller and took longer than it should have. It's supposed to appear at the same time the last word is spoken."

"I may be magic numb, but I'm telling you something is wrong here. Although your magic worked, by your admission it wasn't acting normal." Storm pulled back the threadbare curtains to the outer window, but it was already too dark to see anything outside. "I think we have to keep watches, short ones. Leaving now might cause

more harm than good, but we should be ready if anything happens." He nodded to Keanin. "And as for your
magic; if anything comes through that door and gets past
us, blast it to hell."

Edgar and Keanin both nodded silently, although
Keanin was a few shades paler.

Edgar returned to his sharpening, pausing only to put
the finished blades away and draw out new ones. "I'll
take the first shift, then Keanin, then Storm. I think no
more than two hours at a time; we're all tired and can't
afford to have the watch fall asleep."

———————————

Storm was jerked out of a surprisingly deep sleep what
felt like only seconds later. He instinctively grabbed his
sword and slid it free of its sheath. "Are we under attack?"

"You and I aren't, not yet anyway." Edgar's face was
grim as he stepped back to let Storm get out of his bedroll. "Keanin's missing though."

Storm ran for the door.

"It won't work, they bolted it from the outside. You'll
have to look through there." Edgar pointed at the small
shuttered window that looked down into the main room
below them. "They waited until he was on watch, then
took him, or led him off and sealed us in." Outside their
room, it sounded like a raucous night at a pub. Something that had been lacking when they'd been downstairs
earlier.

Storm tried to be silent as he pried open the rotted
shutters, but there was enough noise in the main room
to drown out any sound they made. Besides, if they were
trapped in here, and he trusted Edgar on that fact, then
whoever trapped them probably didn't care if he and
Edgar were awake. But why take Keanin?

Candlelight flickered down below leaving pools almost
as bright as sunlight, and huge gaps of nothingness. A

crude statue, similar to one Qhazborh's priests might use was set up the corner. Storm was in no way an expert on the followers of the dark gods, but the statue didn't seem quite right; nor did the odd keening taking place below.

The crowd below was large, probably close to a hundred or more. They were gathered around a small area in the middle of the pub in a circle, making a hideous groaning noise; it started softly but slowly grew in volume. A figure walked into the center and turned in a circle with a bow to the entire room. It was the serving maid. Her eyes bore no resemblance to anything of this world. Even without seeing if her blood was green, Storm knew she was a demonspawn. She might not have been before, but she was now.

Edgar saw her the same time Storm did. "We've got to find Keanin and get out of here." He went to the door to keep trying to break through when the noise below grew louder.

Two hooded figures approached the serving maid and bowed. The inhuman moan that came from her filled the room and was echoed by the others in the pub. Her face contorted into a grim smile as she held open her arms. Before Storm could tell Edgar what he saw, another shape was brought out, this one walking stiffly and was covered head to toe in a long robe. The two men pulled back the newcomer's hood and Storm ran to the door. "It's Keanin!" He slammed repeatedly against the door; Edgar finally pulled him away when it wouldn't budge.

They both went back to the window; it was far too small to get through. But they could still see through it. The rest of Keanin's robe dropped. He was shaking and his shirt was tattered and torn. Crude markings covered the skin that showed in the gaps in his shirt but were too murky to be read. The sound from the villagers changed tempo as Keanin's body was walked to the waiting demonspawn woman. She put her hands on his shoulders and yelled an evil sounding spell. One chanted by everyone around her. Keanin stood motionless.

"They're demonspawn, all of them." Storm had no idea what the demonspawn was doing to Keanin, but nothing those things did would be good. He ran back to the door, ready to slam himself against it again.

"Wait." Edgar dove for his pack and pulled out a tiny silver box. "Whatever they're doing is blocking my meager magic, but hopefully a pre-set cuari spell will work. I forgot about these things. Ghortin gave me a few trinkets before we left." He set the box at the bottom of the door and motioned Storm to step back. An instant later both men were almost flattened as the door exploded.

"At least it worked." Edgar was coldly efficient as he sliced through the first two guards outside their door. Four more were behind them in the hallway, and they quickly engaged Edgar. They all bled green as they were cut down.

As Storm ran forward he could see that Keanin had been walked to stand before another demonspawn woman; his soul ached for his friend as the spell was chanted again. Whatever was happening, the horror of it was clear on Keanin's face. He might be trapped in his own body but he was aware and terrified of whatever spell was being worked upon him.

Storm slid his blade through the nearest guard, slicing off its head as he swung the sword back. He knew demonspawn didn't die easily and the last thing he wanted would be these at their backs as they took on the rest.

He decapitated the next guard in one move and saw Edgar had dispatched the other two and was taking on more as they came up the stairs.

Storm threw himself into the melee on the main floor, fighting his way through to Keanin. A demonspawn was about to walk Keanin to another woman when Storm sliced his way through, grabbed his friend, threw a cloak over him, and made his way toward the door. The remaining demonspawn didn't fight but stood watching with dull eyes. Maybe the ones they'd killed had been the only fighters.

He couldn't see Edgar anywhere for a moment, then saw him reappear on the stairs, their possessions in hand. Storm took the chance and ran, half-carrying Keanin, toward the door. Edgar came out seconds after him. They made it to the stable with no one coming after them, but the horses were gone.

"What now? They'll be after us in minutes, and I know Keanin can't run." Storm adjusted Keanin on his arm. His friend still hadn't moved. Whatever spell the demon-spawn had used to get him to move and stand where they wanted was slowly leaving his body, pulling him rapidly to the ground. "And I can't carry him far."

Edgar grabbed Keanin's other side. The spymas-ter turned them around toward the docks. "Only one option."

There was now a second ship alongside the first; the group inside the inn was made up of more than the vil-lagers. Edgar made sure Storm had Keanin securely, then he jumped aboard the new one. "It's empty."

Storm led Keanin up a thin plank. "Can we sail this thing?" It wasn't large but obviously was meant to have a crew of some sort.

"We've no choice." Edgar nodded behind them. A stream of torches was funneling out of the inn. Edgar jumped down to clear the lines, then grabbed a torch from the dock. "Get ready to sail, cast off if you have to. I'll catch up to you!"

Edgar ran down the dock before Storm could open his mouth to argue. A minute later Storm saw the second boat burst into flame, and the dock soon followed. Edgar leaped back on their boat as the crowd of torch-bearing demonspawn hit the remains of the dock.

CHAPTER SEVENTEEN

"YOU'RE CARABELLA. WE'RE your friends," Jenna said soothingly, but Carabella's eyes were still wild and she fought against Crell holding her on the ground. At this point, Crell was sitting on her since Carabella was a good foot and a half taller than her.

"I don't know you." She twisted around. "I don't know me. Where am I?"

Jenna looked to Ghortin, but he was still snoring. Waking him with magic, on top of the other two spells could make a huge mess. Bigger than their current one. There was a memory spell, but she'd only started learning it. If she tried and her magic flared as it did with the other two spells they were in serious trouble. Damn it, she couldn't think about that possible outcome. One thing she fully understood about magic—doubt could mangle or destroy a spell faster than anything.

"Can you do something? She is really strong." Crell grimaced as Carabella flung an arm free and smacked her. She was fighting, but confusion was clear on her face—she wasn't sure why she was fighting.

"Damn it, this might make it worse." Jenna tried to take a calming breath, but her nerves were fried. "Okay, hold her." She went into the chaotic realm for this one. Normally she wouldn't and Ghortin had been working hard to break her of the habit. But in this case, she felt it was justified. Going to the source as it were, gave her more Power, but left her vulnerable as she was just standing there in the real world. Not a good idea during a fight. Hopefully, if there were other attackers out there, they wouldn't decide to charge now.

The chaotic plane was where all magic and energy began—it was beautiful, colorful beyond anything in the outer world, and addictive as hell. Ghortin told her tales of mages who stayed in there until their bodies died of dehydration or outside forces. Keeping his warnings in mind, she gathered the lines of Power around her, then crafted the spell. It would only work if Carabella's memories were blocked, not gone. Jenna left the realm of chaos and cast the spell

Carabella froze as the spell entered her mind. Her eyes locked open and her breathing was shallow.

"Damn it, whatever they spelled her with is trying to push aside my spell." Jenna dropped next to her and took one of her hands. "Fight it! You are Carabella! You're stronger than this!"

Carabella twitched, closed her eyes, and collapsed.

"What happened to her?" Crell moved off her.

"I don't know. Carabella? Snap out of it, Traanafaeren needs you." Nothing. "The cuari need you." Still twitching with eyes fluttering, but no other response. Jenna looked over to where Ghortin continued to snore. "Ghortin needs you!"

Carabella's eyes flew open and she sat up. "Where am I?"

Jenna pulled back. Maybe when Ghortin woke up he'd have another spell they could use. "You're Carabella, we're your friends—"

"I know that. Why am I on the ground?" Carabella looked around. "Ah, yes. Camping. Never did like that. Ghortin's sleeping through whatever happened that left me here—clearly, he and I will need to have words."

Jenna and Crell got to their feet and helped Carabella to hers. She seemed fine, but a bit shaky.

"All of your memories came back? You took off and came back not knowing any of us. Or who you were."

Jenna nodded to Ghortin. "He's out from a spell. The others are the ones who attacked us." Jenna stepped around one of the attackers as she helped Carabella to a rock near the fire.

"I...wait. Yes. I heard my people calling out in the forest. I went after them. Then everything is blank until I woke up over there. Damn it. They tricked me with a will-o-wisp spell like I was a first-year mage. Ghortin is going to love this." She dropped her head into her hands.

Crell handed her two large pouches. "Water is in the right; wine is in the left."

Carabella handed back the water and took a long swig of the wine. "So, while I was gone we were attacked? And they spelled Ghortin? That's not an easy feat."

Jenna sighed and ran a hand through her hair. "I did it by accident." She and Crell quickly filled Carabella in on what happened.

Carabella put down the wine pouch, walked over to the closest attacker, and glared at his feet. "I haven't seen those marks in an extremely long time." She looked up. "Why didn't you kill them?"

Jenna was taken aback at the matter-of-fact tone in her voice. Yes, she'd had to kill to save herself or others, and knew that in this world, she'd most likely need to do so again. But these enemies were defeated, unconscious, and tied up.

Crell tilted her head in question. "I thought maybe you or Ghortin would want to question them."

"No. Kill them all. Now." Carabella started shaking.

Jenna reached out magically and almost got smacked by a powerful spell hitting Carabella. She quickly threw up a shield around her.

Carabella's shaking stopped and she stumbled. And quickly recovered. "Those...twice? They got me twice? I know that weird bubble is waiting for me to use my magic so it can drag me away—but damn it, no one spells me twice!" She looked over to Crell and Jenna. "I'd say good call on keeping them alive. Whoever is behind this wants them dead before they can tell us anything."

Jenna silently held up the wine pouch. She was glad Carabella hadn't turned into a homicidal maniac but she wasn't dropping the shield spell on her yet.

"Thank you, but I think I'm okay." She took her seat. "Nice shield spell by the way. Thank you for thinking of it."

"They were hitting you hard. No idea where it was coming from, but there had to have been more than a single mage behind it. I think my shield only worked because they weren't expecting it." They'd come across triads of mages working together before. All magic users had weaknesses and working together helped cover those holes and gave their spells strength for longer distances.

"That's not good. Nor is my being defenseless." She got up again stalked around the bodies and kicked a sword away from one. "Not bad. Not great, and I have a much better one that I can't access right now. But I think I need a weapon." She looked up. "Can you check to see if it's been spelled?"

Carabella had to talk her through the spell, but now that she had it, it would stay with her. Simple, but not one Ghortin had gotten to yet. He probably didn't think she'd be picking up stray weapons. "It's clear. Checked the belt and scabbard too—they're clear."

Carabella gingerly removed the belt from the attacker, picked up the sword, and came back to the fire.

"I don't think I've ever heard of you fighting with a sword," Crell said.

Carabella demonstrated some fancy, yet old-fashioned sword moves then sheathed the sword. "I haven't used one since the battle crossing the Markare all those years ago. Swords are slow and messy compared to magic, but

I'd had to fight with every skill I had to get us out alive." She shrugged. "I stopped using physical weapons after that."

CHAPTER EIGHTEEN

———◆———

AS THE STOLEN ship bobbed silently in the water, Edgar motioned for Storm to follow him out of the cabin. They'd gotten Keanin settled into what had been the captain's cabin. He seemed physically fine, but at first, he would only stare off into the distance, barely acknowledging them. Finally, he closed his eyes and collapsed into an exhausted sleep.

Edgar nodded as he shut the door behind them. "Come up on deck. I'd rather he didn't hear us."

They had managed to move the ship quite a way away from the village. There was little wind, so they had tried to use the oars. Unfortunately, the ship was large enough that it needed more than two oarsmen. It had taken the entire night and part of the day to get far enough where Edgar felt they could drop anchor. The river was wide and would eventually get them to Erlinda, but Storm's first goal was to keep them away from Shettler's Point.

Storm looked out across the dark waters. They had mage lights, both the ones Edgar could use magically and the ones that were aboard the ship. Edgar had thrown the ship's complement overboard the instant he found them, not trusting the magic behind them. He'd kept his supply unused except in the cabins. It was doubtful anyone could follow them from the village, but better to be sure.

Storm looked over to him. "Do you know what ritual they were doing? Or why Keanin? How badly injured is he?" Edgar was silent for so long, he worried that he'd been spelled somehow.

"It was bad." Edgar took a deep breath. "They weren't

only demonspawn; they were demonspawn working with Qhazborh. Or maybe they were followers of Qhazborh who became demonspawn. I have no idea. Somehow they were trying to use an ancient Qhazborh Power spell to draw energy and more from Keanin." Edgar looked out into the night. "I've seen some horrific things, but never what I saw them doing to him on the magical level. Be grateful you are magic numb, my friend. They attacked Keanin on many levels. They were trying to get to his very essence, his soul. And they wanted the physical as well—they took it from him magically."

"I think we can safely assume the one who sent the demonspawn king after Keanin was behind this as well. They couldn't pull him to their side last time, so they tried to take what they wanted." Storm gripped the rough wood tightly. He needed to fight back somehow, to strike against what attacked Keanin.

Edgar looked at him, clearly not wanting to continue. He finally nodded to himself. "They weren't only taking magic from him as he stood there. There was a fertility spell covering the entire room. The mishmash of spells that were flung at Keanin and through him were terrifying. I couldn't sort them all out and I'm not even sure Ghortin could have."

"Oh, gods." Storm looked back toward the cabin. "What the hells for? To create more demonspawn? It seems to me they're not having trouble with that as it is."

"I wish I knew." Edgar shook his head. "One thing more. They had Keanin under an extremely strong compulsion spell. It was still clinging to him when we left. My skills aren't near enough to remove it. We'll have to watch him carefully."

———◆———

Keanin had fallen asleep on watch in the inn, but now he was awake and a strange woman called to him. She was far more beautiful than anyone he had ever seen. He must go to her, she needed him. In a dream-like state, she called for him to come out of their room. He quietly opened the door and looked out. She was there, waiting, promising him everything wonderful in the world. If he would follow her. He went to her, but suddenly the glamour fell away. She was horrible and vile. The outer shell was that of the aggressive serving maid, but inside was something from the depths of hell—a demonspawn. He fought to break free, but a cold hand grabbed his head and he no longer could move.

"Keanin! Wake up!"

Storm and Edgar ran in when Keanin began screaming. He was sitting upright, his amber eyes locked open in terror, but he didn't see them.

Storm grabbed his shoulders. "Keanin, it's us, wake up!"

With a whoosh of expelled air, Keanin snapped awake. He took a shaky breath and smiled at his friends. "Thank gods it was a dream…" His voice trailed off as he saw the looks on their faces. "It wasn't. It was real. All of it. They—I—" He put his face in his hands as it all came back.

Storm and Edgar sat on either side of him. "It's okay, it's over now," Storm said.

"It's not over." Keanin lifted his face but then looked back down at his torn shirt and the markings on his chest. "I still feel them around me. I need—" He threw off his blankets before Edgar or Storm could grab him and ran for the deck.

"Keanin! Wait!" Storm was right behind him, but he vanished over the railing. Without a thought, Storm went in after him. "Don't do this, you'll be okay. It will be all right." Storm feared the worst; that he was still under the compulsion spell. He pulled back when he realized

Keanin wasn't trying to drown himself, but had pulled free some river kelp and was frantically scrubbing himself clean.

"I'm sorry. I just couldn't stand them being on me one more second." He shuddered. "What they did to me. What they took from me..." Keanin continued to shiver, but it was from far more than the cold.

Storm held out his arm and led his friend back to the ship.

CHAPTER NINETEEN

———◆———

CRELL AND JENNA finally decided to split the watch so they could get some rest. Carabella stayed awake but kept her thoughts to herself. Jenna slept poorly during her brief time, images of devils from her world chasing her friends—mostly Keanin—kept invading her dreams.

She stirred as the sound of voices and the smell of food cooking snuck past the blankets that she'd thrown over her head.

The others were awake, and Ghortin didn't look worse for his double-spelled adventure. But the bodies of the attackers were missing.

Jenna threw back her blankets. "Where did they go?" They needed to get information out of them.

"Easy there, we moved them off to the side. I want to give them some time before I start questioning them." Ghortin nodded to a clump of shrubs next to their clearing. A foot stuck out. "No fear, I have a soundproof spell over them." He tilted his head. "Are you all right, though? I heard you were flinging around a lot of spells last night and you look awful."

Carabella smacked his shoulder. "Never tell a lady that." Then she turned to Jenna. "You do look a bit…pale… however. Did you not sleep well?"

Jenna rubbed her head and found that her hair was sticking up. Ghortin was probably right on how she looked. "I had a dream, something was after Keanin. Then it stopped. But the emotion was so vivid. I could feel Keanin's terror." That had been the worst. She couldn't tell what was happening, beyond the fact her subconscious dream mind assigned his attackers images of the devil, but the emotions had been real. She shuddered. Far too real.

Ghortin came over to her and peered into her eyes. "You and Keanin are close. And the sharing trick you did with your magic all those months ago could have built a bond of some kind."

"Then how come I've never been able to sense him before?" That what she'd felt might be real was horrifying. Made worse by the fact that she knew Storm wouldn't let anything happen to his friend if he was alive to stop it. She squashed that thought to the furthest corner of her mind.

"I don't know, lass." Ghortin's smile was gentle as he put one hand on the side of her head. "I can't see your dreams, but since they are fresh, I might be able to feel if they are more than a dream—and share what you felt."

Jenna nodded. The dream flooded her mind again, but Ghortin tamped it down. Now it only felt like a casual observation.

"I believe there is a connection of some sort between you two, and that something has happened to Keanin." He held up his hand before she could speak. "I think the threat is gone now. At least the immediate one. That was also in your mind, but the terror of the emotions that hit you overwhelmed it."

"Want me to try and call Edgar?" Crell had her taran wand out.

Ghortin patted his pockets. "Yes, I seemed to have misplaced mine."

Jenna handed it back to him. "Sorry, Garlan called to warn us of the group following us. They found a cell of Strann Qhazborh followers outside of Lithunane."

"Thank you." Ghortin pocketed the wand. "I'll contact him for an update once we're on the road."

Crell swore at hers. "I know it works, but it's not reaching Edgar. Yet." She shook her head at Jenna. "No panicking." Then kept trying.

"Hello?" Edgar's voice was a welcome sound even though it was faint and choppy. "We're on the river and reception for these is bad over water."

"Understood. Is everyone okay? Jenna's worried about Keanin."

The silence that followed almost made Jenna jump for the taran wand.

"Storm and I are fine, but Keanin was attacked. He *will* be okay. We will contact you when we're on land again." The call cut off.

"Am I the only one who picked up on the force behind 'he will be okay'?" Jenna was glad they were all alive, but that emphasis of Edgar's was freaking her out.

"Not at all. I caught it too." Crell frowned as she put her wand away.

"You have to hold fast that he will be fine," Ghortin said fiercely. "Now, we can't march without food." He started dishing out breakfast.

━━━━━◆━━━━━

The attackers were next to useless about information—even when Crell stood over each one with her sword in their faces.

"They must know something; why else try to get us to kill them before they regained consciousness?" Jenna kept her voice low as she and Carabella watched from a distance.

"I don't know. There are spells I could use to find out." Her fingers flexed. "They're ones beyond Ghortin's skill level, but don't worry, I won't try."

"Is there anything he or I could do that might help?" Jenna felt like there was something right outside of her mental reach. Something that was giving her a headache.

"*Mindtouch.*" The voice came from inside her, so unless someone else had snuck in it was Typhonel. And she couldn't mention his name to Carabella. "I think I have an idea, maybe a lingering echo from the remains of the mindslave. Let me go check." Carabella started to follow, but she shook her head. "You might want to stay here, just in case." The echo from the mindslave had vanished months ago, but that might be a good way to disguise Typhonel from Carabella—to a point.

Jenna went up to one of the attackers—the one that had held her at knifepoint. She kneeled next to him as her head pounded harder. Something didn't want her near him. "Hi, remember me? I'd like to chat."

He turned away but she grabbed his head.

"Nope. On my terms." She felt Typhonel move forward, but this time he was giving direction rather than taking over. The spell he set out before her was complicated and she doubted she'd remember it once this was done. With it set, she went into the man's mind. Command spells were all around it, but she fought past. He was to grab Ghortin for his master, kill everyone else. She pushed harder—that wasn't shocking. Ghortin would be mindsacrificed to their god, and the Power it raised would bring forth a new world.

There was something else. Something the spells put on this man were trying to hide. She pushed harder, she almost had it.

Then his head exploded.

Jenna's eyes flew open and she tried not to throw up.

Ghortin was there in a minute and magically cleaned her up, then helped her to her feet. "What did you do?" The other attackers all started keening loudly and Crell stepped away as well.

Jenna glanced at Carabella, then dragged Ghortin further away from her. "Typhonel appeared. He said to use the mindtouch spell, set it up for me, then boom."

"That would have been a good spell, and one beyond me. I'd say our enemies knew of it as well."

Jenna told him the little she'd been able to gather. "Damn it, now I've ruined our chances."

"Not at all, they were all triggered against such a thing. We wouldn't have gotten more out of them." He looked her up and down. "Are you sure you're okay?"

"Yes. No. I will be. Thank you for the cleanup." She carefully looked away from the body as they walked back to the others.

Crell had gone through and stabbed all of the others in the heart. "Before you say anything, we couldn't leave them here. That one exploded. And the others were foaming."

"I was going to say that was a good idea." Ghortin glanced at the foam. "We probably don't want to linger here. Dead or not, there could be other traps."

They quickly gathered their things and got back on the trail. Carabella, Ghortin, and Crell all dropped into their own thoughts as they walked.

"Wouldn't it be easier if we had horses?" Jenna finally asked after an hour of trudging. Her fear of the big beasts wasn't near as bad as her fear of permanent blisters at this point.

Carabella reached over and smacked Ghortin in the back of the head. "She's right. You said we could get them once we got further out. I think I'm done with walking."

Jenna laughed at the tone of Carabella's voice, it was as if the entire world had crumbled around her due to lack of four-footed friends. It was nice to see her acting more like herself.

Ghortin snorted but didn't turn around. "I would have explained my plan to you before we left the palace if you hadn't flown the coop without us. We could have gotten some from Resstlin, but we'd have to trade them somewhere and you know how he is about his horses. We can get some at the next village, but we shall have to go in our disguises. I don't want word getting back of us being seen out this far."

Carabella glanced over her shoulder at Jenna. "How long has he been this difficult?" She waved her hands in the air the moment she spoke. "Never mind. I'm sure I don't want to know."

"While I'm used to being on foot, I have to agree on getting horses." Crell came out of wherever her thoughts had taken her. "Not to mention, we look more suspicious tromping through the trails without them. I'll refrain from any disguises unless necessary, however. Unlike you three, I am supposed to be roaming around. But it might be better if I vanish for a bit."

"Agreed. We have company coming down the road, which we are about to intersect. Crell, you take off, you two might wish to don your disguises so we don't give the poor person a heart attack."

Carabella turned and pulled a small bundle of clothes from her pack. She quickly donned the matronly shift and covered her raven hair and ears with an equally bland scarf. Jenna did the same. Ghortin finished pulling on a loose brown farmer's vest, then set the glamour spell on all three of them.

Jenna thought they still looked exactly what they were, a cuari enchantress and Traanafaeren's premiere master-mage, just in odd clothing. Ghortin had shown her the glamour spell over and over in the days leading here. The clothing was to act as a reinforcement of what the viewer expected to see. In theory, anyone coming upon them should see a farmer traveling with his widowed sister and daughter. Crell was gone, but Jenna knew she was watching out for them. Once they got the horses, it would be harder for her to hide like that, but right now it was handy. A backup in case something went wrong.

The glamour spell's last tingles were settling as a dusty

farmer pulling a handcart turned into view.

"Good day, gentles." The tall man bowed, then took a better glance at the widow scarves both women wore. "I share your loss and sorrow." He bowed deeper.

Ghortin matched his bow perfectly. "Good day as well. My sister and my daughter both lost their husbands fighting in the Markare." Ghortin had decided to use their cover story to dig for information and reactions from anyone they came across.

The thin farmer nodded slowly. "Sorrowful thing, that. Troubling that so many died. Had a second cousin's son down near the capital who lost an arm." He looked around as if to see if anyone else was nearby. "They say that King Daylin himself was attacked and maybe even killed by a band of them derawri."

Jenna froze; she knew Crell could hear the man, and most likely had an arrow aimed at his heart. Ghortin quickly put his arm around Jenna's shoulder to settle her. She wasn't sure what people out here would know, but she hadn't expected that at all.

"Nay, that wasn't the way at all. I've good friends whose sons and daughters came back with the tale. People close to the royals, if you take my meaning." Ghortin hitched up his belt with a scratch of his thumb; role-playing was something he obviously enjoyed. "Now the right of it, as I hear tell, is that the good King Daylin was lost, but he was killed by creatures of myth and shadow—demon-spawn for true. A group of derawri saved Prince Corin and other important folks from being lost as well."

Jenna understood what he was trying to do. They couldn't tell people Prince Corin killed the monster pretending to be his father, and clearly, anti-derawri rumors were being spread for one reason or another. Might as well take care of both issues.

The farmer looked skeptical for a few moments, then nodded with a crooked grin. "Aye, you might have the right of it, coming from Lithunane and all. Wasn't sure of the tale myself." His smile faded. "But I'd be careful about who you tell it to if you head further north. More than a few want to start hunting derawris on their own land. They want revenge. King Daylin was a good man." He bent down and pulled up the handles on his cart. "I'd best be on my way; the wife worries these days. Strange things are afoot. Safe journey to you."

Jenna shook her head as the farmer vanished from sight. "Why are they blaming the derawris? Crell and the others with her were trying to fight that thing." She kept her voice at a whisper. Crell still hadn't come out, so there could be more travelers on the trail ahead of them.

Carabella joined them as they started walking. "Aside from sheer cussedness, I'd say our enemies are trying to drive a wedge between Traanafaeren and Derawri. They've already started to separate Khelaran from the rest. I hate to say I've seen it before, but it's an old tactic. You say anyone who was at the battle knew what happened, but not everyone at the battle was on your side. You should expect that some escaped."

"Believe me; none of us thought we'd killed them all." Ghortin snorted. "They'll pick up the pieces of the broken victors if they can get everyone to fight among themselves. Which, while an ancient tactic, is not usually done by warriors unless they are outnumbered. That alone tells us something about our enemy. Right now, they don't feel they can take us all on." He drifted into his thoughts and continued walking and muttering to himself.

Carabella had slowed down, and Crell was still hiding. Jenna dropped back to Carabella as Ghortin walked around a bend.

"Are you okay?"

Carabella nodded. "Ghortin will be annoyed if he knows what I'm about to do. If the news of the battle has already spread to a rural farmer, it won't be long before it's all over the land. Ghortin may not agree, but rumor can cause as much death as an army; often more so." She looked around and raised her hands. "This isn't a spell, not really, so it shouldn't trigger whatever is after me." Before Jenna could stop her, she tossed something that felt like a spell.

And another one of those spell bubbles encased her and knocked her out. Jenna gathered energy for a spell, but she wasn't sure what spell to use. Carabella was fading when she gathered her magic and threw it at the bubble. It burst and dropped Carabella to the dirt.

Ghortin came running around the bend. "What in the blazes is happening here? Did you two want to make sure that any enemy mages drifting around can find us?" He skidded to a halt and noticed Carabella lying on the ground. "What mischief is this?"

"Carabella was attacked by another of those spell balls. She said she wasn't casting a spell, but it felt like one to me. And to whatever is controlling those damn bubbles. I managed to stop it." Jenna went to help Carabella. "No, I'm not sure how. I just threw spells at it. It moved faster this time."

The cuari enchantress was starting to move when Jenna came to her side. "Are you okay?"

Carabella sat up and blinked at both of them. "I think so." She looked at the dirt path she was on. "I do seem to be on the ground, however. Again."

Ghortin reached down and helped Carabella to her feet. She wobbled a bit at first, then her legs stabilized. "What exactly were you doing when you were attacked?" He helped dust her off, but his eyes were narrowed.

Carabella winced. "I was being thoughtless, that's what I was doing." She sighed and shook some last dust off. "I sent off a suggestion to curb those rumors against the derawri. It's not a full spell." At Ghortin's frown, she waved her hands at him. "I know, I said it was thoughtless action. It happened to be even more so than I originally thought." She shook her head as something hit her. "No wonder they captured the rest of the cuari so quickly."

"Agreed." Ghortin snorted. "Since not one of you can go for any time at all without using magic."

"We'll have to move fast if we want to catch them," Carabella said.

Ghortin had already turned to continue back to the road but spun sharply at Carabella's comment. "Catch who?" He folded his arms once he got a clear look at her face. "You can't possibly think we're going to sniff out whoever cast the spell? Here? In the wilds?"

Carabella mimicked his pose perfectly. "And why not? These cretins have captured the rest of my people, attacked Keanin—yes, his attack was tied somehow to the one they flung at me—and have repeatedly attacked me. Besides, I could feel the other cuari more strongly this time. I'm sure I can find out where they are."

Jenna took a step back out of the line of fire and glanced around the woods for Crell. Just in case she needed backup with these two.

"I agree that finding out where the cuari are, and getting them out, is important. But if we don't get that missing book we won't be able to stop Ranz, and this world won't be worth a wooden copper within a year." His anger faded. "I'm sorry, but we can't take the time right now. Or risk another attack on you. Besides, maybe the others were taken as a distraction, to keep us from finding what we need."

Carabella folded her arms and glared. "We need the rest of the cuari to take care of this Ranz person. I doubt he could stand against one of us, let alone all of us."

Ghortin sighed. "You know there are some things that we can't tell you and many of them are about Ranz. Trust me when I say we cannot afford to underestimate his abilities." He stepped forward, taking Carabella's hand before he continued. "I didn't want to bring it up until I knew more, but I have a sinking feeling that Ranz and that creature we fought in the Markare over a thousand years ago are tied in together."

The blood rushed out of Carabella's face and she leaned in toward Ghortin. "But how could…" She stopped and took a shaky breath. "I understand. Can we please at least find out where they are? We don't have to free them yet; we can get the third book or whatever else we need first. But I have to know where they are."

Jenna felt a chill. She was with two of the most powerful beings in this world, and they were both still terrified of whatever had been in the desert all those years ago. Ghortin hadn't told her of his newest theory, but it made sense. If Ranz came from the void beyond the portal, and the portal was in the Markare, then he most likely was somehow connected to that creature. The creature that Ghortin said even Carabella hadn't been able to kill.

Ghortin's frown came back, but Carabella took his arm. "Please? That way if something happens to me, you can rescue them. I'm not sure what we're up against, but I suddenly don't feel so immortal anymore."

"Fine." Ghortin finally gave in. "But I'm not sure how you're going to do it."

Carabella's face lit up and she set her pack down. "I have an idea. I'm going to cast a nice long complicated spell, one that the sphere should love. Let me stay inside it as long as you can, then Jenna can blast me out again. I could feel them this time, Ghortin, much more so than the first time. If I'm ready for it, I should be able to find out where they are."

Jenna jumped in before Ghortin could speak. "I'm not sure I can. That wasn't any sort of official spell, you know. I made it up as I was casting it."

"I know you can do it again." Carabella's smile brightened the entire trail. "Besides, whatever your mentor claims, unorthodox spells are usually the best. And I think this is our only chance."

Ghortin put down his pack next to Carabella's. "Jenna, get ready. If it doesn't work, I'll try as well."

With a nod to both of them, Carabella closed her eyes and began casting her spell. She was immediately engulfed in a light glowing sphere.

They watched Carabella relax into the sphere. Jenna kept reminding herself that whoever was behind that sphere was responsible for untold pain for Keanin. She tapped into that fear and anger. Ghortin shook her back to awareness. Carabella's body was beginning to fade; evidently, the cuari wasn't aware of it, for there was no change in her expression. But the edges of her body were fainter now.

Jenna crafted the bolt of Power just like she had a short while ago. Unfortunately, this time nothing happened. Carabella continued to fade; the trees behind her were beginning to show through her body.

Jenna swore at herself but waved off Ghortin. She could do this, she *needed* to do this. Ghortin couldn't step in every time her magic failed. Shutting her eyes, she focused on Keanin, on Storm, on all of her friends in this world. She made herself visualize what would happen to them if her magic failed. Taking another deep breath, Jenna focused all of that fear and terror into a narrow beam that shattered the sphere surrounding Carabella and cut through the two trees behind her.

A now solid, but again unconscious, Carabella dropped to the dirt path.

Jenna and Ghortin ran to her side and lifted her carefully. Carabella stirred and looked up with a smile. "I told you Jenna could do it." She stood on her own feet and carefully patted herself down. "I seem to be all here; do we still have any wine left?" Ghortin put a wineskin in her hand. After a few very healthy pulls, Carabella turned back to them. "It worked. I found out where they're hiding them. They're in the realm of chaos; on the chaotic plane itself." She waved her hands at Ghortin. "Don't ask how, I couldn't tell that. But they are there. Safe, secure, and unconscious, but there."

"That's impossible, there's no way anyone could stay in there for that long." Ghortin shook his head.

Jenna waved him off as memory of something she'd read hit her. "Wait a minute. Rachael's book. I know there was a section in there, something about this." Ignoring their looks, Jenna ran for her pack and dug out the small gray tome. "I know it was here somewhere…" She muttered to herself as she flipped through the small soft book. Although they had all been written at the same time, Rachael's cuari book seemed far older to Jenna than Ghortin's had. "I thought so. Carabella is right. It says here that it is possible to maintain life on the chaotic plane." Jenna paused and looked at both of them. She wasn't sure how much could be said around Carabella and didn't want to cause her to lose consciousness out in the middle of nowhere. Ghortin caught her look and nodded with a shrug.

"The book talks about signs for the beginning of the end or the end of the beginning. The translation wasn't clear. But it's a change of epochs, not necessarily good or evil, but a major change. It refers to the immortal ones lying in wait in the realm of chaos. They will survive in stasis for one year, and one year only. They will cease to exist if left there for any longer."

Jenna could tell Carabella was dying to get her hands on the book and read for herself. Unfortunately, dying might be the operative word if she touched it. "Well? Does it say how to free them? Shouldn't they give instructions?"

"Well, sort of. I'm afraid this isn't the most direct book. It says we have to get the words of all three books together, then the one who is three and the three who are one will use the knowledge to free the trapped immortals." Jenna shrugged. "Sorry, it's pretty cryptic."

Carabella slumped forward in defeat, but Ghortin perked up. "Interesting, the same people who were mentioned in my book. Damn, I wish I had been able to recall more of it before we left."

Jenna agreed. She hadn't been able to grasp much more than the few spells she'd already learned. She knew it was safer with Rachael, though. Even Ghortin admitted she'd be able to figure out spells faster than anyone else. Maybe if Jenna kept reading this one, something else would make sense.

Ghortin reached over and placed his hand on Carabella's shoulder. "I'm sorry, Carabella, I truly am. We'll try to free the cuari, but I'm not sure if we'll have time."

Jenna re-read a sentence and shook her head. "We'll have to make time. The three books and these mysterious people may be what is needed to free the cuari, but the cuari are needed to save the world. There are other elements as well, most not making any sense. But that part is clear. That *thing* in the desert can't be closed without the cuari."

CHAPTER TWENTY

———◆———

EDGAR GLARED AT the collection of fish Storm held up as he came into the small ship's kitchen. "You would think that after five days of only eating fish, you'd lose your excitement for it."

"You might think so, but you'd be wrong. I never have time to fish normally, and we do need something to eat besides what's left of our dried food."

Edgar sighed and took the string of fish. "Our food issues aside, how is he?" He nodded to the deck above, where Keanin was securing the ship for the night's anchor.

Storm's smile vanished. "Better? I think, but I'm not sure. He's not himself, that's for certain. But who would be after that? He can't fully explain what was done to him."

"I know." Edgar lit the small stove. "My magic is limited, so I don't have much of an idea of what all they did. Just that it was bad. Very bad."

"I certainly don't," Storm said without bitterness. Not having magic had always been hard for him to deal with, but it wasn't right now. "I think they did more than take Power from him though, I'm afraid they left something behind."

Edgar had been cutting a withered onion and almost cut himself at Storm's words.

Storm waved him off. "I think they increased his magic abilities. Focused the Power he has access to, somehow. I wish Ghortin were here, but I'm pretty sure I've heard him muttering spells. I know Ghortin had a hell of a time getting him to memorize anything magic-related."

"That might not be good. Spells take time to master; you can't gift them to someone."

"I know, but I also caught him practicing with mage lights in the cabin and that second coil of rope on deck. In both cases, he'd gotten the items five or six feet off the ground. He dropped them and denied it once he saw me."

"Maybe he's finally working on that training Ghortin started him on? Vengeance can be a powerful motivator."

"Very true. And I know him coming into his full mage abilities would make Ghortin giddy. But only if he's fully in control of them. Can you magically keep an eye on him? See if things seem okay?" Storm knew Keanin had a hell of a lot of Power, but he'd also seen what happened to mages with Power and no training. They usually took a lot of people out with them.

Edgar nodded but kept his words to himself as Keanin sauntered into the kitchen. He'd been trying to act like his old self. Yet his movements and manner were a bit off as if someone was in a play and they'd just been given the part. There was also a hooded shadow in his eyes when he thought no one was looking at him.

Keanin smiled. "Do we have a plan for tomorrow? Or just dock in Erlinda, abandon this boat, and take the first ship we can to Craelyn?"

"I've given that some thought; I think we need to keep a low profile, maybe disguise ourselves. The three of us alone bringing in a ship this size will cause questions even if there hasn't been a report from Shettler's Point. I say we dump this ship a few miles out of town and come in on foot as if we'd been on the trail."

Keanin frowned. "But what if we need to escape in the ship again? Qhazborh could have followers in Erlinda." His voice was tense and his left hand twitched.

Storm watched his friend's hand. Keanin had been casting spells with his left hand each time he'd caught him. "I don't know how this boat could help us in a crowded dock. Escape wouldn't be possible. I agree with Edgar; our best chance is to keep low and not be noticeable."

"We might have to fight. We need to be able to fight. This ship would help us fight. We must destroy them all." Keanin's hand twitched faster and he wasn't listening to his own words. Then he dropped to a chair as what he said caught up to him. "I'm sorry, I haven't been feeling myself lately."

Storm squeezed his shoulder. "It's okay. You've been through hell and back and no one can blame you for wanting revenge. But now isn't the time for it. It's too risky if we're spotted. Qhazborh's followers and the demonspawn working with them will be dealt with. But we need to do it at the right time when we're ready. Not now, when all we'd do is give them another victory. You understand that, right?"

Keanin's hand twitched once, then went still. "Yes. But I'm coming back for that revenge once we've settled this bit with Khelaran."

Storm nodded. "And I promise to help you. We will destroy all of them."

Keanin silently nodded.

They'd finished eating when Edgar's taran wand started shaking. He grabbed it before the other two could. "Edgar here." The wands didn't work well on the water, but there were skirting close to the shore.

Armsmaster Garlan's gruff voice came through clearly. "Where are you three?"

"A few hours hike outside of Erlinda. Why?"

Garlan's swearing was followed by a relieved sigh. "Thank the goddess. We'd gotten some intel that there was an attack at Shettler's Point and rode out here. We found your horses and feared the worst. Two of my scouts have been killed and it appears everyone in the place is inside the inn."

Keanin looked up at that and his left hand twitched before he put his right hand over it to hold it down.

"Kill them." Edgar was calm as he spoke. He handed the wand to Keanin before he could grab it from him.

"You have to kill them all. Now." Keanin's voice cracked and he shook his head. He handed the wand to Storm.

"Surely we need to interrogate—"

"No." Storm cut him off. "That village has fallen to Qhazborh as I'd never seen before. There is no one human left now—they are demonspawn and mindslaves. You must kill them all. But don't let them take any of your people, especially any mages."

Keanin grabbed the wand out of Storm's hand. "If they capture one of your people, kill them. It would be a mercy killing." He took a deep breath and handed the wand back to Storm.

Garlan was silent for a moment. "I understand. We will carry out your orders. And please let Keanin know I am sorry for whatever happened to him here." Nothing had been said, but Garlan was too seasoned not to realize that something horrific had happened.

"Thank you." Storm looked to Keanin but he was calming down. "Don't let any of them escape."

CHAPTER TWENTY-ONE

O VER FOUR HUNDRED miles away, Carabella looked eastward toward the late afternoon sky from atop her horse. "Ghortin, what in the name of the three is that?" She'd stopped scowling once they'd gotten the horses, but the look was back now as she stared at the distant horizon.

"What is what? I was thinking, you know." Ghortin had looked more like he'd been dozing, but Jenna wasn't going to point that out to either of them.

Jenna looked where Carabella pointed, but shook her head. "I don't see anything."

Crell came out of the woods next to them, her small pony fit well between the trees. She was still dressed as she normally was but now had added some knife belts and a ribbon across her chest. Her disguise was as their armed guard. It fit the situation and she didn't like playing dress-up.

"The path ahead looks good; there are a few farms along the way, but they look normal." Her shrug pointed out how quickly normal could end up being anything but. "What are you looking at?"

"Carabella says she sees something. But neither Jenna nor I see it." Ghortin stopped his horse and leaned toward the horizon as if that would help. Then started swearing. "I do see something. A thin, dark line." He shivered. "And not a good one. There's dark magic connected to it. It's very far away, and we're only seeing it because a lot of nasty magic was involved." He looked to Carabella. "I know you can see better than me, can you see what it is now?"

Carabella was silent long enough for the object to be visible to Jenna. A greasy-looking cloud far off in the distance.

Crell swore as she saw it too. "Could that be as far away as Shettler's Point? It's in the direction for it."

Jenna's stomach clenched. That was where whatever happened to Keanin occurred.

Carabella didn't cast a spell, but closed her eyes and reached a hand out toward the clouds. "Yes, it is. Garlan and his soldiers were there." She shook her head. "The magic wasn't from them though. Hopefully, they got clear of that cloud."

"I've never seen smoke like that though." Jenna kept her fear tamped down. She had to believe that Storm, Edgar, and Keanin were all long gone from that place, or she'd find a way to get down there herself.

"Aye, me either." Ghortin held up his hand. "And neither of you reach out to it, again. It's magical, that I can tell. Let me see if I can tell more." He looked toward the horizon and muttered a few spell words too softly for Jenna to hear.

After a few tense moments, he dropped his spell and looked ready to be sick somewhere. "Necromancy." He called up another spell with dark and violent words and sent it toward the growing cloud. The greasy mass slowly dissipated. "Damn them. I hope our people all got free of that before it was released; the cloud itself was deadly and it would have been horrific up close. Whoever was behind the spell used a lot of dead and dying people to create it. And I fear he or she is still alive."

Crell had her hand on the hilt of her sword. "If we need to ride that way, I can get us there." As the leader of her band of rangers, Crell knew every rock in Traanafaeren and many beyond.

"Going down there won't help anything. The mages

in Lithunane would have seen what was done and sent people down to contain it," Ghortin said.

Jenna opened her mouth to speak, but a wave of pure terror for her friends, herself, this world, even her former world, slammed into her. Her mind couldn't fight back. Everything was doomed, why try? Giving in sounded better.

Ghortin turned back to her. "What's wrong? You're white as snow. Are you under attack?"

Jenna heard him but she couldn't speak or move. Part of her mind felt it was best if she stopped everything. She stayed atop her horse only because her legs wouldn't move.

"Crell, stay on your pony and shoot an arrow into any-one who comes near. We've no idea what happened to Jenna," Ghortin said as he and Carabella got off their horses and helped her down from her own. She felt their hands, heard their words, but nothing mattered anymore. They were all going to die.

She forced herself to fight back enough to speak. "Fear. Terror. It's not only me. It's all around me. Inside me." Something was attacking her; it was attacking everyone she knew. In her mind, a massive abyss opened before her. All along the walls were screaming faces and writhing hands. Tortured people reaching out for her, screaming to be let free.

But they were empty now. Just the souls of those left behind. The entire world was filled with these souls, then the worlds behind it.

She was seeing Typhonel's fears of what was to come if things didn't change.

Carabella brushed her brow as they put her on the ground. Her touch brought light into Jenna's darkening world and the images vanished. But the chill remained.

She could move a bit and tried to nod to Ghortin. The terror still grabbed her, but it weakened and faded away.

Somehow Typhonel was involved and that she couldn't risk saying the name aloud in front of Carabella. "Something that happened at Shettler's Point is causing it. Terror and overwhelming uselessness. We can't fight. Can't win."

"You didn't tag along on my spell, did you?" Ghortin's dark eyes were fierce as he tried to see something beyond her. "Damn me. The link between us must have pulled you along. It shouldn't have been strong enough." He said a few soft words, a soothing spell, and Jenna felt the fear slip away further. The presence of Typhonel, lurking at the edge of her consciousness, relaxed.

"Something in your mind grabbed hold of the fear of all the souls who were killed." Ghortin helped her to sit up. "I fear the people of Shettler's Point had been made into mindslaves and your echo would have responded to that."

Jenna hadn't had any reaction from the echo, the remnant of the woman who had been mindsacrificed before Jenna took over her body, for a while. And she couldn't tell how much of the vanishing terror had been from the echo at sensing the victims and what was from Typhonel.

"Is she okay?" Crell had her bow and quiver of arrows out and was watching all around them.

Ghortin nodded. "I believe she will be." He gave a soothing smile, but his eyes were still worried.

The terror was fading, but Jenna was going to have to find a time when Carabella wasn't around to tell him that Typhonel was most likely the source of her terror.

Carabella got to her feet and looked around the clearing they'd been passing through. "Since there is no way you can expect the poor girl to ride after that, I say we set up camp here."

Jenna was about to say she was fine, they still had another hour's ride planned for the day. But she had the strength of an over-cooked noodle at this point. Even getting off the ground was going to be an issue.

Ghortin watched her with a frown, then nodded. "This is as good a place as any. And once you feel better, I think we need to look closer at what happened. That smoke might be gone, but I fear what was behind it and the assault on your mind indicates changes in our enemies."

Jenna was happy to stay seated on the dirt for a bit longer. "Which enemies?"

"All of them." Ghortin moved away and quietly set up their camp.

CHAPTER TWENTY-TWO

THE RUGGED CLIFF face above Storm was cloaked in dying grasses and a dry wind picked up his hair but was too warm to cool anything. He still completely agreed with Edgar's assessment about leaving their stolen ship behind, but it didn't make this part of the trip any less miserable.

A series of oaths and the sound of fabric tearing reinforced that he wasn't the only one not enjoying things. Keanin did sound more like his old self as he chastised the thorn bush that had grabbed his tunic. "Couldn't we go back and get that dingy? Find a way to go further up the coast, we could say we survived a shipwreck. People haven't gone this way in a long time for a reason."

"Which makes it all the better for us." Edgar turned back from the point position. Unlike the other two, he seemed happy hiking through vicious shrubbery. "We would have still had to say what ship we'd been on, where it went down. Too many things to stand out. This way we might make it into town without being noticed."

"Although, if Keanin gets roughed up by any more plants, we might have to say we found him by the side of the road and rescued him." Storm said as he kept climbing.

"Stop smirking!" Keanin said without being able to see Storm's face. "Because I haven't spent my life hiding out in the wilderness is no reason to be mean."

Storm gave a small smile, but it wasn't at Keanin's current misfortune. He was happy to hear something like his normal whine. This was the first day since he'd been attacked that he genuinely sounded and acted like the Keanin that Storm had grown up with. He knew it would take a long time for Keanin to recover from what was done to him, but this was a start.

Within an hour they crested the last hill that would lead down into Erlinda. Storm hadn't been through here in over twenty years and that had been when the royal family made their visit to Craelyn. It had been by ship and quickly done, but even so, Storm was surprised that the city below them didn't look slightly familiar.

The hill most of the city sat on was lower than the one they just crested but still higher than he recalled and odd for a coastal town.

"Am I forgetting things, or has it always looked like that?" Storm knew Edgar would have been out here more recently.

"You could be forgetting things, but this is fairly new. They used mage craft and massive teams of workers to build upon the hill." Edgar pointed to long arms sticking out near the side closest to the water. "They haul larger cargos up with those pulleys. They can be completely protected should they come under attack."

"I'm assuming those lower areas are for the poor?" Storm studied the city portion that was still at sea level. Even from this distance, the structures looked small and badly made.

"Most likely." Edgar started leading them down the trail. "The rich protect the rich. Present company excluded." He nodded to Strom.

Storm frowned. Growing up in privilege meant you took care of others, not left them to live in squalor.

They were approaching the lower level of the city when an arrow shot past all three. Storm spun as it passed; it had been a bit further from him and Edgar, but it was enough to move Keanin's hair as it passed. Keanin appeared lost in thought so he hadn't noticed it. Until he saw both

Storm and Edgar draw their blades and back up closer to him. Keanin reached back for his bow, and slowly pulled out an arrow from the quiver on his back. "Are we under attack?" He sounded almost hopeful, something that was not a normal Keanin response.

All three held still, waiting for the archer to show themselves. There were no further arrows, nor any movement between them and the outskirts of the city. While there was a forest behind them, there was a field with only a few thin trees between them and the city, so hiding would have been difficult.

"Do you see anything?" Storm's vision was good, so was Keanin's, but Edgar's was better.

"No. I don't." He put away his sword but pulled out one of his knives all the while watching the area before them. "If we were on the open trail, I'd say we let Keanin fire arrows back until someone moved. But, that wouldn't be seemly on the edge of a large city. Not to mention, causing an attraction causing disturbance. I'll go in myself." He waited for a nod from Storm then crossed back into the tree line behind them and moved toward the city.

Keanin gave a low whimper as Edgar vanished. "They found me. How did they find me so fast?" He was still holding his bow, but Storm gently removed the arrow from his shaking hand.

"They didn't find you. You're fine." He forced Keanin to look up. "We won't let that happen."

Keanin grabbed Storm's sword arm. "Promise me that you'll kill me before they can get me again." He looked frantic but the grip he had on Storm's arm was tight.

"I'm not going to kill you. And they're not getting you back. *Ever.*"

"No, they will never get me back. But I don't know that I'll have the chance to end my life in time." Keanin was calming down in appearance, if not in words. "You'll have to do it. It's the only way."

Storm started to shake him off, but Keanin kept talking. "No. You have to. You don't know what I saw, what I felt. If they get me again they can use me to do things, horrible things, portal-end-of-the-world things." He stepped forward to stare into Storm's eyes. "Corin, I love you like a brother; you must do this. They will use me against Jenna. Against everyone we hold dear. I won't be able to stop them."

Storm put his hand on top of Keanin's. The fear in his friend's face was horrible to see, but it was for what he would be forced to do if captured, not for himself. Storm slowly nodded. "In all but blood, you are my brother. If it comes to that, I will end your life. They will not take you." He tried to shake off the feeling of doom that crawled into his soul at his words. "But you have to tell your shade to leave me in peace."

Keanin gave a shaky smile and hugged Storm. "Thank you, I feel better already. And my shade will leave you alone if you promise to take care of Jenna for me." His smile said he didn't think that would be a hardship.

Edgar came back, skirting the edge of the trees as he dragged two semi-conscious people with him. A human male and a kelar female. "Found who was shooting at you."

"Just two?" Storm looked down at them. Neither was trying to get up.

"There were three more, these are the only ones who survived." Edgar gave a grim smile at the look of surprise on his prisoner's face. "They refused to stand down or answer my questions."

Storm leaned down and lifted the man by his collar. "Who do you work for?"

The man tried to turn his head away, but the woman lunged over with a small dagger aimed at Storm's throat. He grabbed her hand, but she had a second small blade and stabbed herself in the chest before he could stop her.

Edgar grabbed her, but she was already dying. She gave a bloody grin as she watched Storm. "Royal blood will be ours. Qhazborh bring me..." She stiffened and died. The blade had to have been poisoned. Both Edgar and Storm dropped her.

Storm wiped his hand on his tunic. Hopefully, her poison had stayed inside her.

Edgar quickly patted down the unmoving man but came up with nothing. "I'm sorry, I can't believe I missed the jack-blades in her bodice."

Keanin put away his bow and arrow and came forward to nudge the dead woman with his foot. He tilted his head, then gave a grim smile. "She was the leader."

The man squirmed in Edgar's grasp. "Who told you that? Are you a spy?"

"No." Keanin stepped forward quickly. "I'm your executioner. Give my regards to your god." Before either Storm or Edgar realized what he was doing, Keanin tried to slit the man's throat.

CHAPTER TWENTY-THREE

JENNA SIGHED AS she took in the sad village ahead of them. They'd gone through a number of them, but they were getting shabbier and more depressing they traveled.

She'd briefly been able to fill Ghortin in on Typhonel's melt-down and assured him she was fine. But the reality was the despair and terror that had flooded her mind still lingered—and places like the village they were heading to didn't help.

A single, rut-grooved lane plowed through the leaning mortar and wood buildings of the town as if it was afraid of getting too close to either side. Jenna didn't blame it.

"Couldn't we bypass this one?" She was trying to keep from sounding whiney, but they didn't need supplies, and this wasn't a planned stop. For the most part, they'd been sleeping in their tents, not in town. Even Carabella had stopped complaining about that as the towns grew worse. Crell had stayed silent but she also had ridden ahead this time to see what was beyond the village.

"I agree it's not in the best condition. But with the fields around it, this is the fastest way. We will be through it before you—"

Before he could finish his sentence, a rag-clothed man ran out from the trees next to them. A bloody knife was clutched tightly in his hand as he charged Carabella.

Carabella automatically raised her hands to cast a spell, but Jenna knew whatever that spell bubble was that had been haunting her would attack as soon as she cast any-thing. Breaking Carabella of spellcasting was like trying to make someone stop breathing.

Jenna got her spell in first, a simple relocation, short distance, but should be enough to drop him. He should have landed safely on his ass until they could figure out who he was and what he was doing.

Should have.

Instead, his eyes grew unnaturally large and he exploded.

Ghortin dropped the hand he had raised to cast his spell. "What in the seven hells of the abyss happened?"

Luckily, before he exploded, the man had been relocated a good twenty feet back so his remains didn't get on anyone. Jenna still felt like she was going to be sick.

The remains did hit the forest behind him. They were close enough to the town that people were coming out to see what the noise had been.

Carabella looked at the crowd, then rode toward Jenna, took hold of the reins to her horse, and started leading her away.

"But I didn't mean to do that." Jenna was in shock.

"I'm not certain what you did or didn't do, child," Carabella kept her voice down as she watched the crowd closing in. "It would be best if we weren't involved. Angry mobs are never good."

Most of the mob came from the town and stopped in front of Ghortin. Two farmers came out of the fields and blocked Carabella and Jenna's horses as they tried to go back down the trail.

"What happened here? How did you destroy him like that?" The first farmer grabbed a hold of the reins to Carabella's horse. He didn't sound angry, but not happy either.

Carabella started sobbing hysterically. "Oh, help us! Our guard had to ride ahead, then that thing ran at me... then exploded. Why did this happen? I can't take any of this. My niece is in shock. Help us." The words were so muddled by hiccups and sobs that Jenna almost believed her.

The farmer nearest to them let go of the reins and both farmers took a few steps back. "I'm sorry for whatever happened. Someone will figure it out." He leaned forward. "Neither of you are injured?" At their nods, he waved to the second man. "Faslin, get these two ladies to the Swan and Goose, get some food and ale in them." He gave a smile to both and darted off to the rest of the crowd gathering around Ghortin and the remains of the attacker.

———◆———

Ghortin overheard the farmer and nodded to Carabella. Going to the pub would help get the two of them out of sight and hopefully, out of mind. Besides, Jenna didn't look good.

He kept trying to answer questions from the crowd while scanning for magic residue from what had happened. And keeping an eye out for Crell. It would be better if she stayed out of this completely. By the look on Jenna's face, he didn't think she'd intended to kill the man. Her spell could have gone awry though. He knew neither he nor Carabella had done it.

There was an odd magical taint to the remains that tugged at his memory. Alas, with the crowd of town's folk growing larger, and all shouting questions, he couldn't chase down where he'd felt it.

"Will everyone please shut up?" His bellow shocked the people around him into doing just that. Carabella glanced back but she and Jenna continued following the farmer into town. "Thank you." He sought out the most prosperous-looking person there while his mind continued to try and follow the magic behind the dead man. "Could you please explain what happened? Or do all of your people magically explode? It was quite disturbing."

The large man stepped forward and the way the crowd

moved out of his way told Ghortin he'd picked a leader of the town. "That's what I was about to ask you. Our folk don't abide by magic." He folded his thick arms and settled into a glare.

"Then how did he explode?" Ghortin ruffled himself up to look hurt and insulted. "You can't think *I* did this? I am a merchant, simply returning with my daughter and sister after market down south. Our guard has ridden ahead, and look what has happened." He nodded down the remains. "And if your people don't trust magic, then why did he have one of those amulet things? Been warned about them—bad magic." As he spoke, Ghortin pointed a shaking hand down to the bloody ground. There lay a large Qhazborh pendent. Of course, Ghortin had magicked it into being and it would vanish in a few days, but it would give them something to focus on. No idea if this man had been a follower or not, but the red blood all over indicated he hadn't been a demonspawn.

A slight woman wearing riding leather stepped forward. "He's right, Jolie, I've seen one of those before, so has Hoijt. Grolian wasn't one of us at all, stuck to himself, odd like."

Voices grew as members of the crowd all collaborated on the woman's story. From the sound of it, anyone who hadn't grown up in this town was suspect and the dead man had only been there since the previous spring. No one was paying much attention to Ghortin as their speculation grew louder.

Ghortin coughed and turned toward the man, Jolie. "I'm afraid my sister and daughter are scarred. Where did you send them?" Ghortin's weariness wasn't completely feigned. Making that pendent had taken far more out of him than it should have.

Jolie pointed down the road, where a pub sign hung. Ghortin nodded his thanks and quickly left. Still no sign of Crell, but she was almost as good as Edgar at staying hidden when she needed to.

The pub was dark but he heard Carabella's theatrical words as soon as he walked in.

"There he is, thank the stars he's not been injured. My brother is safe." Her eyes were bright with tears, From the sympathetic looks being flung her way, she'd been working this for a while.

He refrained from growling at her as he took a seat. "Just what are you—"

Carabella leaned back as she cut him off. "Dear brother, meet our new, most valiant friend." A man seated behind them had been blocked by Carabella and the general darkness of the pub. "This is Linton the bard."

He was human, as everyone Ghortin had seen in the town was. This close to Strann that wasn't too surprising. But these small towns had been far more mixed when he'd last come through. Of course, that would have probably been thirty or more years ago. Thick blond hair and wide deep brown eyes. His face was pure innocence until he smiled. He reminded Ghortin of some long-snooted predators who lived in the warmer and wetter parts of the world.

Ghortin nodded. "Ah, well, hello. Please excuse us, trauma outside and all." The last thing they needed was a nosy bard watching them.

"Ah, yet I could not stand to leave such fair ladies alone in such a time of distress." His accent was that of Strann, his phrasing was more suited to the Khelaran high council.

"Then it is a good thing they are not alone, isn't it." Ghortin folded his arms but the bard refused to take the hint. His grin grew wider.

"Yes, tis true." He smiled at Ghortin as if they were long-lost, favorite cousins. "From where do you hail with two such lovely women? Could you not welcome another's company to help keep them from harm?"

"I'm not in the habit of explaining myself to strangers. However, these are my sister and my daughter, both gone through a recent trauma. If you will excuse us?" When Linton made no move, Ghortin helped Carabella to her feet. "Come, sister dear, we should see to our rooms."

Carabella's eyes narrowed but she nodded. Jenna got to her feet, but not before Linton took her hand and kissed it.

"Until we meet again, fair one." He rose to his feet quickly and left the pub.

Ghortin spoke to the pub owner-innkeeper about a room but was told their guard had already secured one for them.

"Ah yes, that was the plan. Just checking. Up the stairs to the right you say?" He forced a smile. Crell could have set up their rooms—or it could be something else entirely.

He led the way to their room, a large family-style setup. He motioned for Jenna and Carabella to stay behind them as he opened the door cautiously.

To find Crell on one of the beds. "Took you long enough. Been waiting up here for a while. Which one of you blew up that man?"

Ghortin shut the door after Carabella and Jenna came in. He also slipped a warding spell on it. The man who attacked them might not have been alone.

"I don't think I blew him up?" Jenna dropped her pack.

Carabella scowled. "Something happened on the chaotic plane that caused an event. Jenna relocated him, and most likely did not cause his explosion, but it was likely an interaction between the prior chaotic event, her spell, and a new chaotic event."

"I'm glad you felt that event or rather those events from the chaotic plane. They were so faint I couldn't pinpoint them." Ghortin turned to Jenna as she dropped her pack. "Did you notice anything odd when you cast your spell?

Or perhaps directly before that?"

"Not at all. As Carabella said, I was trying to relocate him." Jenna's frown returned. "Do you think that man was against us specifically?"

"I think we can't ignore that possibility. We can't check his feet for the marks though."

"Which leaves us with what happened to that man?" Carabella held up her hand. "Yes, I shouldn't have thought of drawing a spell, instinct, you know. But I know what I felt. There were two distinct surges of chaotic energy, before and after Jenna's spell. Ones that I don't recognize at all."

CHAPTER TWENTY-FOUR

STORM GRABBED KEANIN'S arm and jerked the knife away before he could kill their prisoner. Edgar dragged the prisoner out of reach.

"What in the hell? We need to question him, not kill him." Storm leaned close to Keanin. He hadn't tried again but he was shaking in anger. "This isn't like you."

Keanin took a deep breath. "I'm not like me anymore. Those bastards made sure of that. But I'll let him live if he tells us what he knows. Quickly." He gave the prisoner a dark glance and stalked off into the trees.

It was well done; the prisoner knew he'd almost died. But if Storm or Edgar had done that, it would have been to get the man to talk. Keanin had been ready to kill him. They were going to have to watch him carefully.

The body of the woman stiffened and darkened. The prisoner squirmed to move away from it. He now appeared more concerned about being near her body than whether someone was going to slit his throat.

Edgar kept a hold of him and dragged him back further into the trees. "Some poisons can cause more trouble after the user is dead. We probably don't want to stick around here."

Keanin stayed further in the tree line. His jaw was clenched so tightly, it looked ready to snap.

Storm nudged the man as Edgar tied his hands and feet together. "I'd advise you to start talking quickly. Our friend over there has had a few bad days and really wants to kill someone."

The prisoner stayed silent until Keanin took a single step forward. "I'll talk! Don't let him near me. That woman was the Hilt, a position in our organization that leads us in doing our god's bidding. We knew royal blood was coming this way and needed to gather it. Qhazborh will not be pleased." He was so matter-of-fact about admitting to being a follower of the dark gods that Storm was taken aback. The woman had shouted the name, so perhaps he felt hiding it was pointless. But it was still odd to hear it so easily shared.

"But who is a royal? Who told you to attack us?" Edgar shrugged. "I don't see any royals around here."

The prisoner glanced to Storm, then to Keanin. "We were told to watch for you. Another group is watching the docks in case you came by sea. We know who we are looking for." He kept glancing between the Keanin and Storm indicating that they hadn't been specific as to which one was.

"And what were you going to do when you brought this fictitious royal back? Where were you taking them?" Edgar flipped one of his knives in the air.

"Not taking them anywhere." His look was an odd combination of a smile and a grimace. "Needed their bodies. Must complete our task before the portal opens." He started twitching and his eyes went wide. "He found me. I tried to do what you said, I tried!" He started foaming at the mouth and Edgar leaped back to the others.

"We probably want to get far from here."

They took off running as the man's pleading turned to screams.

"Our evil deities don't seem too happy with failure." Storm kept Keanin in front of him when he drifted behind.

Edgar glanced back but kept moving further from the now silent body and the town. A low-level explosion followed quickly. "Not at all. And I wonder why they think Keanin is royal too. Are you sure you don't have royal blood?"

Keanin shook his head. "Not that I know of. I'd think someone from Khelaran would have come forth long ago if I was a missing heir." He increased his pace to catch up to Edgar. "Can I have my knife back now?"

Edgar shrugged and brought them to a stop. "Can you keep yourself under control with it? You've been through things we can't imagine. But it's dangerous out here— now more so because someone wants kelar royals—dead apparently. And they think you're one. You can't do what you want." He looked to Storm. "I think from here on out, we go in disguise."

"I promise to try." Keanin held out his hand. "But things have changed in me. I will try to be more like you. When I can."

"That'll work." Edgar gave him the knife back. "Let's see what I can do to make us all look less like us." He dug through their packs.

An hour later three weary travelers approached Erlinda from the west. Keanin hadn't been happy about the extension around the town to change the direction they were coming from but he gave in when Edgar had him dress in his finery. He might have changed, but he still loved dressing up. There were enough changes that unless someone knew him well, they wouldn't know who he was. Hopefully, the people after them would be fooled long enough for them to get on a ship to Craelyn.

They'd briefly discussed going back to Lithunane. But even Keanin felt they needed to see if Khelaran had truly fallen. Edgar used the taran wand to notify Tor Ranshal of what was going on—he and Rachael could pass it to Resstlin.

Storm and Edgar were disguised as the sell-swords hired by a Khelaran merchant. Keanin was content playing foppish dress-up, and Storm and Edgar were more comfortable in rough leathers. Storm was disguised as a Crailian sell-sword. The Craili were a band of deadly fighters from the far north of Khelaran. They were respected and deadly and he had the skill of the blade to back it up.

Edgar was also a sell-sword, but his lack of height would have been unheard of in the Craili, so he went for a regular thug.

"I still say I could wear the patch." Keanin studied both of them. "It would make me look dashing. I admit this is foppish even for me." He gestured down to his elaborate outfit with a wince.

Strom grinned and adjusted his eye patch. "Nope, I get this. Many Craili are proud of their injuries and missing limbs—this builds into that." He also had dried ink around his other eye and a jagged mark on his left cheek. Both would identify him as a Crailian.

"Sorry, it does work better with him," Edgar said. They were still far enough from the town not to be heard, but that wouldn't last for long. "But we forgot names. Storm, you shall be Hawk's Flight—close enough to the Crailian names to work. Keanin, Lanian shall be your name. You dabble in fabrics and were attacked going home to Craelyn. I shall be Syl, a former spymaster fallen on hard times."

From his grin, Storm knew there was most likely a long tale behind that persona, but they didn't have time to discuss it.

"Who goes there?" A pair of city guards armed with both pikes and swords at their sides marched out of an outlying building to greet them as they approached.

Edgar bobbed his head. "We are escorting a merchant back to his home and need to take a ship. I don't recall guards last time I came through." He rocked back and rested his hand on the hilt of his sword.

"Times have changed recently." The guard looked to say more but the second one coughed and cut him off.

"We have to confirm everyone who enters here."

Edgar shrugged but also didn't drop his hand from his sword. Storm stayed back but did the same.

Keanin shoved past both of them and gave an exaggerated sigh. "As you were told, I am *Lanian*. I'm sure you have heard of me and my glorious fabrics." He looked around the edge of town. Erlinda wasn't particularly small or run down, but the sniff he gave indicated both. "Then again, you might not. My wares are for…a different station of persons. But never mind that. We are taking a ship home, so if you don't mind…" He flung his fingers at both guards.

"What ship?" The first guard couldn't fold his arms because of the pike he carried, but he leaned back in a way that suggested it.

Edgar nodded. "*The Golden Sparrow*. We leave tomorrow."

The second guard snorted. "Not unless you want to swim there. *The Golden Sparrow* sank two days ago before she could return from Craelyn. Freak storm." He nodded to the first guard and they stepped out of the way. "You might be able to find passage on another ship, but the cost will be steep."

"We will find another passage then." Storm didn't move but pitched his voice low. The guard had to take a step forward to hear him. "We have been hired; we *will* complete our job."

The guard went a shade paler than before. "Of course, you will. Crailian sell-swords are trusted beyond all. Try the third dock, better options there." Both guards quickly moved away.

Storm was certain the guard had been about to say something else instead of trusted but thought better of it. He nodded as they passed by.

"Good call on the ship. A missing ship gives us time to look around and see what's happening. And how they react to the bodies you left. Good thing we came in from the north." Storm kept his voice low and pulled up his hood. No one seemed to be noticing them, but that could change.

Edgar frowned as he watched the people around them as well. "I picked a ship that usually makes that run. That would have been the one we'd take. Am I the only one who missed this storm? Two days ago we were on the water. Granted further south, but a storm strong enough to take out one of the ocean ships would have been felt."

Keanin sighed. "Can't we solve something, anything, before adding more to the pile? How can this all be connected?"

"No idea." Edgar looked around at the bustle surrounding the docks. "I believe our benefactor is exhausted from his journey, and we should take rooms first. Then we can see about a ship for a few days out."

Storm looked around but didn't see whatever Edgar had. They did need to see if Erlinda had fallen to Qhazborh's followers, it was a major connection town for many people in Traanafaeren. But they should be able to do it in a day. The way Edgar was scowling around them he was serious about a few days.

"You can explain later," Storm said. "What inn do you prefer?"

It took longer than it should have to find one that Keanin felt fit his station, yet also showed his loss of income from his fictitious attack. Well off, but not over the top.

By the time Edgar got them booked, Storm was ready to tie up Keanin and shove him in a closet somewhere.

They picked a single larger room and the innkeeper nodded in understanding when Edgar told him of their tale of woe.

"Understandable. I'd keep people around me as well." He nodded to Keanin. "I can promise you weren't attacked by our people. Good and upstanding, stay out of trouble we do." He handed a key to Edgar. "Second door as you go up the stairs. Travel is light right now, so I'll keep the rooms on either side of you open as long as I can." He nodded to them all and turned back to the kitchen.

Edgar led, with Keanin in the middle, and Storm, still hooded but with it pushed back enough to show his Crailian face marks, following. He made sure to give a slow glance to the pub before he went up the stairs. He might not have magic like the other two, but there was something dark lurking through this town. He intended to find it and destroy it.

CHAPTER TWENTY-FIVE

A LTHOUGH THEY'D TAKEN the rest of the afternoon debating it, neither Ghortin nor Carabella got
any closer to what caused the man to explode. Jenna gave
up trying to provide suggestions after the first hour, and
instead opened the small gray book Rachael had given
her before they left. Crell rolled over and took a nap.

Unlike Ghortin's book, this one seemed to be specifically made for Guardians. And was so boring that it made
her fall asleep almost every time she tried to read it. To
her, it seemed to be full of minute details about people
long dead that had no bearing on her current issue or
what was happening now. The important bits were doled
out in tiny drabs between pages of drudgery. The portal
was barely mentioned.

Unfortunately, the book was spelled, differently than
Ghortin's had been, but still enough to make things difficult. The damn spell book could tell when a page had
been read and refused to allow the reader to skip ahead.

"Any luck?" Carabella walked to where Jenna sat. "I
know I can't help you, nor even look at the words, but
you look upset."

Jenna closed the book. "It's the damnedest thing. I have
to read to move forward but I get sleepy every time I try
to read. Why create these things, then make them impossible to use? I'd like to go back and throttle the people
who created them."

"That does seem rather pointless. Although, couldn't
you do a spell to stay awake, and just plow through it? I
know Ghortin said the books can't be spelled, but what

about one on you?" Carabella's hands were twitching toward the book. She finally pulled both hands back.

Ghortin looked up from the spell book he was studying at Carabella's words. "What now? Suggesting spells to my apprentice?"

"She has a good point. Once we get the third book and get the cuari back, we do have to figure out how to close that portal." Jenna patted the book. "In theory, that's what this book and I can do. If I can get through it. This book is incredibly dry and wordy. It's going to take a while to get through it. We might not have that time."

Ghortin looked at the tiny window, it was already getting dark outside. "It's coming time that we can go search the town for clues as to what our friend was up to. Do you want to stay here and read, or help?"

Crell had appeared to be sound asleep but at Ghortin's words, she rolled off her bed and stood there waiting. "I'm ready to go. Look what happened the last time I left you folks."

Jenna put the book back in her bag. He had a good point. Not to mention a non-sleeping spell this close to bedtime would leave her cranky and far too awake if it worked.

"Dinner first? Then come back up here, change, sneak out, and lurk about? It would be suspicious if we weren't seen for dinner, even in a place like this." Carabella was a bit too excited concerning the lurking-about aspect. Using magic or not, there'd be plenty of trouble she could get in. From the looks on Crell's and Ghortin's faces, they were thinking the same thing.

"I prefer the term investigate to lurking. I don't lurk." Ghortin tugged on the edges of his tunic. "But yes, that is the plan as it were. And no magic. Either of you. We've not figured out what those bursts of chaos were or why that man exploded. If we need magic, I'll do it." He nodded to Crell. "Keep up the guise of our guard, if you would."

Crell gave a bow and put on her sword belt. "Yes, sir."

They went downstairs. It was too early for the pub to be busy, but there were a few people at the tables having dinner.

"I don't see Linton," Carabella said as she surveyed the room.

"Why would you care if he were here?" Ghortin looked over to Jenna and rolled his eyes. "Oh."

"What?" Jenna looked to both. She wasn't going to admit that she had glanced around for him as they came down. "He's a nice guy. There are some of those around you know." She actually thought he was a bit sketchy, but it was nice to talk to someone new.

"And him being good-looking has nothing to do with it?" Ghortin waved to the innkeeper and pointed to a table in the corner. "You are an engaged woman after all."

Crell covered her laugh and schooled her face to look stern as she escorted them to their table.

"I'm not engaged. And I am not interested in Linton. Aside from the fact it's nice to talk to someone who doesn't know who I am and isn't trying to destroy the world." Jenna slid into her seat with a sigh. "I wish we knew how the others were." They'd agreed to keep the taran wand usage minimal, but if they hadn't heard from Edgar or the others within a few days, Ghortin said they could try again. The problem was timing since the wands were dicey on the water.

Ghortin patted her hand. "Now maybe you have an idea why Storm tried to keep you in Lithunane. The worry is horrible."

Jenna dropped the conversation as the innkeeper came up. Ghortin quickly placed their order, including three ales and a glass of wine.

Carabella took a sip of the wine when the drinks arrived, then looked around for a place to spit it out.

She ended up spitting it back into the glass. "That is vile. Seriously, awful." She pushed the glass away from her.

"I can order something else?" Ghortin had finished half his pint already.

She shuddered. "No. Someone needs to stay sober."

Jenna took a sip of her ale. It wasn't as bad as Carabella's reaction said her wine had been. But it was pretty nasty. She pushed it aside.

Crell took one sip of hers, then pushed it away. "That is bad. Besides, your guardswoman should stay sober too." She grimaced as Ghortin finished his. "How can you drink that? That tastes like shoe water. With the feet still in the shoes."

"It's fine, you don't appreciate the rougher ales." Ghortin took a sip of Jenna's abandoned ale then spat it back into the glass. "That was not what I drank. Damn it, something is wrong and if they did something to your drinks, I'm afraid what they'd do to our food." He glanced around. "But it would be suspicious if we left suddenly."

Carabella gave a small smile, rose to her feet, and then swooned. Jenna caught her before she hit the ground, but Carabella was taller than she was. Crell kept everyone in the pub away from them. In the process, she *accidentally* knocked Jenna's, Carabella's, and her own drinks to the floor.

"My sister has fainted!" Ghortin scooped her up and went for the stairs.

Jenna darted to the innkeeper. "I am so sorry; my aunt has been ill and the attack today has made her weak."

He watched her, Crell waiting sternly next to her, then Ghortin going up the stairs. "I'll send food up in a bit."

She wanted to tell him not to bother, no way was she touching anything he made. But it would look odd to do that. "Thank you so much." She and Crell turned and ran up the stairs, but Jenna caught a familiar blond head leaving the inn as she reached the top. Linton had been in the pub—and he'd made sure to stay in the shadows. *Damn it. So much for someone normal and not trying to destroy the world.*

Ghortin and Carabella were already packing when Jenna and Crell got there. Crell checked the locks on the door twice, then moved a chair under the handle. "No, I don't think anyone will try to break in, but I didn't think anyone would try to poison us, either. Better to be safe than sorry." She hadn't taken anything out of her bags before so pulled up another chair next to the door and sat.

"Linton was in the pub. I think he was watching us; he took off as we came up the stairs. I take it we're leaving immediately?" Riding at night wasn't her favorite thing to do, but better than stay and wait for someone to try to poison them again—or something else.

"Not immediately, but I want to be ready to go quickly and soon." Ghortin pulled more things out of his bag.

"How is making a mess the same as getting ready?" Crell tilted her head.

"I'm ready. I'm looking for a vial, one with...ha!" He pulled out a small wrapped bottle. "I have no idea what was in the drinks. There are poisons that a single drop can complete their job. This is guman root." His smile was wide, Carabella's fell.

"That is a horrible potion." She shuddered.

"You never developed a taste, it's a bit sharp but refreshing." Ghortin unwrapped the bottle and shook it. "Just one drop. Let it sit on your tongue as long as possible before swallowing it. And keep your tongue extended. I might be able to determine the poison, or poisons, from the color change. Once you swallow it, it should neutralize whatever they got you with."

Crell came away from her door. "That little thing can neutralize all poisons?"

"Well, the ones you survive long enough to take it for

anyway." He held up the bottle. "Who is first?" He lifted the stopper off the bottle.

"Shouldn't you take it too? You did sip my ale." Jenna wrinkled her nose at the smell. If it only tasted half as bad as it smelled, it was going to be nasty.

"Ah, yes. I shall. But someone will have to look at my tongue, and I'd rather you each see it a few times first. Although mine wasn't as bad tasting as yours, there might have been something in it as well." He turned to Jenna with the dropper ready.

She stuck out her tongue and tried not to think about the smell. The taste put that completely out of mind. Burnt rubbish with a side of rotten fruit hit her tongue. "Oh, gawd." She was limited to what she could say with her tongue out.

Ghortin studied her tongue, making muttering sounds to himself. "You said you saw Linton downstairs?"

"Un-huh."

"Damn it. This looks like a compulsion spell, a malth de rein. The caster would have had to have been within a short distance after it was taken."

Carabella stepped forward and also looked at Jenna's tongue. "A dark love spell? Why would someone put that on us?"

"Might not have been on all of us." Ghortin frowned then nodded. "You can swallow now."

Jenna swallowed. It wasn't any better that way. There hadn't been many people in the pub, and Linton had definitely been hiding from them. "You think Linton drugged me to fall in love with him? What the hell?"

"I agree it looks like he is involved. But it wouldn't have been love," Carabella said. "You would have been dying for his touch literally. A person under that poison must have the object of their desires until they die. No one has used those poisons in eons."

Ghortin's scowl etched its way in deeper. "I know.

You're next."

Carabella's nose wrinkled as he dropped it on her tongue, but she held steady.

"Nope. No malth de rein for you. He must not like older women. Damn, almost as bad though. Death drop."

Jenna wasn't happy that Linton had singled her out for something special. "What's that?"

At Ghortin's nod, Carabella swallowed the elixir. "I would have also been under his spell. A mindless zombie killing whoever he ordered until I died. I'm sensing a theme here, and again, sight-of-spell is required for it to work. I can't believe I was polite to that weasel."

Crell silently stuck out her tongue for the drop.

"He was building an army. Death drop in Crell's drink as well."

"I will kill him myself." Crell stepped back. "Unless Jenna wants the honor."

"We can all do it." Jenna nodded to Ghortin. "Your turn."

Carabella took the dropper and released one drop on his tongue. "Damn, confirms his master plan. You have both malth de rein, most likely from Jenna's drink, and cout la spades. Nice. Sex slave, two warrior zombies, and a dark mage rising from the dead. He was setting himself up for something."

Jenna shook her head. "How could he be certain who got which poison? We didn't see him down there and if he hadn't moved under the torches as he left, I wouldn't have seen him leave. Yet he not only spelled our drinks *after* we ordered them but got them placed in front of the right ale drinkers?"

Crell started swearing. "Which means that at least the server and possibly the entire town were in on it. We have to leave, now."

Ghortin put away the things he'd dug out, then went to the window. "The streets are too empty for this early. I don't like using magic, we're leaving a trail for any mage trying to follow us. But I agree, we need to get away from here." He started pacing. "The only one of us that drank their entire drink was me, and everyone in the pub saw that. They will be expecting me to go into a death-like coma. We should oblige them."

Jenna narrowed her eyes. "And then what? They also would know the three of us aren't under their control. They'd just come after us another way."

He deflated. "True. Not to mention without the guman root, even a small amount could have made you react differently."

Crell lifted her sword. "Look, I don't like picking fights, but they started it. If the whole town isn't working with that creep—or if it was another creep entirely—they still are involved. None of us are bad fighters, and Ghortin and Jenna are mages. We leave and fight if they try to stop us." She grinned. "And if Jenna explodes a few bad folks, accidentally, I say good riddance."

Jenna was about to point out that she didn't know how it happened before. But right now she was so pissed she wouldn't mind if Linton blew up.

CHAPTER TWENTY-SIX

STORM WATCHED THE street below them and the long pair of wharves beyond that. Everything looked normal down there. Merchants buzzing back and forth, passengers getting on southbound ships—the north-bound ones to Craelyn always left in the morning. But there was a good amount of people heading south. Not a single thing that didn't look like a busy coastal town going about its business.

Edgar took off as soon as they got to their room. Three hours ago. There was no way Storm was leaving Keanin alone to go after him and he knew Edgar had counted on that.

"Has the view changed?" Keanin removed some of his fineries and was lounging on the bed he'd claimed.

"No. Nor is there any sign of Edgar." Storm dropped the curtain and sat in one of the wooden chairs. "Damn it. The longer we stay here the bigger risk we take of someone figuring out who we are or ties us to the people Edgar killed. We have to get on a ship."

"If it's any consolation, I don't feel anything." Keanin pulled out a mending kit and starting fixing the tears in the clothing he'd worn on the way in. "Rather, I don't *not* feel anything. You were right in Shettler's Point, they'd had a magic dampener. But here I feel the normal ebb and flow of magic." He'd been focusing on the needle and thread, but looked up at his last words.

"I know you've been practicing magic," Storm said with a small smile. "And I know Ghortin was afraid of you using it without him. But no one knew what you'd be faced with. I think he'd understand if you trained on simple defensive spells."

Keanin looked back to his mending. "Thank you for understanding, I wasn't sure how to tell you and Edgar. But I want more than just defensive magic. Ghortin didn't teach me much, but I need to be able to destroy them." He didn't look up but there was a viciousness in his voice that Storm had never heard before.

Storm wasn't a magic user, but even he knew using spells that you didn't know very well was a good way to get yourself, and probably anyone around you, killed. "You have to be careful, Keanin. At least work with Edgar—he knows some spells."

"I will. I just…it feels like they did something to me." He held up his hand. "I know they did, but somehow I feel more in touch with my magic than before."

Storm sat back in his chair. Until Edgar came back, they weren't going anywhere. "It could just be anger. You're more aware of things because of it."

"Oh, it is partially that. I am aware of that. This is something more. Isn't it curious that I never noticed my magic until Jenna came to our world? Magic is inherited and according to records I found, my parents were both strong mages—yet I didn't show anything until this last year?"

"Are you saying Jenna gave you magic?"

"No, but who she is, and the former mindslave whose body she took over, could have released a block within me without any of us being aware of it. Maybe what those monsters did to me on the magical level released more of it."

"Which would imply that someone put a magic block on you when you were a baby. Damn, I wish Ghortin were here." Storm leaned forward. Keanin was being too calm about this. "Promise me, unless it's a matter of life or death, you will stick to defensive magic."

Keanin focused on the tunic in his hand for a few minutes. "I will try. Sorry, that's the best I can do."

Storm got up and clasped Keanin's shoulder. "That's a start."

A pounding up the stairs and the sudden flinging open of the door had Storm drawing his sword and Keanin cupping his left hand for a spell.

"Just me." Edgar shut the door quickly behind him. His eyes were bright and he didn't look upset.

Storm sheathed his sword and Keanin shook out his hand. "Where were you, why were you running, and why in the hell do we need to stay here a few days?"

"It's complicated." Edgar paced around the room running his fingers through his short hair as he walked. "Well, not really. Sort of. From what I can tell there was an incursion of the followers of Qhazborh a few months ago. The town killed or chased them all off." He held up his hand to stop the expected comment. "Obviously, they didn't get them all, based on the ones in the forest, but hopefully that indicates the town isn't turned."

Keanin set down his mending. "Who are you and what did you do to Edgar?" He said it lightly, but Storm noticed that he'd dropped his left hand under the tunic he was fixing. Most likely to hide a spell ready to be thrown.

Storm agreed on the caution. Edgar hadn't grown up in Lithunane, but they'd been friends for over thirty years. The only time he'd seen him like this he'd been incredibly drunk.

"Were you drinking?" Storm stepped closer. At first, he didn't smell anything, then a whiff hit him. "Gorgon ale-wine? What in the hell?" The stuff was incredibly potent and judging by the smell, massive quantities had been involved.

Edgar nodded slowly. "No, I smell like that to make others think I was drunk. They talk better that way."

"You're starting to list to the left." Storm walked him back to his bed. The minute the back of his legs hit it Edgar fell back and stayed there.

"Not anymore." Edgar's laughter was almost hysterical.

Storm took out his dagger and sliced Edgar's arm. "Nope, not green."

"That wasn't nice." Edgar didn't seem upset about the cut, nor the implication that he might be a demonspawn. "This town is really quite lovely."

"Keanin? Can you tell on a magical level if anything has been done to him? The Gorgon ale-wine is coming from his clothes, but not him."

Keanin grimaced and came over. "I can try? The spells Ghortin taught me were mostly defensive."

Edgar looked like he was falling asleep but he waved a hand wildly at them. "Traliu spell...Tailue spell... Therilia spell. That one. Defensive."

"I think even I've heard of that one. Wouldn't call it defensive though. Isn't it just to see past a lie?" Storm grabbed Edgar as he started rolling across the bed.

"Sort of." Keanin stared down at Edgar. "But I think if I use it against him it might work. It should get past any compulsion spell that might have been put on him to not talk." He spoke a few soft words, then cast a spell at Edgar. "Are you drunk?"

"Nope." A green aura appeared around Edgar. "Spelled. Yup. Didn't notice it. Bottle in my pack." His voice sounded more like him, but he was still slurring and dropping words. And he was trying to roll off the bed.

"Damn it. What spell?" Storm asked as he dumped the contents of Edgar's pack on the bed. There was only one bottle, a slim orange one. "This?"

"Dunno. Bad one. They were good. My spell protection was better, so they didn't win. But still snuck part of it in. Break bottle near my face."

Storm wondered what the spell was supposed to do if

this wasn't winning. Edgar was so out of sorts; anything could have happened to him in this state and he couldn't have fought back.

Keanin helped sit Edgar up and Storm snapped the bottle under Edgar's nose. A light-yellow smoke came out and he started coughing.

"Keep it there." He choked out the words. "Okay, that's enough." He rubbed his head and blinked at them. "I have the worst hangover."

"I thought you didn't have anything to drink?" Storm stood back. If there was something else wrong with Edgar he could reach him before he did anything.

"I didn't. I thought I was being so tricky. Caught sight of one of Ravenhearst's henchmen when we came into town. Tracked him down, acted drunk—and he zapped me. Got something in my drink."

Keanin silently handed him the water pouch.

"Thanks. Damn, I haven't been caught like that since I first started spy school." He polished it off and Keanin got him a second one.

"I'm still trying to figure out how and why there is a spell to make you drunk." Storm knew there were a lot of spells out there and creative and powerful mages were making more. But this one seemed a bit odd.

"It should have killed me. It was a lassin spell. Lower level, so whoever hit me with it wasn't a strong magic user or wasn't close enough to hit me fully. Or might have wanted a weaker version. It cuts off the oxygen to your brain. They can slip it into water and have a person keel over in a few minutes."

"And therefore made you appear drunk as it went through your body." Storm recognized the name of that spell. Ghortin once had an apprentice almost accidentally kill himself with it about a hundred years ago.

"Yup. Weak execution, plus, my own spell breaker." Edgar pulled out a small amulet hanging around his neck.

"Took three years to have it made. It's tied to me and me alone, but it takes out weaker spells and slows down others." He dropped it back into his tunic and flopped back on the bed with a hand over his eyes. "How long had I been gone?"

"Almost three hours."

"Damn it. I take back what I said about that being a weak spell—my spell breaker had to work too hard to slow it down. From what my shattered head can recall, I started feeling odd about two and a half hours ago. If I hadn't had this, you would have been looking for me floating face down in the ocean."

CHAPTER TWENTY- SEVEN

———◆———

JENNA TRIED TO focus the anger she felt about Linton into calming her nerves as they readied to escape. So far it wasn't working as well as she'd hoped. She wasn't certain that she agreed with Crell about the entire town being involved—she thought they would have been more accommodating and friendly, like Linton, if they had been. But that still didn't exclude any of them from working with him. Especially the innkeeper and his staff.

They'd been ready to leave for a half-hour, but Ghortin and Carabella were having a heated, albeit low volume, debate as to the best way to get out. Carabella felt that she could support a large spell, as long as she didn't create or cast it. She would just be loaning Power to Ghortin and Jenna and felt that the spell that was hunting her wouldn't notice.

Ghortin—and Jenna although neither had asked for her opinion—disagreed. He planned for them to sneak out the window, creep over to the stables in stages, and ride out across the field behind them. Jenna certainly wasn't going to say what she thought of Ghortin climbing through a window.

Crell had been tossing a knife in the air, but the look of annoyance on her face was getting worse.

"We could just go down the stairs and leave like normal people." Jenna had enough. At this point, they wouldn't be leaving before daybreak. "They wouldn't be expecting that. Especially if it didn't look like we had our packs with us. Ghortin and I can hide them magically, then we all leave."

"But for what reason? We need a ruse." Ghortin was too vested in his sneaking-out plan.

"I have no idea. Make something up? Without our packs, they probably won't think we're taking off."

Carabella smiled. "Much better than climbing through windows. You know, it would work better if Ghortin wasn't with us. Make things more believable, since he should be sick under the spell they slipped him. Can you hide him as well?"

Jenna looked at the packs and Ghortin. The spell was a simple one, but hiding a few packs was easier than a person. Ghortin wouldn't be able to cast it on himself and he was the most likely to stay behind to make their story work.

"I think so? But you need to stay right behind me. Can you cover the packs?"

Ghortin's annoyance at them rejecting his plan vanished. "I'm so proud of you! Yes, that will work. I can set up an image spell here making it look like myself and the packs are still in place, in case someone gets nosy." He rubbed his hands. "Excellent thinking."

He cast the spell and a pale version of himself appeared on the bed. Images of their packs leaned up against the wall. "It won't hold if someone touches any of it, but hopefully they won't check for a while."

Crell reached for the door. "I'll go first, with Jenna and Ghortin next. Carabella last, maybe some tears and concern for Ghortin?" She nodded as everyone lined up, Ghortin cast a misdirect spell on their packs, and Jenna cast her spell on him.

"I still see everything." Crell pulled back from the door.

"You're too close, and you know what to look for. Step back a few feet. Both of their spells are more misdirect than actual hiding." Carabella motioned at her to step back.

"Okay, I still sort of see the packs and him, but also sort

of don't. Let's go." Crell opened the door.

Jenna focused on maintaining the spell over Ghortin but also tried to look sad and worried. Not hard, considering what might happen if they were caught. The spells she and Ghortin were using needed a lot of help and wouldn't work well in daylight—she just hoped the moon outside wasn't bright enough to give them away.

The innkeeper nodded to Crell. "I was going to send up the food now."

Jenna drew herself up. "Unfortunately, my father is very ill. We're going to get some herbs to help him, but we don't need food yet." She bit her lip to make it look like she was trying to keep from crying.

"I can have a healer sent up." There was a quick flash of some emotion in the innkeeper's eyes—something dark.

"No, no," Carabella said. "He has a condition. Please don't let anyone up. We will be back momentarily." She was good. Enough pained concern flowed through her voice and her face had a tragic, suffering look.

Crell kept walking for the door, so Jenna followed. She almost yelped when Ghortin hit the back of her foot. She took a deep breath and focused on maintaining the spell.

"I will keep everyone out. Take care, there have been odd creatures out at night." He looked ready to say more, then went back to polishing a glass.

They picked up their pace as they went for the stables.

"I feel like someone is aiming an arrow at my back," Jenna whispered as she followed Crell closely.

"I think we all do," Carabella said.

Ghortin had to stay silent for Jenna's spell to hold but she felt him follow closer. He didn't step on her heel this time though.

They'd made it to the stable and gotten the horses packed when yells came out from the inn.

"Drop your spells, they won't help us anymore." Crell took the lead and they raced out of the stable and around toward the field.

Jenna glanced back. People were coming out of the inn, but they were running away from it, not toward them. Then it burst into flame.

"Damn it—neither of you did that, did you?" Crell glanced back but kept her pony at top speed.

"Not me. What happened?" Jenna didn't want to risk another look back, but they were still close enough that the flames cast an eerie glow to the sky ahead of them.

"It wasn't me." Ghortin dropped back behind Carabella. "I have a spell ready if they follow, but so far they're focusing on the flames."

They had dropped out of a gallop after a few minutes but didn't stop until an hour later. The field gave way to heavy woods and Crell slowed them down.

Ghortin took over and led them to a small clearing not too far inside the forest. "We need to rest; our horses are exhausted."

Crell nodded and took the saddle and pack off her pony. "I will walk back and make sure no one followed us, but that fire should have kept them occupied. However it happened, I think it saved us." Derawri didn't often ride horses or ponies, usually traveling by a mile-eating run they could keep up for days. Crell was off before anyone could stop her.

"I still don't get how a fire happened just at the perfect time to cover our escape." Jenna settled her horse and rubbed her down as best she could.

"Are you certain neither of you did anything?" Carabella narrowed her eyes at both of them. "I felt a magic flare right before the flames started."

"Considering that we were both running spells, I doubt either of us had the energy to cause a fire." But Ghortin watched Jenna carefully.

"What? It wasn't me. This was the first time I've held a misdirect spell like that. Trust me, that took everything

I had." She'd take Carabella's word for it about sensing the magic, she didn't sense anything. She did try to reach out to Typhonel, maybe it was him. But she didn't get a response. If it had been the lost god, he'd already taken off again.

They had the camp set when Crell came jogging back.

"They got the fire out, but the inn is nothing but cinders. Oddly, nothing near it burned. It was as if something wanted that inn to burn and stopped the flames when it reached the end."

"That has to be magic." Carabella's fingers were twitching.

"You can't cast a spell to find out. Not even a small one. Not a just-helping-with-some-Power one. Nothing." Ghortin glared at her until her fingers stopped moving.

"I doubt you'd fare much better if you couldn't access your magic." She handed out dried rations.

"I wouldn't know what to look for," Jenna said. She didn't add that she was also exhausted from holding the spell on Ghortin. Even if she knew what to look for, she'd probably fall over if she tried.

"I'll see if I can sense anything, it won't be much at this distance but might give us an idea of what happened." Ghortin got back to his feet and stepped just to the edge of the clearing.

Jenna felt him send forth a subtle spell, one more of inquiry than of command. One minute the spell was flowing from him. A second later he collapsed.

CHAPTER TWENTY-EIGHT

STORM WATCHED EDGAR make light of almost being spelled to death, then finally cut him off. "You took a pointless risk. We had no idea who you'd seen or what you were after." His eyes narrowed. "That's not like you. At all."

Edgar looked up from where he finished wrapping up the cut Storm had given his arm. "Thank you for checking before you ran me through, by the way." He sighed. "I'll admit it, I was rash. Impulsive."

"Foolish." Storm folded his arms.

"Fine, foolish." Edgar glanced to Keanin who was back to focusing on his mending. "I needed to do something and I thought...I don't know what I thought."

"You thought you could help Keanin?"

Keanin looked up but didn't say anything.

"In a weird way, yeah, I guess so. When I saw Raven-hearst's man—it was just too perfect. We couldn't all go; he might recognize you two. But I figured I could sneak in under disguise and get some answers."

"How'd that work?" Keanin finally said. "I know you want to help me, but going out on your own isn't going to do it." He turned to Storm. "For any of us, even me."

Edgar laughed and shook his head. "Now I know things are changing. But you're right, none of us should go off alone."

Storm sighed. "I probably would have done the same had I been in your shoes. But we need to stay focused. Was this man of Ravenhearst's the reason we're waiting a few days? I think we might want to leave if that's the case."

"No. I not only saw him, I saw Mikasa. He wasn't with her; she was surrounded by ladies-in-waiting like she was a royal. But he wasn't far behind. They're waiting for a ship to Craelyn. I didn't think us being trapped on a vessel with her and whoever she's working with was a good idea."

"Damn that woman." Storm got up and paced. "Did you recognize anyone who was with her? Anyone else, aside from the man who spelled you?"

"Not a single one. The ladies and the guards were all kelar, that was clear. The man who spelled me was human."

"I wonder if I would recognize the courtiers with her." Keanin looked to both. "Seriously, I know you're a spy, but neither of you pays attention during court events. They most likely are Khelaran nobles."

"No." Both Edgar and Storm said at the same time.

"I'm just going to stay in here, while you two skulk around for a few days?" He picked at his clothes. "I need a better disguise. The merchant can get sick, and you two can bring on another sell-sword."

Storm was shaking his head when Edgar spoke.

"He has a point. We need to see what's happening in Khelaran. Granted, this isn't Khelaran, but it's the most common way into the country. And the only one that doesn't involve five weeks of land travel. If something is going on here…" He shrugged. The rest of his point was clear.

"Damn it. Fine." Storm didn't like the idea, but they needed to get to Khelaran and they needed to see how far the issues went. It was like an infection, they just kept finding more.

Keanin's face perked up way too much at that. "Excellent. Can I have an eye patch too?"

"No." Edgar started picking through Storm and

Keanin's clothes and shook his head. "I'm going to have to get more clothing. We probably would have anyway before we left. A bit suspicious if even sell-swords are wearing the same clothing every day."

"Not to mention nasty." Keanin wrinkled his nose. "None of my clothing will work. The black pants and boots will, but the rest is useless."

Edgar went for the door but Storm blocked him. "Not alone. I'm close enough to Keanin's size we can get clothing for him that way." Storm turned to Keanin. "This will only work if you stay here. Alone. Not leaving. You shouldn't be looking out the window if we're claiming that the merchant is ill."

"I'll stay here." There was that far too happy look again.

Storm narrowed his eyes. "I'm serious. There's too much going on for you to go on a revenge hunt. I can go and find clothing that will fit you, or I'll stay here and guard you and you just get what Edgar guesses at."

"You do like yellow, right?" Edgar added a few more knives hidden about himself as he smiled. He then pulled out a new tunic, vest, and hooded cape and quickly changed. "Clothing is a memory trigger and I don't want my friend to notice me, by chance anyway. I want to find him before he realizes who I am."

"Yellow is a horrible…I get it." Keanin leaned back. "I will stay here. Either of you have mending?"

Storm watched him for a few more moments, then he and Edgar left. They couldn't watch Keanin all the time and if he was going to be a problem, better to find out now than in Craelyn.

They'd started this trip as a gesture of goodwill to the Khelaran royals, to reassure their king that Traanafaeren wasn't behind the recent attack. But the more they were finding, the more it was clear that Khelaran might have already fallen to the followers of Qhazborh—or worse.

The town looked about the same down here as it had

from the room, but the smell of fish and the ocean was far stronger. Yells echoed around as the two ships heading south prepared to set sail. There was only one other ship and judging by the lack of activity, it was the one heading north to Craelyn in the morning.

Storm pulled up his hood, again making certain that enough of his face showed to make the Crailian markings noticeable. Then Edgar raised his as well and adjusted his posture.

"You spotted your friend?" Storm didn't look at Edgar as he spoke but examined a knife vendor's small booth they'd been passing.

"I believe so. I see one of the men who had been near him at the bar, and there is a man in a familiar cloak behind him. Amateurs. Always change up your clothing." Edgar picked up a small throwing knife from a vendor's table. "I'll take this one, any more like it?" His voice changed as he spoke to the vendor, it was now lower and rougher.

"Aye. Three more. Want them all?"

"Only probably need two, but better to be sure." Edgar stored the small blades and handed over the coins.

"They're still at the fish booth. They don't appear to be too concerned about anyone looking for them," Storm said, then lowered his head as the second man flung back his cape. "Damn. Let me guess, the one you ran into was Lord Hilten?" Not only was he part of Ravenhearst's crew, but he'd also been one of Mikasa's followers. He came across as flighty and a typical courtier. He didn't look that way now.

"Yup, the same. They really must think they took me out of the game. Not only foolish but cocky and foolish." He'd kept his voice low but watched them as he led Storm past two other booths. "But even foolish people can get the drop on you. He did once, not this time."

The two left the fish booth and wandered down toward

the waterfront. Neither seemed the least concerned about being watched or followed.

"I'm assuming you'll want to question them before you knife them?" Storm kept an eye on them but they could have been out for a stroll in a garden somewhere for all the concern they showed.

"Oh, the throwing blades were just to have—not for our friends. I'm down to one and they are handy, but you don't always get them back. Now, who's this?"

Two new people were following Hilten and his friend. Both wore dark cloaks but moved like the military. The dark gray skies had many people keeping their hoods up, but these two dropped theirs as they approached Hilten. Both were women, and judging from the bit of metal that showed when they dropped their hoods, both were members of the Khelaran army.

"What are they doing here?" Storm reached for his sword but kept his movements subtle. "Have they forgotten that this is still Traanafaeren?" The town of Erlinda marked the start of the borderlands between Traanafaeren and Khelaran. Active military coming through without clearing it through Resstlin in Lithunane could be an act of war.

"Their swords are peace bonded." Edgar had sharper eyes than Storm but a movement of the woman in the back showed the leather tie on her blade.

"They are still in armor. Or at least partially." Storm wasn't a stickler for rules and these border areas were usually fairly lax. But with everything that had been happening, that laxness couldn't continue.

Edgar put his hand on his arm. "Are you planning on marching up and announcing who you are? That'll be nice."

Storm released the grip he had on the hilt of his sword. "No. Damn it. Two human criminals working with two Khelaran military members isn't good, though."

"Stay here." Edgar slipped away before Storm could respond.

Annoying, but Storm kept his focus on the scenario. The stance of the two women wasn't friendly and Hilten looked disturbed at whatever they were discussing. His friend kept taking steps backward, slowly heading toward the alley behind them. Probably what caused Edgar to take off. Questioning them one at a time would be easier.

Hilten and the first woman started yelling at each other until the second woman took hold of the first one's shoulder.

She let herself be pulled back but then spun back to him. "We can't do anything to you here, Hilten, but if you step one foot across the borderlands, you're mine." The growl in her voice and the automatic reaching for her bonded sword indicated it would be a short and painful meeting—for him. "Oh, and your friend is abandoning you." She threw the last bit over her shoulder as the man with Hilten stopped being subtle and took off running down the alley.

Hilten glared at the departing soldiers, turned to run after his partner, then instead ducked behind the row of vendors. Storm wanted to go after him, but there was no way to tell Edgar and he'd been right about them sticking together. They'd spend too much time trying to find each other if they split up. If they had to leave town suddenly they all needed to be together.

Edgar's head popped out of the alley and nodded. The way he didn't come out indicated he'd found his prey.

Storm glanced around to make sure no one was watching—Hilten had started running once he got past the vendors—and went into the alley.

Edgar was toward the far end of the alley holding up an unconscious man.

"Hard to question them if they're knocked out."

"He fought back and ran into the wall. Knocked himself out." He started tapping the man's cheek. Finally, he pulled out a small button and slapped it on him with a word. An arc of light jumped out of the button and into the man. He jumped and started scrabbling about. "Garlan always swore by shock tabs. I'll have to tell him thank you." Edgar's grin was evil as he dragged the struggling man to his feet.

Storm put a hand on Edgar's shoulder and leaned forward. "Let me. It has been long since my blade has drunk blood." A low-level threat as far as the Craili went, but Edgar's prisoner looked ready to jump out of his skin.

The benefits of taking a persona feared by so many.

"I'll tell you anything—just keep him away from me." The man's voice went higher. Even in the darkness of the alley, he'd dropped a few shades of skin color as well.

Storm dropped his hand from his sword hilt, took a step back, and folded his arms.

"Good choice. He's a bit prickly. Now, how long have you been working for Lord Hilten?"

"Who?" The man shook his head as Storm leaned forward. "No, seriously? I don't know that name."

"Who was the man you were with? The one you helped spell me in the pub a bit ago?"

"Pouth? He's not a lord, he's a scam artist. I just met him; I swear. Claims to be royalty in disguise. We didn't mean to hurt you, and you seem fine now. He said you two knew each other and it was a game." He glanced to Storm. "It's not, isn't it? He hired me to slip the spelled potion in your drink. I'm a pickpocket, so I usually take things, but it works the same." His words were beating each other up in their attempt to all get out at once.

"That man is a criminal wanted by the Traanafaeren king for high crimes against the kingdom. You're working with him. Why shouldn't we turn you over?"

"I...I heard things." He nodded madly. "We'd been working together for a week or so, he'd have me slip

things to people, then he'd get what he wanted. Different
ways of robbing, but to each their own. He's waiting for
some other royals. Some from Lithunane heading this
way. Needs to bring them into Strann."

Storm sighed. "A royal who was hunting other royals?
You realize how ridiculous that sounds?"

"I might have guessed he wasn't who he said he was."
The man winced. "But the money was good. More
when we caught the royals he was looking for. Could
have set me up for a year. Especially once they shipped
the others up here and he got them too." He'd muttered
the last bit.

"Others?" Storm took a step forward.

"Yeah, some woman on the run with one of them cuari
and another mage. They have a trap set for them. They
were going to lure them into it, grab them, and send
them and the royals who were coming here off, and I'd
be rich." He twisted a bit. "I told you good information,
right? You'll let me go? Bygones and whatnot?"

CHAPTER TWENTY-NINE

JENNA AND CARABELLA jumped forward as Crell pulled out her bow and arrow and watched the woods around them.

"Was he hit?" She didn't turn toward them.

Jenna patted Ghortin down but didn't see any blood. "Not that I can tell, at least not by an arrow." He was completely unresponsive.

Carabella sat next to them and flexed her fingers. "Don't worry, no spells." She pulled a small charm out of her pack. It started swaying immediately. "But you need to cast one, we need a protection spell now. Crell, move closer. Something is searching for us."

Jenna didn't see or feel anything, but Carabella was close to being hysterical as she watched the pendant swing. There wasn't much Power left for Jenna to draw on, so she closed her eyes and focused on the chaotic plane to pull in Power from the source. There was something wrong with the chaotic plane. It wasn't as bright and beautiful as it usually was and she wasn't tempted to stay. She didn't linger but just took enough Power for the one spell.

She came back, opened her eyes, and flung a protection spell around them. She still felt drained, but she covered them. "What am I protecting us against and what attacked Ghortin?"

"I'm not sure. But this pendant doesn't lie. Something is pulling in a lot of Power and focusing it this way." Carabella held Ghortin's head off the ground. A strong protection spell might have cut off whatever attacked him—but it might not. And Jenna was too close to collapsing to try a second time.

"Could it be an attack because he is half-cuari?" Crell stepped closer but remained with her back to them as she kept her arrow on the woods. Good idea; this protection spell was for magical attacks, not arrows.

Carabella was calming down. "I'd say that could be a valid suggestion, but this attack felt different. It's still rolling around us. Jenna, you don't feel it?"

"No, but I'm so tapped out right now that I had to go into the chaotic realm just to cast this. Which probably won't hold long. Do you have any idea what is attacking us?" A nudge, almost like someone trying to open a locked door hit her. "Okay, that I felt. Whatever it is, it's pushing against the protection spell."

"I don't see anything. Nor did I sense any physical presence before you created this." Crell lowered her bow slightly, but it was just to adjust her stance.

"We have to do something—I really can't hold this." Jenna turned to Carabella before she could respond. "Don't think it."

"I wasn't. Okay, maybe. Ghortin? Can you hear us?" She patted the side of his face.

Crell gave a barely perceptible jump as Ghortin's vest pocket started buzzing. "Damn it, whoever is calling needs to pick better timing."

Jenna got up and took the taran wand. "Bad timing. Is it an emergency?"

"We're too late." Storm started swearing. "Jenna, you all have to watch out, Ravenhearst's people have set up a trap for you. Unless it's already happened?"

"Damn it—probably. There was a setup with poisons in a village we stopped at. We're in the woods now, but something magical took down Ghortin and is somehow surrounding us. We think." She looked to Carabella for confirmation. "It feels trap-like on a few levels." She wanted to tell him that she was also losing control of the protection shield, but saying that out loud wasn't a good idea if whoever was behind the aggressive spell was nearby.

"Where are you? Outside of what village?"

Jenna could almost see the amount of strain in his words. Wherever he and the others were, they weren't close enough to help. And it was tearing him up.

"Tell him it's Quarterbane. Edgar knows where it is." Crell kept watching the forest as Jenna repeated where they were. She had stopped asking the names of towns and villages that they rode through a week ago.

"Hold on." Storm made some rustling noises, then Edgar's voice came through the wand.

"You're making really good time and in this case, it is to your benefit. Put the wand near your ear, it will mask my words from anyone other than you."

Jenna shrugged. "Done."

"Good, now you have to go to the exact location I'm going to tell you. Moving Ghortin won't be easy, and it'll just have to be you and Carabella. I'm assuming Crell is keeping watch with her bow and arrow, and she needs to keep that up. The information we had was this was a physical trap, not magical. But the one giving us the information is clueless, so who knows. You'll need to ready everything, packs, horses, yourselves and run for the caves I'm going to tell you about." After a bit of going back and forth, trying to figure out where they were in relation to the caves, the plan was made.

Storm's voice came back over the wand. "I want you to contact us the moment you are in those caves. Remember the cave near Ghortin's cottage? He stole the idea from the ones in that part of the land. Move fast and you'll be inside before whoever is after you can get you. You can't wait. Be careful." He cut the call.

Jenna went to Crell and Carabella to whisper the plan

to them.

Carabella nodded at the plan but didn't look happy. "I know the caves but didn't realize we were that close. Dropping your shield will confuse whatever's after us magically, but not for long. And if the spell caster is nearby, we'll have even less time."

"Which is why we go now," Crell whispered.

"Why am I here and why are you whispering?" Ghortin opened his eyes but didn't look happy about it.

Carabella shoved him down. "Please shut up. We're under attack." She quickly filled him in. He seemed to think he could run, and that would help—but they still were taking a risk by dropping Jenna's spell.

Not that it mattered. Jenna felt her protection spell starting to unravel. She wouldn't be able to hold it much longer and she didn't have time to go back into the chaotic plane for more Power. Not to mention, aside from the cuari possibly being held there—going too often was a way to be trapped there for good.

"On my count, we all run for the horses and the closest cave." Crell still watched the woods and kept her voice low. "No magic. They didn't go after Jenna with this protection spell, but we can't take the chance. Ready?"

When all three murmured their agreement, she yelled and ran forward. Jenna dropped her protection spell, Ghortin staggered to his feet with Carabella's help, and they ran.

The horses must have felt something was wrong, as they came along easily. The caves were closer than Jenna thought, but not close enough. She'd stayed in the back and felt a stab of pain lance through her middle just as they ran inside the cave.

Her back was on fire and she thought it had been an arrow, but she didn't feel any blood. Crell pulled her further in, passed her to Carabella, and then she blacked out.

Swirls of chaotic energy passed through her, along with more of the stabbing pain. Jenna tried to open her eyes, but her eyelids were like lead. It was normally silent in the realm of chaos but tortured screams echoed around her. Slowly the voices became sharper, louder, and she realized it was Ghortin talking to someone near her.

Or maybe it was to her. She pushed away from the chaos of her dream and tried to sit up. Screaming in pain, she managed to open her eyes. "I…" Pain flooded her before she could say anything else.

Ghortin was next to her and trying to make her drink a light purple drink. The part of her that recalled how bad some of his potions could taste tried to pull back. Then she remembered that they usually worked.

It took both Carabella and Ghortin to help her drink it, but immediately she felt a cooling sensation flood her body. "Thank you." She tried sitting up further, but couldn't. "What hit me?"

"A spell. I would have been watching for it if I hadn't been so addled myself." Ghortin shook his head. "Damn them, whoever is out there, they know us too well. The spell after me was based on my sending a search spell. The one after you was attached to your going to the chaotic plane. They were trying to push you back to it so you'd be trapped."

"But I did that to fuel the protection spell, why didn't it hit…oh. It didn't hit immediately *because* of the protection spell. When I dropped it, it got me." She looked around the cave. Larger than the one Ghortin had put in near his cottage, it was equally not completely natural. "Are we safe here?" She tried again to sit up and with their help, she was able to move closer to a rock and lean against it.

"For now," Crell said, from near a large pile of rocks. "Setting this in place wasn't hard, but if they know where we are, they can force us out eventually."

"At least they can't use magic against us while we're in here," Carabella said.

"And neither can we." Ghortin magicked the glass he'd given to Jenna into nothing. "Except inside here. The cave has magic blockers both naturally and built into it. We can't magic out and they can't magic in."

"What did they build these for? Edgar made it sound like there were a few out here." Jenna knew that Ghortin had built his escape cave because the woods around him had been overrun by monsters for a few years. He'd needed a safe spot in case he couldn't get back to his cottage.

"There was a mage battle, long ago. When we were just setting up Traanafaeren as a kingdom, mages came to challenge us. Usually, we just let them fight it out between themselves." Carabella shook her head. "I only stepped in when absolutely necessary."

Ghortin smiled at her. "These rocks, before they became caves, had a blocking element, so we'd try to get the mages to fight down here. We're only a few days east of Irundail. One battle created a lot of misbegotten monsters—killed the mages in question but left a mess. Carabella created these, and I copied them near my home. But they can't hold forever. They are meant just to provide a safe hideout for a short while."

Jenna felt her strength slowly come back but still felt like she'd run a record mile sprint. And everything hurt. "How did they know I'd go for the chaotic plane? You, I get. Of course, you'd try and see what caused the fire. But you've told me many times, mages don't go directly to the source."

"They don't. Whoever is after us knew you do."

"How? That's not common knowledge."

He shook his head. "No idea, but whoever is after us is strong, patient, and knows too much."

CHAPTER THIRTY

S TORM GRABBED THE man and lifted him high in the air. "You will tell me everything you know—who is tracking them?"

Edgar lowered his arm and held out the taran wand where the man couldn't see it but Storm could. "Maybe it would be best if you contacted some people we know? I can work on our friend." He smiled, but it wasn't a nice one. He held a knife in his other hand.

Storm took the taran wand and stepped away from where the man couldn't hear him. He was grateful to hear Jenna's voice but terrified that the trap had already been sprung. He talked to her, but they needed information he didn't have. He removed his hands from the speaking position on the wand and walked back to Edgar.

"Edgar, can we take care of this now? I need you took look at something." He held up the wand.

Edgar nodded and sharply hit the man in the head with the handle of his knife. He knew exactly where Jenna and the others were and quickly guided them to what they needed to do.

He handed the wand back to Storm and went back to their unconscious pickpocket.

There were a lot of things Storm wanted to tell Jenna, but couldn't. He said what he could to warn them, then ended the communication.

"He's not going to tell anything useful; I believe that he hasn't a clue." Edgar tied their pickpocket up. "They'll be fine." The words were there but Edgar was a bit too focused on what he was doing and wouldn't meet

Storm's eyes.

"They're in danger. They didn't have to be."

"There's a good chance that both Strann and Khelaran have either fallen to the enemy or are compromised. We have to go to Khelaran to get intelligence and see how screwed we are. From what I understand, they need that book—without it, nothing we're doing matters."

"They should have waited for us." Storm knew he was being pissy, but he couldn't help it. He'd just found Jenna; he couldn't lose her.

Edgar folded his arms. "And what if the Strann borders closed before we got back?"

"Logically, I know you're right." Storm sighed. "I know they had to go. But damn it."

"Agreed. And trust me, I know she's just as worried about you." He looked down at the pickpocket. "I don't know how much more he would have been able to tell us; he was just a hired flunky. He should get free in a few hours—or maybe the guards will find him. And maybe he'll stay clear of Hilten now."

"Sorry I didn't chase down Hilten. He was fast. Whatever those two Khelaran guardswomen said to him upset him." They walked out of the alley and back to the vendors and docks.

"Which makes one wonder why Khelaran guards would care about a Strann minor functionary." Edgar pulled up his hood. "There's never been a lot of love between the two kingdoms, but that almost looked personal from what I saw."

"Agreed, and he was personally disturbed. Do we try and find him? Unlike his friend back there, he might have more information."

They walked closer to the docks and were about to turn down one when a familiar high-pitched voice came out of the crowd behind them.

Storm swore. "Damn it. That's Mikasa. I'd recognize

that screech anywhere." He turned to look over the water and tugged his hood lower over his face.

Edgar did the same, but Storm saw was also managing to keep watch of the group coming onto the dock. "The two Khelaran guardswomen are bringing up the rear—they must be assigned to her and her people. No sign of Ravenhearst or Hilten though."

The entourage clomped up the dock behind them without notice. Mikasa's voice was shrill as she passed. "I'm telling you; he was a wild man in bed. But I'm sure my new fiancé will be even better." Mikasa's annoying voice was only surpassed by the tittering laughs of her ladies.

"You slept with her?" Edgar kept his voice low.

"What? She wasn't talking about me; she must have had some other fiancé." Storm shuddered. "Gods, I only kissed her once and it was all her doing."

"Well, good to know that imaginary you is good in bed." Edgar leaned forward to watch the group move toward their ship. "My question is, who is she engaged to now?"

"Hopefully, some nasty old reprobate. The Khelaran king gives out noble titles like paper." Storm glanced at the women but turned away quickly. "I think the guardswoman with the short black hair recognized us."

Edgar pulled out a longer dagger. "Yet she's not doing anything about it. Not even telling her partner, from what I can see. Interesting." He put the dagger back.

"Even more interesting, why in the hell are they getting on their ship now? It can't depart until morning." Storm didn't turn back. He was certain there was recognition in the glance he'd had of the guardswoman, but there was no way to know why she wasn't acting on it. Yet.

Erlinda was a major shipping town, and they kept a tight command of their departure times. The winds and tides were best in the morning to head north to Craelyn, so that was when ships left.

"Another damn good question." Edgar sighed. "I'd wanted to investigate the dock more, but even if Mikasa didn't notice us, I think you're right about the guard-swoman." He started walking toward the dockmaster's building. "Let's just see what we can find out?" He pushed back his hood, straightened up, and immediately looked less disreputable.

Storm hung back.

"I say, my companions and I were looking at a ship to Craelyn. We were told they were only going with the morning tide, but one of my friends met some of those ladies last night. They are going back to Craelyn as well." He nodded toward the ship.

The dockmaster was a solid derawri female. She snorted as she looked at the ship. "Them. Sorry, that ship is booked full. The lady in charge demanded access to it tonight; she fears someone is after her on land. I warned them, no wild parties on any ship docked here. Highly unusual."

Edgar gave a small smile. "They paid well?"

She snorted. "Double what I would have taken." She looked past him to Storm. "He with you?"

"Aye, sometimes good to have muscle when traveling. I was robbed on my way here and need to go buy some more clothes. Any suggestions?"

She told him of two shops that had cheap but service-able garb, then leaned forward and lowered her voice. "He really a Crailian sell-sword?" Her whisper was loud enough for half the dock to hear.

"Yes, I don't want to spend a lot on my clothing, but my life is another matter."

She nodded slowly, still watching Storm. "Be wary, we don't get his type this far south very often. Someone was already looking for one a few hours ago. Asked if one got on any of the ships."

Storm kept his face neutral.

"Maybe we'll find this other one. Might be a friend of Hawk's." Edgar raised his voice. "Ya have any friends down here, Hawk?"

Storm shook his head. "But I haven't been home in a long time. Someone could be earning their leathers." He pitched his voice low and with enough of the accent of the north to sound legitimate.

Earning their leathers was a coming-of-age ritual of the Craili. Although that could be what was going on, he doubted there was a real Crailian in town. Someone was looking for him.

Edgar told the dock mistress he'd be back to book their travel, thanked her for her information, and they left the dock. "Let's get our new mercenary some clothes. Might pick up a change or two for me as well, we should have a merchant with us after all."

"Since someone is already asking about me, maybe I should drop this disguise."

"Or we wait until we find out why they are looking for you. If they are after you, Storm, we kill them. But it could just be some local thug wanting to prove himself by fighting a Crailian and living through it."

"True. I have to admit, I kind of like the looks people give me when they think I'm not looking." Storm grinned as two men moved widely out of his way and ducked their heads. "Much better than having people fawning over me back home."

Edgar laughed, then stopped, swore, and took off running.

Storm didn't ask what he saw, just took off after him.

Whoever Edgar was following, they darted down an alley and into the rows of houses that loomed above the row of shops.

Storm caught up to Edgar easily but running at full speed with a sword wasn't fun. He still wasn't sure who

Edgar was after as there were more twists and narrow roads. He might not know who the prey was, but Edgar did.

Edgar sprinted and tore off around a corner. Storm was less than a few steps behind but pulled up short when he saw nothing but an empty lane. Then he heard scuffling and spun to find a huge blade being swung in his direction. The person holding the blade was a tall kelar, one with short hair that clearly showed the tip of his right ear had been cut off.

Storm blocked him and swung back. The escaped prisoner—the removal of an ear tip was only for Khelaran prisoners on death row—had good form but he wasn't as fast as he should be. Storm got in a slice against him, tearing a slash across his chest. The blood was red, so that was good.

The attacker stumbled back, fell to the ground, and didn't look like he was getting up.

"Who are you? Why did you attack me?" Storm kept his voice as low as he could but the fact was if his opponent hadn't been already injured, Storm could have lost this fight.

That was an extremely uncommon occurrence.

"I hired him." Hilten came from around the corner with Edgar's dagger at his back. "I figured if your friend here hired you, I should hire someone as well. As I told him, I was just given the stuff to put in his drink. Money drop. No idea who was behind it." He winced as Edgar pressed forward with his dagger as he pulled back on his collar.

"You just happened to come across an escaped Khelaran prisoner?"

The prisoner in question appeared to be bleeding out, he'd stayed where he fell and didn't look good.

"That isn't from what I did to him." Storm put away his sword, but like Edgar, he took out a dagger. Much better for close work, which was why Edgar rarely carried his sword. He kicked away the Khelaran's sword, then flicked open his cape with the tip of the dagger.

A massive amount of blood had pooled on his tunic and was running onto the ground.

And it was beginning to turn green.

CHAPTER THIRTY-ONE

———◆———

"HOW LONG ARE we staying here?" Jenna was feeling better, but it had been at least eight hours since they'd come into this cave. They couldn't hide here forever. The horses were being extremely patient with their confinement, but it felt as if Ghortin was running a low-level de-stress spell at them.

Considering how relaxed she felt, he might have been flooding the cave with it.

"I believe we got in here unseen. We need to wait until they've gone," Ghortin said, without looking up from his spell book. "Whoever is out there, we're not up for a battle."

He'd tried opening Jenna's cuari book a few hours ago, but it wouldn't let him. Just like every other time. Rachael said her book was attuned only to the Guardians. But Ghortin kept trying just out of perversity.

"Were they after us magically or is someone out there?" She was asking the questions but didn't feel like she needed to know. Nothing mattered right now. "Damn it, are you seriously spelling all of us?"

He looked up at that. "What? No. Just a low-level spell for the horses." He glanced over to where Carabella was asleep and Crell was nodding off near her. They'd all taken naps in shifts, so both women should be awake. "Oh. I might have lost my focus on it." He said a few words and the feeling of laziness fled. "Sorry."

Jenna shook her head. "So, when do we get out?"

Crell stretched. "I can check the woods around us. They are after you magic users—not me. And no one sees me in the forest if I don't want to be seen. Do you think that weasel Linton is behind this?" She switched her sword and bow and arrow for a long dagger and some knives.

"I don't know." Ghortin raised his hand before she could complain. "Not about you going, but if our friend Linton is involved. I didn't feel he was a magic user, but he could have been hiding it well. He could have done what he tried to do with the poison with a spell for less effort, though. Far less effort. That doesn't mean he's not involved." He got to his feet and they moved enough rocks out of the way for Crell to crawl out. "Be careful and don't go any further than you have to."

She grinned. "Yes, mother." Then she ducked out the hole and vanished.

They rolled the rocks back into place.

"I think your spell is wearing off the horses too, they're getting jumpy." Carabella went to one and started petting it. "Any idea what they used to trap both of you?"

"No. My book was of no help." He looked over to Jenna.

"Nor mine, but to be fair, this isn't a general spell book. It's more focused on trying to stop the end of the world." She wasn't trying to be defensive about it, but there were priorities.

"Which is quite nice of it." Carabella widened her eyes. "Not sure why I didn't think of my library earlier." Before either could stop her, she spoke a spell and a small glowing rectangle appeared before her. She grabbed a pile of books from within it, and it vanished.

Jenna held her breath waiting for the spell bubble to grab Carabella. Then she started laughing. "So these walls can stop magic from a possible group of deities? What did you put in them?" They looked like normal cave walls to her, but there was some extremely serious magic in them.

"A *lot* of spells." Carabella smiled at the cave. "Some that I've forgotten. I should have realized they would block the cuari hunting spell." She patted the books. "Remember these?" She held up a small yellow one to Ghortin.

"My primers?"

"Well, this one was." She handed it to Jenna. "I know things have been happening, but your training of your apprentice has been lax." The grin she gave Jenna indicated she didn't hold Jenna at all responsible. "These others are older spell books that I'd kept in a pocket of my library back at my tower. We seem to be facing people who are going back to the old ways and we need to be at their level. I didn't recognize it until I took my second nap, but it was an inarit spell bomb that took out the inn. I felt something when it first exploded, but it didn't pop through what it was at the time. Those haven't been in common usage for a few hundred years. It's an unstable spell, and better ones have been created since then."

Jenna leafed through the small yellow spell book. She recognized some spells, while others were completely new. "I told him long ago that I needed more training."

"He got distracted with something, didn't he? Hid away in his vortex hole? Never changes."

"Exactly! I ended up calling a bunch of elementals to get him out." Jenna wished they could go back to the time in the cottage—before she realized how terrifying everything was.

"And then *she* used a Command spell to stop me in place." Ghortin took one of the other books from Carabella and paged through it. "And no, I didn't teach that to her."

"Interesting." Carabella leaned closer. "He probably deserved it. If you want to freshen up on Command spells, try this book." She handed over another book, this one a bit larger than the first, but narrow and green.

"Thank you. It was instinct, but might be handy to actually know how to do it. Is there a system for the coloring of spell books?"

Carabella shrugged. "Not that I know of. That one used to have a lovely paper cover. Baby Ghortin chewed it off." She flashed him a grin that he deflected.

"Since we're trapped here at the moment, maybe I could hear some of those stories?"

Ghortin took his book and stomped off toward the back of the cave.

"That is a wonderful idea!" Carabella walked toward a pair of seat-sized boulders.

Before they could get started a rattling sound came from the side of the cave near Ghortin.

"Is that a voice?" Jenna strained to pick out the sounds. It sounded like someone was pounding on the side of the cave and yelling.

Ghortin glanced at the entrance and the pile of rocks there. "I left a small gap for Crell to call to us when she came back. But it's not coming from there."

"Could they have captured her and know we're around here somewhere?" The voice was too muffled to clearly hear anything of the words or the tone. There could be anyone out there.

"And they are yelling at us, instead of trying to break in through the entrance? It wouldn't be easy, not with my spells holding this side down, but a persistent and strong enough mage could get through that." He pointed to the rock barricade. "So why aren't they trying?"

The voice yelled again, but she still couldn't understand them. "We can't spell them, but can we spell us to hear them? Or at least one of us?"

"I can do that." Ghortin cracked his knuckles and waved off Carabella. "My turn. Besides, we don't want you getting used to using magic until this issue of the missing cuari is done."

She held up her books. "Or I find a way around it. But yes, by all means, go ahead."

Ghortin nodded to Jenna, said a few words that she

could barely hear, and cast his spell.

A flash of bright light caught her off guard and when she could see again, she was five feet off the ground and in danger of smacking her head on the ceiling of the cave.

"Was this what you intended?" She held her arms up and stopped her upward movement by pushing against a lower part of the ceiling. She had no idea there was a floating spell but wasn't sure how this would help. She was closer to the voice though.

"Sort of. Didn't plan on you flying like that. The cave must be messing with spells. Go on then, move over to where the noise is. Who knows how long the spell will last."

Jenna pushed herself along the ceiling until she heard the pounding. Then the voice came again.

"It's Crell!" Now she could hear the voice, but the words were still difficult. "Crell, don't know if you can hear me, but what happened?"

"There's a spell bubble blocking the entrance. Looks like the one that was after Carabella. The woods are clear, but I can't get through the bubble."

Ghortin snorted. "Good to know the deities couldn't get through the cave, but they definitely felt you casting magic." He rolled up his sleeves and stomped toward the rocks blocking the front. "I'll just pull these back and zap that damn thing. Make sure Crell saw no one else around."

"I'm pretty sure she wouldn't be yelling like this if there were." Jenna started drifting lower as the spell faded. She'd have to learn this one. Even if it was short-lived, floating could come in handy. "Hold on, Crell, Ghortin is coming out."

Ghortin removed two medium-sized rocks and was reaching for a third when a substance started flowing inside and heading for Carabella.

He didn't seem to see it, but Jenna did. She landed and ran over. "Put them back! Something's coming in."

Carabella smiled and then collapsed but there didn't appear to be any sign of the bubble.

"Damn it. Whatever is inside those things to knock out the cuari just came in." He yawned. "Might be affecting me a bit too." He didn't collapse like Carabella had but he looked like he seriously needed a nap.

Jenna put the rocks back and rolled another over for good measure. "Damn it. A magic user needs to break the bubble and we're all inside." She looked around. Ghortin was close to being asleep and Carabella was lightly snoring. "Great."

She didn't have any cuari blood and didn't feel different from the gas that had seeped in. If she moved fast, she should be able to get a spell out to burst the bubble blocking the entrance before too much of it entered.

Of course, she still hadn't nailed down exactly what she did the first two times.

Crell yelled again from the outside, but Jenna couldn't hear the words clearly. Hopefully, they weren't something akin to there being a bunch of archers right past the bubble waiting to skewer her when she broke out.

She shook her shoulders and thought about the spell she needed. The first times had been done out of panic; this time she could craft something. Hopefully. Equally hopeful was the belief that the gas that seeped in only went after cuari and couldn't change things up on her.

She built the spell slowly, creating it in the form of a spear to make it go through the entire bubble. It felt as ready as it was going to get, so she held her breath, moved a stone at eye level, and let it fly.

More of the gas whooshed into the cave, but the popping sound indicated it was from the bubble exploding. Unfortunately, it also completely knocked out Ghortin.

She checked, but the faint color in the air that had been

created by the spell bubble was gone, so she started moving more of the stones. Crell came through the gap and helped. The stones could be removed from the outside, but they were spelled in such a way to make it extremely difficult.

"I take it no one is out there?" Jenna swore there were more stones and small boulders than when they set them in place. A glance told her neither Ghortin nor Carabella had woken up yet.

"No, and I went close to that village. They are already rebuilding the inn."

"I wish we know if the entire village was bad, or just a few." Jenna's back was glad to see the last stone gone.

"I think we have to assume the entire village. I've been reporting our progress to Garlan. I'll let him know this one is a problem. He doesn't have enough people to send them everywhere, but between him and my rangers, we'll get answers."

Jenna turned to the other two. "Why aren't they waking up? The gas from the spell put them to sleep, but they shouldn't still be out." She shook Ghortin, but he didn't flicker an eyelid.

"This cave must be keeping the gas here." Crell went to Ghortin since he was the closest. "Help me drag them out."

They'd pulled Carabella and Ghortin out of the cave and brought out all of the supplies and horses when Ghortin finally started twitching.

"Where am I?"

"Why are we on the ground?" Carabella responded. Both still sounded groggy but were at least conscious.

"You'd think with the number of times both of you have woken up in the dirt on this trip, you'd figure it out." Crell reached down and helped Ghortin to his feet.

Jenna did the same for Carabella.

"That is so annoying." Carabella dusted herself off. "At

least we know that it will go after a half-cuari too."

"Wait, so neither of you can use magic now?" Jenna was feeling more confident in her abilities, crafting that spell and having it work had felt good. But no way was she up to being the only magic user on this trip. She knew they had to get that book, but they might need to wait.

"I wouldn't go that far," Ghortin said. "The bubble itself has yet to come for me, but we now know that the gas will get me, so I'll avoid the gas."

Carabella looked ready to argue but stopped before she said a word and silently got on her horse. "We keep going? Strann is just two days ride, day and a half if we ride quickly—and avoid towns." She glared at Ghortin.

"Not only are we on a mission to get the book, but finding out what areas have been compromised is part of our trip. Tor Ranshal appreciates our information."

Crell tied the lead to her pony to the back of Jenna's saddle. "Going direct means going through these woods. I can do better recon on my own feet." She patted the pony. "No offense." Kelars had more of a horse whisperer thing going, but the way the pony nodded it appeared that derawri did as well.

Jenna and Ghortin both got on their horses and made their way through the woods. Carabella almost immediately dropped into reading her books and Ghortin was busy picking out the trails and trail markers left by Crell. So Jenna pulled out the yellow spell book. She wasn't as adept at reading and riding as the other two—she'd seen Ghortin read a spell book while racing through woods before—but she could manage it.

She was deeply into the spell for transmogrification when she looked up and the others were gone. She didn't appear to be in the same forest at all.

CHAPTER THIRTY-TWO

STORM STARTED SWEARING as more green blood pooled out on the ground and the Khelaran prisoner transformed into a demonspawn. He didn't have to check to know it was dead; those things returned to their natural form when they died. Or most did. He whirled to Hilten and grabbed him from Edgar.

"You're working with demonspawn? What in the hell is wrong with you?"

Hilten squirmed. But it seemed to be as much as trying to get away from the dead demonspawn as getting away from Storm.

"That's…not…no. Ravenhearst told me…that's a…?" He now looked ready to take his chances with Storm if he could stay away from the body.

Edgar stepped over to the body, carefully avoiding the blood. He patted it down and came back with a packet of papers and a bag of coins. "Yours?"

Hilten looked ready to throw up. "The coins are mine. Were mine. Never seen those papers before. Are you going to kill me?"

"Not if you start talking fast. And I mean everything about what you're doing here." Edgar nodded to Storm. "My friend has a bad temper and he hates demonspawn. You can understand how he'd like to kill you slowly. I can make sure that doesn't happen if you talk."

Storm adjusted his grip on Hitlen's arm and twisted it up slightly.

"Okay! Just keep him from hurting me." He was carefully not addressing Storm directly and his terror was

real. He had no idea who Storm and Edgar were. Storm
had seen too much of him while he was at the palace to
think it was an act. The man was an opportunist but not
bright.

"And we're talking?" Edgar removed a smaller dagger
with a short, wicked-looking, hook from his tunic and
stepped forward. Hilten pulled back until he remembered who was behind him. He stood where he was and
twitched.

"Lord Ravenhearst asked me to watch this town. Keeping an eye out for some royals from Lithunane who were
going where they shouldn't. Haven't seen them yet, but
he also said to be ready for other contacts, and take what
jobs they dropped my way. One of them told me to slip
you that drink. Didn't realize you were with a Crailian. I think Ravenhearst is trying to disrupt the shipping
industry here, but what do I know, right? I'm being paid.
The work was easy, and so far no idiot princes have come
my way."

Storm didn't shake him as he wanted but contemplated
it. He didn't care if he thought Storm was an idiot, but he
wasn't giving them anything useful.

"Which *princes* are you looking for?"

"If I tell you, can I go?"

"No. But you won't find out what a Crailian sell-sword
can do to your arm. And the rest of you."

Storm lifted Hilten enough that he rose onto the balls
of his feet, then dropped him down to emphasize the
point.

"Prince Corin and Prince Keanin. They don't call him
a prince; did you know that? That fop Keanin is apparently a prince of a lost Khelaran line. I heard the king
wasn't happy when the Empress of Strann shared that
information with him. She was extremely happy about
telling him though." He was getting too smug, so Storm
pressed his dagger into his side. Not hard enough to get

through his layers of clothing, but enough to knock him down a bit.

"Which king?" Edgar asked.

"King Philia of Khelaran. Didn't you hear? Your king is dead."

Edgar gave Storm a sharp look. Good thing he did. Storm was thinking of seeing how much faster Hilten would talk if he was bleeding out.

"I would watch how you speak. The dead have ears and I don't think you'd like to join them." Storm made sure his voice was low and accented.

"Sorry. No harm. Look, you grabbed my hired help and killed my guard, how about you just let me go? I didn't know that guy was a demonspawn. I saw those things in Lithunane at the ball—I wouldn't hire one."

Edgar tilted his head and smiled. "Why were two guard-swomen of the Khelaran army so interested in you?"

"Just a misunderstanding."

Edgar shrugged and turned away. "Kill him."

Hilten twisted but couldn't get away. "No, really. I know things. The guards are protecting Lady Mikasa, and she's my friend. They wouldn't let me near her and I might have said somethings before they chased me off. They were just making sure I stayed away from their ship."

"And?" Storm grunted out as he lifted Hilten completely off his feet.

"And told me if I ever came near her they would kill me."

Aside from finding out for certain that Ravenhearst knew they were on the move, they hadn't gathered much information. Keanin's change in circumstance could just be a nasty rumor spread by the Empress of Strann—that would be dealt with once they got solid information. The bit about Mikasa had raised a question though.

"Who is Lady Mikasa engaged to?" Hilten wasn't Kelar, but he seemed to have a fair amount of information about that kingdom. The guards keeping him away from her when she should be able to claim him as a friend could mean that the sanction against non-kelars was spreading, or something else entirely.

"Lord Jila. Stuffy old man, a close confidant of the king." Although Storm had asked the question, Hilten leaned toward Edgar. "Rumor is, she's going to be the king's mistress, but is wedding Jila as a cover."

The sound of heavily booted feet marching their way cut off any more questions.

Five of the town's guards came around the corner, then froze as they saw the situation. All dropped their hands to their swords.

"We heard there was a fight going on back here," the tall, blonde, kelar captain said as she stepped forward. "What is that…thing?" She nodded to the dead demon-spawn.

Storm gave her serious regard for staying calm in front of the horrific monster before them. Either she was as tough as she looked, or a dead demonspawn wasn't a surprise to her.

"This man is wanted in Lithunane for conspiring against the royal family and working with traitors." Edgar walked toward the demonspawn. "This is a demonspawn that he was working with. He even paid it." He tossed the coin bag to the captain.

She stared at the demonspawn for a few moments, then slowly nodded. Storm was ready to throw Hilten at the guards and fight their way out if it looked like she and the guards with her were on the wrong side.

"I've heard of them. One of my cousins was killed by one at the ball last year." She had her sword out and held at Hilten's neck before Storm could move. "Why shouldn't I kill you where you stand? Are there more of them here?"

The rest of the guards stood ready but didn't move.

Hilten started shaking. "I didn't know what it was. I was at that ball. I almost died. I wouldn't..." The rest of his words were lost in sobs.

The captain stepped back and sheathed her sword. "I take it you two are just waiting for a ship?"

Edgar smiled. "We are. This one tried to poison me earlier, so I was trying to find out why."

Three of the guards moved to Storm and took Hilten. He let him go. There wasn't much more to learn from him, and his connection to the dead demonspawn would keep him locked up for a long time. Unless Ravenhearst sent someone to take care of him in jail.

"A Crailian sell-sword is uncommon around here. I'd heard from others that you were passing by." She was almost as tall as Storm and kept her gaze steady. "See that you continue to move on."

Storm nodded silently and she went back to her crew.

"I think we should go back about our business. Thank you, Captain, for your timely appearance." Edgar turned and they walked back down the alley.

CHAPTER THIRTY-THREE

JENNA SWORE. NOT only was everyone else missing, so was her horse. And she was sitting on a dirt trail. She quickly scrambled to her feet and looked around. The forest they'd been riding through had been full of old pine trees. This one was newer and full of twisted bright green trees that she'd never seen in this world. They reminded her of a tropical jungle back on Earth. The light was odd like it came from the setting sun, but it wasn't twilight.

She stopped walking and focused on listening. Not only did she not hear her friends, or her horse, she heard nothing. No birds, animals, not even bugs.

Her clothes, weapons, and what she could see of her body looked the same, so that was a good thing. A spell gone wrong by a priest of Qhazborh had been what pulled her consciousness through to her current world. She was going to be pissed if something tugged her to yet another world and another body.

"Hello?" The silence was getting to her, but her softly spoken word felt like a yell in the dense jungle. The trees were massive and had long strands of vines tumbling off of them. They seemed to augment the sound and echo it back to her.

Her pack was still on her horse, hopefully, with Ghortin and the others. But she'd had the yellow spell book that Carabella had loaned her in her hands and still did. No food, no water, no horse, but she might be able to find out where she was with a spell.

There were a lot of spells in this book, but nothing

helpful for finding out where she was. After the quick page through brought nothing, she sat on a rock to read through them slowly. Reaching out to Typhonel brought no help either, as he showed up on his own timeline and it seemed that he was still functioning that way. She was a quarter of the way through the spell book when she heard a low growling.

She dropped the book, grabbed her sword, and spun. To be bowled over by a mass of fur, claws, and teeth that knocked her sword out of her hand and slammed her into the ground. She rolled away, barely missing a swipe by a massive paw armed with long needle-like claws, then smacked it in the head with a nearby rock. It stopped going after her but didn't look nearly injured enough.

It was a scirett, one of the hyena-looking creatures she and Ghortin had run into when they'd traveled to Lithunane months ago.

Rather, it was a scirett who'd been taking steroids.

The sciretts who had chased them before had looked like a combination of hyena, baboon, and a large cat. They'd only been a few feet high but were brutal killers.

The one facing her now, shaking its head as if it wasn't sure what had happened, was the size of Crell's pony. Maybe she'd been transported to their homeland and this is what they really looked like. Except that Ghortin was certain the things had been shoved through the portal in the middle of the Markare by the cuari and had started trickling out along with other monsters as the portal weakened. No sciretts had been reported after she and Ghortin returned.

"Oh, damn," Jenna swore for a bunch of reasons this time, but the second most important was that her sword was lying behind the monster scirett. The first reason was worse. If this was where the sciretts were, had she been flung through the portal?

No time to sort that thought now, as the scirett recovered and lunged for her. She threw up a shield spell, slowing it down but not stopping it. She pulled out her dagger and started running into the jungle.

The jungle became thicker the farther she ran and the trail was mostly overgrown with vines and plants. Wherever she was it wasn't near any population centers.

A growl from behind her increased her speed. She needed time to figure out what spell to use, but her mind couldn't sort anything out. She'd seen the smaller sciretts run, and the one behind her should have easily caught her. A glance back showed that the thing's massive front legs and powerful shoulders were slowing it down. It was as if someone had altered the monster for upper body strength but forgot that they ran on all fours.

Staying ahead of it long enough to get a spell sorted out in her head wasn't going to be easy, but she had a better chance than she'd thought.

Or she did until a second growl, a roar really, came from her left. Another scirett was coming through the jungle. She was grateful the trees were getting thicker as it was slowing the creature down. She tried to run faster, but she was running out of steam.

And jungle. What looked like an open meadow wasn't that far ahead. The jungle was slowing the sciretts down more than her—all bets were off if she went out in the open.

Thinking of a single spell to hold them back wasn't working, but maybe she could combine a few. Ghortin had taught her a lightning spell a few days ago, or the basics for it. It would call down a lightning bolt to your target. But her aim was always off. Maybe if she combined it with the spear she'd created to burst the cuari hunting bubble she'd have a chance.

She'd have one shot. The second scirett was now a few feet behind the first one on the thin trail. This worked or she became scirett chow. She gathered Power from the chaotic realm, formed her spell, and sent two arcs of lightning at the creatures. She also flung herself out of the jungle and into the field.

"What happened?" She staggered to her feet. Her hands were tingling and the tips of her fingers looked burnt. They were numb at the moment, but the damage looked bad. She held her dagger in front of her, but it hurt to hold. Not to mention, it wouldn't save her from the sciretts.

But they weren't coming out. Nor were there any sounds of them dying from her spell. Had she been wrong and the meadow wasn't someplace they would venture? The odd light that she'd attributed to the jungle was still there, but there was cloud cover so she couldn't see where the sun was. Standing here with her dagger out was ridiculous, not to mention she needed to get her sword and that spell book. Either her spell had taken the sciretts out, or they'd kill her.

With a sigh, she walked back to the edge of the jungle. An odd crackling sound accompanied by a nasty odor of burnt fur hit her a few paces inside the jungle. Her spell book and sword were both behind two snapping, popping, and frozen in place, sciretts. Their jaws were locked open as if their final act had been to try and bite the lightning.

Arcs of electricity danced between them. While both were still upright they were clearly dead. She walked around them at as much of a distance as she could. Got her book and sword, and moved further away.

The spell had hit them with such force that their feet appeared to be bolted to the ground. And the spell was still running. Her Power wasn't behind it anymore, but it was still functioning.

She looked at her fingers. Both hands had scorch marks and the pain was just settling in. How much Power had she pulled through herself for that spell? And how?

"That was a bit overkill, wasn't it? Not that it couldn't have happened to two better creatures." The voice was low and masculine and apparently came from nowhere as spinning in a full circle didn't show her who was speaking.

"Who said that?" She winced as she adjusted the spell book in her hand. She'd sheathed her sword when she picked it up but didn't have a place to carry the book. Her fingers were getting worse and she was starting to shake as the burst of adrenaline faded.

"Me. Sorry, forgot you probably can't see me. Neither could they, so they were never a threat. But they were awful and would have killed you in a moment." There was a flicker off to the left. "I didn't know people were coming through now or I would have cleaned the place up."

The flicker turned into a small tree, then a deer, then a bear of some sort, one that had horns, then a man. He wasn't human, nor kelar, nor derawri. He had to be a cuari, but unlike Carabella he looked older than Ghortin.

"There you are. I could only see the edges of you before. You're not supposed to be here, I don't think." He came closer but still stayed on his side of the jungle.

"Where is here?" Jenna put the book under her arm and cradled her hands. Hopefully, he didn't mean her harm as right now she couldn't fight off an army of three-day-old kittens.

"Now I know that you're not supposed to be here. You're on the chaotic plane." He looked across to her hands. "Oh, dear. You pull your magic from here, don't you? Got a bit more than you bargained for, didn't you?"

"I've seen the chaotic planes. They are wild and beautiful and dramatic. This is a jungle and a field." Jenna moved to a large rock and sat. Sitting might be a sign of weakness, but it was better than falling which was her next option.

"You mean like this?" The cuari, which must be what he was, raised both hands and the jungle and field vanished. The odd sunlight remained, but the world looked like what she'd seen on the chaotic plane. Bright, crazy, and exhilarating. Ghortin hadn't been happy that she pulled her magic from the source. And he'd made sure she understood that staying here too long could leave her stranded or mindless.

But this was it. Maybe she was crazy and not actually speaking to an unusual cuari.

The cuari snapped his fingers, and the jungle and field came back. The dead and still crackling with electricity sciretts never left. "That is what it looks like in reality. But most psyches, including cuari, sciretts, and humans, can't handle it for long. An overlay pops in to keep our minds from overloading."

"How did I get here? I'm Jenna by the way." She grimaced as another wave of pain shot through her hands.

"You really did hurt yourself. Fascinating." The cuari came closer but still stood a few feet away. "We don't feel pain. None of us do. I almost miss it."

"How did *you* get here?" Maybe there was a way out.

"We lost a battle we never should have started. My people were proud and rash. We ended up here." His face fell as he looked around them. "We deserved this."

Jenna thought he'd been one of Carabella's friends, one of the ninety-nine missing cuari. But his comment and the depth of sorrow in his voice and face told a different story. He had to be cuari from the before time. The ones who had supposedly been killed by the gods and goddesses themselves thousands of years ago. If this was a ghost, he was fairly solid-looking. Of course, he had popped in out of nothing.

"You're a cuari." She was going to say from before but wasn't sure what she could say to a being who should be dead in a place that shouldn't exist.

"I was. Now I am simply Meith. Hold out your hands, Jenna, let me help you." He didn't come closer but raised his hands.

Having a strange and possibly dead cuari offer to use magic on her wasn't the best idea. But the blackness from her fingers was working its way up her hands and heading toward her wrists.

She held both hands up and facing him.

He smiled, waved his hands toward her, muttered a few magic-sounding words, and flung a ball of light at her.

That went right through her. Her hands still hurt and the darkness was up to her forearms now.

"Now see here!" Meith looked up into the trees and stomped his foot. "You brought her here, one way or another, you know you did. She didn't know what would happen if she used magic. Let me fix her."

Jenna wasn't certain who he was yelling at but she hoped that he wasn't pissing off deities on her behalf. "If I could go back to where I was, Ghortin can fix me. Just get me back there." She spoke to Meith but kept looking into the jungle above them. She'd no idea if this was where the gods and goddesses lived or if they just kept an eye on things. That fact that at least one of the original cuari was still more or less alive was going to rock enough of Rachael's and Ghortin's world—she didn't need to add more drama by meeting a deity.

"You'd better let me do it this time," Meith yelled up at the vines overhead. Then he rolled up the sleeves of his robe and rubbed his hands together.

Jenna was just going to tell him that maybe they should wait when a sharp light ran through her. It didn't hurt per se, but it was akin to being pushed into an icy stream. The light vanished as quickly as it came, along with the bodies of the two sciretts.

She flexed her hands. No pain and the burnt look was

gone.

Meith folded his arms and glared up into the trees. "Thank you. But I could have done that too. And don't tell me that you're bringing those two back. Phela messed with them and made them worse than nature intended— which you specifically forbade. They need to rest."

This time the beam of light was in between Jenna and Meith, roughly where the two sciretts had been. There was a shape inside of it, but it was too bright for her to see what it was. "Hello, child. You have come far. You weren't supposed to be here anymore than you were supposed to be in the world you just came from. We can't solve the mystery of how you came to the chaotic plane, but we can send you home. Your true home."

A flat swirl of light broke off and images of Los Angeles appeared before her.

CHAPTER THIRTY-FOUR

"HOW MUCH TRUTH do we think there is to that story about Keanin?" Storm kept his voice low as they walked away from the guards working on moving the body of the demonspawn. None of them looked happy about their job.

"Someone believes it. It explains about those Qhazborh followers thinking we had two princes with us."

"And no one was able to sort out much when Keanin was brought to us. I'm only a few years older than him, so I recall little about his arrival. But I know my parents would have reached out to the Khelaran kingdom about him. They kept him as they were told he had no family—or so they said." He pulled his hood up as they came to a crowded street. "I don't know that we should tell Keanin—at least not yet." With everything that went on, knowing he's a target because he might be a prince, one who the Khelaran king wasn't happy about, might push him over the edge."

Storm and Edgar made their way to a narrow lane of clothing shops. Unlike the ones closer to the docks, these were smaller. And perfect for what they needed.

"Agreed." Edgar walked past the first two shops, then started into the third. "He's already aware of having to be careful, let's not push him too far. And now I'm grateful he's changing to a mercenary. Anyone who knows him would never guess who it was."

"And you get to play merchant. Nice change." Storm ducked under the shop's sign and followed Edgar inside.

"Indeed. I can't recall the last time I did that." Edgar

stopped in front of a worn but serviceable dark blue coat. "Now this is what a man of former success would be wearing." He slipped it on for size. Immediately his demeanor and stance changed. "We will take this one." He took it off and handed it to Storm.

Edgar not only had a sharp eye for enemies and thieves, but he was also excellent at picking clothing. He blazed through the shop, looking for items for all three of them, and tossing his finds to Storm as he went.

"Not many people have a Crailian sell-sword as a valet." The old man had been in the back and only came out once Storm's arms were full. "You must be someone of great importance."

"Ah, good sir." Edgar's voice now had a slight tremble to it. "I am but a humble merchant. I have been attacked too many times not to travel in this land without guards."

Storm kept his face neutral but adjusted the clothing in his arms slightly. He doubted the shopkeeper was up to something, but they'd also hadn't thought that there were demonspawn roaming around. He could have his sword out in a second if needed.

The shopkeeper didn't say anything but nodded. He also kept glancing at Storm.

Edgar picked up one more shirt, for Storm or Keanin by the look of it, and put it on the counter. Storm dumped the clothing he was carrying and then stepped back a few feet behind Edgar.

"Are they as deadly as the rumors say?" The shopkeeper started sorting the clothes.

"More so," Storm answered.

The man's eyes widened, he gave a quick nod, then went back to totaling their cost. He quickly wrapped the clothing up in a pair of tight bundles.

Edgar paid him, then they left. The shopkeeper sighed as they left. Most likely from holding his breath.

"I am rethinking choosing such a noticeable persona.

It's nice to be respected, but annoying too." Storm was used to people watching him, and he didn't like it normally. It was one of the reasons he stayed out of the palace as much as he could. But seeing fear in people's eyes wasn't great either.

"Nope, unless we have a serious reason to, I think we need you to stay that way. You are noticeable, but people will remember the Crailian sell-sword, not who was with him. And since it sounds like Ravenhearst knows that we're traveling, it's better no one figures out who you are. Or any of us."

"I will have to drop it at some point if we're having me make an official presentation to the Khelaran royals. But it can wait until we get there. Do you think we have enough clothing?" The bundles were tightly packed but still large.

"I'm still sorting out Khelaran. But yes, we'll figure that out on the way." Edgar looked down the lane and then shrugged and turned back toward their inn. "I would like to get a few more options. But I don't like leaving Keanin alone too long."

The area around the docks was less busy now, mostly because it was neither time for the morning sail to the north nor the evening sail to the south. Storm watched everyone around them carefully though.

The appearance of that demonspawn was disturbing. He believed Hilten that he hadn't known what he was working with, but had it been a random hire, or had Ravenhearst set it up? His bet was on Ravenhearst. Part of him hoped he was here so he could kill the bastard.

The pub on the ground floor of the inn was mostly empty as they passed through to their room.

Edgar was reaching for the doorknob when the door rattled and there was the sound of breaking glass. Both Storm and Edgar dropped their packages and ran inside.

To find a slightly smoky and sheepish-looking Keanin

standing in the middle of the room. He'd pushed the beds aside and was standing in the middle of a murky circle on the floor.

Edgar grabbed the packs and shut the door behind them, but a second later the door rattled.

"I said, keep it down! I know you're up to something in there, but you'll be paying for anything you break." The innkeeper didn't open the door but the exasperation in his voice indicated this wasn't his first time up there.

"Sorry!" Keanin and Edgar both yelled.

Storm heard a grunt of acknowledgment through the door, then heavy footsteps descended the stairs.

"What the hell did you do?" Storm picked up a chair that was on its side. Like the floor, it had what looked like scorch marks on the legs.

"I've been practicing." Keanin's smile was too broad for it to be good. "There's a spell that can heat things to where they will explode. From the inside."

"That's kind of sick. Wouldn't it be easier to just run them through with a sword or arrow?" Storm picked up the pack he'd been carrying and tossed it on one of the beds. They could move furniture around after they talked about his spell choices. He wasn't a magic user, but he'd spent far too much time with Ghortin to not fear the spells Keanin was messing with.

"Sometimes you don't have that option." Keanin sniffed.

"Those are walthi level spells, aren't they? A few dozen levels above where you should be?" Edgar busied himself by opening both packs of clothing and sorting them into three piles.

Storm let out a whistle. Even he'd heard of walthi level spells. They were some of the most powerful and danger-ous class of spells known. Jenna had asked Ghortin about a walthi water spell once and he'd told her it would be years if not decades before she would have the ability to control one of those.

Keanin was silent.

"How did you learn them?"

He didn't want to answer at first but finally gave in with a sigh. "I found a spell book a few months ago. It was with the gear we found when we packed up to leave the Markare after the battle." He held up a small, blood-red book. "I figured if I told Ghortin, he'd take it from me. So, I just carried it around." He at least looked a little embarrassed.

"Damn it, Keanin. Didn't you wonder who might have left it? There were some nasty magic users there." Edgar fished out his taran wand and spoke into it. "Ghortin? We might have a serious issue."

"You too?" Ghortin's voice was as stressed as Storm had ever heard it. It was all he could do to not tear the wand out of Edgar's hands.

"Keanin found a spell book in the Markare when we fought the false king. It has walthi level spells in it."

"Don't let him try anything!"

"Too late. He was messing around with a fire spell."

"Damn it all. Keanin…you…defend yourself with easier spells. You have the book I gave you, stick to that. It's never safe to pick up an unknown spell book. Edgar, can you get a somin bag?"

"I have one in my gear. Good to keep magical items from causing trouble."

"Put the book in there. And keep it with you. Is Keanin okay?"

"He is. The room is singed, but he's unharmed. Now, what's wrong on your end?"

There was a pause on the other end. "Jenna has gone missing. It just happened, but we'll find her, tell Storm to settle down."

Storm was reaching for the wand but took a step back.

"Was she kidnapped?"

"No idea, but doubtful. It only happened a few moments ago. We were riding through the forest and then she was gone. Her horse, pack, and everything else are still here and none of us heard or saw anything."

"Keep us updated. I'll keep Storm from charging off to find you. By the way, we came across a demonspawn in town. Dead now, but there could be more."

"Damn it. Keep Storm calm, Keanin from that damn book, and all of you stay out of trouble." Ghortin cut the call.

"How in the hell did they lose her?" Storm was trying to stay calm, but vanishing into thin air? It had to be the followers of Qhazborh.

"Easy there," Edgar said. "If it just happened then Ghortin hasn't had a chance to search for her. Not to mention it would take us at least a week to get to them. It wouldn't help her or you. Let Ghortin and Carabella figure it out." He took the red book from Keanin, pulled out a thin fabric bag from his pack, and dropped the book in it. Then he tucked it into his tunic and turned to Keanin. "And you—work on defensive spells." He smiled. "Protecting yourself is always a good idea, accidentally blowing yourself up, really isn't."

Keanin nodded and then put his hand on Storm's shoulder. "I know Ghortin and Jenna will sort it out. The more I accept my magic, the more I realize how strong Ghortin and Jenna are. Wherever she is, you know she is fighting to get back."

Storm sighed. "Thanks. I just…yeah. Having nothing I can do bothers me."

"Agreed." Keanin pulled a chair up and sat. "Now what was that about demonspawn?" He didn't seem as concerned as Storm expected. Perhaps that was a plus side of him finally accepting his magic.

Storm filled him in on Hilten, Mikasa, and the demonspawn while Edgar started trying on clothes. His merchant persona wasn't as high-end as Keanin's but he looked like one who'd fallen on rough times.

"I always hated Hilten. The man was a weaselly jerk. If you didn't kill the demonspawn, who did?"

"Damn good question, and one we would have asked Hilten if the guards hadn't shown up." Edgar posed in front of the small wardrobe mirror and made minor adjustments to his ensemble. "Although, there's a good chance Hilten had no idea either. We'd only seen him and his pick-pocket friend roaming around, the fighter was a new addition. The wound looked new from what I could tell."

"I got a strike in, but I didn't kill it. Even injured, that thing was fast." Storm looked at the clothes Edgar handed him. Dark green, gray, brown, and black were about the only colors and the designs were simple and fit his persona better than his current clothing.

"We're going to hunt them, right?" Keanin's smile was grim. And uncommon for him.

When they'd been in Lithunane, Keanin had wanted to hide in his room to make sure no demonspawn could get him. Now he wanted to launch a hunting party. Storm was glad that Keanin was able to defend himself better now, he just wished there hadn't been such a brutal reason behind it.

Things looked bad, and they weren't sure of the extent of the issues. A courtier wouldn't last long if war came; a pissed-off mage could.

"Unless you've found a way to pick them out of the crowd, and I remind you this one looked kelar and bled red for a while before we saw the green, we wouldn't know who to look for." Edgar tossed a pile of clothing to Keanin. They weren't as dark as Storm's but still looked like they belonged to someone used to blending in.

Keanin looked through them with a frown. He might like the idea of dressing as a mercenary in theory, but his taste in clothing was still upper class. "Fine. But if anyone acts weird on our ship north, I get to check them. I assume since Mikasa and crew have taken over the ship leaving tomorrow we have to wait?"

"Yes. I'll try to book us tomorrow, but might be a day or two as they still haven't replaced the ship they lost." Edgar had slicked back his black hair with water and done something to his cheeks to make them sharper than usual. "What do you think? Nasler Starling is reborn."

"Wasn't there a character in those old children's tales named Starling?" Storm admitted that if he passed Edgar in the street it would take him a while to recognize him. "And what happened to Syl?"

"Yes, a successful merchant of tapestries. I've used this persona before, although not in a long time. It seems to make people comfortable when dealing with me during negotiations." Edgar shook his head. "And Syl was a common thug, Nasler is a different class completely. Anyone can tell that."

"You have nothing to sell. We're not merchants."

"Not right now, but my luck might improve and leave us with a chance to make some money." He rubbed his hands together, then shook himself and looked more like Edgar again. "Sorry, I haven't had much of a chance for disguise these last few years. Didn't realize how much I missed it."

"Dinner here or down in the docks?" Keanin had changed into his mercenary garb.

Edgar frowned. "You don't look like a merc. Your hair is too...you. Let me see what else I have." He rummaged through items he'd just bought as well as things he had with him. Finally, he pulled out a large black square of fabric. "I still want to dye your hair; it's just too well known. But start with this." He narrowed his eyes as Keanin covered most of his hair with the fabric and tied it. "You wouldn't let me cut it, would you?"

Before Keanin could do more than open his mouth, yelling and screaming came from outside their window.

Pounding came up the stairs as the innkeeper ran through. "Everyone to the docks! They're on fire!"

CHAPTER THIRTY-FIVE

JENNA WALKED CLOSER to the swirling light. Although she had lived in the outskirts of Los Angeles, she'd never been a fan of the city itself and rarely went downtown. The view before her was the L.A. skyline and she was surprised at the wetness in her eyes. She wasn't sure if the being who created this moving and very real appearing image was a deity or a powerful cuari, but she somehow knew it spoke the truth.

After over a year of living with Ghortin, Storm, and the others, she could go home.

"My body in that world is gone. I saw it." When the mage had pulled her through unintentionally into the body of a mindslave, he'd murdered her former body. She now guessed that it had been Sacaranz from the level of Power he'd supposedly used.

"You would go back as you are."

And freak out her family and friends. She shook her head. It was more than that. There was real longing at seeing that image, her heart reached out and wanted her old life back. But only for a moment. Then her current life, and all of the people dear to her, came to mind. "That isn't my life anymore. The world I have been in is under attack. And while you seem to not be doing anything about it, I'm with people who are trying to save it."

Meith smiled. "She's got you there."

"We can't interfere."

"Are you one of the deities?" A chill went through her at the realization of who she might be speaking to. Having Typhonel in her head was one thing, this being was an active god.

"As you would know them, yes. But none of our kind can have sway in the worlds, beyond tiny movements—such as returning you home."

"Then why is Qhazborh giving Power to his priests and mages? They are bringing forth demonspawn—Helikin, I believe, was the old term."

Meith wasn't smiling anymore.

"None of us can do that. You must be confused."

"Search her mind," Meith said.

Jenna nodded. "If it means that you'll believe me, do what he just said. Search away. I give you permission or whatever you need." It was terrifying that the other gods and goddesses might be unaware of what Qhazborh's people were doing.

"That won't be necessary."

"Will you help us? Things are going to get nasty down there very quickly. We need help."

The pause was long enough that she wondered if the deity was still there or if he'd just left the beam of light on.

"Very well. This will open your mind, not only to us but also to yourself. Long-lost memories will be brought to the surface. Some may not be pleasant."

There weren't many options. She needed to get back and they needed help. "I understand. What do I need to do?"

"Remove your sword and dagger. Put down your book. Walk toward us. We will take care of the rest."

Jenna did as he said. As she walked forward, she turned to look at Meith for encouragement. Unfortunately, his smile looked forced now. For good or bad, this might be her only way out. It also might get the people she loved some much-needed support. Taking a deep breath she stepped into the light.

She'd expected it to feel like *something*. When they'd

healed her hands the light had been cold and sharp. This was neither cold nor warm. It was as if she was engulfed in something that was her exact temperature. She and the light were one. She'd just started to feel like she was floating when images appeared around her. They were from her memories and the first was of being on the trail with Ghortin and Carabella.

The sights, sounds, smells, and feelings of everything she'd ever experienced flowed around her growing stronger until she thought she would burst.

"There, there. Are you feeling better now? They've left." Meith stood near her looking down at her in concern. She was on the ground and the light and whatever deities had been within it were gone.

"I think so." She took a deep breath and tried to sit up. "Nope. Not okay, not sitting up." She hadn't moved much but even that hurt. Memories drifted around her head, but none came too close. Hopefully, it would stay that way. The flood that had hit her while in the light had forced her mind to shut down. Not to mention that her body felt like a steamroller had run over it. And reversed.

"Did they get what they needed? How come I'm still here instead of back home?"

"I don't know. I believe so. You were in there for a long time, then they brought you out unconscious. I couldn't touch you, but you were breathing, so I gathered you were alive." He peered down at her. "You don't look good though."

"Why can't you touch me? Did they say anything?" She felt like she was never going to be able to move again, and she had no idea if it had done anything to help her cause.

"Different planes of existence. My people weren't all killed, despite what the stories down in the below world say. But we were transformed." He patted his chest. "Sounds solid, right? Watch." He leaned over and tried to touch her head. His hand went through her.

"Yup. Different planes. How do you feel?" He sat on a rock. "This isn't one of yours either. Sadly, those two sciretts were in your plane."

"I feel horrible. Whatever that deity or deities did to me, I don't think it's supposed to be done to a human mind or body. There are planes within this plane?" She held up her hand as he opened his mouth to explain. "No, never mind. My brain is leaking out of my ears, and I can't have any other ideas running loose in there right now."

"I'm sorry that you're stuck here, but it is refreshing to see someone new. I think my friends want to come meet you." He looked around the empty jungle. "Eventually."

"Do they mind if I'm lying down at the time? I seriously can't budge." If those sciretts came back, she'd just have to die. Movement wasn't going to happen.

His laugh was warm. "I don't think so. And it's only a small group of us who didn't try to overthrow the gods and goddesses, but who also failed to stop it." There was a deep sorrow on his face as he looked away.

"What happened to the ones who did try to do it?" She didn't know how Meith or the gods and goddesses would feel if they knew she had Typhonel in her head. If the thing with the light opened everything to them, the deities now knew. Maybe they could help. Having a displaced god in her head had proven to be helpful many times, but she didn't think it was a good situation for either of them. Typhonel had spent the last thousand or more years in a quasi-slumber in the minds of the Guardians. It couldn't be a coincidence that he was now waking up and becoming aware of the world he was in.

"They were destroyed." His voice was flat. "They weren't killed, they were unmade. But we all paid a price we deserved." He nodded and a small smile came back. "I saw a cuari in your memories, Carabella. She was one of the good ones—she fought against what our people did. It's too bad she doesn't remember any of that time."

Jenna slowly rolled onto her elbow, then sat up. "Are the rest of her people here? She felt them and has been under attack by a spell bubble."

Anger flashed across Meith's face. "That I don't know. I knew they were under attack, but no one listens to me. If they are on the chaotic plane, then they are in a pocket far from here. What do the cuari books say? We helped create those, you know."

"We only have two of them. The locked spell one and the one for the Guardian. Ghortin has been having trouble with the first one and the second one isn't proving as helpful as I'd like. We're traveling to get the third."

"You...you are a Guardian?" His eyes teared up but his smile was huge. "I came up with those, I did. That was my idea. The gods fought me on it for a long time. That might explain why you were brought here. But not really, no other Guardians have come up. Interesting."

"Do you think that me being one of the Guardians will get me back home?" Finding this out was interesting, and most likely Rachael and Ghortin would be chewing up this new information for months once things settled down. But she needed to leave.

"It might, but I've no idea how you got here, so that's just a guess. Tell me, where are the other two books?"

"Aren't there only three? Rachael, another Guardian, said there were three."

"What? No, there were five. This is not good. Were memories from the first Guardians removed? I need to speak to someone. Stay here." He gave her a nod and then vanished.

Jenna swore. He'd left her alone, in some weird pocket of the chaotic plane, and told her to stay put. She moved a bit back and was able to lean against a rock. There was no way to tell the passage of time here, the odd twilight sky was still there, but she felt like she'd been here for days.

A chill wind drifted through the jungle. The light stayed the same and the vines weren't moving. But down the path where she sat, a wind came through. Then it came back in the other direction.

"Who's there?" If Meith couldn't touch her, maybe other planes couldn't be seen.

"Why are you here?" The voice was hollow, like an old-style recording done by a machine.

"Who are you? Show yourself." Her sword and spell book were out of reach, but her dagger was still with her. She pulled it out and debated rolling the five feet or so to reach her spell book and sword.

"Tilthan. Flori. Bace. Rha. Maeve. Jaili."

She waited a moment to see if there was more. "Those are your names?"

"Those are your ancestors. The ones who came before you. You can't stop this. There will be more names after you are gone."

"I'm not from your world. My ancestors are far from here." The voice was no longer hollow, but the coldness was worse. It chilled her soul.

"William. Mathis. Lucy. Joy. Susan. More ancestors. No more will come after."

Jenna pulled her legs up close. There was still nothing she could see to fight, but she needed to be ready to move if she had to. Susan was her grandmother's name. Joy had been her great-grandmother. She didn't recognize the others before them, but she could guess. "Who. Are. You?" She calmed her breathing and focused on the air around her.

"I am death."

She rolled away a moment before a flash of lightning shattered the rock she'd been leaning against. She grabbed her sword and spell book and scrambled into the jungle. Whatever it was hadn't shown itself even to throw the lightning. She'd been staring at the spot the lightning appeared from. She cast a spell shield, but it flickered and failed. Her magic was there, she felt it, but the shield was useless.

Death was a personification from Earth. Her new home didn't mention it as a person and saw it as more a rite of passage. So what was she facing?

"You can't hide. It is predetermined. I called you here so your energy upon death would feed the chaotic plane. It hungers." Another bolt came, this one snapping a tree a few feet from her. But this time she'd seen a flash of something. A person, shield, monster—something had appeared in the tiniest moment before the bolt fired.

She needed a spell to blast that thing apart when it appeared. There was a good chance anything she tried would do nothing—Meith couldn't touch her. But it was better than nothing. Two more lightning bolts hit as she moved around the jungle. Each time she saw the flash before the strike a bit longer. It was coming from one area. No matter where she went, the lightning came from the same direction.

Made it easier to guess the next attack.

The simplest spell that might be useful was a wind spell. She'd been slowly pulling Power from the chaotic plane around here with each move and now felt ready to burst.

The flash was brief, but she got off her spell with all the force she had. The jungle exploding around her wasn't expected.

CHAPTER THIRTY-SIX

"**D**AMN IT. KEANIN throw this hood over you too. We'll need to work on you looking less like you, but the innkeeper knows we're up here, so we have to go downstairs."

Keanin added the hood to his outfit, then put a protection spell on their room and all three ran out the door with their sword belts on. The weapons wouldn't help in a fire, but it seemed that flames were being used by the other side. Storm was almost expecting to hear that the inn was on fire after what happened to Jenna and the others. Sneaking around wasn't his style, and he sorely wanted to fight something directly.

Preferably something that wasn't an already mortally injured demonspawn.

People ran out of the inn and pub, racing toward the waterfront. Thin shoots of flame rose into the air between the buildings.

"Get the ships away from the docks! Damn you all, get them clear!" The dock mistress' bellow was heard long before they saw her.

The scene was bedlam. Most people ran toward the source of the fire, a large shed on the far side of the dock, but a few ran away. The three joined a fire brigade as buckets were brought out.

"I know I'm new to magic," Keanin said quietly. "But don't most places use magic to help put fires out? I could try—"

"No." Storm and Edgar echoed each other.

"Sorry, it's a good thought and if lives were in danger,

that would be worth the risk. But you're a merc." Edgar slung the buckets to the next person in line. "And I'm not saying there aren't mercenaries with magic, but it's rare. And noticeable. We already have our sell-sword, we don't want to stand out too much."

Storm watched the people around them. They'd kept their words low, but more were crowding in. At least the ships that had been secured at the dock were finally moving out to sea.

There were three, and none of them had been that close to the burning shed. But considering that they, like the rest of the dock, were made of wood moving them was the safest course.

The shed was completely engulfed, so the trick now was just to keep the flames from destroying the dock and the town's livelihood.

A half-hour later, the fire was out, most of the dock had been saved, and two of the ships who'd fled were on their way back.

"Where's the *Golden Harpy*?" The dock mistress pulled out her glass and scanned the horizon. "Damn Croft, he just kept running. Not sure what he's thinking—can't go north until morning anyway."

A group of men came up to her dragging a body. Whoever it was had been dead for a few hours; dried blood covered his chest. "Croft ain't on that ship. Someone killed him." They dumped the body in front of the dock mistress and stepped back.

Storm, Edgar, and Keanin faded into the gathering crowd, but not so far that they couldn't hear what happened. Storm couldn't have told anyone the name of the ship Mikasa had been on, but he knew it hadn't been either of the two that returned. Was this fire, murder, and missing ship a ploy by Ravenhearst working with Mikasa? Or something else completely?

The dock mistress looked down at the body and shook

her head. "Where was he?"

"Out down behind the Fool pub. Thought he was drunk at first, then I rolled him over." The man shook his head. "Ain't no one drunk enough to sleep off a slit throat."

Guards came down the dock as someone must have told them about the body. The same guard crew who'd taken in Hilten were there, along with five more.

Storm pulled his hood down lower. It had seemed as if the guards weren't following secret orders and the disgust at the dead demonspawn had been genuine. But that was a lot of armed people for a single murdered ship captain. And a missing ship, but he doubted they were going after it.

"Who was on the *Golden Harpy* when she took off?" The woman guard captain stepped aside and two of the other guards loaded the late captain onto a gurney.

"I thought he was." The dock mistress pointed to the body now being carted off. "He should have been there along with the rest of his crew since that…woman… demanded to be let onboard tonight. And her crew of maids and guards of course. Two guards, five ladies-in-waiting." She snorted and leaned forward. "She was afraid someone was after her, so why have only two Khelaran military as escorts?"

"How many crew should have been on the ship?" The guard captain didn't appear to care about the dock mistress' opinion.

"Seven, plus a cook crew of three. They paid extra for that. Only a two-day trip, they shouldn't have needed that much food."

CHAPTER THIRTY-SEVEN

———◆———

T HE EXPLOSION WAS possibly the most surreal
thing Jenna had ever seen. The entire jungle lifted
around her and filled with wild colors of light and odd
impossible shapes. The movement of all of the reality
around her slowed down until she had to stare at a single
spot to see that it was still moving. The space in-between
was a dusky gray with no depth.

Then everything collapsed in on itself.

A moment later she was back in the jungle just as it had
been. But no one was flinging invisible lightning bolts at
her this time.

"What just happened?" Her question wasn't directed
at anyone, as she didn't think anyone was there. The area
felt empty. "Hello? Anyone around?" She got to her feet,
retrieved her sword and spell book again, then walked
face-first into an invisible wall.

Swearing and rubbing her nose, she stepped back a few
paces. "Is someone there?" Tucking the spell book under
her arm, she felt the seemingly empty space in front of
her.

Solid.

She put the book in her right hand and kept it up in
front of her as she trailed the invisible wall with her left.
After about fifteen feet her right hand hit another wall.
"Seriously? Someone has me in a box? Meith? Can you
hear me?" She was glad whatever or whoever had been
flinging deadly bolts at her was gone, and that no sciretts
reappeared, but a tiny box?

With silence being her only response, she continued

to map out her small enclosure. She completed a second lap and paid careful attention to the distance. Not that it would help get her out, but knowing your enemy was always a good idea.

As far as she could tell it was a roughly fifteen-by-fifteen-foot box and was too high for her to tell if it had a ceiling or not. No matter how close she got to it, she couldn't see it. Her nose still hurt from where she walked into it initially but the jungle around her still looked the same.

After ten minutes, she was ready to crawl the walls and hope there wasn't a ceiling. There was a single boulder to sit on, so she sat and looked in the book for any spells designed to blow up an invisible box. Funny, not a single one was listed.

She found one that might work and mentally sent an apology to Ghortin. He'd drilled into her how important practice was to new spells. Now she was making up spells and about to try one she'd never seen before.

It looked simple, which usually meant that it wasn't. It was supposed to send an electrical charge into a focused spot. Sort of like what she'd used to destroy the sciretts, but this worked on magic instead of bodies or buildings. It disconnected the magics holding a spell together.

In theory.

She read the actions of casting the spell through a dozen times, formed the spell in her mind, reached deep inside for Power, and fell off her rock face-first. There was nothing there.

Swearing loudly, she got to her feet and reached out for the chaotic plane. Considering that she was inside it, the reach shouldn't be far and she was more afraid of over-powering the spell than under-powering it.

She'd stayed on her feet, but was dropped to the ground anyway as her failed attempt at gathering Power slammed into her. If what Meith said was right, she was in the chaotic plane. The source where all magic came from. How could she not access it?

Unless this damn box blocked magic.

She grabbed a handful of dirt and threw it toward the closest side of the wall. It spread out over the invisible flat surface. Some of it stuck but eventually vanished into the wall and became invisible. If this cage was blocking her access to magic, while it itself was magic, it was using a lot of Power to just exist. Part of its existence was staying unseen. Maybe she could overwhelm some of those magic circuits.

She threw more dirt at the same spot. More stuck and it took a little longer to be absorbed. There was a lot of dirt and plant debris in her fifteen-by-fifteen-foot cage. She started flinging it as fast as she could at the same spot. The section took a bit longer each time as it needed to access more Power to absorb the debris.

Ghortin had warned her about spells being pushed to their limits and how it could backfire on the spell caster. She hoped he was right in this case.

She was getting to the end of the easily accessible dirt and debris within the box and was keeping an eye out for anything she could dig with when the cage cracked. Just a small dark line, right in the center of where she'd been flinging dirt. But it gave her hope.

She doubled her efforts with the last of the dirt. This time, the dirt that stuck didn't vanish. Then the crack widened and a hole appeared.

In theory, and according to Ghortin, overloading the spell that was creating the cage should have collapsed the cage. Or exploded it. And hopefully snapped back at the spell caster.

Neither happened. While she could still see the jungle through the rest of the cage, the widening gap where she'd been targeting showed nothing but darkness.

Her options were limited and there wasn't enough dirt

to continue overloading the spell. With a heavy sigh, she sheathed her sword and dagger, tucked the spell book into her tunic, and crawled out.

There was ground under her hands as she crawled, but it felt more like asphalt than dirt. A light breeze ruffled her hair bringing with it the scent of…smog? Cars? The scents were familiar, but not anything she'd smelled in over a year. And not ones that should be in a jungle in the chaotic plane.

Maybe it was an aberration of some sort. A trick of her mind trying to fill the void around her. Just as she thought there should be sounds, car horns echoed in the distance. Then headlights barreled for her and she barely rolled out of the way as a car sped past.

The driver had to have seen her, their lights were right on her, yet the car tore by without slowing down.

"This is where you belong." The voice was similar to the one who'd been flinging bolts at her but different. Still invisible though.

"Are you the one that locked me up? Who are you? Why are you doing this?" Another car tore by, its lights shining on her as she sat by the side of a road. One barely wider than an alley from what she briefly saw. Again no slow down.

"You are an aberration. The true world can't function with you in it. Change has to happen." That was the difference, the voice was less confident and weaker now. Probably the same being though.

She got to her feet. It smelled like L.A., and the faint glowing strip in the distance was coming into focus looked a lot like downtown L.A. But it seemed like things were coming into being as she thought of them. She immediately thought of how she missed flying in L.A. and was slowly lifted off her feet. She hadn't specified how she flew and whoever was messing with her just took her word for it. "I wish I had my wings back."

Nope. She thought the words before she said them and no wings appeared. Whatever was controlling this was reading her thoughts.

"If you want we can give this to you."

"I hurt you with my spells, didn't I? Then you put too much magic energy into that box and now you don't have enough to control me. This. Isn't. My. Home." As she said the words, she flung an illumination spell into the air. The light flickered, then held. She was in a dingy alley in L.A., but one that had a faint shadow of a jungle lurking around the edges. "Let me go or I will keep pushing until I destroy you." Before she said the words, she'd imagined grabbing her attacker by the throat. A dark form materialized in her hands. Because she didn't know what it looked like, the form was vague, but it struggled enough to know she was hurting it. She closed her hands tighter on its throat.

"You can't..."

"You said I was an aberration. You don't know what I can do." She separated her hands, pulling the vague form apart. She hung on when it started screaming. The alley flashed to the jungle and somehow she knew that was real and not inside the box. She kept pulling. "Put me back where you found me, or your essence will be scattered throughout the known worlds." She felt another presence in her mind at that last bit, but couldn't stop to check. Hopefully, it was Typhonel and not some random freeloader.

The being yelled once more and then everything was ripped away from her. The alley, the skyline, the smells, then the jungle. With a thud, she dropped about five feet to land on a dirt trail.

"How did you get here?" Crell came running out of the woods; she looked battered and bloody. The woods were smoky and blackened trees filled them. "We've been looking for you for months."

Jenna looked around. Months? "No. Back *when* you took me." In her mind, she hung onto the form and pulled on it again. The world spun around her and she found herself again being to land on a dirt trail. Her horse was in front of her, with Crell's pony tied behind. Ghortin and Crell came running out of the woods at her arrival and Carabella got off her horse to run over as well. All looked more or less as they had when she'd vanished. More importantly, Crell didn't look like she'd been on the losing end of a few battles.

Ghortin reached her first and helped her to her feet.

"How long was I gone?" In a small corner of her mind, she still held onto the being from the jungle. It feared her and she wasn't afraid to use that fear if she needed to.

"Almost three hours," Ghortin said. "I was getting quite worried."

Jenna sent the entity in her thoughts a threat of what would happen to it if this was fake or it ripped her out of reality again, then let it go. Everything stayed put around her.

"So was I." At some point, she'd deal with whatever had happened in the first drop—where she'd been missing for months and Crell had seriously had her ass kicked—but not right now. Hopefully, that reality vanished when she forced them to put her back here. She realized everything ached and while she wasn't sure how long she'd been gone, it felt long enough to leave her hungry and exhausted. "Could we set up camp soon?" She walked to her horse and pulled out some dried fruit. "I'm starving and worn out. Plus it'll be easier to tell you everything if I'm sitting." She hadn't been hungry or thirsty wherever she had been, but it was smacking into her now.

Crell nodded. "While searching for you, I found a nice grotto back in the woods a bit. Figured we could use it if we needed to wait to find you."

Carabella stood in front of her with her eyes narrowed.

Even not using magic she was clearly seeing something of what had happened. Dancing around Meith and who he was while she was in earshot wouldn't be fun.

"You were on the chaotic plane, weren't you?" She tilted her head. "Did you see my people?"

"I was there—or so I was told. I'll tell you all when we're settled. But no, I didn't see your people." Not a lie, she'd only heard that the ninety-nine cuari were there. The only one she'd met had been outside of that group.

Carabella held her look a bit longer as if she could see everything that remained unsaid. Then she shrugged. "It was a longshot. I doubt you could have gotten them free anyway. We need your untouchable books to get them free and then to stop this entire mess." She draped her arm around Jenna's shoulders and started following Crell. Ghortin and the horses followed.

That was a fun thought, how she was going to tell Ghortin there were two more books of the cuari. They'd need to tell Rachael and Tor Ranshal as well. She had no idea of the implications, but Meith was extremely disturbed that all mention of the other two books had been lost. Which most likely meant someone or something had fought hard to suppress them.

Crell's grotto was a small clearing with heavy forest on three sides and ancient trees that extended their branches over it. Jenna relaxed as soon as they walked into that green embrace.

"You sit before you fall, we'll set up camp." Crell and Carabella aimed her toward a fallen log then joined Ghortin in picketing the horses and setting up camp.

He started to make a fire ring, took one look up at the trees, and created a pile of mage lights instead. "Not a worry, we're grateful for your protection. No fire will come here."

Although they were glows and not an actual fire, they still gathered around to eat. Warm food would have been nice but not at the risk they'd piss off the forest. Jenna hadn't heard of sentient trees before, but if they did exist in this world—these were them.

Jenna sighed. In her time jump, this forest had been burnt and battles had taken place. Each step away from that was a good thing.

CHAPTER THIRTY-EIGHT

STORM TRIED TO hear more, but the guard captain spoke too softly to her crew for him to hear anything else. Whatever she said caused them to break up. Half went down to what remained of the shed, the rest began interviewing people standing around.

Edgar wove through the crowd with Keanin and Storm on his heels. But they weren't fast enough. The guard captain had disbursed her people then moved to where Edgar came out past the crowd.

"You two, again? And a new friend? I don't think Captain Croft was a demonspawn." She waited until they weren't right near the crowd to approach them and kept her voice low. She also was watching the crowd more than them.

Edgar took point. "We're staying at the Swan Inn, and they called for everyone to help with the fire. We might be passing through but didn't seem right to hide in our rooms."

Her gaze hit all three. "And you always run out fully armed? The Crailian I get, but you two? And you were looking a bit more like a merc when I saw you two before." She tipped her head. "I'm Captain Talia Cilone. And you are?"

Edgar laughed and held out his hand. "Honored to meet you. I'm Syl, this is Hawk and Lanian—he was back in our rooms when Hawk and I went out to replace some of our stolen clothing. He's my personal guard. Hawk was added after one too many ambushes."

Talia looked Keanin over. He still wore the hood but

it was pushed back further than Storm's was. "He looks like he can fight too. You three traveling to Craelyn, I'd gather? Going for the tourney?"

Storm was surprised at that, but Edgar saved him from asking.

"I'd heard they'd had an attack a few weeks past. They're still going on with the tournament?"

The Khelaran tournament was a massive, overwrought event. Storm would never have agreed to go into Craelyn if he thought they'd still be holding it. More reasons not to show anyone up there who he really was. If the Khelaran kingdom had truly fallen to the enemy or was working with them, it wouldn't matter if Prince Corin of Traanafaeren made an official appearance. As a visiting royal of a certain age and known fighting prowess, he knew he'd be expected to take part in the tournament.

He'd rather face another demonspawn than put on borrowed armor and pretend to battle other nobles. He'd attended exactly two Khelaran tournaments in his life. First when he was a kid. It was glorious and wonderful—until his older brother Justlantin told him it was all for show and that the results were determined in advance. Real tournaments did happen, but this was the king's tourney and nothing was left to chance.

He hadn't believed him and as soon as he was old enough he made the trip up and jousted. It was rigged to show support for the Khelaran military and visitors always lost. He'd never been back.

Talia shrugged while she kept watching the crowd on the dock. "We heard that as well, but then three days later word came that they'd fought them off and the tourney would be a celebration of Khelaran life. You realize that with the missing ship, going north will be problematic, right? They already lost one ship to a storm a few days ago. The *Golden Harpy* was the only one left making that run until the ship that left yesterday comes back."

"Do you think that the other ship was destroyed to keep people from going to Craelyn?"

Talia looked sharply at Edgar and narrowed her eyes. "Why would you say that? The ship's only been missing less than an hour. Is there something you'd like to tell me?" Her hand slid down to the hilt of her sword.

"You have someone on that ship, don't you?" Keanin had been silent but spoke before Edgar could.

"My brother was supposed to be staff on that ship. I'll check his usual haunts, but I have a feeling he was on it." She looked around the dispersing crowd and motioned for them to follow her a bit further away. "I'd like to hire you, all of you, to help me find my brother and bring back that ship." She turned to Edgar. "You're dressed like a merchant now, but I know a fighter's walk when I see it. I can pay well."

"We don't have a ship. And unless Erlinda pays far more than Lithunane for their guards, no, you can't afford us." Edgar smiled but there was no warmth there and his hand was within easy reach of this sword.

Storm dropped his hand to the hilt of his sword as well. The only way to get to Craelyn via land was a five-week journey. That wasn't an option, but might be their only choice if they had to fight their way out of here.

"Easy there. I'm not tricking or trapping you. My brother and I are the children of former Khelaran nobles. Our parents moved down here for reasons not made clear to us when we were kids. They died a few years ago, leaving both of us extremely comfortable. We work because we want to, not because we need to. I can pay." She smiled. "And I have a boat, the *Reef Dancer*. Doesn't need much of a crew if you're all willing to work. We find the ship, rescue my brother, and I promise to get you to Craelyn in time for the tourney."

Edgar didn't look at the other two, but Storm was close enough to watch him think it through. Finally, he nodded. "We keep to ourselves though, you and whoever else you bring leave us alone unless we have to work together on something."

Talia's smile brightened her face. "Agreed. How quickly can you be ready? We can't catch the tide north until the morning, but neither can the *Golden Harpy*. I'd like to catch them down here before they head north."

"We can be packed and out within an hour. I'll think of an excuse for us to be leaving suddenly to the inn-keeper—I'd rather it didn't get spread around town."

"Meet me at the small dock just off the market street. The *Reef Dancer* is docked there. Oh, and the innkeeper is a gossip but will stay quiet if paid enough. Two golds and he'll swear on his mother's grave you three were never there." With a nod, she jogged off to join her guards.

"Are we certain this is a good idea?" Keanin carefully watched her go.

"She's our best chance for getting there, and if this ship going missing has anything to do with Mikasa or Ravenhearst we have to find it." Storm turned Keanin's head back toward them as he realized he was still staring. "She's a captain in the city guard. You're a much better swordsman than you want to admit, but she'd probably slice you to ribbons if you're too forward."

Keanin blushed, sure sign he'd been thinking how attractive she was.

Edgar sighed and led the way back to the inn. "No military for you my friend. Maybe when this whole thing is over, and the world is safe, you can come back and reintroduce yourself as yourself." He glanced over his shoulder. "A braid, we can get your hair in a braid and put some lampblack on it. And stay clear of her."

"I just admired a strong and attractive woman. Honestly." Keanin pushed past both and went up the stairs to take his spell off the door.

"Is this really our only option? I agree with Keanin on

that concern. We've no idea of who Talia is, nor anyone she'll be bringing. We don't have a lot of options if things go bad while we're at sea," Storm said as they entered the inn.

Edgar held up one hand, then walked over to the inn-keeper. "We have an emergency and have to go back south. We would appreciate it if our being here was for-gotten. Captain Talia said you were a man we can trust." He slipped the coins into the innkeeper's hand.

He weighed them without looking then nodded. "Talia's good people. You were never here. There's a sec-ond exit at the far end of the stairs, which will keep anyone down here from seeing you." He gave a curt nod, then went into the kitchen.

"Either he and Talia are in cahoots, or I think we can trust her. I slipped an honesty charm on the coins right before I handed them over." Edgar took the stairs two at a time.

Storm followed. He didn't like this but had the inn-keeper lied he would have started choking because of the charm Edgar put on the coins.

Keanin had gotten a head start on packing, but he had more clothing tossed about. He'd already darkened his hair and twisted it into a long sloppy braid. There wasn't time for a full dye job, but between the braid, the hood, and the lampblack he wouldn't look as much like himself.

"All settled? By the way, my spell held, but someone had been trying to get around it." He folded the last of his shirts into his pack and tied it shut.

"Are you sure they didn't get in and then reset the spell?" Storm looked through his things but they didn't have time to find out if they'd been robbed—or had items added to their belongings.

"I learn from the best." Keanin held up a twig. "Jenna told me of this trick. Put it against the back of the door when you set your spell. If anyone opens it without removing the spell, then the twig will drop. It was still there, but there were odd magic signatures on the door."

"Thanks for setting that up, but we'll have to hope whoever they are they aren't with Talia. We have to get moving." Edgar had his hand on the handle when his shirt pocket started vibrating. He looked to Storm.

"They might have news of Jenna, answer it."

"Or something unrelated from one of the other wand holders." He held up his hand then gave the wand to Storm. "It's all yours."

"Hello?" Storm had been trying to keep his worry about Jenna tamped down but it came out now.

"Storm? Ghortin said he told you I went missing. Just wanted to let you know that I'm back."

Storm knew the goofy grin on his face was completely at odds with his Crailian persona, but he didn't care. "And you're okay? What happened to you?"

"I'm fine and we'd burn out the juice in these wands if I told you everything. Also, it involved some things a certain cuari can't hear."

"As long as you're all fine. When will you get to the Strann border?" There were many more things he wanted to ask, but this wasn't the time or place.

"We're all good. We're adding an extra day, so hopefully in two days. Is everyone okay out there?"

"We are. We'll be at sea soon, so I'm not sure how that will impact these wands." He looked to Edgar, but he just shrugged and slightly shook his head.

"Understood. Don't do anything heroic or fearless, okay?"

He laughed. "I'll try. You neither. Take care."

"Bye, Storm." She ended the call.

"Good to know she's back, but I am extremely curious as to where she went." Edgar took the wand back and went for the door again. Keanin followed him out.

Storm shut the door behind him and trailed the other

two down the hall. It was that odd time of evening when folks hadn't come in yet for dinner and the daytime drinkers had left.

They left the alley and Edgar stuck to the shadows as much as possible as they went to the distant dock. This one was much smaller and mostly had fishing boats around it.

"Is that her?" Keanin pushed back his hood a bit and pointed to the boat at the end of the dock. A figure waved to them then ducked below deck.

"Pull your hood back down." Storm tugged his own hood lower as they walked toward the boat. Most of the fishing boats had been in for hours, judging by the lack of activity, but there were still people around. Talia hadn't said this had to be a stealth mission per se, but it was probably best if as few people as possible saw them leave. Not to mention, they hadn't found out if Ravenhearst had other spies in town. Knowing him, Hilten wasn't the only one. For one thing, there was whoever gave Hilten the order to knock out Edgar.

There was no one visible on the boat, but the name was clear, the *Reef Dancer*. Edgar stepped forward and three people in dark clothing ran on deck. Their faces were mostly covered, but none looked like Talia. He gripped his sword and saw Edgar and Keanin do the same. Talia might have appeared to be honest, but that looked questionable now.

CHAPTER THIRTY-NINE

———◆———

JENNA FIGURED SHE must look pretty bad, as everyone waited to ask her questions until after she'd eaten. Night was falling, and honestly, she would rather sleep and deal with it all in the morning. But she needed to tell them some of what happened.

"Now, how much of what happened can you talk about around me?" Carabella asked. "I'd rather go out of ear-shot than collapse again."

"I think most of it. There are some things I'll need to tell Ghortin about alone, and he'll need to tell Tor Ranshal and Rachael, but I'll save those for the morning." Not only was she tired and being lulled to sleep by the glows and a full stomach, but she also didn't think any of them should be wandering the woods. The image of that battle-weary Crell was going to linger in her mind for a while.

She started with the sciretts. After Ghortin's third interruption for details that she didn't have, she held up her hand. "I'm tired. I'm telling you all that I recall. Maybe I can just tell you my version, you take notes, and when I'm more coherent you can ask away. My brain will work much better then." He wasn't as surprised about the jungle or the sciretts as she would have expected—so she would need to ask him some questions too. Later.

"Fine. Continue. You were about to use a very unorthodox spell on some primordial sciretts." He waved his hands at her. "That's what you described."

"Sorry, no one covered what spell to use when giant, mutated sciretts attack you in a strange jungle." She finished the rundown as best she could and completely avoided mentioning Meith.

"You were back in your world? How was it?" Carabella was more interested in that than anything else.

"Unfortunately, they put me in a dirty part of town. If I was really there. No one can fly in that world, yet when I thought how much I missed it, I rose into the air. I have a feeling it wasn't Earth but a trap as much as the invisible box had been. Whoever was behind it had a lot of Power. But they were afraid of me."

"You gave them a good reason." Ghortin yawned. "And you're not the only one who has had a long day." He spoke a word and the glows changed color to a dusky orange and flew around the edges of the camp. "We should still keep watches, but the lights will signal if anything gets within a dozen feet. I'd forgotten that spell, but it's a handy one."

The other three overruled her offer to stand watch and divided into three shifts. Jenna would have continued to argue but it was hard when her own body was on their side. She finally crawled into her sleep sack and fell asleep.

To be woken by yells and all screams around her. She wasn't in the camp anymore, now she was back in L.A. It was daytime and pockets of darkness were ripping open the sky letting horrible creatures in. All teeth and nails they didn't look like they should be able to move let alone fight, yet they started attacking people as soon as they hit the ground.

Glowing red and gray balls came through the holes as well and lightning shot out of them and into the buildings. The yelling got louder as the buildings toppled.

Jenna ran forward, pulling in her magic as she did so. She tried to use her own lightning spell to stop a green monster with fangs and eight legs charging for a group near her, but nothing came out.

"Jenna! Why are you doing this?" Voices all around her

yelled and screamed her name as they died.

"Jenna! Wake up!" Carabella's voice echoed the other screams but broke through the horror and rattled her out of the nightmare.

The terror she just went through left her heart racing and she fought to open her eyes. Carabella held her hands, Crell was sitting on her legs, and Ghortin looked ready to blast someone. Hopefully not her, but it was hard to tell.

"What happened?" Jenna looked around frantically. Images from her dream were fading slowly. Carabella and Crell eventually let go of her, but it wasn't a good sign they had to restrain her like that.

"That's what we'd like to know." Ghortin dropped the spell he'd held in his hands. "I was on watch and you started tossing and fighting. Then screaming. We woke you up at the screaming. It took a bit."

She sat up slowly. "I dreamed that I was back in my former world, but it was under attack. Tears in the sky were allowing weird monsters in and the people were blaming me."

"Well, you did just have an odd experience on the chaotic plane. It's natural that your mind would try and deal with it—nightmares are usually things we're afraid of or left unfinished." Carabella peered closely into her eyes. "Your people don't time travel, do they?"

"No. No one can, can they?" Aside from her popping ahead a few months in that divergent timeline. Something she hadn't told them about yet.

"The cuari had been able to when the one hundred were first created. It turned out to be a very bad idea." The way Ghortin kept glancing at Carabella, Jenna had a feeling there was more he couldn't mention in front of her.

"Some of my people misused it. But there's a lag when it occurs, a slight changing of the eyes for a few hours.

It's been a long time since I've seen it, but your eyes look affected. It might not have been a dream."

Jenna hadn't told them about her run-in with future Crell. If there was something in her eyes it might be from that. She'd been hesitant because of all those old tv shows where someone messed up the timeline by knowing something they shouldn't.

"You have more, don't you?" Carabella asked.

"When I forced whoever who grabbed me to let me go, I first came back a few months from now. Things weren't good. I made them bring me back to when I was taken."

"That could have done it." Carabella got to her feet. "Or the dream you just had was a time hop."

"But it wasn't here. My dream, or whatever, was my former world. And it looked like the current time—or at least like a year ago had looked."

Carabella tilted her head. "Time passes differently between worlds. But there's no way to know what truly occurred. Not without more spells than I have access to right now."

"For now, let me give you something to sleep. It'll make more sense in the morning." Ghortin held up a glass, one that hadn't existed a moment before. The liquid was surprisingly clear.

Jenna narrowed her eyes. "What's in it?" Ghortin seemed to have an endless supply of potions. They worked but they almost all tasted nasty. They were often a vile color combination too. Clear made her even more suspicious.

"You have no faith in me." He tried to look wounded, but since no one believed him he handed over the drink with a flourish. "It's a sleep aid, nothing more. We don't know if what you just experienced was a nightmare, or some odd reality popping in for a visit, but it is clear you're exhausted. Nothing funny tasting, I promise."

Jenna took a cautious sip. She'd once had a potion of his literally crawl down her throat. This tasted like water, nothing more. He made the glass vanish as soon as she finished, which was a good thing. She was asleep before she hit her pillow.

CHAPTER FORTY

STORM TURNED TO look behind them. Three more attackers, same clothing as the ones of the boat, stood between them and the town. They were all carrying long thin blades, more common to the desert tribes than a town like this.

Edgar glanced back, and he and Keanin took positions to watch both sides.

"Options?" Storm's stance was relaxed but he was ready to do whatever was needed to get his friends out of there. They couldn't go back to the inn since the innkeeper seemed to be working with Talia. If this was a setup, they were either expecting them or were damn quick with planning.

"It seems that we fight. I'd say we misjudged our good captain." Edgar raised his voice. "We don't want trouble. Just thought you were someone else."

A ruckus came from inside the *Reef Dancer* and the three people on it all ran below the deck. The other three started down the dock, then turned and ran as one of their companions on the ship was thrown overboard.

Keanin started after them, but Storm grabbed his arm. "I don't think we have to worry about them." Two guardsmen coming up the dock grabbed the three and easily disarmed them. They looked like they'd been waiting for them.

Talia came out on the deck, holding one of the culprits. She spoke to him harshly, but not loud enough for Storm to hear, then threw him overboard. Two men came out holding the third and likewise tossed him into the water.

"Take those three in and fish the rest out. Keep them in lockup until their parents come to get them." Talia waved to Edgar. "Damn kids. They went too far this time. Come aboard."

Storm stood back and let Edgar lead. He'd been in charge so far and it was better they keep that up. They received nods from the two men on deck, both of them were guards who had been with Talia before, but like her were not wearing a uniform now.

"Sorry about that. A gang of junior thugs. I knew they were around the dock, didn't realize what they were doing."

"Were they dressed like Khelaran acubi?" Edgar watched as more uniformed guards dragged two of the cloaked people out of the water. Now it was clear they were shorter than they'd looked, especially since the two were kelar.

Storm hadn't noticed their choice in outfits until Edgar mentioned it, but now he did.

"Yes. They go through stages as to who they are emulating. The infamous desert tribes' people are the current fad." She laughed as the two being escorted past watched Storm with wide eyes. "And I have a feeling that next week we'll have a pack of Crailian sell-swords on our hands."

"You have an interesting town." Storm watched the guards and kids walk off. Now that they'd been caught, all of the soggy fighters slouched like teenagers.

"And you also have an interesting boat." Edgar walked over and lifted a wide swath of canvas that ran the length of the boat on both sides. It was covering ports for rowing stations. "I don't know that the six of us could row this thing."

Talia laughed. "That's just a backup. This was an old longboat from the south—the far southern continent. My brother and I refurbished it and added the mast and sails." She handed Edgar a scroll and a quill. "The contract for this job." She nodded to the two men on deck. A tall human and a shorter kelar-human mix. "This is Hon and Flini. They've sailed with my brother and me before. To be honest, I'm hoping that I'm just hiring three men to help us catch the missing ship and not three swordsmen. But better to be prepared."

"True. Someone took that ship and might not be willing to give it back." Edgar looked over the short contract then signed it. "Is there a place we can store our gear?"

The kelar named Flini nodded. "We have some rooms below decks. I'll show you."

The boat was larger below deck than Storm would have guessed and had seven small rooms. None much larger than a cot and chair, but they worked.

"They redid this area too." Edgar patted the wood framing on the door.

Hon grinned. "Flini and I helped Diath rebuild this— he's Talia's brother. Washed up on shore ten years ago and took five years just to get the framing done. But the *Reef Dancer* is a fine boat. You three are from the south?"

"Aye. Just outside of Lithunane. Heading for Craelyn for some work and these two might enter a tournament. Get us some renown to get more jobs."

Hon led them back up after they dropped their packs. "Thought you were a merchant?"

"I dabble in many things. And if others are will to pay what your captain is paying for our current services, I might be looking at a new line of work."

Talia quickly got everyone in position and started moving the boat clear of the dock.

"The sails aren't up, how are we moving?" Keanin came up close behind Talia until Storm gave him a look and he took a few steps back.

"Ah, now I know you're not from here." Talia laughed. "There are three docks in Erlinda, and all three have spells for setting sail and coming back. Once we're out of the main channel, we take over. But for now, it's all magic."

Storm was impressed. Lithunane wasn't a coastal city but he'd spent time as a boy down in the fishing towns a few days' rides away. The coastline of Traanafaeren was tricky and boats needed extremely skilled captains to leave the coast. "How long have you had that? There are towns to the south that would love that ability."

"Five years. It's been a huge boon. It was one of the reasons Diath figured he could rebuild this boat."

They moved into the open sea and Keanin nodded. "I have some small mage craft; I just felt the spell let go." He gave Talia one of his court smiles, then tried to tone it down and ended up looking awkward.

She took it for what it was intended and smiled back. "Not too many mercs have magic, but good to know in case we need it. Flini has some hearth magic, but that's it." She and the other two ran the sails up and they moved away from the coast.

"I spoke to the captains of the other two ships. All three stayed close to each other at first, then the *Golden Harpy* went north. The other two thought nothing of it, thinking she was just waiting until it was safe to return. By the time they headed back, she was out of sight."

"How could that be? It's clear out here." Storm wasn't on the open ocean much, but he could see quite a distance right now.

"They both claimed that an odd fog bank appeared when they were out further." Talia scowled. "Neither wanted to tell me that at first."

"Did they seem spelled? Wouldn't we have seen something that heavy from land?" Keanin asked.

"They were extremely questionable. But getting more out of them or their crew was going to take too long. They did seem genuinely concerned about the ship going missing and I've known both of them for years.

My guess is someone on the *Golden Harpy* cast the fog spell, or two people on both of the other ships cast a spell on the crew and captains to think they saw fog."

"Neither is good." Edgar had his spyglass out and watched the horizon. "We're not prepared to handle any heavy magic users." He started swearing. "I see the ship."

Talia had her glass up and looked in the same direction. "I don't. Are you sure?"

Edgar handed his glass to Keanin.

"I see it too." He handed it to Storm.

"Damn it, it's a spell only magic users can break. I don't see it." Storm looked across the horizon but couldn't see a thing.

Talia handed her glass to Flini.

"Yup, sitting right out there. It's not close and getting further away, but it's out there. Heading straight out to sea."

"Mikasa must have some magic users with her. Strong ones. Damn it, what is she up to?" Storm muttered and handed the glass back to Edgar.

"Lady Mikasa? That annoying, self-absorbed, self-described princess?" Talia asked. "You three know her?"

"Sadly. She was in Lithunane for a bit." Keanin rolled his eyes.

Storm kept watching the horizon, but with or without the glass, he couldn't see a thing. "What's out this way? Or rather, the way they're heading."

Talia looked out over the sea. "If you go far enough that way you would eventually hit the Qini empire. But they don't like visitors and getting there by sea would take months."

"Is Thoali out here? I know it's to the north." Edgar continued watching the ship through his glass.

"The pirate hideout?" Hon laughed as he turned the wheel over to Flini since Flini could see where the other ship was. "That's a myth."

"No, it's not." Edgar's face was worried. "You don't have trouble with pirates, do you? Thoali is real and rumored to be in the north."

"We used to have problems, at least the old-timers say we did," Hon said. "It was before my time. If there's a primary hiding spot for pirates this close why wouldn't they have been harassing our ships?"

"They wouldn't if they didn't want to draw attention from Erlinda. And why would Mikasa be heading right for it?" Storm added Ravenhearst's name in his head but he wasn't going to go through explaining that connection. Talia and her people seemed trustworthy, but they had just met them.

"There's an island ahead, and they've turned toward it." Flini didn't sound happy about that but he turned to follow the ship. "It's pretty far out there, though. Keep following?"

Talia ran her hand through her short hair. "Damn it. Not only magic users hiding ships but an entire island. We can't take on an island of pirates."

"So we turn back?" Flini didn't move the wheel but looked ready for whichever direction she said.

She stayed silent for a bit, then slowly shook her head. "We can't do that either. At least I can't. Diath wouldn't have left me behind and I can't do that to him. I can send you three back to the dock in the dingy. It's not much and you'll have to row in, but I'm not paying you three enough to take on a bunch of pirates."

Keanin stepped forward before Edgar could answer. "I will stay and help. Your devotion to your brother is admirable."

"And your speech sounds more courtier than mercenary." Talia's eyes narrowed. "You three are good, I'll give you that. But you're not what you seem." She had her sword point at Keanin's throat before he could flinch.

"Tell me who you three really are or I'll make sure you all go in the water with enough holes to draw a mess of sharks."

CHAPTER FORTY-ONE

JENNA WAS GRATEFUL that there'd been no more nightmares, or whatever happened to her. But they'd been up and riding for almost two hours now and she still felt like she needed to sleep for a few more hours. It didn't help that the trail was monotonous, and everyone now agreed that villages were dangerous, so Ghortin had them avoid as many as possible.

"If you fall off your horse there's a good chance you'll land on your face." Crell was back to riding her pony but had drifted behind her. Jenna had a bad feeling it was because she was afraid she would fall off. Or if Jenna vanished again, they wanted to make sure that someone saw it happen.

"I'm just so sleepy." Jenna yawned. "What did you put in that drink, Ghortin?"

He glanced up from the map he was reading. "Just the normal things one puts in them. I'd say this is as much, if not more, the result of your odd traveling about between planes as it is my drink."

He started to go back to his map when Jenna's tired brain caught up with yesterday. She hadn't told him about the books. She could bring up that there were two missing books of the cuari in front of Carabella, but she wouldn't be able to say where the information came from. Meith could have been lying about who he was, but her gut told her that he had been telling the truth.

Which meant no bringing him up in front of Carabella.

She'd meant to pull Ghortin aside before they started

riding today and tell him about it, then pass the information to Rachael and Tor Ranshal. But her brain just wasn't firing right. She'd only managed to get ready to leave on time with help.

"Crell, you know where Ghortin's taking us, right? I need to talk to him about some stuff from yesterday."

Crell looked to Carabella. "Yup. I'll make sure we don't get too far ahead." She rode past, said a few words to Carabella, and passed Ghortin at a canter.

"Here now, I'm going slow so we don't wear out our horses."

"I told Crell to go ahead, there were some things about yesterday that I couldn't talk about in front of Carabella. I'm so groggy that I forgot."

Ghortin nodded and brought his horse back to her. "I thought as much, but didn't know if it was sensitive or just Carabella-sensitive."

"Carabella. There was someone besides the sciretts with me. Someone besides my invisible enemy with the lightning bolts and traps too. A cuari named Meith."

He scowled and tented his fingers in front of his mouth. He did that when he was searching his memory but wanted to look like he was thinking deep thoughts.

"Nope, the name doesn't ring a bell. I thought you said you didn't see them there?"

"He claims to not be one of the one hundred. Says not all of the first ones were killed. Those who didn't actively go against the gods and goddesses were allowed to live in the chaotic plane. He remembered Carabella from before." She gave a small smile. "He said she stood up to the rest of the cuari when the atrocities happened."

"I...I have no idea how to process that. I also don't know how to tell if he was lying or not." Ghortin rarely looked confused, but he was heading that way now.

"It sounds odd, but I think he was telling me the truth. Also, Typhonel never showed himself in my self-consciousness, but I had a feeling from him...he knew Meith and didn't hate him."

"I don't believe anyone has ever thought any of the other cuari survived. But I suppose if the gods and goddesses didn't want it known, it wouldn't be known. This is important information, for certain. And it was a good idea you kept that from her. Like Ranz, your friend's real name could drop her. Was that it? Not that this isn't huge, it is, but it will need to be shelved for now."

"No. He asked about the books of the cuari, as he was one of the ones who helped write them. All *five* of them." She didn't think shoving such a fact aside right now was a good idea. There were too many things that were interwoven to ignore anything.

"Five?" Ghortin scowled and blinked his eyes as if someone smacked him in the head. "There have never been five. Rachael has been a Guardian for over a thousand years, she would know how many books there were. There have always been three. Although I wasn't aware of them as I should have been."

"Unless it happened before she came along. Meith was extremely disturbed that we only knew of three. He left to go speak with someone—there are other non-hundred cuari there, according to him—but he didn't come back before the lightning-bolt being showed up."

Ghortin's face went through several contortions as he processed that those two extra books might be needed to stop whatever was about to occur from happening. They hadn't even tracked down the third one yet.

"Maybe he didn't come back because one of the others didn't like what you told him." He looked like he wanted to jump off his horse and start pacing, but held off when she glared at him.

"I was thinking that as well." Okay, not seriously at first. She'd been running for her life. But it had crept into her mind. Yes, the cuari who had been saved were supposedly not bad. But Sacaranz was out roaming about, hell-bent on world domination. The thought that he might have cohorts beyond the demonspawn working with him had been shoved aside as an issue to face when things settled down. They couldn't afford that thought anymore and Meith might have come across someone working with Sacaranz.

"We have to tell Rachael and Tor Ranshal, they need to know. How are we going to find these books? We need clues." As he spoke he pulled out the taran wand. "Rachael? This is Ghortin. Are you with Tor and preferably in a secure location?"

Jenna moved her horse closer to Ghortin. Rachael had a quiet voice sometimes and she must not have been in a secure location based on her whispering.

Ghortin could hear her though. "Damn. Okay, can you sneak out? Sorry, but we have some important information to pass along to you two." He nodded at something she said, then moved his hands so his words wouldn't carry through the wand. "She was in one of Resstlin's meetings. Unfortunately, by her being a victim of the dakair attacks, he's now realized her importance and is bringing her in on things. Just give her a few moments to escape. Once we tell her, she can pass the information to Tor Ranshal as he's in some meeting elsewhere. Resstlin never met a meeting he didn't like. Even if he's not in it."

The taran wand made a low chirp before Jenna could respond.

Rachael's voice was clearer now. "Much better. I'm in the new rooms he assigned me. Annoying, but no one can hear me in here. What's happened? Is everyone safe?"

Jenna smiled at the genuine concern in Rachael's voice. Not only did she miss Storm, Keanin, and Edgar, she missed the others back in the palace.

"I can't fill in all the details right now. If I can find a mage-sender in the Traanafaeren embassy in Strann, I'll send you a full report. But we've solid information that there are actually five books of the cuari, not three."

"What? Who could say that? Tor Ranshal and I have studied the lore for centuries—there are three. The lost cuari created them at the deities' command."

"It was one of them who told us. Rather, he told Jenna. When she was taken up to the chaotic plane. He claimed he wasn't the only non-hundred cuari who survived."

Silence. Ghortin handed the wand to Jenna.

"Rachael? Are you there? The one I met was named Meith. He said that only the ones who had been actively trying to overthrow the gods and goddesses were destroyed. That he hadn't been directly involved."

"I do recognize that name. But only from a long list. I'm sorry, I just can't see how we've not known all of these years. Is there any way you could have been fooled? Things are never what they seem on the chaotic plane."

"I…hold on a second." Typhonel had been more forth-coming in his appearances. He was more aware of who he was so he wanted her to know when he was present. She felt the mental equivalent of a tap on her shoulder. "*Let me?*" "There's someone who wants to talk to you. Might sound like me, don't know."

Typhonel felt like a breeze against her mind, then his voice came out of her mouth. "Guardian, do you know who I was?"

Jenna felt a chill as just a small portion of his essence showed itself. It was amazing that he hadn't blown up prior Guardians although he hadn't been aware of what and who he was. Still, that was a lot of being to have in your head.

"I believe I do. Typhonel?" Rachael sounded subdued, which was better than the close to hysteria she'd been before. Well, as close as Jenna had ever heard.

"Yes. I felt the being Meith while my vessel was in the plane. The chaotic plane would not let me make myself known, but that was Meith. He was one of the original cuari. I can't see the books you all speak of, but he wasn't lying. There are five that he created for use by the Guardians and Protectors."

"I believe you. Oh, how I wish I could sit and speak to you." Rachael no longer sounded concerned, just extremely wistful.

"If you succeed in saving these worlds, I will join my brothers and sisters. If you fail, I will die with you. There will not be time until your task is finished."

"Understood. I know I have a responsibility, and now Tor Ranshal and I have a few more. But I am weary."

Jenna knew that Rachael had first thought perhaps Jenna was to be her replacement. Rachael was old even for the long-lived kelar, and while not being morbid about it, was ready for her life to be over.

"I know, child. Your time will come. These final battles will save all or doom all. We all have our parts and no one can say what the outcome will be." With that, Typhonel vanished from her mind.

Jenna was grateful for being on her horse as his sudden departure probably would have made her fall over had she been standing. As it was she shifted a bit more than her horse would have liked, judging by the way the mare looked back at her.

"Thank you, Jenna. I will talk to Tor Ranshal and notify you if we find anything about these books. At least we have a name to start with. Take care of each other." Then Rachael cut the contact and Jenna handed to wand back to Ghortin.

"That was weird." She rubbed the side of her head. It was almost as if Typhonel's presence was echoing around in her mind.

"It was disturbing to watch. Your face was still you, but had an odd overlay to it as if someone else was imposed over your features." He secured the wand in his vest.

"Hopefully he won't have to do that very often. I know little of Guardians or Protectors, but I can't imagine that having a displaced deity present itself like that is a good thing."

"On the plus side, I'm no longer sleepy." Of course, using a god as a wake-up was sort of like using a ten-pound mallet to flatten a leaf.

"Then shall we join the others? It is going to be difficult not to speak of this around Carabella."

Jenna nodded and followed him down the trail.

CHAPTER FORTY-TWO

———————

EDGAR HELD HIS hands out from his sides and Storm and Keanin froze. "We won't harm you. Just some mercenaries trying to make things right. I *was* a merchant—once. I went to fight for our king in the Markare. What I saw there…we have to fight back."

Talia didn't waver in her stance, but she did nod to Hon and Flini to stand still. Both were drawing their swords. "That doesn't sit right. Part of it does. You were in the Markare. But a lot doesn't." She pulled an old pendant out from her shirt with her free hand. "I lack magic, but I can sense truths with this stone. You're good, I'll grant you that. It only now started indicating something was wrong. Will you take it in your hand and repeat what you said?"

Edgar paused only a second, then nodded. He took the pendant but stayed near Talia and Keanin. Storm had no idea what his plan was but was ready for anything. Keanin looked remarkably calm considering one slight move would send her sword into his throat.

Edgar wrapped his fingers around the pendant and nodded. "My name is Edgar. I am from Lithunane and serve the royal house. I have been a merchant, among other things. I promise that as long as you are not working for the demonspawn or Qhazborh's priests, we mean you and your people no harm. We are trying to get to Khelaran to find out what's happened. The things that attacked and killed our king were only pushed back; they weren't destroyed. This world is under attack. It's subtle now, but it will only get worse if we don't stop it."

Storm hadn't been expecting that and judging by the surprise on Talia's face, she wasn't either. She took the pendant back carefully. "Sir Edgar Lafavei I believe is what you are more commonly known as." She tilted her head. "I am honored to meet you. Your reputation is a worthy one." She looked to Storm and Keanin. "I trust Sir Edgar and my pendant enough not to question you two. But I believe we are honored to have you both onboard as well." She sheathed her sword, slipped the necklace over her head, and tucked the pendant back into her shirt. "Shall we go after that ship?"

Hon and Flini said nothing but went about their jobs. Flini kept the wheel, while Talia and Hon adjusted the rest of the lines, cables, and sails.

Edgar stood at the railing and kept watching the ship and the island it was obviously heading to.

"Was that wise? We don't know them," Storm said quietly as he stood next to his friend.

"We didn't have much choice. Yes, we could have fought, but enough people have died. I'd rather keep the innocent out of it. Besides, I'm not sure which side Keanin would fight for." Edgar nodded to where Talia was showing Keanin how to handle some of the lines. His hood was back a bit more than it should be and the look in his eyes was obvious.

"He's smitten. Don't know that he's gone for a guard before." There had been one who'd gone for him, Marta. He hadn't returned the interest and then she'd been replaced by a demonspawn and tried to kill him.

"He's got it bad. She is a good distraction though. He's not as on edge as he'd been, but I know he's still dealing with what happened to him."

Storm watched as Keanin laughed at something Talia said. "True."

"What's our plan, by the way? I know coming along on this was my idea, but do we have a plan?"

Storm leaned on the railing. "I know we need to stop whatever Mikasa's up to. Yes, that ship could have been taken against her wishes, but the entire bit about her demanding to stay onboard overnight? A little too much like a setup. What I don't get is what was the point? The ship could have veered off course when it left in the morning and have been far less noteworthy. This was extremely noticeable."

"Or it is to us because we know and don't trust her. Talia was the only one talking about sending someone out after the missing ship. If it had vanished during its normal travels perhaps more people would have been interested in finding it." He shook his head. "Or not. I am perplexed on this one. Think Mikasa will tell us when we get there?"

"How well do you two know her? Lady Mikasa, I mean." Hon had been nearby, but not close enough to hear their conversation at the near whisper they'd kept it at.

"I had a few run-ins with her," Storm said. "She was unpleasant."

Edgar laughed. "More than unpleasant. Why do you ask?"

"There was an altercation when she first came into town a few days ago. Nothing big, the captain wasn't involved. Just wondering if she was prone to fighting."

"Not at all. She was fighting with someone?" Storm's mind went to the obvious—Mikasa had been replaced by a demonspawn.

"More like someone was fighting with her. Or at least he was yelling loud enough. I don't think they actually came to blows, but he left when we approached to investigate the yelling."

"Who was he?" Edgar put down his glass.

"Never seen him before or since. Tall, blond, human. Dressed like someone important. He took off with some

locals who have since gone missing as soon as we came
to see what was going on."

Ravenhearst most likely. Storm watched as Edgar's
mind made a further connection that he hadn't yet.

"Any chance the locals were three women, four men?"
Edgar went on to describe the ones who had attacked
them outside of town. At least the two he'd dragged
out to the forest. Storm hadn't seen the others but anyone who knew them would recognize them from the
descriptions Edgar gave.

Hon's face grew grim. "Aye. That's them. Not people
you'd want to mess with. Part of an odd religious group
who moved in a few months ago. Mostly kept to themselves."

Storm knew Edgar would have hidden the ones he
killed well, but they'd been close enough to town that
someone should have found the bodies by now. Most
likely someone else from the group they belonged to
took the bodies away.

"This blond human, he wasn't known to you?" Storm
was getting sick of dodging around looking for Ravenhearst while keeping him from finding them.

"Nope. He arrived in town a few hours after Lady
Mikasa did. Then they had a screaming match, then he
left with the locals. Haven't seen him since."

"So, the fight between the two was only verbal?" That
fit in much better with Mikasa's behavior.

"Mostly. When we walked up she'd had his arm twisted
behind him and was lifting it high. She dropped it before
we got close. Not that a slight woman couldn't do that,
but it seemed odd for someone claiming to be nobility."

Edgar's look was grim and Storm felt the same. She
might be able to fight better than they'd assumed based
on her time in Lithunane. But that she would have done
that against Ravenhearst? Maybe they'd misjudged who
was following who in this situation.

"Thank you for that information. We'll need to watch her as well as the pirates if she's working with them." Edgar went back to looking through his glass.

Hon gave Storm a tight nod, then went to help with the ship. There wasn't a lot of wind, so they were having to make adjustments to the sails to catch what they could.

"What is going on? I thought Ravenhearst was in charge. Mikasa didn't think beyond the next court gossip. She might have fooled me about a lot of things, but her inanity was genuine," Storm said. There was no way the woman he'd known could have been a mastermind of anything. Ravenhearst might have simply pushed her too far.

Or she *had* been replaced by a demonspawn.

Talia walked over to them. Keanin drifted behind her but not too close. "We need to figure out what our plan is. If that island is Thoali, we can't charge in there."

"I wish we knew who was in command on that ship and why they're going to a pirate hideout. Even with these glasses, they're too far away to see what is happening," Edgar said.

"Which also means they can't see who's following them any easier than we can see them. Diath also had a spell put into the hull which deflects magic. It won't stop anything strong magic-wise, but it'll seriously slow down or reflect anything mid-range."

Flini laughed. "He didn't think you knew he'd added it. Was so proud of sneaking it into the wood."

Talia shook her head and turned back to Edgar and Storm. "It's illegal, as it can also stop a legal magical scan of the ship. But that law primarily refers to the big ships and this falls under a fishing boat category. Still, I officially don't know about it."

Edgar had turned back to watch the ship through his glass. "They're going into whatever dock is on there."

Talia handed her glass to Keanin. "If you have some

magic, see what you can see too."

Keanin started swearing almost the moment he put it to his eye. "They're setting it on fire!"

CHAPTER FORTY-THREE

JENNA WAS STILL thinking about the two missing books when they caught up to Carabella and Crell. They waited at a fork in the trail and had been chatting when Ghortin and Jenna arrived.

"All the secret things are taken care of?" Carabella held up her hand. "I know, I know. Trust me, if I get sucked up into that bubble, I want to go down throwing spells as no one has seen before. Not to be captured for hearing the wrong words or information forbidden to me."

Crell leaned back on her pony. "As much as I would like to say I know where I'm going, and I do, I'm not sure where *you* intended to be going. You can reach Strann either direction."

"This is true. And I had been planning on going to the left, but some new information is making me want to take a slight detour to the right." He smiled at all of them, then started down the smaller trail.

"And does this information contain things I can't hear or are you just enjoying being difficult?" Carabella fell in behind Ghortin with Jenna and Crell behind her.

"A bit of both really. The other two have no idea what I'm doing either, but *they're* not complaining." He was too smug with himself to sound annoyed.

"I was in my head," Jenna answered. She must have missed whatever great secret Rachael released. "To be fair, I wouldn't know one path from the other, but it would be nice to know why you're changing our direction."

"Something Rachael said triggered a memory. There

was a temple out here, way out here and long before we created Traanafaeren."

Carabella burst out laughing. "You're looking for the lost temple of Duliane? Seriously? That's a myth. Has always been a myth. And will never stop being one." She looked back to the other two with a sad shake of her head. "I thought he grew out of believing in things like that a thousand years ago."

"I've never heard of this temple and I'm sure Jenna hasn't either. Why are we detouring if the possible fate of the world is hanging in the balance?" Crell didn't sound any happier than the rest.

"It's not a detour. As you said, both trails get to Strann and this one might be a bit closer to Lawri, the town where the book we are looking for was spotted. There are some relics, other books to be exact, that Jenna found out about on her recent adventure. I think the temple of Duliane would be the perfect spot to look."

Carabella turned back to Jenna. "The temple supposedly was founded before the one hundred cuari were made by the mythical beings who came before us. They gathered the knowledge of the world as they knew it, then they all vanished. No one has been able to find it in thousands of years. *Thousands*, Ghortin. Including the sixty that you spent looking for it."

"He spent sixty years looking for it? How can you think you know where it is now?" Jenna knew they needed to find these two extra books, but her book hadn't mentioned them, so taking time to look for them now wasn't a great idea.

"Rachael mentioned something in our talk. I can't go into it, because it might trigger someone. Actually, Jenna mentioned it first. Your *friend*."

"I don't see how that knowing that name told you to go to a mythological ruin." Jenna had almost said Meith but caught herself.

"It didn't." He turned with a pleased smile. "But, I've always believed part of the reason no one could access the temple was because they didn't have the right *list*." He gave a nod and wink at the word list.

Jenna rubbed her eyes with her free hand. He thought that Meith's name would open the temple. Which might or might not have anything to do with the two missing books.

"Try looking up the lost temple of Duliane in your book. See if it has anything." Ghortin didn't wait for a response, just nudged his horse into a canter. The rest increased their speed, but it took Jenna a few moments to get her gray spell book out. She waved Crell to go ahead as Carabella was already out of sight. They shouldn't get separated and knowing Ghortin he wouldn't notice no one was with him for ten minutes.

The gray book had drifted to the bottom of her pack, so she stopped her horse to dig through it. She'd just closed her pack back up when a cold wind circled her and her horse.

"Who's there?" She put the spell book under her arm so she could keep one on the reins and one ready for a spell. Her mare didn't seem to notice the first pass of the oddly cold wind. She did the second. Her ears flicked back and she stomped in place. "I agree. Let's get out of here."

They'd just started down the path when the horse froze. Nothing Jenna could do would move the mare and she wasn't blinking. "Who is doing this? Show yourself. I have the ability to make you visible but it'll hurt you badly." She didn't have a spell to do that, but after her trick with the dirt in her invisible cage, she had some ideas. Sadly, it probably wouldn't actually hurt whatever was doing this.

"You need to stop." The voice sounded like many voices and all drifting along with the wind. If the wind could talk, this would have been what she expected.

"Stop what? I can't stop doing something if I don't know what it is." She mentally pulled together her version of a dirt-throwing spell. It would surround her and her horse in a mini cyclone of dirt and debris. Then it would push out until it exposed the things causing the wind.

In theory.

"Everything. You are the tear between the worlds that will undo us all." The voices grew louder and her horse unfroze. Which just meant she was freaked out even more.

"It's okay, I promise." Jenna kept her voice low and soothing as she patted the horse's neck. She also gathered the spell she'd put together and pushed it out. At first, nothing happened beyond the wind growing stronger and colder. She wasn't certain but a dark spot in the sky seemed to appear directly over her and her horse.

Then the dirt, debris, and pebbles started flying around them. She comforted her horse and leaned low as the debris storm circled them and slowly moved outward. Dark shapes appeared but they vanished before she could get a good look. With a popping sound the dark hole above her closed and she let her spell drop.

"What's taking you so long?" Crell came jogging back down to her. "I yelled at Ghortin to wait up, but he and Carabella got a good lead."

Jenna nudged her horse and she slowly took a few steps forward. "Something ambushed me. I'm fine, so is my horse, but I think we need to stick together. I'm not sure if whatever it was came from this world. It reminded me a bit of the being who was after me in the chaotic plane—just more of them this time." She shivered; that was a thought to process in a nice warm pub far from here. Not on the open trail.

"We can check the area if you want." Crell had her sword across her lap and watched the trees around them.

"I didn't see anything, but something was there. Let's catch up to them before Ghortin decides to do this on his own."

Crell didn't put away her sword, but she nodded and turned her pony around. Jenna moved her mare to stay close behind. The horse seemed more than happy to do so.

Carabella and Ghortin were arguing about something as they caught up with them, but as usual, dropped their conversation as Crell and Jenna came around the corner.

"Is everything all right? You had us worried." Carabella looked shaken at whatever Ghortin had told her, but she wasn't unconscious or in a spell bubble, so it probably didn't have anything to do with the other cuari.

"Something spoke to me and then tried to stop my horse and me. It froze the horse for a while, but just caused a lot of wind from what I could tell. Until I convinced it that it needed to move on." She rubbed her arms as a remnant of the chill came back. "It reminded me of whatever was after me in the chaotic plane."

"Were you casting any magic?" Ghortin asked.

"No. Not until I called up a spell to make whoever was attacking visible. They vanished instead."

"That's it, we stay in teams, preferably all of us together. No one goes off on their own." Carabella had recovered from whatever had upset her but was now focused on Jenna.

"Now I know the world is ending." Ghortin turned his horse and started slowly walking down the trail. "A cuari admitting it is safer to work with others."

"Ha. I always work with others, just not you." She dropped in closely behind him.

Crell shook her head when Jenna motioned for her to go ahead of her. "As the only non-magic user in this bunch, I seem to be the safest. I want all of you where I can see you."

Jenna shrugged and followed Carabella. "Why did you hide from him for all those years?"

"We fought…or was it that he broke a vase? Damaged one of my long-running spells?" She waved her hands. "Something. I don't remember, do you Ghortin?"

He didn't look back. "No, but I wasn't the one pouting."

"I don't pout. Whatever it was, it wasn't big enough to remember. After a while, it became a game. I was hoping to get to a thousand years. My plan was to drop in on him as if nothing happened on the first day of the first month of that thousandth year. Alas, reality reared its annoying head, and I had to break it off early." She turned to Jenna. "But nine hundred years, eleven months, and three days is still not bad."

Jenna opened her mouth to say something about how perverse that was, then decided staying out of it was a better idea. "Life is extremely different for you immortal folks. You do realize that's not how regular people function, right?"

Ghortin laughed. "You are not normal, my dear. You're unique and we've no idea what your abilities or skills truly will become. Nor how long you'll live. Kelar aren't immortal but they do live for hundreds, if not up to a thousand years. Rachael is eighteen hundred years old. Who she is as a Guardian has given her an extremely long life."

That was interesting and not something she'd thought of before. If she were truly human any relationship she and Storm had would be short by his lifespan. She was an extremely modified human, but the fact that Ghortin didn't know her possible lifespan didn't comfort her.

"Easy there. Just means that you're like him." Carabella let her horse drift back to Jenna. "He's the only half-cuari in the world, and he will always be the only one. The one hundred are supposed to be sterile. There can only be one hundred of us you know. Rules. Anyway, a few thousand years ago, I fell in love with a knight. A human knight. He was funny, brave, charming, and like all mortals, too short-lived. He died before I realized I was pregnant." She got a wistful smile. "No one could explain how I conceived, but then this one came along and changed my entire life."

"What was his name? He was from Strann, I assume?"

"Jhantin. He was. Back then travel between the kingdoms was unheard of except for the hundred. We cuari found it easier if we kept the lands apart from each other. As you've seen, they don't always play well together."

"Does Ghortin look like him?" Jenna didn't add that he didn't look like Carabella at all aside from their height.

"He does. He really does."

"Not only is the cuari now wanting to work together, but she is also now becoming melancholy. What is this world coming to?"

"You are so droll." Carabella shook her head and turned to Jenna. "Did you find whatever you were looking for in that book? The whatever it is that I can't know about that might give us a better direction than Ghortin's hunch? Please say you have."

"I haven't had much time. But I did find the name in question. Was this temple we're looking for ever called the lost floating city? I found a reference to that."

Both Ghortin and Carabella shook their heads. Jenna figured if she refrained from saying the actual names of places and people, they might not trigger Carabella. The lost floating city was called something long and unpronounceable, but she got the point across by just what it was.

There had been two sections that mentioned Meith, and a lot of other cuari. But the going was slow and the stories dealing with them long and tedious. So far nothing indicating there were two more books or that not all of the original cuari beyond the one hundred were dead.

Ghortin picked up a little more speed, Carabella rode in behind him, and Jenna went back to her book.

An hour later, she was almost dozing off when a line of text caught her eye. It was the third passage with Meith's name listed and it mentioned the time of treasure and all lost things. It called it a secret temple of sol. That was a little too obvious, but she was willing to work with it. "What about the secret temple of sol? 'A light in the darkness lost to all but the blind.' Does that make sense to you?" It certainly didn't to her.

"Yes! There was a mention of that and the light! Although did the book say sol or sun?" Ghortin turned in his saddle.

"Sol…wait…now it says sun. I know I'm tired, but what the heck? The words changed." Jenna kept watching them but nothing else moved. She rubbed her eyes.

"Ha! You doubted me, but we're almost there! I've found it!" Ghortin got his horse to a jog and took off down the trail.

CHAPTER FORTY-FOUR

"WHAT? THE SHIP?" Edgar focused his glass. "Oh, crap—the dock. People are running off of the *Golden Harpy* and they have torches. I can't see who, but I'd say more people were on board than we'd been told."

Storm looked in that direction but while he could see there was an island, a ship, and flames, that was about it. The people were too small.

Flini was still at the wheel, but Hon came over to take it so he could use his glass. "They are burning the dock and the town." He looked over to Talia. "Why? Most people in Erlinda didn't even know this island was out here, whether it's pirates or not. Why steal a ship to attack the island?"

"I say we find out. Where there was one demonspawn there could be more." Edgar turned to Talia with a bow. "Captain, we await your orders."

Talia slowly shook her head. "It's madness, but you've all joined in. I want to find out what happened to Diath and any more of our people who might have ended up on that ship. And hope by all that's holy that none are demonspawn." She turned to Edgar. "Do you know how they change them into people? Could they have all been changed on that ship? Is it a spell?"

Keanin stepped forward before Edgar could respond. "I know more of them than the others. I am also more than just a little bit of a magic user. Those things can and do take the likeness of the people they replace, but it takes longer than a few hours. And the people they replace are murdered. If they were going to call forth enough demonspawn to replace the people on that ship, they would have done so overnight, which might have been what their initial plans were. Something changed them." He glanced to Storm then pushed back his hood. "And I would be honored if you called me Keanin. At least for as long as we may survive." He gave one of his extravagant bows.

Talia's eyes went wide. She might have figured he was a courtier, but Lord Keanin Plantarie was almost a prince.

"Thank you. I am honored."

Edgar and Keanin looked to Storm.

"Fine." He shoved back his hood as well and lifted his eye patch. "I'm keeping the Crailian markings as it might throw enough people off when we go on our suicide run. Second guess before they challenge a Crailian. But I'm Corin. I prefer to be called Storm, and definitely not prince."

Talia had almost been ready to bow when he shook his head. "Nope. No bowing either. Just Storm. It could mean your lives as well as ours if the wrong people find out who we are."

Hon let out a whistle. "Well, at least if we're going down, we're going down with a nice class of people."

Flini started to say something when an explosion came from the island. They'd gotten closer, but were still far enough that the explosion was more of a series of distant popping sounds. But the subsequent waves were large enough to rock the boat.

"Change course! Larger waves are coming. The explosions are coming from under the water." Talia and Hon adjusted the rigging as more waves, these much higher than the first, raced for them. "We don't want them to hit us broadside. Tie yourselves to something!"

The boat turned barely enough to present a smaller target for the waves but the jostling wasn't as bad as it had looked ready to be. Still, everyone was tossed about a bit.

"How and why are they blowing things up under the water?" Hon looked more than a little rattled as he watched the water.

"My guess would be caves," Edgar yelled as another series of waves came their way. "But whether it's the ones being attacked who are destroying what they have or the people from the *Golden Harpy*, I have no idea."

Talia paced the deck in between waves. She couldn't go far as she needed to hang on to the webbing. "I still need to know what happened to my brother. Again, I'm offering anyone who wants to leave to take the dingy." She was pointedly looking at Storm and Keanin.

Storm recognized the look and laughed. "You don't want to go down in history as the person responsible for killing nobles."

"I don't want to be responsible for killing a prince *and* nobles. No offense, but that's not a good thing to have tied to my memory."

"Trust me, he's tougher than he looks." Keanin started laughing. "Okay, when he's not dressed like that. He does make a good Crailian with that scowl, though."

Storm laughed at Keanin's comment. "We have our own tasks, and one of them is tracking down possible demonspawn incursions. This trip so far has been more dangerous than expected, but better to find out now than when it explodes and takes out the entire kingdom."

"Or the world." Edgar kept watching the island but the waves were dying down. "What we faced in the Markare and what seems to be happening all over Traanafaeren is minor compared to what will happen to the world if the followers of Qhazborh and the demonspawn win. The enemy is conducting feints right now. Tests to see how easy it would be to destroy us all."

"Far too easy." Keanin also kept his eyes on the island. His face was grim, but Storm knew he wasn't thinking of what was on the island.

Talia glanced to Storm but he shook his head. Keanin was still working through too much. He'd talk about it when he was ready.

"Then we all go." She nodded. "I promise I will not do anything out of the ordinary to save any of you. At least anything more than what I'd do to save my crew."

"Agreed." Edgar nodded toward the island. "They are still attacking whatever else was by the dock, most likely a town or hideout of some sort. But no more explosions that I've seen. The back of the island is too steep for us to go over. The fighting would be done and our people gone by the time we got to that side. But if we go around the island and come from the other side…we might be able to land at that beach and approach on foot."

Edgar's eyes were better than Keanin's or Flini's, and the non-magic users were still having trouble seeing anything. But first Keanin and the Flini nodded as they saw what he was talking about.

"I see it. Captain?" Flini took back the wheel from Hon.

"Do what the man suggested. It's better than charging into the place, cannons blazing." Talia grinned. "Yes, we have cannons, hidden like the rowing stations, and only two, but there are cannons. I'd rather not use them unless we have no other choice. They take forever to load, reload, and they rock this boat badly."

Hon laughed. "Diath almost capsized it completely the first time he used one. More of a danger to us than anyone else in my opinion."

"Agreed." Talia made some more changes to the sail.

"But you still want me to get them ready."

"Yup." She flashed him a smile. "Always be prepared, even if it's just to die."

Hon muttered to himself as he went below the decks.

"I'd like to see them if you don't mind?" Edgar closed

up his glass and tucked it away.

"Be my guest, Hon can tell you what to do." Talia turned back to the island but directed her next question to Storm. "What's it like being a prince?"

Storm laughed. "Not near as much fun as some would think."

"Which is why he spends all of his time out of the palace." Keanin perked up and came over. "The tales I could tell you!"

"I will take you up on that. I know the best little pub on the outskirts of Craelyn. I take it you'll still be in disguise then?" She turned to Storm.

He flipped his patch down and tugged his hood up. "For as long as I can. We need to see what happened to the ruling family when they were attacked. If I have to go in as Prince Corin, I will but that wouldn't be my first choice."

The ship rocked and Hon popped his head up from belowdecks. "That wasn't us, honest."

"That was something deep below. Extremely deep below." Talia used a glass, then started swearing. "You don't need magic. Look there." She handed her glass to Storm and Keanin looked through his borrowed one.

"What are we looking at?" Keanin kept looking at the horizon but Talia tilted his glass down.

"Here it comes again. Hold on!"

Storm finally saw the wave coming toward them. Unlike the ones caused by the explosion, this wave seemed to have a figure in it. A massive figure. "What in the hell is that?" The thing vanished before hitting the boat, but the boat rocked wildly again.

"I have no idea. Flini, get us to the other side of the island. Hopefully, shallow water will get it to back off. If it hits us directly, we're done for."

Hon motioned below deck. "Edgar and I have both cannons loaded and ready. If it makes another pass, do you want us to fire?"

"Damn it. Hitting anything underwater isn't easy. I'd guess if you were able to fire right when it gets closer to the surface, maybe the water wouldn't slow down the cannonball so much? It would be better if it would come out of the water, but I don't know that we want that if the cannonball doesn't hurt it."

"Are there sea monsters in your waters? A friend told me about ones that used to terrorize coastal town a thousand years ago, but he said they were long gone." Storm now wished that he'd paid more attention to Ghortin's tales.

"He'd have been right. We don't have anything beyond children's stories about them. But whatever this is, it's huge."

"And it's coming around again," Keanin yelled as he pointed to the front of the boat. The arrow-shaped waves were coming right for them.

"I'm trying to turn but we won't make it in time," Flini swore as he turned the wheel, but the movement of the boat was far slower than whatever was out there.

"Hang on!" Talia shoved a rope into Keanin's hands. Storm had already grabbed one when the ship went airborne and long tentacles reached over the deck.

CHAPTER FORTY-FIVE

JENNA, CARABELLA, AND Crell took off after Ghortin.

"I thought we were staying in pairs?" Jenna didn't see him but the trail was narrow and twisty. The trees had owned it for a long time.

"He agrees to rules unless they pertain to him," Carabella said as she ducked beneath a branch. "Slow down, darn you!"

Ghortin waited near a clump of trees. "It's this way."

Crell brought up the rear but caught his words. "How did knowing that another term for this place was mentioned in the book Jenna has make you conclude it was this way?"

"The trail is here. We'll have to go slow; it's never been large and I'd guess no one has been this way in hundreds of years. As for the how, mentioning the temple of the sun in the book she has connects it to the lost temple of Duliane. And I know where the temple of the sun is. Found the ruins when I was looking for Duliane, but since I didn't have that book, I didn't realize they were the same." He held up his hand to make a point. "But the tip-off was the phrase, 'A light in the darkness, lost to all but the blind'. That was always used in references to the lost temple of Duliane." He looked at the thin trail. "I think we'll do best to walk our horses in. If I can find a safe shelter, we might secure them before we go in too far."

Jenna put her book back into her pack and got off her horse. She had her sword and added a dagger. What she wanted was a flashlight. The forest grew dark extremely fast and while she or Ghortin could use glows, she didn't because he wasn't.

"Is there a reason you're not lighting the place up a bit? My eyes are good, but it's getting darker in here." Crell stayed in the last position but she was close behind.

"If this is the lost temple, which I'm still doubting, magic of any kind is a trigger for disaster." Carabella carefully led her horse around a huge tree root. "The ground itself will open and the invaders will be swallowed. Or so it's claimed. To be safe, no one should use magic until we're back out on that nice actual road." The tone in her voice indicated what she still thought of the wisdom of this excursion.

"That would have been good to tell us before we walked in here, Ghortin." Jenna had held off on the glows just because he had. But as it was getting darker with each step, she would have probably been reaching to pull some up.

"Pish, I knew Carabella knew and figured she could tell you. Now everyone be quiet for a moment." He paused and lowered his head before nodding to himself and veering off through some trees.

"Are we close? Not very well hidden if it's this close to a road." Jenna wasn't getting threatening feelings from the trees around them, but she didn't think they were happy about them walking through their forest.

"What? Oh no. I just recalled where I used to camp when I was searching out here. It was a nice little clearing and perfect for the horses." He shoved some struggling saplings out of the way. "A bit rougher than I recall, but it'll still do. Right, boy?" He patted his horse on the nose as he walked out into a small sheltered area. There was a small stream and grass, so once their packs were off, the horses were happy.

"Before we go, let me do something. This isn't magic,

but a gift I have." Carabella turned to look her horse in the eye. "We would appreciate it if you stay here and wait for us?" The horse tilted its head, then nodded. She did the same to the other two horses as well as Crell's pony.

"How do you do that without magic?" Jenna adjusted her sword belt as they followed Ghortin out of the clearing.

"It's something we can do. The one hundred were created to watch over all of the sentient beings in this land, including animals."

"That would be a handy talent at times, I'd think." Crell was staying to the back and had drifted further behind as they left the horses. A glance back confirmed that Crell's hand was on the hilt of her sword and she watched everything around them as she walked.

"It is," Carabella said. "Now, Ghortin, I know you're excited, but if you break a leg on something out there, we're leaving you behind. Without magic, we wouldn't be able to move you."

Ghortin didn't say anything but noticeably slowed down. He patted a stone marker they passed. The writing was almost completely worn away, but it appeared to say Temple of the Sun.

Not being able to pull in magic was going to be hard. Jenna doubted that they were just going to be able to walk up and get the books and whatever else was in there without a fight or challenges. She patted the hilt of her sword and reminded herself that she could do this. But after spending the past year learning magic it was going to be hard not to reach for it.

"What are you sighing about?" Carabella dropped back to walk near her.

"I was just realizing that a bit over a year ago I'd never seen anyone with magic, let alone used it myself. Now I'm having a hard time reminding myself that whatever happens out here, I can't use it."

"It becomes harder to not use it the stronger you get. It's easier for me right now as that damn bubble keeps trying to grab me. But we magic users become dependent on our magic skills far too easily."

"Shh." Ghortin held up his right hand and stood still. He was listening for something, or to something, but unlike finding his old campground, he didn't look happy. He motioned for them to come close. "We are being surrounded. I'm not sure by who. And no, Crell, this wasn't your fault. It's mine. I forgot that there was a sensor just past that last marker. I never triggered it before because I never came through with a cuari before. I should have realized that would be an issue."

"How screwed are we? And why would Carabella trigger it? They liked the cuari, right?" Jenna caught herself before she said it had been the cuari who had made this. They *were* the cuari. The story of a lost race was in place to keep the one hundred cuari from exposure to things they couldn't know.

"They did. But the trigger means that we can open the temple if we get to it. I wasn't a threat before, so while I'd heard rumors there were safeguards nothing ever triggered with only me." He nodded. "We might have to fight something, but we do have a chance of getting in. This is good news." His smile wasn't as reassuring as it should be.

"I can go back and wait with the horses if that will help." Carabella looked torn, she clearly wanted to see what was in the ruins too.

Crell shook her head. "I was briefly a treasure seeker in my youth. If you being here triggers the defensive response, then you being here is the only way we get in. This better be worth it, Ghortin. I can feel something around us now."

"Then let's go faster. I know where to go, even with this overgrowth. We might be able to get into the ruins before they stop us." Ghortin returned to walking but kept a slow pace. "When I raise both hands, we all run, directly ahead. Don't stop. Oh, keep as quiet as you can—magic won't be the only thing causing a deadly response here. Or in the ruins"

Jenna held on to her sword. Running with them wasn't easy even without being in a very dense forest. And being hunted by some unknown but most likely supernatural enemies. Then Ghortin raised his hands and they took off running.

There were faint noises in the woods around them but their attackers didn't show themselves until Ghortin had burst out into a clearing in front of a massive ruin.

Four beings in such heavy padded armor it was impossible to tell what gender or species they were appeared from nowhere in front of the entrance to the ruins. All raised wicked-looking two-handed-long-swords and charged forward.

Ghortin and the others spread out to fight. And Jenna soon found herself facing one of the armored beings.

She swore as the attacker swung high and barely missed her head. She'd gotten better at using the sword in the last few months, but this person was far better than her. Carabella's admonishment not to use magic was looking less and less feasible. She didn't want them to be detected magically, but she also wanted to stay alive.

She made a feint with her dagger, then managed to nick their leg. Unfortunately, the heavy padding they wore kept her from getting a flesh shot but they did take a step back.

The others were holding their own against their attackers, even Carabella. Jenna hadn't seen her fight before, but she knew what she was doing. Her attacker was bleeding from a few strikes she'd gotten in.

Ghortin ran his through, shoved the person into the heavy brush, and raced into the temple. The attacker she

faced turned to follow and she bolted after it. A swipe
at the back of their legs brought him down. They rolled
and tried to get up, but couldn't. At first, Jenna thought
she'd really hamstrung the person, but then she saw one
of Crell's throwing stars in their back. The being flickered
then vanished. The attackers weren't living but were still
deadly. Crell and Carabella were still holding their own
so she ran after Ghortin.

The ruins started shaking as she entered the main doorway. Using magic or not, something knew they'd come
inside. The entrance was a spacious foyer that led to three
stone arches with dim hallways behind them. All looked
the same and there was no sign of Ghortin. The books
could be in any of them or none.

"Damn it." She'd said it to herself, but the ruins shook
harder. Ghortin was right about the sound sensing too.
She shut up and took the archway to the far left. The
dust on the floor was thick and undisturbed. No one
had come this way in a long time. She ran to the middle
doorway—the same.

With a sigh, she ran to the third doorway. The temple
was shaking harder now and she almost fell twice. Still no
sign of Crell or Carabella having come inside yet.

The dust was disturbed in this hallway and dim lights
sputtered to life as she walked past them. They were
ancient, battered-looking, and faded as soon as she passed.
They were better than nothing, but it was still dim. Not
sure if the lights were a good sign or not, she kept going
until she stumbled over something large.

Ghortin was on the floor ahead of her. His eyes were
locked open and his body was stiff. She dropped to one
knee and felt for a pulse. It was there, slow, extremely so,
but it was there. He was alive but something had stunned
him. They couldn't use magic, but that didn't mean that
the place itself couldn't.

Jenna stayed down as if she were still checking on

Ghortin. It could have been a spell triggered by his coming down here. Or there was someone else in here.

The corridor was silent and a faint light came from the far end. Enough dust had been stirred up by her and Ghortin's arrival to show tiny lines of light crisscrossing the area. If she hadn't dropped when she did whatever spell hit that Ghortin would have struck her as well.

The lines of light looked like something you'd see around banks or in high-end museums back on Earth. But those were lasers and she doubted the technology was the same.

But dealing with them might be similar. She carefully pulled Ghortin off to one side of the corridor. She wanted him out of the way, but moving him also stirred up a lot more dust and pointed out where all of the light lines were.

It looked like the lowest beam of light was a bit below her hips. She could crawl through, providing that there wasn't a person at the other end. She waited a few more moments just in case Crell or Carabella came in. While she waited she grabbed handfuls of the small stones scattered along the edges and wrote out, "duck". They might not have much time before this place shook itself apart and she couldn't waste it waiting for them. She patted Ghortin—he seemed to be breathing easier now—then kept low as she crawled toward the weak light.

CHAPTER FORTY-SIX

S TORM WAS THE closest to the long bluish tentacles
slapping the boat. He grabbed another rope further
up the deck and started attacking the tentacles with his
sword. The tip of the closest one was the size of his thigh.

Luckily, they were flesh and when he sliced through
the end of one, all of the tentacles pulled back. The part
he'd cut off flopped on the deck like a lizard tail.

Flini kept turning the ship to get away from the monster. He got them turned around but they weren't moving
quickly.

"I think the monster is hanging on to us," Talia yelled as
she came up to Storm. "Damn, that thing smells awful."
The part that Storm had sliced off had stopped moving,
but he agreed on the smell. It was longer than his leg and
slimy-looking, so picking it up wasn't an option.

The boat started shaking, but if the size of the tentacles
were any indication, the beast below the water was large
enough to rip the boat apart without a problem. So why
wasn't it?

"It must be working with someone." Keanin made
his way closer. "There are spells for controlling animals,
it takes an incredibly strong mage, but it can be done.
Something is controlling it."

"Makes sense. That blow had to have hurt, yet it's not
leaving us." Storm made his way to the back of the ship.
The water was churning and it looked like they were
being pulled in reverse, but he couldn't see the creature.

Hon and Edgar ran on deck.

"The cannons are ready, but I don't know they'll do

any good," Hon said.

Edgar took out his glass and started swearing as he ran to the side of the boat. "The ship is leaving the island. It looks like there had been two other ships docked there, but they're both burning."

"Which direction is she going?"

"Looks like north. How far away is the channel your ships use for safe passage along the coast?"

"They could go north for a while before they'd have to cut in. If they don't do it by the Gillion reef, they'll end up smashed." Hon was trying to adjust the sails to give them more power, but whatever was holding them wasn't budging.

"So they stole the ship and went to a secret pirate lair, just to destroy it? And let that monster out?" Keanin looked over where Storm was trying to see the creature.

"I'd guess it's a kraken. But letting it out could have been their focus if they knew it was located there. Think of what a kraken would do to local sea travel if it was free." Edgar was still looking through his glass, but the flames had increased on the island. Also, once the *Golden Harpy* cleared the area, even the non-magic users could see the island.

The boat shuddered and groaned. The kraken had decided grabbing it on the deck was a bad idea, even something that large wouldn't want its tentacles being hacked off, but it still wasn't letting go.

"If someone from that ship was controlling it, shouldn't it have backed off once they left?" Flini was holding the wheel steady, but the muscles in his arms were showing how hard he was fighting.

"One would think, but I'm not a magic user, so I'm not cognizant of spells." Talia looked at the limp sails. "Many sea creatures are territorial. If we could jerk free and pick up a good wind, maybe it would back off."

"I can try." Keanin didn't sound confidant but he lifted

his shoulders when Talia looked toward him. "I could try and get us free and get some wind for the sails. Well, not real wind, Ghortin warned me to never muss with the weather. But I can create something to move the sails. I think."

Storm knew that Keanin's outlook on magic had changed drastically since his attack, but this was surprising even with that consideration. Keanin often fell for women quickly, but this was fast even for him.

"Might as well try, just don't break the boat." Talia and Hon readied the sails as Storm and Edgar kept watch for the kraken.

Keanin closed his eyes and held out his arms. Storm felt a rumble under his feet and a tingle that went through the thick soles of his boots.

Then the water below them started frothing as two tentacles darted out, and one grabbed Storm around the waist. Edgar was there in a second sawing at the tentacle and Storm tried punching it.

Keanin dropped his arms and the water stilled but the tentacles kept coming.

"Keep it up! The magic is hurting it, that's why it's fighting back!" Storm dropped to the deck as Edgar cut through the tentacle.

Another took its place.

Edgar wasn't a strong magic user, but he ran to the next closest tentacle and flung a spell at it at the same time he swung his sword.

The kraken pulled back all of its remaining tentacles and the boat snapped backward.

"Damn it, my spell has the sails moving but we're going toward the island, not away from it." Sweat was falling down Keanin's forehead as he fought to hold the spell to get them some more distance. The kraken had let them go but could grab them at any time.

Edgar watched as the island grew closer. "The kraken,

or whatever it was, isn't following us anymore, and maybe we can see if what's left on the island will tell us where that thing came from. I have a feeling Ghortin would be interested in another mythological creature appearing."

Storm watched the *Golden Harpy* vanish from sight. "I'm thinking catching up to them before Craelyn isn't possible?"

"No." Talia looked in the same direction, then turned back. "They're on the run. They'll have to find a place to wait overnight. There's no way to get into the channel to Craelyn until the morning tide shift. But this was too well planned, I'm sure they have a spot to hide. It's no longer just a missing ship and crew, they left Erlinda with an agenda."

"We'll get your brother back. I promise." Keanin was still focusing on keeping the boat moving but glanced toward her with a smile.

"Thank you. Looks like you three get a detour before Craelyn anyway."

The fires on the island went out the moment the *Golden Harpy* was out of sight. Edgar looked through his glass. "I'm not sure they did burn it. Okay, the two ships that were at the dock are gone, but with the amount of damage we saw earlier, there should be nothing left." He handed his glass to Storm.

Storm looked, but the scene was as Edgar described. Two very large ships listing as burnt husks at the dock, but a mostly intact group of buildings near the dock. "I don't see anyone. Damn. I'm missing a lot of reasons why here. How I get. They used magic, but why?"

"Hopefully getting on that island will give us some answers." Talia and her crew brought the boat around. The dock wasn't stable, but they could get close enough to secure the ship with the anchor and take the dingy to shore. Flini would stay onboard, ready to cast off if things went bad.

"If those were their ships, where are the pirates?" Hon asked as they pulled the small craft up on the shore. "If they were pirates."

Edgar picked up a tattered piece of black fabric floating on the foam at the shore's edge. "Missing part, but pretty sure they were pirates." He held up the familiar black and white flag. "But that doesn't answer where the people are."

Everyone had their swords at the ready. It looked like there was no one here, but they also hadn't seen any bodies. The three nearby buildings showed no people, alive or dead.

"What's that back there?" Keanin had gone closer to the back of the building they'd just searched but was pointing behind it. "I hear water down there."

"You three check that, and we'll make sure no one is hiding in the far building." Talia and Hon walked down along the water.

Keanin looked torn.

"Go with them; they're more likely to run into something than we are." Storm waved toward the other two. Keanin smiled and took off after them.

"Seriously, I've never seen him like this." Edgar shook his head.

"Me either. Hope she doesn't get annoyed at his behavior," Storm said as they walked toward the back. The building was almost built into a black rock wall, but the backside of the building, the plants, even the dirt around the back were also black. Unlike the rock, they hadn't started that way.

"The underwater explosion we saw was here." Edgar rubbed some of the soot between his fingers then wrinkled his nose. "Cinderbrush. Flammable and reacts strongly to focused magic. And grows in the desert, not in the middle of the ocean. They brought it with them."

A narrow flight of stairs was cut into the rock wall and

that was also where the sound of water was coming from.

Both put their swords away, there would be no room to swing them, but drew daggers. Edgar spoke a soft spell and a glow appeared over his hand.

"Something stinks, and it's more than just the cinderbrush."

"It smells like that kraken, or at least the parts on the boat." Storm covered his nose as best he could as the smell grew worse near the bottom. The tunnel spread out to a shallow bay completely encased in the black rock. "Are those bars?"

The water was dark, so seeing through it was impossible. But a cave opening near the end of the tunnel let in a bit of light. It also had what looked to be heavy iron bars at its end. Or did. They were twisted and stuck up in odd angles. Something broke them, then something else widened the gap.

Edgar let out a low whistle. "They used more than just the cinderbrush and magic. Rather, they used *a lot* of cinderbrush and magic."

"The pirates were holding a kraken here? And the people with Mikasa knew, broke it out, then are just sailing up to Craelyn for the start of the tournament?" Storm had no idea what was going on. They'd had monsters and animals from myth appear out in the Markare. The theory was that they had come back through the portal. They were nowhere near the portal now. So where did a kraken come from and how did the pirates get it?

"Doesn't make sense, and I wish I knew who was in charge on the *Golden Harpy*. But those would be my guesses."

Storm looked around but there wasn't anything else of importance here. How a group of pirates captured a mythological sea monster would be a good question for when they found the pirates. "Let's go up and see if the others found anything."

Edgar still had his small glow so Storm followed him up. Edgar was at the top of the stairs when he started swearing.

"Come up slowly with your hands raised. No weapons. I have three archers ready to shoot you where you stand."

CHAPTER FORTY-SEVEN

———

JENNA CREPT FORWARD on her hands and knees. It probably wasn't doing her scabbard or sword any good being dragged like this, but the choices were slim. The lights continued to flare faintly on, then off once she passed them. At least the shaking had stopped.

She'd thought the hallway she was in ended up in a room, but it was just another open space with two more arches leading different directions.

"Seriously? Is this a mousetrap?" The rumbling that followed her words reminded her to keep her voice inside of her head. She went to the middle of the space, grabbed some dirt, and tossed it up near her. Yup. More magic-powered light bars crossing the area. If she found these books in here she might have to be carried out, her knees were already aching. Unlike the other section, no one had been down either direction for a long time and the dust looked the same in both.

The annoying thing was that with a spell or two she could have probably disabled the sensors. And possibly brought the entire thing down on her head.

She closed her eyes, took in a deep breath, and tried to reach out with anything other than magic as to which direction she should go. This would be a great time for some insight from Typhonel, but he wasn't hanging around.

The left side seemed more likely, although she couldn't say why. She tossed some more dirt that way to verify the bands of light were still at about the same level, then crawled on.

The hall was mercifully much shorter and did end in a room. An empty room.

She rubbed her eyes and kept her swearing inside her head. All of this and it was the wrong side. Or both were empty and she'd just keep crawling around until her knees gave out or the building collapsed.

More dust got in her eyes. She'd stirred a little up when she came in, but it still shouldn't be floating around. Unless there was a crack in the walls somewhere.

It took a few minutes, but she found a thin line between the stones on the far wall. It was too neat to have been a natural crack so she started pushing on it. It wouldn't budge so she threw her entire weight against it and tumbled into a small room when it gave way. The door started closing but she got a rock in the way to block it first.

The room was dim but glowed softly. When she'd first come to this world, she and Storm had to hide out in a cave and the walls had this glowing moss. This light was the same. The room was empty aside from a good-sized chest.

That wouldn't open.

She sighed after trying everything to open it. Getting herself and this thing out down both halls without triggering the sensors, or getting so frustrated that she resorted to magic, wasn't going to be easy.

"Jenna?" Crell's whisper came from the crack and was low but the ruins still rumbled in response.

Jenna scooted as close as she could but didn't push open the door. That rumble had been sharper than the others, they might have limited time.

"I'm here." Another jolt. "Found something. Must move fast." She cut her words but this time the ruins shook sharply and continued. Dust and what felt like ceiling debris rained down on her.

Crell didn't say anything but the door started to move. Jenna scrambled back to the chest and pulled. It wasn't as heavy as it could be given the size, but still heavy enough that dragging it while crawling wasn't going to be good.

She and Crell got the door open as wide as possible, and with Crell pulling and Jenna pushing they got the chest out.

Crell leaned forward to whisper to her. "We got Ghortin out. Carabella is trying to work on a non-magical way to block the sensors."

The ruins gave a smaller rumble, but Jenna still kept her response to a nod. Then they push-pulled the chest down the hallway and through to the next. Crell did point to it once with a questioning look, but Jenna just shrugged and tugged on the lock. It looked old enough to fall apart in her hands, but it hadn't budged yet.

They made it to the main foyer, but still no sign of Carabella, so they'd stayed on their knees.

No one had said anything, Jenna hadn't used a bit of magic, but the moment they crossed into the foyer with the chest, the walls started shaking and didn't stop.

Carabella came dashing back into the ruins. "Use your magic, Jenna. This thing is going down whether you do or not."

Jenna stumbled around, cast a spell to lift the chest, much harder than it should be but it got it off the ground, and the three of them ran out of the ruins.

The shaking got worse and they moved further back to where Ghortin was still unconscious. Seconds later the entire structure collapsed in on itself.

Crell let out a whistle. "I hope whatever you're looking for is in there. No one is going back now."

Ghortin started groaning and sat up. "What happened?" Then he saw the dust rising from the collapsed building. "What did you do?"

Jenna pointed to the chest. "We got that out. But we didn't get much of a chance. That place was collapsing with or without us."

Ghortin stiffly got to his feet and went to the chest. "This was it? No rooms full of riches? No secret arcane relics? Maybe they're still in there." He started toward the wreckage but Crell stopped him.

"There's nothing left. Trust me."

"But…" He let his words drop when Carabella stood next to Crell. Neither of them looked like they'd had an easy time with their attackers.

"Maybe we should look in the chest?" Jenna looked around. They were in the open here and there was no way anyone within a few miles didn't hear and probably feel that implosion.

"You always were my favorite." Ghortin spun on his heel and marched to the chest.

"Maybe not here, though." Jenna grabbed one handle and Crell quickly grabbed the other before Ghortin could reach it.

Carabella folded her arms and scowled at Ghortin. "Agreed. His campsite isn't much, but it's more secluded than this."

Ghortin sighed and led the way back to his camp. "I doubt anyone would be out here. The Lawri trail is far less traveled than the one that goes to the capital."

Carabella strode at his heels. "While I'm sure we are all grateful for your opinion, we all almost died back there trying to get this chest. I for one do not want it to be stolen in front of us."

The horses nickered softly at their arrival and a thin green shield dropped as they approached. Ghortin's shield still being in place was a good sign. Provided no one had followed them.

"What are you glaring at? I thought Ghortin was the one who wanted to go back?" Crell asked Jenna. She let go of her end of the chest, prompting Jenna to as well. But Jenna kept looking around the woods.

"I don't feel secure. It's like someone is watching us. I

felt it when we ran out of the ruins but wasn't as aware of it as we were trying not to die. Now I really feel it." It was as if no matter which direction she turned, there was always someone behind her.

"It's okay, no one followed us." Ghortin had dropped his hand on her shoulder right before he spoke and she jumped.

"I'm telling you; I feel something. Might not be a someone though." She rubbed her arms as a chill ran through her.

"Let me check." Ghortin rubbed his hands together and sent forth a spell. It was a tricky one that seemed simple but usually ended up not working right for Jenna. When done right, the spell gently reached out and exposed people who might be hidden from sight. When done wrong it ended up grabbing random palace maids from two floors away and dragging them into the room where the spell was cast. Jenna stopped trying to practice it after the third unplanned visit.

Jenna waited, but Ghortin continued to stand there. His smile was slowly fading. Finally, he dropped his hands and scowled at the trees.

"Well?" Jenna asked the question, but Crell and Carabella looked ready to do the same.

"There is something out there. You're right. But it deflected my spell. The only way I know it's out there is because it pushed the spell back to me a little too hard." He sent out another spell, this time a faint green shield surrounded them. "This is going to take a lot of Power to keep up around all of us like this, but I've no idea what's out there. It's a presence more than anything, but we can't count on it being on our side."

"Can we try to open this chest now?" Carabella stood over it but hadn't touched it. She looked ready to grab it regardless of what Ghortin said.

"There's a nasty lock on it." Jenna stepped over to it.

She wasn't completely certain the shield would stop something that was a presence more so than an actual person, but it did cut the feeling of being watched down a bit. "That's why we had to bring the entire thing."

Ghortin pulled on the lock expectantly. Nothing happened. He tried again, then shook his head. "I hate to try a spell on it, it could damage the contents."

"Or blow it up." Carabella had moved to the edge of the clearing.

"That's possible too. But we can't lug this chest with us on our travels. If there are items of use inside, we can spread them out among us."

Crell shook her head and looked at all of them. "None of you ever picked locks in your youth? Carabella excluded."

"Sorry, no." Ghortin stepped closer as Crell pulled out a small bundle from her pack and dropped next to the chest. "I'd like to learn though."

She shook her head. "Not in a single lesson you won't. Tell you what, when we're back safe and sound in Lithunane, I'll run a class for all of you well-behaved children."

Carabella had returned closer to the chest once she was certain Ghortin wasn't going to be blowing it apart. "And me. I didn't have a childhood per se, but I believe I would like to learn how to pick locks. Even when I can use my magic, there are times when it's not the best option."

Crell nodded then went to work. Ten minutes and one annoyed Crell later, a soft click sounded and the lock opened.

Jenna, Ghortin, and Carabella had all sat on rocks around the chest after the first few minutes.

"That was an example of an evil lock. It's impossibly old and I swear was changing as I worked on it." Crell pulled it off but didn't open the lid. "I think Jenna should have the honors; she did find it."

Jenna pulled up the lid before the other two could comment. A dusty blanket, one that looked older than Carabella, covered the top. She gently set it aside, then jumped back screaming as a massive snake lunged at her.

CHAPTER FORTY-EIGHT

S TORM SWORE, TUCKED his dagger away, and stepped up with his hands raised. Four soot-covered and injured human males stood there. All were heavily armed, but only one had a bow.

The one who spoke had an arrow aimed at Edgar's head, and even a bad archer couldn't miss at that range. "Good to know you can listen." He nodded to the one next to him. "Tie them both up but start with the Crailian."

Storm held his hands out slowly, watching the area around them. There was no room for them to have any other archers, let alone three of them. And these four people were in bad shape.

As soon as two of them came forward to tie Storm's hands, both he and Edgar moved. Storm swung out with his leg and took both of them down.

The archer fired but Edgar was already on him with his dagger to his throat. Storm punched one of the ones near him when he tried to get up, and he stayed down. Storm grabbed the one that looked the most injured and held him like a shield toward the only one still standing. "I would drop your sword immediately if I were you."

The man looked to the one on the ground with Edgar standing over him, then dropped his sword.

"You don't belong here. Letting him loose wasn't enough? You came back for more? Everyone who couldn't get out is dead." The one at Edgar's feet didn't move, but he was pissed.

Edgar now had his sword out and pointed toward the

man at his feet. "We didn't do anything. We were looking for a missing ship and saw the attack. How in the hell did you people have a kraken?"

"He's always been here. Well, as long as any of us have been here. He keeps us hidden from anyone. But somehow those people saw through whatever magic he did." The guy shrugged. "Didn't know what he was called. We gave him fish, he stayed in his cave, and cast his hiding spell. It was a good deal."

"And now it's loose." Storm released the man he was holding, but only after he'd removed a few knives from his tunic. "What were you hiding here besides that? You said they killed everyone else?"

"We tried to defend the creature, but those people on that ship overpowered us with magic. Two of our ships got away, the other two you can't miss. Aside from us, everyone left was killed or taken."

"Odd question. When you were fighting these people, did any of them bleed green?" The one at Edgar's feet shook his head, but the one still standing nodded.

"Aye. A female Khelaran guard. I got a good strike into her before her companions joined in. She fell and was spurting green blood. Never seen the like."

"Demonspawn." Storm kept his voice low but all of them heard him.

The one who'd spoken laughed. "Those aren't real, everyone knows that."

"They're as real as that kraken you had here, and just as deadly." Edgar looked around, then took the ties they'd been about to use on them from the one on the ground. "We're not going to kill you, nor take you with us. But we can't have you roaming around." He and Storm tied them up and left them sitting where anyone near the beach would see them. Maybe the ships that took off would come back for them.

No sign of Keanin, Talia, or Hon though.

Storm held his sword close to the nearest one. "What did you do to our friends?"

The man first shook his head, then Storm pressed his sword against his neck.

"They're at the post. Left them there hoping the creature—kraken if that's what you say it was, we never called it anything—would come back."

Edgar had a knife out as he dropped close to the man. "Where?"

He nodded to the left. Down the beach, a large rock rose out of the water. A rock with three figures on it. "The post is a rock of logite, so no magic user can cast any spells."

Storm and Edgar went down the beach, once closer it was clear that all three were conscious but gagged and tied up. There was a small boat on the beach that had probably been used to get them out there.

Storm and Edgar rowed out, removed their gags, and were working on untying them when Hon's eyes went huge as he looked past them. "That thing is coming this way!"

Storm glanced back to see waves starting to swell but kept working on freeing Keanin as Edgar worked on Talia. Edgar pulled Hon into the boat, binds and all. Talia got in as well but the waves being created by the kraken swimming toward them bounced the small boat too much for Storm and Keanin to get in.

"Go! Get out of here!" Storm yelled as the others tried to get back to them. "You can't stop it."

The issue became pointless when the waves from the kraken pushed the boat further away from the rock.

Storm turned, expecting to see Keanin upset but instead, he looked oddly calm and relaxed. A small smile appeared as he closed his eyes and raised his hands. He pulled in enough Power that even Storm felt it. This type of rock stopped the basics of magic from working, yet not only was he pulling in magic, but the air around them crackled with it. Then Storm realized he was standing in a puddle of water and was pulling Power from the sea.

Keanin reached toward the kraken as its head rose out of the water. It was definitely a kraken out of myth. Wide-set eyes narrowed as it first looked to the drifting boat, then to Storm and Keanin. It reached for them but then froze, a tentacle hanging dripping in midair.

"You froze it?" Storm wasn't sure whether to be happy or not. Keanin might have saved them, but controlling something that large was madness. Ignoring the issue about the magic blocking rock. If they survived, Ghortin was going to have a field day sorting this out.

"No. *He* stopped himself. I'm telling him that we're his friends. Not food. He's glad to be free."

The kraken slowly pulled back his tentacle but watched Storm with one yellow eye.

"Put your sword away." Keanin opened his eyes and smiled at the monster. "You did attack us first after all. We were simply defending ourselves. You have the ocean again, go be free. Go make friends somewhere."

Storm put away his sword but kept his hand on the hilt as Keanin laughed.

"He says thank you for putting that away. But he is the only one of his kind. He will leave us be though, he prefers the depths of the deep ocean."

The kraken pulled back his tentacles and submerged. The waves went out of the bay and away from land.

Keanin's eyes went wide then he started to fall. Storm grabbed him before he tumbled off the rock.

Keanin blinked a few times and stood. "That's not good." He watched the waves fade. "He wanted to go to the deep ocean because while he's alone now, he won't be for long. I would have made him explain more before he took off if I'd known that." He glared at the departing waves.

"You do realize you were communicating with and mentally chastising a mythological monster that probably wouldn't have noticed if it swallowed us, right?" Storm knew Keanin's magic was unpredictable, but that was scary even to him and he wasn't a magic user. "And the rock we're on should have stopped you completely."

With the waves from the kraken gone, Edgar and the others were making their way back to the rock.

"I...I did. It was odd, it just felt natural. Like you can communicate with horses. I don't know what made it happen—it wasn't anything Ghortin taught me—but somehow I knew the way to reach out to it." He looked down at the puddle and rock under his feet. "Maybe water is a workaround for the blocking properties of this rock. And I discovered it."

"Unlike that kraken, horses aren't going to eat you. Not to mention that I can't hear inside horses' heads. When we rejoin Ghortin and the others, you have to have a long talk with him about what you just did. The bit he added about more coming is disturbing, but I'm also not sure about you talking to it."

The boat got closer and Edgar held it steady for them to get on board. "Not that I'm not glad to see you both, but shouldn't you be in that monster's belly by now?"

"Keanin has a new calling." Storm smiled at Talia and Hon. For right now they were all working together, but he'd never heard of any mage strong enough to do what Keanin just did. Of course, this was the only kraken in the world, so it was hard to judge. He still didn't think they should spread this information about Keanin's new trick around.

Keanin must have finally caught on that what he did was unusual as he shrugged it off. "I was able to chase it off with some small magics that I worked through the water, it wanted to leave here. I think. Glad you came back when you did."

Talia gave him a sideways look, but let it ride. "Before we were captured, we found the bodies of about twenty people—all pirates. And two decapitated demonspawn."

"Damn it, the pirates we found said there was at least one demonspawn. We need to catch up with the *Golden Harpy*." Edgar was rowing them to the beach to get the dingy from Talia's boat. The pirates who survived would probably find another place since the magic they'd been using from the kraken would be gone now.

"I don't know how. That ship had a lead on us, even before we came here." Hon helped get them back on board the larger ship.

Keanin flexed his fingers. "If I were able to keep the sails full could we do it? I feel oddly refreshed."

Storm looked at him carefully. "You were struggling when we came in here and you had to keep the sails filled." He looked to Talia and Hon. "I'm thinking this would be keeping it up for a few hours?"

"At least." Talia shook her head. "I understand that you need to stop these demonspawn and whoever is working with them, and I haven't given up hope that my brother is still alive, but you won't do anyone any good if you drain your magic."

A real fear. Storm knew Jenna had lost her magical ability at one point due to overuse. So had Tor Ranshal. Jenna's came back, but Tor's still hadn't.

CHAPTER FORTY-NINE

———————◆———————

JENNA STUMBLED BACKWARD, bowling over Ghortin as the snake struck out at her. "Get back!" She didn't know why the others weren't moving, but that snake was big enough to reach any of them without leaving the chest.

Ghortin got up and grabbed her arms. "What do you see?" His voice was too calm.

"The same thing you should be seeing, a giant snake. Don't you hear the rattle? It's a massive rattlesnake."

"A rattle what?" Carabella was standing inches away from the snake, then she walked right through it.

"A rattlesnake." Jenna could still see it although the others didn't and Carabella had moved through it twice now. "A poisonous snake from my world…that would never be that large…and would be seen by you three if it was real." She ran her fingers through her hair. She had always been terrified of rattlesnakes. As a kid, one of them bit her best friend when they were playing in the hills around their home. Her friend had survived, but the terror around that moment never left.

"I can move the blanket?" Crell was closest and reached forward.

"Nope, thank you. I think this might be a test. You know hidden relics, always a test." She glanced around but all three were still giving her a questioning look. Maybe like the rattlesnakes, tests for treasure were a thing only on Earth. But something had made her see that snake. None of them saw it. Either she was losing her mind or it was a spell triggered by whoever opened the chest.

She forced herself to walk through the snake and it faded away. Letting her held breath out, she pulled aside the blanket. A tray of gold trinkets glimmered on top as if they'd just been placed there. Nice, but not what they were looking for. She lifted the tray out, handed it to Crell, and pulled aside another blanket. Then started swearing.

"The books aren't there?" Ghortin said as he and Carabella crowded forward and Crell put down the tray and joined them.

"They might be. Who knows?" She lifted up a handful of pages. "There are hundreds if not thousands of sheets." A few layers down she saw some dark gray covers. "How thoughtful, we also have the covers." She held up the empty gray pieces for two books. Each page had been carefully removed with a knife, not torn out, but removed. Then gathered and hidden away. "Why?"

Carabella took a few steps back and sat. "I'm not sure, but I feel a bit off. Those books lost some of their magic when they were taken apart, but they are still powerful. Just by my reaction, they are far stronger than the one Jenna carries."

Ghortin picked through some of the pages, shaking his head and swearing under his breath as he did so. "The one she carries has been out in the world for a few thousand years, and that daily exposure wears down magic. These have been locked away. Did you see that gold? Like it was just made. The chest protected everything from aging. I wish we could talk to your friend from the chaotic plane about this."

"I'm not going to try and find him. Not to mention, he didn't know that no one was aware of these two books, so he wasn't the one who did this." There were enough pages that moving them without the chest was going to be awkward.

"I can carry the gold, that is assuming you're not planning on leaving it here?" Crell was starting to wrap the pieces. They were small statues and some jewelry.

"What?" Ghortin glanced over from his contemplation of a page. "Yes, please do wrap them up. I think the safest place for these would be my library in Irundail. I seriously doubt that anyone would go into my rooms in Lithunane, but the protection on my library is far more impressive."

Jenna tried reading a page or two, but they weren't in any order and seemed to be a lot of naming of people and things. "First off, are we going to Irundail or Strann? Secondly, wouldn't your vortex be the safest place?"

"We're going to Strann. I have a way to reach into my library, not unlike Carabella pulling out her spell books from hers. My vortex, however, can't be reached that way."

"I'm going to stand by the horses; those pages are disturbing me." Carabella waved her hand in front of her nose as if something nasty smelling had come her way. She didn't wait for a response but went to pet and talk to the horses and Crell's pony.

Ghortin spoke a few faint spell words and a square hole in the air in front of him appeared. Jenna would take his word for that being his library, as it was a jumbled mess from what she could see through it.

He scowled at the hole, then motioned for it to drop lower. Then he shoved the entire chest in. "Easier than risking losing a page."

Crell held up the blanket she'd wrapped the gold in. "Did you want these to go in as well?"

He paused then shook his head. "They aren't probably worth much—well, aside from being gold. We might need to barter for things in Strann. If you don't mind carrying them, let's keep them for now." He closed the portal when she nodded and put the bundle back in her pack.

"If they aren't valuable, why lock them in a secret chest in a secret temple?" Jenna hadn't gotten a good look, but the pieces looked well made.

"Thief deterrent probably. The real treasure is those pages. But if a relic hunter or common thief found the chest they'd take the gold and not worry about the papers. It's not that uncommon with academic finds. But, they could come in handy at some point. I'll take a better look when we're in Strann."

Carabella came back to the group. "Which should be tomorrow? Unless you've another detour planned?" She turned to Jenna and Crell. "This is why I don't travel with him. Takes forever to get anywhere and he rarely goes anywhere interesting."

"You have no sense of adventure. But yes, we should get there within a few hours in the morning. I don't expect trouble, but best we enter away from the capitol and keep a low profile."

They set up a small camp, this time with a fire instead of the glows. The trees didn't give off the same awareness the others had and Jenna was still feeling chilled.

"Are we leaving that there all night?" Crell pointed to the flickering shield as she finished eating.

Ghortin looked to Jenna.

"Don't look at me. I'm not sensing anything with the shield raised. But who knows what's beyond it." She rubbed her arms. "I'm still cold though."

Carabella reached over and put the back of her hand against Jenna's forehead. "You're burning up." She looked to Crell. "You were further in the tunnel like she was. How are you feeling?"

Crell shrugged. "A little tired, but not bad. You think something in those ruins is making Jenna ill?"

"I think that very thing." Carabella dug through her pack. "I don't have any trialio root, do you?"

Ghortin shook his head. "No one has hidden plagues

in ruins for eons. And it should have hit me if they did, I was the first inside."

"And you got zapped by the spell they had running and never made it further than the first part of the first corridor. They had beams of something crossing the halls that triggered it and knocked you out. We had to crawl in." Jenna wasn't sure if it was because she was paying more attention to how she felt, or if she did have something. She was feeling worse and just wanted to sleep somewhere for a week or so.

Ghortin magically created two full glasses. Unlike the prior one that he'd given her, these weren't clear. Nor did they smell like anything she wanted anywhere near her. "No trialio root, but this should help."

Carabella brought her one glass and he took the other to Crell.

"That is nasty, I'm not drinking that." Crell pulled back. "Nothing wrong with me that a good night's sleep won't take care of."

"You're not being hit as hard yet because it is targeting magic users. Those would be the ones the spell caster protecting the chest would most want to protect against. But you will feel worse if you don't drink this." Ghortin glanced to Jenna. "Both of you will."

Jenna looked at the glass, then at Carabella. There was too much sincerity and concern in those exotic cuari eyes to not take this seriously. "Fine." She tried to keep from breathing in the smell, but that was pretty much impossible. She gulped the contents of the glass down, then smiled. "I think it worked. I feel great." She rose to her feet to demonstrate and immediately dropped. Every nerve in her body was on fire and her brains were trying to batter their way out of her head.

CHAPTER FIFTY

STORM WATCHED KEANIN carefully from the far end of the deck as they traveled after the *Golden Harpy*. The channel opening that would allow ships to safely sail into Craelyn wouldn't be available until the tides changed at sunrise. But the closer they could get to it before that happened, the better. The *Golden Harpy* was larger and faster than their boat, even with whatever magic Keanin was using to fill their sails.

"He's far more than a casual magic user, isn't he?" Talia leaned against the railing next to Storm and watched Keanin as well.

"Yes, but I'm still worried about what he's doing."

"Me too." Edgar came over to join them. "He says that he's perfectly fine. Not even breaking a sweat and we're moving fast."

"I have to say, you three aren't what I would have expected from royals and nobles." She laughed. "Particularly you, Storm. There's not a lot of information about you, but the rumors are that you live in a cave in the woods and only go to the palace when you have to."

Edgar's sharp laugh made Hon, Flini, and even Keanin glance over. "That's an accurate statement. But he hides out with a wily old mage in his magic cottage. The bit about not being in Lithunane unless he has to is spot on though."

"You mean Mastermage Ghortin? I seriously thought he was a myth. There have been fewer strong magic users up here over the years, at least according to the old drunks in the pub. They claim magic is waning." She smiled at Keanin when he glanced over. "Good to know the mastermage is real and magic is still growing."

"Ghortin is an interesting character, to say the least, and I feel far more comfortable out in the woods than in the palace." Storm looked around the open ocean. "But I have to say, this isn't bad either. As long as monsters from the deep aren't trying to eat us." He turned to Edgar. "Can you check the taran wand? I know it doesn't work well on water, but the others need to know about the kraken."

"Taran wands are real too?" Talia's eyes grew large. "Yes, I don't have magic but my grandmere did and she used to tell us wonderful stories. There was one where some lost adventurers used a pair of those wands to escape the depths of the abyss itself. That story always scared my brother." Her smile dropped and she looked out over the ocean.

"There's a chance he's still alive. We've no real idea why they did what they did. Nor what they're doing." Storm clasped her shoulder. He'd been frantic to find his father when he was taken. Talia was handling this much better than he had.

"Thank you. And if anyone can survive, it'll be Diath. I have to focus on getting to that ship, finding out what's happened, and killing some demonspawn. Any tips on fighting them?"

"Not that I know. I almost died in my first battle with them."

Edgar had the taran wand out but kept scowling at it. "There's a slight tingle when it's live, but I'm not getting anything. I agree we need to get the information out about the kraken, especially since it seems to think more will be coming. But it might have to wait until we get on land."

"The *Golden Harpy* is anchored not far from here," Keanin shouted. He had his head tilted as if he was listening to something, but his hands were still making tiny adjustments to the sails with his spell. "Can we drop anchor? Too much closer and they'll see us." He dropped his hands and shook them out. "Unexpected side effect, I have no feeling in my hands."

Hon had the wheel. "There's a sand bar not far from here. We can settle in for the night."

"Move us over to it." Talia grabbed some of the riggings. "Thank you, Keanin, for your gifts. We never would have made it anywhere close to here otherwise."

He smiled and gave an elaborate bow. "I live to serve, lovely lady."

Storm caught Talia's blush before she turned away and adjusted more lines. "Yes, well, thank you."

The sand bar wasn't much, barely a berm of sand in the ocean. They'd be staying on board tonight for certain. But it was enough for anchoring.

Keanin came over to Storm and Edgar after the boat was secure. "Any more luck on the taran wand? I'm not trying to be pessimistic, but if we don't survive, we need to get the word out on the kraken."

"True. But so far I can't get through." Edgar looked over the side of the boat to the thin strip of island rising out of the water. "Maybe that's enough land to ground it. We can't see most of it, but there's probably a good amount of island under there." He explained what he was doing to Talia then took the rope ladder down to the sand.

"How are you feeling?" Storm was watching Keanin still for any problems with the magic he'd been doing, but he seemed perfectly fine. However, that and the commonplace comment about them possibly not surviving was making him worried. It wasn't that long ago that Keanin had been trying to hide in the palace because he didn't want to deal with changes. Now he was changing so fast it was frightening.

"Surprisingly, I feel okay. I'm still working through what was done to me at Shettler's Point, but I'm finding out that I'm stronger than I knew. No matter what happens, no one will ever attack me like that again." His eyes were distant. "I'm sure she's fine, by the way."

"What? Who?"

"Jenna. I can feel it. Something has happened to her, but she's going to be fine." His smile should have made Storm feel better. But the words didn't.

"What's happened to her?"

"That I can't tell you. But she's not in any real danger." He tilted his head as if he heard something far away. "She's going to have many stories to share when we get back together, that's for certain."

"You're not making me feel better." Storm leaned over and called to Edgar. "Any luck getting through to Ghortin?"

"No. I seem to be making the connection then something blocks it. Crell too. I'll see if I can reach Rachael so the information is with someone. Even just one of those things could destroy all of our coastal towns."

"They'll be fine. Trust me." Keanin smiled and patted Storm's arm.

"How do you know?" Storm knew he had to trust that Jenna and those with her could defend themselves, but it still made things difficult knowing something was going on, but not what.

Keanin smiled and shrugged. "I just do."

Edgar climbed up from the sand bar. "I got through to Rachael and Garlan. Both say the situation in the palace is normal. Resstlin is preparing for his coronation, but Queen Areania and your siblings haven't left Irundail yet. The theory is they believe in the impending threat more than Resstlin does and don't want to risk the coronation becoming a target for an attack. It was suggested that he move the entire event to Irundail since it is far more secure."

Storm shook his head. "And he took that well, I'm sure." His eldest brother was a showman. Irundail was safer by far, but not very flashy. The beauty of the palace in Lithunane would be a better backdrop for his coronation. After this was over, Storm was going to consider moving to Irundail just to be free from any obligations Resstlin might try to put on him. And to be away from Resstlin himself.

"He said it was a move motivated by fear and that he couldn't condone that. Having it in the palace would be a show of strength. Yeah, those were his words. Garlan sounded like he was repeating them through clenched teeth."

"He probably was. I have a feeling once he feels things are settled, Garlan will be retiring. He's given decades to our family and deserves better," Storm said. "I hope Resstlin does it before we get back; that's one event I can do without."

Once the boat was secure, they made a rough meal, set watch rotations, and went to sleep. There was nothing out here except darkness and waves, but having a useless watch was better than waking to a nasty surprise.

Storm had just finished his watch and was settling into his cot when the screams started. He bolted to his feet and ran to Keanin's door. It was locked, but those were screams of terror.

Everyone came out except Flini, who stuck his head down from the deck.

"Nothing got past me, I swear!"

"Do you have keys or am I breaking this down?" Storm rattled the door handle. "We're coming, Keanin, hang on!"

Edgar fussed with the lock and the door popped open. He also sent in a glow as the room was pitch dark.

Keanin was on his cot, bunched up against the wall and

screaming. His eyes were wide open but he didn't appear to see them. His voice was odd and discordant—not like him at all. His hair was matted in sweat. "No! Don't let them! Stop!"

Storm grabbed his shoulders but was knocked off his feet as Keanin shoved him away.

"They are making monsters. My monsters! Stop them." His voice sounded more like his own now, and he seemed to see them all. He was still shaking so badly it was as if he'd been dumped in ice. "We have to stop them." He grabbed Edgar's shoulders. "*We have to.*"

Storm came back to the cot. "What happened?"

Keanin ran his hand through his tangled hair. "At first it was a nightmare. I've had them every night but haven't said anything. But then I had a connection to something else…not all of those women died. At least two survived and they are about to give birth."

Talia looked to Storm but he shook his head. He'd explain later if Keanin wasn't ready to.

"It can't have to do with what they did to you. The births, that is. It wasn't long enough—"

Keanin cut Edgar off. "They aren't of this world. They don't need the time our people take. They took something from me and others from beyond the portal. They are making monsters."

CHAPTER FIFTY-ONE

JENNA WAS STILL conscious, but doing anything beyond breathing wasn't going to happen at the moment. Everyone crowded around her as she lay on the ground until Carabella chased the other two off.

"Let me see what's happened." She rose her hand before Ghortin could speak. "I won't use magic. I do have abilities beyond that, you know."

"Hard to tell since you're always using magic. Or so I've heard." But he stepped a few feet back, along with Crell.

"Just someone please do something? I'm not twitching as much anymore, but nothing wants to work." Jenna tried to move, but still nothing. It was as if all of her nerves just decided to shut down. "Are you certain it wasn't in that damn drink? That thing was awful. Although I don't seem to be running a fever now." That would be a better plus if she could move.

Ghortin looked minorly insulted but Crell shook her head. "It did nothing to me, aside from whatever it was supposed to do. I feel fine, but I didn't feel that bad before."

"That was a spell attack, one on top of what you were already facing. My potion helped you. It's not my fault there was more than one layer to the attack. And a tricky one at that."

Carabella brushed back her hair and dropped into a low, soothing voice. "It's okay, you're safe. Ghortin, bring me a lonive root from my pack? It's in the blue bag." She kept brushing back Jenna's hair and muttering soft words. "You've had a nasty attack on your nervous system. Probably the same spell that made you see your snake friend. But we can fix it. Just relax. You're safe and among friends."

Carabella's voice worked, Jenna started to relax and her nerves settled down to almost normal. She still couldn't move though.

Ghortin came back with a short yellow root. "Topical?"

"Yes, I think that will be the best way." Carabella took the root, touching it as minimally as possible, then snapped it in half. She carefully applied the broken ends to Jenna's forehead.

A soothing coolness flowed from the two spots where the wet root touched her head. Followed by a lovely numbness. The final bit of twitching in her nerves subsided and all of her muscles relaxed.

She struggled to sit up again, but this time she made it. "Wow. Okay, that wasn't fun, and that root...I'm extremely relaxed now. Like maybe too much. Do we have anything to eat?"

"She'll be fine." Carabella smiled and got to her feet. "You might be a bit sore once the lonive wears off, but you'll recover. It was a lingering trap spell. One I haven't seen since before Ghortin was born."

"What was it trying to do? Shake me to death?" Jenna rubbed her arms and got to her feet. She did feel better but there was still a lingering tingle from whatever got her. The flu-like feelings were gone though.

"No, but its purpose is to disable, not kill. Had you panicked it would have pressed harder onto your nervous system and been more difficult to get rid of." Carabella put the root pieces back into the small pouch. "If the illusion of your fear, that snake from your home world, didn't get you to back off, then this spell would lock you down so the protectors of the chest could come to stop you. It's tied to magic users only. The spell was still working, obviously, but it was weaker than it should have been. I don't think whoever left the chest in the ruins expected it to be there as long as it was."

"Good thing we're not planning on traveling anymore today." Crell started setting camp. "You look like a two-year-old could push you over with a feather."

"Thanks. So now what? We have those two books but can't look at them now. And no idea if all the pages are there. We just stay with our plan?"

"I believe we have to. Regardless of what these new books have in terms of information, we know we need the third one. If we can get the cuari free, we'll have a better chance facing the demonspawn."

Crell's taran wand started buzzing. "What? Seriously? Hold on." She'd originally kept the wand near her ear but now held it out. "Tell me what you just said."

"Hello everyone." Rachael's voice was a little murky but it was clear who it was. "They're fine, but Storm and the others faced another creature who shouldn't exist." She quickly told them about the kraken. And the fact there might be more coming. "They are having trouble reaching out to either Crell or Ghortin because they're still on the sea but were able to get through to me. Are you running a shield of some kind?"

"Yes, too long to explain, but we are. It's enough combined with their own issues to not let them through." Ghortin looked around the woods and focused in the direction the ruins were. "And there could be other elements involved. Any clue as to how something like that creature appeared? It's not as if they could have come through the portal."

"Not at all. Tor Ranshal and I have been going through everything we can in the library, but nothing. Simply, they shouldn't exist." She paused. "How are all of you doing? There're some odd auguries going on. Ones that predict something bad, but I can't tell where."

"I'd say we're finding bad all along the countryside. We hit it, Storm, Keanin, and Edgar hit it. The country might not be under a direct attack, no armies are marching yet, but we are facing some serious problems. Has the royal family come south yet?"

"No, much to Resstlin's annoyance."

"Good. See if Tor can work his talents in keeping them in Irundail as long as possible."

Rachael laughed. "You, Edgar, and Storm have the same thoughts—it was suggested that the coronation be in Irundail."

Crell let out a laugh at that and even Carabella shook her head.

"That would never happen. Not sure how Resstlin turned out so different from his parents and siblings, but he did. We should reach Strann early tomorrow. A few days to meet with the bookseller, see what else we can easily determine, and we'll be home before you know it."

"Good to hear. Safe travels." Rachael ended the call.

"I'm ready for bed. That root really did relax me too much." Jenna wished that Storm had been calling instead of Rachael, but it was still good to hear her voice—and that all three of the others were okay.

"Good idea. We'll have to move briskly tomorrow; I don't want to cross the border at night. Even in the best of times, the Strann border can be questionable." Ghortin looked down at Carabella. "And I can pass as human but you definitely do not look human. People in small villages might think you're just an exotic kelar, but city folks will know you're not."

"We'll discuss it in the morning. I've got a few ideas." Carabella grinned.

———————

Jenna was enjoying a lovely dream. She was living in a palace with all of her friends nearby. Storm was there, but he wasn't quite himself. He wanted her to let him into the room she was in, but he couldn't pass the door frame. His face morphed and she realized it was Linton. She woke with a start.

The bard was in ten feet in front of her.

"Let me in. They won't know." His face was contorted but it was him. Dark shapes hovered behind him, but none of them were clear enough to see. And none of them crossed the flickering line of Ghortin's shield. Her friends weren't moving, and judging by the way Ghortin was sprawled he'd been on watch when hit with something. So much for his shield completely blocking magic.

"Why?" Jenna's mood wasn't good. She'd been enjoying the nice dream and was getting tired of things taking that away. She got to her feet and folded her arms. "What are you and why are you following us?"

Linton pulled back a bit. He must have been counting on her being under some spell. "You should come with me, with us. You don't belong here."

Jenna stared at him. Or rather through him. "You're not really here, are you? Just some wispy little figment of my mind." She stalked forward. "You know what? I'm tired of everything pushing me around." She sent a spell right at Linton. The shield should have stopped it, but it still shoved him back.

"My master can give you all that you want. You can have your dreams, this world, and your old." He smiled. "Yes, we know you're not from here. But you can have all of your dreams together. Join with us."

"Does that work? Ever? Seriously, even if I wasn't already pissed, that wouldn't work. It wouldn't work on anyone with half a brain. Is that how they caught you?" She fired another spell. These were a smaller variation of her spears and seemed to work well on whatever Linton was sending. He and the beings with him were growing fainter.

"Leave. Me. Alone." She accented each word with a flung spell spear.

Linton's face was now filled with fear and his image started moving away from her.

"Oh, that's good then. I *can* hurt you in that form. Thank you for that." She sent the same arcing spell she'd flung at the sciretts. He screamed, then he and those with him vanished.

"Who's yelling?" Ghortin scrambled about, sat up, and looked confused. "See here, what am I doing in the dirt?"

Jenna found herself shaking, but it was with unused Power more than fear. She really wanted to blow something up. She shook off the feeling before turning to Ghortin. "You've been ending up there a lot as of late. Me too and I'm personally done with it. Linton sent an image of himself, one with some friends and enough magic to take you out. I pointed out he should leave us alone."

Crell and Carabella both stirred, and Crell was on her feet with her sword in her hand immediately.

"What happened? I had strange dreams." Crell looked around slowly.

"I did as well." Carabella hadn't pulled a weapon yet, but her dagger was next to her.

"Linton came for a visit." Jenna paused as pieces connected. "That bastard was who I felt watching us. He's probably been following us since that village but we didn't notice."

"He managed to knock me out? Within my own shield?" Ghortin was on his feet and looked pissed.

"Join the angry club." Jenna forced herself to settle down. The power behind her anger was good, but the lingering feeling of violence wasn't. Fighting back was good. Pushing it too far was how villains were made.

"How did we not notice him? You guys can sense other magic users, can't you?" Crell put her sword away but kept it close as she readied a quick breakfast.

"To some extent, yes. Jenna sensed him in this case, but only recently and it wasn't clear. I didn't pick up on him as a magic user when we were in that town, nor anytime afterward. I'd say he has someone running blocking for him." Ghortin glared at the woods around them.

"Qhazborh." Jenna felt sick as she realized the presence that had been behind Linton's sending. "He spoke of his master, and I now know what I felt. Qhazborh. Or rather the gods and goddesses that form the representation of Qhazborh."

"That would explain how he got through my shield to get to me. But if I dare say so, it held well enough that he couldn't get further in. He needed you to drop it." Ghortin had recovered his brief annoyance at having his shield partially breached.

"Is there any way we can keep him and his friends from following us?" Jenna was feeling less angry but more freaked out. If he'd been following them the entire time, he knew everything that was happening.

"I'll work on that." Ghortin narrowed his eyes as he watched her. "Most likely he's managed to connect to you and that's who he's following. We're just incidental."

"Great. Is there any way we can block him from following me? That's worse, by the way." Jenna finished breakfast and loaded her pack onto her horse.

"I might know of a spell." Carabella pulled out one of her spell books. "Might take a while, it's basically an anti-possession spell, but you and Ghortin should be able to modify it. It's the only one that I know of that works against spiritual manifestations." She finished loading her pack but kept the small blue book she'd pulled out with her.

Ghortin dropped his shield, but then stood where it had been. They were still going to have to walk the horses and pony out until they got to the main road, but he hadn't taken his yet.

Jenna and her horse came behind him. "Are we waiting for something?"

"Just trying to figure out why my shield didn't block the attack completely. I shouldn't have been unconscious and you shouldn't have been in a dreamscape with him." He stood there for a few more moments, then shook his head and went back for his horse.

"Trickier spells don't always work the way they should. I taught you that when you were a child. The more complex a spell is, the more likely that some part of it will slip." Carabella took the lead as they started walking. "That shield of yours was a conglomeration of at least three different ones that I could tell. It's surprising it didn't fail completely." She turned back to Jenna. "The classics are the best spells. No matter what he says."

"Ha! Jenna makes up new ones all the time. And that's the best way. Mark my words, things are changing in this world. If magic users don't adapt we'll not survive." Ghortin walked faster to catch up to them.

Jenna looked back at him then her eyes widened as she saw what was behind him. Or what wasn't behind him. The woods were gone. "Look out, there's something behind you!"

CHAPTER FIFTY-TWO

NO ONE WAS ready to sleep after Keanin's attack.
"I'm okay now, but I think I'd like to be alone.
I didn't get enough information to know where they
went, or what they're creating, but I felt the evilness. We
can assume they fled to the Markare after they escaped
from Shettler's Point. We'll need to try and pass that
information along before we leave the sand bar tomorrow." Keanin rubbed his face then looked up at the four
watching him. "Seriously, I will be okay." He turned to
Talia and Hon. "I'm not ready to fill you in on what this
was the result of, but maybe my friends could tell you
after I speak with them?" He didn't look frightened or
angry, just extremely tired.

Talia nodded and led Hon out on deck with Flini.

Storm shut the door behind them. "Are you sure you're
okay? Why didn't you tell us you were having nightmares?"

"Because they're nightmares? They happen to everyone." Keanin busied himself with fluffing the sad pillow
on his cot.

"And for magic users, they can be far more than that.
I know Ghortin would have told you to watch out for
things like that on your first lesson." Edgar folded his
arms.

"Fine. I didn't want to keep bringing up what happened to me. It was bad, very bad. But right now there's
a lot of bad happening all around us. For once I don't
think the world revolves around me. I will have to deal
with it, but not while other lives could be in danger." He

yawned. "And I think showing off with my wind spell wiped me out. Do you think she was impressed?"

Storm laughed. "You've never gone for fighters before. What brought this change on?"

"Not sure, sometimes you see someone and you just know. Obviously, I won't make any moves until after we've saved the day." He paused. "We are planning on saving the day, right? Rescue her brother and anyone else kidnapped on the *Golden Harpy*, see if Khelaran has fallen, check out the tournament, then head back home?"

Storm shook his head. At least Keanin sounded more like himself. "I wouldn't stay up too late if I were you. We're keeping you off the watch, but if we need you tomorrow, you need to be rested." Storm paused. "Are you certain you want me to tell all three of them about what happened? They won't pry if we tell them you're not ready." He didn't think Talia would and the other two would follow her lead.

"I know. But they need to know why I might do the things that I might do. If we come across any demon-spawn...they just need to know." His face was grim and resolute.

Storm nodded. It was his call. And it might be a good warning for Talia. If her brother was no longer himself, Keanin would do his best to kill the creature who had replaced him. That it would still look like her brother was the issue.

Talia and the other two were on deck waiting for them.

She held up her hand as they approached. "Before you say anything, please know that he doesn't need to tell us. We don't need to know."

"Yeah, he wants you to know. We're probably going to face some harsh fighting when we catch the people from the *Golden Harpy*. You need to understand what's behind his actions." Edgar looked to Storm but Storm nodded for him to go on. Edgar told the events faster and clearer than Storm would have. It wasn't that he didn't care about Keanin, but Keanin was like a brother to Storm and emotionality would get in the way.

Even in the faint lights around the deck, Talia's face went pale as he finished with the implications of these two pregnant demonspawn. "Why? I get them attacking and fighting, but why do that to him?"

"We don't know," Storm said. "Keanin's magic is new. I've known him almost all of my life and he never had any indication of magic until a few months ago. It's wild and unpredictable. And apparently extremely strong. The demonspawn monster who murdered my father was trying to bring Keanin back to wherever he came from. When we do find these demonspawn, Keanin's going to try and destroy them all, and they're going to try and take him."

"We won't let that happen." Talia nodded.

"There's a chance that your brother has become one of them." Edgar looked at all three. Hon and Flini were Diath's friends. "If this works as we hope, we'll come in not long after the *Golden Harpy*. We might have issues if any of us are recognized."

"I understand. If we fight, we fight." She nodded. "I'm taking the watch now. Good night gentlemen." She went to the wheel and looked out over the dark ocean.

Hon stepped closer. "Talia has been through some rough times herself. But she'll do what needs to be done. And we'll all stand by Keanin."

"Thank you. I think I'm going to stay on deck for a while." Storm watched the other two leave, then turned to Edgar. "You could go to sleep too, you know."

"So could you," Edgar said. "I think we should stay in disguise when we come in, and play it by ear when we get to the castle."

"If we go to the castle. I don't think the original reason for us going to calm the worried Khelarans has any merit anymore. They have to be involved in what's going on." From the beginning, Storm didn't want to appear as himself in front of the Khelaran king and give assurances that the Traanafaeren kingdom wasn't doing anything wrong. But this hadn't been how he'd wanted to get out of it.

"Now we don't know that. They could be victims and people like Mikasa are coming in to pick them off." Edgar shrugged.

"Damn. Do you think she's a demonspawn? I know the pirate said he'd seen one during the fight, but why else would they have taken her ship? She's going to wed someone close to the king, perhaps already has a relationship with the king. A demonspawn looking like her could take over the kingdom easily."

"If she is one, whether recent or a while ago, why bring her in now if they already are controlling Khelaran?" Edgar asked.

"For reassurance and to solidify their stance? I mean the entire bit of them being attacked, then the attackers left? That's odd at best. That it was Mikasa who helped get them inside, yet it wasn't? And that now she's going to wed a high-ranking official? There are more layers than even you can easily sort." Storm let out a sigh. "I just want to fight who needs to be fought and end this. Sneaking around isn't my way any more than being a courtier would be."

"You are a basic soul. I respect that, I do. But I think you're right about sorting the layers. If the attack on Khelaran did happen, it's not common knowledge to anyone in Traanafaeren beyond the palace, even those near the Khelaran border. Before I was drugged in that pub by Hilten, I made some general inquires. Aside from recently losing a ship, there's been no indication of anything wrong with Khelaran. And they blame the weather for that, not Khelaran."

"True. Which means if it was a real attack and Mikasa had been involved, no one in Erlinda would know. But people in Craelyn would know."

"If it happened." Edgar glanced at the still dark sky. "I think we need some sleep. Hon has the last watch after Talia and if we have to fight anything tomorrow, I don't want to doze off."

———◆———

The next morning brought no new intel, but a very groggy Keanin.

"You stayed awake all night trying to figure out where they were, didn't you?" Storm hadn't gotten a lot of sleep, but more than his friend.

"I tried. It was reckless to trace a vision dream like that, but I had to try. I couldn't push past anything beyond the room. The women were there and others who I couldn't see. Light blue walls. One window. That is it." Keanin rubbed his face but still looked ready to fall over.

Hon came over with some mugs. "Hot klah tea. It'll wake you up." He handed a cup to each of them, then gave some to the others.

Storm took a whiff and pulled back. "I'm not sure you even have to drink this stuff; it's waking me up from a distance." He'd had klah tea before, but not often. It was common with fighters on heavy campaigns where sleep might not be an option. Traanafaeren hadn't been at war with anyone in hundreds of years, but some of the older guards drank it out of fondness for the old days. He took a tentative sip. The stuff Hon handed them would have been strong even for someone who regularly drank it.

"Ah, love this stuff." Keanin took a long sip and perked up immediately. "Did you know that the courtiers who stay up all night at their parties use this regularly? If we're going to be out and about longer, I want to make sure we start packing this." Another sip. "I almost feel normal again."

Edgar walked over. "I'm going to try Ghortin and Crell again, let them know what happened. We've no idea where your dream took place, and they need to be aware."

"Of any pregnant human-looking women? That's going to be easy." Storm shook his head. "Sorry, didn't sleep and this stuff is nasty."

Keanin had finished his, so he gratefully took Storm's mug.

"Agreed. But better to pass along what we know. If I can't get through, I'll contact Rachael again, although it'll be early in the morning there. Do you want to come?" He added the last part with a smile to Storm.

There was a limit on how much they could use the wands, made even more difficult by the ocean around them. But he missed hearing Jenna's voice. "I think I should, just in case."

They went down to the sand bar as Talia and her crew readied the boat for departure.

"Do you want to try?" Edgar handed the wand over.

"Sure." Storm put his hands in the right spot and tried to contact Ghortin. Nothing. He tried Crell and forced the worry to leave his mind. If Ghortin had tried to contact Edgar while they were on the water, they wouldn't have gotten through either. The route to Strann was completely landlocked but there could be other things blocking them. He shook his head and handed it back to Edgar. "Nope. Tell Rachael we still can't get through."

Edgar got through to Rachael, gave her the information about what Keanin had seen, and mentioned Ghortin and the others. He was about to ask if she'd gotten through to Ghortin when the call dropped. He tried calling back, but it went nowhere. "Damn. I think she got the information, but she was responding when it dropped."

"Hopefully they're all fine. Now, can we go fight something?" Storm was concerned about Jenna, Rachael, and the rest. The wands seemed to increase their anxiety instead of making it better. He just needed to stab something.

"Ho there, you two ready? The tide is changing, and we have a ship to catch." Talia yelled down from the boat. She looked ready to kill things too.

CHAPTER FIFTY-THREE

GHORTIN SPUN TO look behind him at Jenna's yell, then turned back to her with a shrug. "I don't see anything; what do you think you see?"

Jenna would have shaken it off as her mind just being exhausted, but she still saw a dark blob behind him. Slowly the trees began to reappear as the blob faded. "There was something there. Or rather not there. I didn't see the trees, the trail, anything. There was a weird shadow appearing behind Ghortin." She looked to the other two. "I swear I saw it."

Ghortin walked back a few steps, closed his eyes, and held out a hand. Then came back toward them. "Whatever it was, it's gone now."

"There are spells that could be triggered to just a single person." Carabella gave Jenna a reassuring look.

"But keep telling us if you see things—everyone needs to keep an eye out. You were right about the odd presence watching us and it turned out to be Linton. There's no way to tell when something that any of us notice will be important." Ghortin moved to lead then turned back. "Oh, disguises? Carabella? You had something to wear?"

Carabella had been wearing a huge crimson cape since she rose and Jenna thought it was because she was chilled. But she looked far too excited as she flung back her cape and revealed tan leather pants, fitted tunic of the same color, and black boots. Then she lifted a black square of cloth that had been tied around her neck and covered her ears with it. "I like this. And as a fighting woman, I should be leading, don't you think? Us non-magic users have to protect the magical ones, don't we, Crell?"

Crell laughed but nodded. "Agreed. I like it, you look suitably dangerous and not like a cuari. Aside from the eyes."

Carabella's green eyes looked normal until someone looked closely. Her pupils were more like a cat.

Ghortin shook his head but didn't comment on her outfit or persona. He walked closer to her and put a spell on her eyes. They were now a very human-looking dark brown with normal pupils. "Since you worked this out, and since you can't use magic, you might as well lead." He turned to Crell. "I take it you will be our rear guard?"

"Someone has to keep an eye on you magical lot." She waved them forward.

Carabella hit the main road first and was on her horse with her hand on her sword hilt before Jenna even got off the smaller trail.

Ghortin snorted behind her. "If you're going to strike a pose every time we stop, it's going to get old."

"I think she looks great." Jenna smiled. "Lead on, fearless leader."

They came across a small caravan of merchants within a few minutes. Luckily they'd passed by before Carabella and crew had come off of the smaller trail. Explaining where they were coming from might have been awkward.

"Hail and well met!" Carabella's voice was so cheerful and welcoming Jenna almost didn't recognize that the words came from her at first.

They were approaching the slowest moving cart and Carabella's yell caused the two old men driving it to turn around. She cantered alongside them.

"Hello?" The first one didn't seem worried but also wasn't sure about what to make of Carabella. Her garb and attitude were a bit out of the norm—not only for her but for the entire country of Strann.

"My companions and I have been on the road for many days and it's been a long time since I've been back to Strann." She beamed at them. "Any news?"

Ghortin sighed heavily as he rode next to Jenna.

"She doesn't get out of the city much, does she?" Crell whispered from behind them. From Carabella's twitch, she heard her, but the two men didn't. Both were human, so they could be from Traanafaeren or Strann.

"Not often." Ghortin's whisper was louder than many people's speaking voices so both men turned around. He smiled and rode a bit forward.

The men turned back to Carabella. "Not much new going on. Empress still takes her share when we bring in goods, though don't she?" The first one shook his head. "That's been getting worse, I guess. She's paying for changes to her castle, but I ain't seen none."

The second one leaned forward. "She's building an army is what I've heard. On the money we need to feed our families." He looked around and ducked as if he'd said too much.

They'd slowed down at Carabella's approach but the rest of the caravan kept moving.

"Don't you need to travel with them?" Jenna didn't think that the two shabby-looking guards riding along-side the other carts and wagons would be much help against anything serious attacking, but they must have been traveling together.

"Eh, we're close enough to the border. And I'm think-ing this lady can help defend us if need be." The man turned back to look at the three of them again. "You three as well. Not sure about a derawri heading into Strann though. Less tolerance being shown for the other races." He put his hand over his heart. "Not me, mind you. Kelars and derawris are good people. Just make sure they know you're just passing through."

Carabella looked back to Crell. "Let who know?"

"The border guards. They check everything and everyone. As long as you don't have anything of questionable ownership, you won't be bothered."

The second to the last cart slowed down and the driver turned. A middle-aged woman who looked like she won far more barfights than most, rose from her seat. "Get moving, you old beans. We left with five carts, we come back with five carts. I'm not explaining that we lost one at the border." She dropped back onto the bench and moved her cart faster.

"Aye. She'll be awful to deal with if we don't move. Take care, young lady." He looked back to the others. "You too. Remember to let them search your bags without a fuss, you're passing through, and none of you are magic users." He clicked to his horse and caught up with the rest of the train.

Carabella stopped. "That was useful but troubling."

"If I had a choice, I'd say we don't go." Ghortin watched the carts vanish around a corner. "But we need that third book. I'm glad I put the rest of the chest in the library, but Crell's got the gold. I don't think any of the pieces are dangerous or even magical, but until we look at them more closely, we can't be sure. And all the spell books we're carrying would ruin the idea that we're not magic users—not to mention they could confiscate them."

"Can we just open one of those door things to your library again and toss everything in there?" Jenna didn't want to give up her spell book or the other one that she'd borrowed from Carabella, but she also didn't want them taken from her.

"That's our best option. But not here on the road. If they have guards at the border it's hard to tell how far down the road they wander." He looked around then led his horse off the path and back into the woods far enough that they wouldn't be easily seen from the road.

He waved his hand for his spell, but nothing happened.

He tried again.

"I thought you knew how to do that spell?" Carabella was splitting her watch between him and the road they'd left.

"Something is blocking it." Ghortin shook out his shoulders and stretched his hands to get ready for his third try.

They all froze as the sound of running horses echoed down the road. Whoever they were, they were heading toward Strann at a pace that said they knew the road well or didn't care if they ran into anything.

Jenna couldn't explain it, but something about those horses, or the people riding them, suddenly terrified her. Not a single rational reason but she knew they shouldn't be seen by them. Her hand dropped to her sword as her mind was too frozen with fear to complete a spell.

"Jenna? What's wrong?" Crell was right next to her, but even so, kept her voice low.

"No. No one speaks." Jenna barely whispered as the riders came closer. She knew if whoever was on the road found them they would kill herself and the others. Nothing as to why she knew it, but it scared the life out of her.

Ghortin and Carabella moved slightly but no one spoke.

A group of masked riders rode past, but the same trees that were helping Jenna and her friends hide also hid the riders so there wasn't much to be seen. But they were eerily silent aside from a creaking of leather, the clang of metal, and the pounding of hooves. They were past them in moments.

Jenna closed her eyes and listened until not a sound from them was heard. Then she opened her eyes, carefully got off her horse, went into the bushes, and threw up.

Carabella had been closest to her and jumped off her horse. She waited until Jenna was through and then patted her back. "Are you okay?" she whispered.

"I think so. Those...whatever they were. I've never been so afraid in my life." She couldn't help it, she still whispered. Logically and emotionally she knew the riders were gone. But some part of her wanted to go crawl in a dark, quiet hole for a few months just to be certain they couldn't find her.

"I agree," Ghortin whispered, then coughed and spoke normally. Softly, as they still didn't want anyone to see them from the road, but deliberately not a whisper. "They are gone now."

"What were they? They felt like grim riders or they were close enough to the tales that my da told me growing up to be them. I swear it's going to take days for my bones to unfreeze." Crell was pale and kept rubbing her arms. It was the most disturbed that Jenna had ever seen her.

Aside from Carabella, they had all faced a powerful and crazy demonspawn king—and they had been less disturbed than this.

"What are grim riders?" Jenna shivered and got back on her horse. "Agreed on the freezing bones. I always thought that was just a saying. Not anymore."

"They are a tale best told from a warm, safe, and secure pub on a rainy night. Not one I'd be telling now." Ghortin shook his shoulders. "I felt the cold as well and would be willing to dismiss this as simply all of us being overwrought, but there have been too many strange, dangerous, and what should-be-mythological things going on. Suffice it to say, if those were grim riders, your instincts were sound." He looked around and took a deep breath. "Let's try this again, shall we?" The small portal window to his library in Irundail opened on the first try and he quickly put the gold pieces and the spell books inside, then shut it again.

"It worked fine now. So, I'm thinking our friends who

just passed are magic users?" Even though Jenna wasn't sure what these grim riders were, she didn't want to say their name.

Ghortin started to lead them back, then paused and motioned for Carabella to take his place. "More that they *are* magic. If they are what we think. But those don't exist. However, if they did, they embody chaotic magic."

Carabella got them back to the road, but she paused before they came out of cover. Her hearing was the sharpest of all of them and if she didn't hear anything, that was good enough for Jenna. She led them out onto the road.

"The chaotic plane has a personification?" Those things hadn't felt anything like the realm of chaos did, not even this last visit where things were trying to kill her.

"They are wild chaos magic. The plane is where chaos magic began. The story is that someone evil stole some of it, twisted it, and made them out of it." He waved his hand. "But we're not talking about them here and now. However, whatever they were, it reinforces not to use magic while in Strann unless absolutely necessary. Even if we fight, wait as long as you can before using spells."

"Shouldn't we do something about our magic signatures? A strong magic user will sense all three of us." Carabella was still leading, but she was keeping her horse to a slow walk. The road was wide enough so Jenna road alongside her.

"Do you think we'll need it?" Jenna was getting less comfortable about going into Strann the closer they got. Spells used to hide magic were tricky and uncomfortable. Ghortin left one on her for almost an entire day when he was first teaching her the spell. She'd felt like she couldn't breathe and her skin was itchy for days afterward.

"The words about no magic users combined with whatever rode past us, makes me say yes," Carabella said. "I would normally count on my ability to mask my Powers, but since I can't touch my own magic…Ghortin?"

"Agreed. Although we should have done it when we were still off-trail. We're about an hour from the border still, but who knows how far out they have monitors. Let's just get this done then." He stopped his horse and the rest did as well. "This isn't going to be fun, ladies." He said a few spell words; some spells needed verbal reinforcement, some didn't.

Jenna knew the moment the spell hit—the itchiness started.

"That isn't holding." Ghortin scowled at himself and Jenna and Carabella.

"It feels to me like it is." Jenna fought to keep from scratching her arms.

"It's in your head. Let me try again. The spell slid off all of us." He flexed his fingers and muttered the spell words with more force. Again the tingle, again him scowling. It took four tries for it to stick to his satisfaction. "I had to work far too hard at that. Whatever Strann is doing against magic, it's got a reach. Also, be wary if you do have to use magic while we're here. The amount of work on that spell means accessing your magic will be delayed."

CHAPTER FIFTY-FOUR

STORM DID WHAT he could to help keep the sails in the right position. He wasn't that familiar with boats but it was something physical to do. Keanin was working his magic on the sails again, and Edgar had climbed to the little-used crow's nest and was watching the horizon.

Talia shook her head at him. "We don't use the crow's nest much, Diath added it on, but the boat isn't big enough for it. Not to mention, not sure if most of us are as limber as Edgar is."

"He's never found a place he couldn't get into, at least not that I've heard." Storm watched his friend. "How are you doing? I lost my father to these things, it's terrifying because they seem so much like our loved ones. I believed the thing we rescued was my father."

Talia nodded. "I've been steeling myself for this. One way or another I get him back. Either we're bringing him home or he's already gone and I'm freeing his memory. I had no idea what this was going to turn into, nor who I was asking for help. But I'm glad you three are here." She clasped his shoulder then went to go check on their movement.

Storm couldn't see the channel they'd entered, but Talia knew where it was. Khelaran had gone through some rough decades, long before Traanafaeren was created. They'd locked their borders a little too well, including their waterways. None of their mages had been able to reverse the changes, or so they claimed. Storm's parents had believed the Khelaran king just liked maintaining control over access, but couldn't publicly admit to it.

"Land ho!" Edgar yelled down. "I've always wanted to yell that. Anyway, I see the coastline. I'm assuming the dark mass rising out of the sea is the back of Irundail?"

Talia nodded. "Aye. Someday I'd like to see it from the front. Not much to see from this end, but damn impressive."

Irundail was contained in a long and deep valley and the castle at the far end was backed up against massive obsidian cliffs. The same ones they could now see. At a thousand feet high, no one was getting into the valley from that way. Storm admired them as the channel flowed past. He'd been this way before but it had been a long time ago.

"Something is floating in the water," Edgar called down. "A bit ahead. A few somethings. Damn, it looks like bodies."

Storm moved to the bow and used his own glass. The small forms were still a bit ahead of them, but they did look like bodies.

"Did they kill everyone on the ship?" Flini had the wheel but was trying to see into the water.

"No idea. They did take many of the pirates with them. These could be them."

"Why would they do that?" Hon asked from the lines he was working. "Kidnap them and dump them at sea?"

"Demonspawn." Keanin had been focusing on his wind spell but he opened his eyes briefly. "They replaced them. They have to murder the people they take over."

"Damn it." Storm looked around the deck. "Do you have hooks of some kind?"

"We have this wench. This was a legitimate fishing vessel until my brother got bored with it." Talia brought forward a long arm that had been across the aft of the boat. "We can scoop them up."

He looked to Talia. "They might not all be pirates."

Talia handed her rigging off to Hon and put the fishing net arm in place. The net was far newer than the rest and was meant to hold large catches of fish from the big schools further away from the coast.

Storm knew they couldn't get all of the bodies, there were at least thirty that he could count. But he knew for Talia's sake if they saw any that looked like her brother, they needed to be brought aboard.

"You three have never seen Diath. His hair is short and blond like mine, only a bit longer." Her voice was mono-tone, the type people got when they were trying like hell not to cry or lose control.

Storm nodded and focused on the bodies they were approaching as Talia and Hon took over the net. The first ones were most likely pirates, long hair and mismatched clothes. Storm was grateful they were face down. Blood trailed from them, which meant the sea predators would soon be after them. A woman floated by, she was facing up and the few pieces of Khelaran armor she still had on hadn't pulled her down yet. Nor had it protected her from a jagged slice across her neck.

"One of Mikasa's Khelaran guards. The one that watched Edgar and me on the dock." He'd been pretty sure she recognized something about either he or Edgar, but they'd not find out now.

A blond kelar male and two humans, both face down and both with long hair so they could be male or female were the next on their grim passage. "There's a blond kelar male, starboard side." He kept his concern out of his voice. Talia didn't want it at this point, and he respected that.

Talia and Hon swung the netting rig to the right side and dipped it into the water. The blond kelar that was hauled up dripped as much blood as water. Whoever it was they'd gone down fighting.

"I can't see his face." Talia's voice was under control but the tension lines in her face and the way she gripped the rigging said she was anything but.

Storm ran over and pulled the netting closer. "Does your brother have a tattoo on his left arm? It looks like a sea monster?" Unless they brought the body on board, which they would if it was Diath, he couldn't get a good look at the face.

"Thank gods, no. He hates needles." Talia wiped her eyes and swung the arm back over the ocean. "We can't take them with us, but they'll rejoin the sea."

Two more women looked like the ladies who had been with Mikasa drifted past, but no more blond men. And no Mikasa. They continued to Craelyn.

Talia started shaking after they got past the bodies. Once they'd secured the hook and net she turned around. "We're not going to need to do much for the next half hour or so. The Khelaran kingdom is a heavy believer in magic. Their system will bring us in. I need to go to my room for a bit."

Everyone nodded and Keanin dropped his spell. "I'm a good listener." He stood by her but didn't block her.

At first, she looked ready to shake her head, but then she nodded. "I might not have much of worth to say."

"I'll be the judge of that." He smiled gently then they went below the deck.

Hon was watching from the aft as the bodies faded from view. "That's horrific. Not that I like pirates. But no one deserves that. How do we tell if we're fighting a demonspawn again?" They all moved toward the wheel so Flini could be involved.

Edgar came down off the crow's nest. There wasn't much to watch for since the Craelyn ship system was pulling them in. Storm had thought the system in Erlinda had been impressive—this was miles away and still able to control the ships and boats.

"They'll seem normal, that's the problem," Storm said. "But they are stronger and faster than us. If you press them and manage to gain an advantage, you'll notice that right off. They bleed green when cut deep enough, but the one we found in Erlinda was bleeding red for a while before it bled green. They usually return to their real form when killed."

"But not always. We don't know why but a few didn't turn back after the fight in the Markare." Edgar was sharpening his knives as they spoke.

"And some will change for the shock value. They did that at the ball, but I'd think since we now know they exist, that wouldn't be a great tactic," Storm added. He wished he had a way to identify them on sight and have a better defense than just 'fight for your life'. But there hadn't been time to study them enough. Which was probably why they kept poking to keep things off balance.

"We can't win against them, can we?" Flini remained by the wheel making minor adjustments but most of the steering was being done by the Craelyn system.

"We did in the Markare." Storm forced more sincerity than he felt into his voice. He'd led people before and while this fighting force was tiny, they still needed to think they could win, or there was no point in trying. Fear and self-doubt lost more battles than swords ever did. "It's not easy, I won't lie. But it can be done. In the Markare the one who'd replaced my father was their leader. Once he was killed, the others fell or vanished."

Edgar nodded. "We just have to figure out who the leader is."

CHAPTER FIFTY-FIVE

JENNA TRIED TO keep up with the increasingly wild fictitious tales Carabella wove as they traveled to the border. No more signs of grim riders, merchants, or anyone. And without her spell books to read, nothing to do.

Except listen to Carabella.

The cuari woman could spin a tale, that was for certain, but following the stories was a bit dicey as she seemed to be making it up as she went.

"And that is how the hole in the middle of the ocean came to be." Carabella nodded serenely as if she'd just given the secret of the universe to Jenna. "If you could go out there, way out there, you'd see. There's a hole to the other side of the world through the water."

"Maybe someday when this mess is over—" Jenna's words cut off as everything went dark.

"—I'll be able to do that." The words she'd been saying came out even though she wasn't facing Carabella anymore. And she was standing near a sooty circle that she was pretty sure once held a pair of giant dead sciretts.

She was back on the chaotic plane. This time she landed on her feet, but the area looked far worse than it had in her prior visit. The trees were dying. According to Meith, this version of the plane would be easier for the human mind to understand, but it should still be a reflection of the real plane. And right now it looked extremely sick.

"Hello? Is anyone here?" Hopefully whoever brought her back wasn't the one who'd been trying to get her to return to Los Angeles.

"Jenna? Thank the stars." Meith came scurrying out

from a few trees away. Like the area around him, he looked worse for wear. His robes were shabby and torn. He shook as he ran forward and took both her hands. "I didn't know if the spell would work. It's been so long since you were here, but the realm of chaos is under attack."

"I was just here a few days ago. What happened?" She looked down at his hands holding hers. "And how are you touching me? You said you were on a different plane of existence and couldn't touch me." She pulled her hands free. "You're not Meith."

He looked over his shoulder. "We have to hide. I am Meith, I am. The planes...the walls between them are crumbling. We can't stay here. It's been years since you were here before and I wish I had time right now to tell you everything. But all I can do is warn you. There is a battle going on that is going to determine reality. All of it. The world you live in now, your old world, and every world in existence. And there are thousands. All, plus the chaotic plane and everyone who exists here, will be destroyed. Time is already jumping, which is why you're out of time from me right now." He waved his hands in panic. "No time. I brought you here to warn you, what happens in your world is the key. It can save everything or lead to the destruction of all."

"What? How do we stop it?" She had so many questions but his frantic looking around was getting to her too. They didn't have time.

"Stop the war. There cannot be a war, the nations must hold strong. No war. The realm of chaos is being pulled apart, divided into warring factions. That can't happen in your world too—one will impact the other." He glanced around. "They are coming now. I wanted—"

Jenna's world went dark and she tumbled to the road next to her horse.

"Damn it!" She pounded the road in frustration. She

needed more information than that. They were already trying to stop any wars from happening in both Strann and Khelaran.

"Did you fall off your horse? I didn't notice." Ghortin had been right behind her and Carabella, he should have noticed that she vanished for a few minutes.

They stopped and she got up and dusted herself off. "No. I was in the plane, the chaotic plane. None of you noticed I was gone?" She wanted to test what just happened by trying to go to the chaotic plane and pull in magic—except that Ghortin's spell hiding her magic would have to be reset and they were only a few minutes from the Strann border. Not to mention that she might not have seen what she thought she just saw. Meith had said that it had been years since she'd been there. She had no idea what caused the jump in time, but it might not be something she could control.

"You were there on your horse and then you were on the ground." Crell had been a bit to the side of Ghortin but stepped forward. "I thought that I'd blinked and missed you falling off."

Carabella shook her head. "Whatever happened this is a bad place to discuss it. Guards are riding our way."

Jenna started to get back on her horse then stopped at Crell's shake of her head.

The guards cantered three abreast down the road, two rows of them, and stopped in front of Carabella.

"Was there a problem? We heard you coming down the road, then you stopped." The leader smiled but it was a flat cold smile. They'd hoped to catch people who didn't want to be seen by them.

"I wasn't paying attention and I fell off my horse." Jenna raised her dusty hands. "They were making sure I was okay."

The leader nudged his horse forward a few steps to investigate her hands. He sniffed and nodded. "Very well.

We are going further south; something was going on a
ways down the road. You didn't see anything, I assume?"
He asked the question but didn't seem interested in the
answer. He'd already dismissed them.

Carabella shrugged. "Nothing that we saw. But we did
hear something off in the woods last night." She pointed
the opposite direction that the ruin had been in. "It was
late, so we weren't going to investigate. But it was loud
whatever it was. How far is the border?"

The guard's horse stomped his feet. "You'll see it in
about fifteen minutes. Be prepared to be searched." He
didn't say anything more, just led his people through
them and toward the south.

"This is going to be fun," Ghortin said once the guards
had picked up speed and moved out of sight. "Probably
wait until we're someplace more secure to tell us what
just happened to you."

Jenna got back on her horse with a grimace. She'd hit
the road hard this time. "And hope I don't get pulled out
in front of anyone in Strann—especially guards." She had
no control over being pulled into the chaotic plane, but
she was praying to anyone who was listening that they
would leave her alone for a while.

The border was even closer than the guard said and
staffed with extremely bored-looking guards. All human,
all male. The guard troop that had ridden past them was
also all human but equally male and female.

Jenna had been living in Traanafaeren for the past
year—all three species called it home. She didn't realize
how odd it was to only see humans.

"State your name, your purpose for entering Strann,
and how long you will be staying." The guard stood in
front of them. He was on foot, as were most of them. But
there were two waiting on horseback for anyone who
tried to run.

There must have been some recent changes to Strann.

Jenna had never heard of it spoken in glowing terms, but it also was never mentioned as being as closed off as Derawri or Khelaran. That had changed.

Carabella toned down her perky-adventurer voice and calmly stated her made-up name, reason: to see a friend, and time of leaving: one week. They didn't ask for the name of her friend but did ask where the friend lived. She stated a town Jenna had never heard of before.

"Ahh, that's a good day's ride to the north. Travel well." The guard seemed appeased by the fact she knew someone in their country.

"Thank you. These are my traveling companions. Lisin, Herbert, and Fiane. They shall be accompanying me and have the same destination and length of time."

Jenna let out a mental sigh in gratitude at Carabella's words. She hadn't been looking forward to making something up. Not to mention she knew nothing of Strann's geography. Carabella picking a town far from here hopefully helped them.

"Thank you, we have noted the names. We do have to search your packs for contraband."

"Of course, we would expect no less." Carabella got off her horse and handed her pack to the guard.

The search was fine except when the guards came across the taran wands in Ghortin and Crell's packs. Each guard raised them in question.

Ghortin bustled forward. "You had the other one, Fiane! No wonder I couldn't find it last night." He plucked them both out of the guards' hands. "Firestarters. They don't work if you only have one." He grinned. "I can show you if you'd like? They're fascinating."

The guards waved him off. "No need. That's clearly what you would use two sticks for. You're all clear, you may carry on." From the wince on his face, he was afraid Ghortin would try to bore him to death talking about wood.

"Thank you." Carabella nodded and quickly walked away from the booth. The trail away from the booth looked a lot like the mostly empty land they'd just ridden through, clearly having a large population near the border wasn't common.

"Let's keep moving, shall we? I'd like to take a break in Lawri before we continue and our time will be close." She'd raised her voice louder than needed.

Jenna came alongside her and dropped her voice. "We're being followed?"

"More than that," Carabella said softly. "They put something in each of our packs, most likely a tracker of some sort. I saw it when Ghortin was showing off the wands." She looked around and smiled as she waved to the trees and raised her voice. "You are right, it is wonderful to be back here. Such a lovely land."

"Are we going to be okay looking for the book? We need to find it, but if they take it from us once we do?" Jenna kept her voice low as she plastered on a smile and she looked around the trail. Yep, same trees as to the south and she'd have to take Carabella's word about followers as she didn't see any.

"I'm hoping we can lose whoever is after us in the town and remove the trackers."

They rode for another ten minutes, all of them making small talk about their trip and the excitement of going to Lawri. The other two either saw their followers or assumed they were there. Jenna still saw and heard nothing, but the other three were more likely to notice them.

They got to a dip in the road when three men in masks rode in front of them.

"Thinking you didn't pay the empress's toll. Pay or we can't let you cross."

Jenna saw other followers in the woods now. Three more were standing back in the trees.

Carabella rode forward. "There's no toll in Strann,

friend. I'd thank you to stand down." She had her hand on the hilt of her sword. Jenna and Ghortin did the same. Crell had her bow and an arrow ready so fast that all Jenna caught out of the corner of her eye was a blur.

"There's four of you and eight of us."

"No, there's four of us and six of you. With those odds, I'd stand down." Carabella didn't look concerned and folded her arms.

There was a movement in the woods and Crell released an arrow, then had another arrow out. "Five now. Seriously, listen to the pretty lady and back down." Crell hadn't even looked at the ones facing them.

CHAPTER FIFTY-SIX

———◆———

THE APPROACH TO Craelyn was anticlimactic considering they'd just sailed through bodies of people murdered by demonspawn. They'd dropped the bodies far enough out that no one near land would have noticed. And once the sharks and other sea creatures got to the bodies, there would be nothing left.

The sounds from the dock as they approached seemed normal. Yells of commands and orders as ships were unloaded, the smell of fish, and the cries of seabirds hoping to get some of the fish.

"Where's the *Golden Harpy?*" Edgar leaned against the railing next to Storm as they came in. There were several docks and they seemed to be going to the smallest. Made sense, they were a much smaller boat compared to the large ships coming in. Even the fishing vessels were much larger.

"Probably at the far dock," Talia said as she and Keanin came up from below. Her eyes were red, but she seemed back in control of herself. "The ships from Erlinda usually get a good spot. Yup, look there." She and Keanin came to the bow and she pointed a ship out.

"It looks like they already unloaded. How'd they get that far ahead of us?" Storm used his glass on the ship in question but it looked empty.

"They shouldn't have been able to," Hon said from behind them. "The system that brings the ships in works the same for each ship."

"Unless someone in the channel guard is working with them." Talia shook her head. "I'd hoped to catch them on their ship, or at least near the docks. The further they travel the harder it will be to stop them."

"And the more likely they can spread demonspawn duplicates around." Edgar closed his glass. "We dock, find out where they went, and track them down."

Keanin put his hand on Talia's shoulder. "And we find your brother."

"Thank you." She touched his hand. "My guess would be they'd be heading for the castle if they're getting Mikasa to her groom."

"We need to get them before that happens." Storm said. "If she can replace him with a demonspawn, they can get more of their kind in there and replace the king and the entire royal staff. King Philia isn't a great ruler, but he's better than demonspawn."

They had just started securing their boat when a phalanx of armed militia marched toward them.

"Is this a problem?" Edgar asked as both Keanin and Storm pulled up the hoods on their cloaks.

"They can't be coming here. It must be another ship," Talia said but she looked worried.

"Hail, *Reef Dancer*, prepare to be boarded." The leader of the phalanx, a tall kelar male with long black hair, looked like he smelled rotting fish as he approached them.

"By whose orders? I have permission to dock here. We're from Erlinda." Talia kept her hand on her sword as she yelled back.

"By orders of King Philia. Your boat was seen attacking another vessel and leaving the dead in your wake. Including a guardswoman of the Khelaran military."

Everyone on the ship dropped their hands to their swords as another smaller ship, one they hadn't seen, came into the dock behind them. It blocked the only way for the *Reef Dancer* to get away and looked like it had a bunch of bodies lying on the deck.

Mikasa's crew had known someone was following them

and used the bodies to lock down those who would stop them.

"Drop your weapons overboard and stand with your hands over your heads. We would prefer to bring you in alive for your crimes." The look on his face was at odds with that. He might just be doing his job, but he wanted them to fight.

"That is probably not going to happen." Keanin hadn't been as close to the rail as the rest, but he stepped forward now. "We're not going anywhere. But you are." He lifted his arms, spat out a few sharp-sounding spell words, and the entire phalanx rose in the air. "When I drop them, you all might want to run." He grunted as he spoke and the sweat running down his face indicated how hard it was to hold them aloft.

He didn't drop them so much as fling them into the bay behind their boat and in front of the one blocking them. The guards were all wearing armor and the frantic motions of them trying to take it off before they were pulled under got the other ship's attention.

Talia and Keanin led the others over the railing but there was no time to lower the ramp. The people on the dock were stunned at what happened and while they were trying to sort things out, the six ran past them.

"This way!" Hon sprinted to the lead and led them down a side alley. Then two more, each getting narrower. He finally slowed down but kept moving. "Finding us in here will be hard, but we need to get to the center. It's the poor part of Craelyn and running will cause too much unwanted attention." He looked around. "Probably a good idea to sheathe your swords too."

Talia patted him on the back. "Good call. It's been too long since I've been in this area and it's changed drastically. I'd never be able to find my way out." The pathways became smaller and the homes darker and dingier.

"Why aren't there people here?" Storm looked around.

He understood when they were running—armed people running through a poor part of town was never good. But they'd been walking for a bit now. Yet not only was no one out but no one was even looking through windows, as he looked closer, he saw things on the ground that shouldn't be. Washing, wet from the bucket, dumped in a pile. Rough toys left out where any other kid could take them.

"They're hiding," Hon said as he led them further in.

Edgar stopped and reached down. "Food. Fresh stew, dumped on the ground." He touched it and looked closer at the dirt around them. "No one living here could afford to drop food. It's still warm. And look at the ground."

Storm squatted down as well. "Boots." He pointed to a distinctive mark. "And that's the tip of the boots of a Khelaran soldier." He looked around the dirt road. "A bunch of them. Damn it, they cleared out the poor section of town? Why?"

Keanin didn't drop down but grew pale as he studied the dirt in front of him. He finally looked up. "They needed more bodies. They were taken to become demonspawn."

"You don't know that." Flini looked around. Finally, he went to the nearest house and knocked on the door. It swung open as soon as he touched it. They all went to houses and knocked. All of them were unlocked with no one inside.

"We probably want to leave before someone tries to blame this on us too," Hon said. "I know somewhere we can hide, but we'll get a bit close to the castle."

"Since that's where we need to be, lead on." Edgar nodded and they all followed Hon.

Storm let out a breath as they heard the welcome sounds of kids running and playing as they came out of the poor area. This neighborhood wasn't high-end, but the houses were well maintained and spread out. A group of kids was running at the far end of the street chasing each other in a game that involved a lot of laughing.

"No one noticed what happened in the poor quarter?" Flini shook his head. "How could all of those people have been taken and no one a few blocks away noticed?"

"People don't notice what they don't want to. Especially when it comes to the invisible poor." Storm looked at the houses as they passed. The kids might not have noticed, but a few worried glances from adults inside the houses watching them said that they knew something had happened.

They got out to the main road to find bright banners and signs hung everywhere. The tournament was in one day.

"Damn it, think of all of the people they could kill and replace if they went after the tournament? Fighters from all of Khelaran and beyond come to this event." Talia had been mostly quiet, but she was visibly upset along with the rest.

Hon looked down where the road bent. "It sounds like something is coming this way. Might be for the tourney…"

"Might be people looking for us or grabbing more victims," Talia finished for him. "Get us out of here."

Hon ran across the street with the rest close by. He ducked behind a wall and motioned for them to sit. "We need to wait here. Whoever they are they're too close and would spot us if we go further."

The clomping of heavy boots and hooves grew louder. People from the nearby houses came running out waving brightly colored streamers.

Storm swore under his breath as the first riders came around the corner. It was King Philia and his entourage, in tourney regalia. On his right rode a heavyset older kelar not looking happy to be on his horse. Directly behind him, with an entourage of her own, rode Lady Mikasa. And the two Khelaran guardswomen they'd seen in Erlinda. At least one was a demonspawn duplicate as it was the woman they'd seen in Erlinda and floating in the water on the way here.

Keanin's hand started twitching and it wasn't to go for his sword.

Storm reached over to grab his hand before he cast any spells. He shook his head when Keanin looked over. He was furious and Storm didn't blame him after what had happened to him. Knowing that there were probably many demonspawn riding past—possibly Mikasa herself was one—didn't make it easy for any of them.

But giving away their location right now would just get them captured or killed. They needed to find a place to recoup, make a plan, then see how many they could destroy. Getting out of Khelaran alive was looking less likely. But he would take out as many of the demon-spawn and anyone working with them as he could before he went.

Keanin sucked in a gasp and started shaking and Storm turned back to the people marching by. Another group of women, lower middle class, but still connected enough to be in this parade, were riding by. Including a few very pregnant ones in an open carriage.

"That's them. I recognize them." Keanin's voice was little more than a whisper and his golden eyes were wide with a combination of terror and fury. He also looked ready to do something he shouldn't at any moment. Short of gagging and sitting on him, Storm had no idea how he could stop him.

Talia was on the other side of Keanin and reached over to grab his arm with one hand and turned his face to her with her other. Her voice was too low for Storm to hear the words, but the tone was soft, soothing, and understanding.

The tension left Keanin, and the parade continued its march down the road, eventually following the long road to the castle.

Hon waited a few moments for the stragglers; people who weren't part of the parade officially but joined in any way to follow the crowd, and for the rest of the people return to their homes. "Okay, it's not far." He kept low and zigzagged behind a few merchant buildings into a small wooded area. "Found this place a few months ago. Diath and I were working with another ship crew and decided to stay over. No one's been in it for years." He crept over to a small ramshackle hut in the middle of the woods. There wasn't much to it and it appeared ready to collapse if anyone looked at it for too long.

But it was better than being exposed.

As beaten as the hut was, the door was solid. "It sticks a bit, but here we go." Hon swung open the door and Edgar sent a glow in.

A beaten blond man sat hunched over a broken table. He raised his head wearily. "Who are you? Do what you want, I'm not going back." His tunic was torn and covered in green blood.

Talia stumbled forward, stopping when she saw the tunic. "Diath?"

CHAPTER FIFTY-SEVEN

———◆———

JENNA ADJUSTED HER grip on her sword and patted her horse's neck. The three attackers facing them didn't respond much when one of their people had been killed. Then they got off their horses and stomped forward.

"Seriously? This woman has a bow and can kill all of you before you get near us." Jenna had no idea what their plan was unless they wanted to get shot.

"Get off your horses and fight us." The first one slowed down but didn't stop. Until Crell put an arrow in his shoulder. It could have been a fatal shot; she was holding back.

He kept coming.

She fired an arrow at his other shoulder.

"Now that's not fair," the voice didn't come from the attackers and sounded more like a disgruntled older woman. "You should have at least fought a little bit. It's not easy to make these mannequins react, you know. The empress ain't any fonder of magic than me." A moment after she spoke, the five remaining attackers vanished into a puff of black smoke and an older gnome female appeared before them.

"Who are you and what are you doing? Also, do you think you can vanish before she puts an arrow in you? My patience is wearing thin." Carabella leaned over her horse to glare at the woman. From the way her hand was twitching, Jenna knew she wanted to hit her with a nasty spell.

The gnome was not impressed. "Eh, I have to protect

my livelihood now, don't I? Not many magic users in Strann get to be as old as me, especially ones that ain't human, like three of you fine people are. I had to make sure you weren't magic users come to trick me. Had you been magic users, you would have blasted my mannequins apart in a blaze of magical glory. And ya would have never found me." She folded her arms. "You *are* here for the book, I take it?"

Jenna leaned back; she was going to let Ghortin deal with this one. He's the one who'd found out that the cuari book was here—she'd no idea if these sources told this woman about them coming to get it or not.

"Are you known in certain circles as Falcon?" Ghortin rode his horse forward. It was hard to tell if he was concerned about meeting this woman out here or not.

"The one and only. If you need it, I can get it. As it happened, I've got a lot of books including the one you're looking for. I'd show you the way, but like my mannequins, I'm not really here. I will see you at the bookshop soon. You can't miss it, it's the only one with books." With an odd half bow to Ghortin, she vanished.

"Okay, what was that?" Crell got off her horse and retrieved her arrows where they'd stuck into the ground. "I swear I heard them thunk into flesh."

"She's good." Ghortin rubbed his chin. "I wasn't even sure who we were dealing with, but if that's the only shop in Lawri, then that must be her. I trust the sources the information came from." He started down the path.

"I'm not sure *I* trust her. Testing to see if we're magic users?" Crell got back on her horse but kept her bow and quiver out. "Even I know it took a lot of magic for her to pull off those damn mannequins."

"Agreed." Carabella followed behind Ghortin. "And I would have dearly loved to have smacked her magical self away from us. Alas, we have to deal with what we deal with. I do wonder how she hasn't been stopped if the empress is forbidding magic, however."

"She's selling people out to them," Jenna said softly, but it felt right. "Think about it. She says it's for her protection, but I'm sure that if we'd used magic, the next visit we'd have would be with armed guards, not hollow images." There might not be magic on Earth, but that kind of behavior was sadly not unknown.

"You could be right." Crell rode alongside her as Carabella traveled next to Ghortin. "I say we get your book, then get out of this land and back home as soon as possible."

"Agreed. There is something wrong here—Strann was never against magic before. We need to report what we can." Ghortin didn't reach for his taran wand though. "Once we're back in Traanafaeren." From the delay, he'd been about to reach for the wand, then thought better about it.

Jenna wasn't sure if there was anyone still following them or if that had been Falcon's spell they'd felt before, but all of them stayed quiet as they rode.

The road finally opened wider as it went into the small town. This was clearly the main road as all of the shops huddled along it. Houses lurked behind the shops but even they weren't too far from the road. All in all, not a place Jenna wanted to stay long at.

"Ah, there it is." Ghortin had been looking into the open shops as they passed since only half had signs out front. But he'd spotted a sign with a scroll and open book toward the end of the row.

They spread out more as they followed the road, all of them with their hands on their sword hilts—even Crell had her bow put away and kept her hand on the hilt of her sword.

"Are you going to take all day?" The woman—Jenna had a hard time thinking of her like a falcon—walked out of the shop and stood there glaring until Ghortin reached her. "Leave your horses there and get in here. I don't have all day and there are other customers interested in it." She stomped back into her store.

Jenna moved her horse next to Ghortin as they led them to a hitching post. "There are others? No one else should even know the books exist."

"I know. This might not be our book. I trust my source implicitly, but they did vanish not long after passing the information along. Be wary. Remember, there will be a lag if you have to break my spell hiding your magic."

That wasn't reassuring. After being admonished not to use magic, being reminded what would happen if she did made the spot between her shoulder blades ache. Like they'd all just become targets.

Horses secured, they walked into the shop. Aside from it being mostly open to the front, and being full of books in languages never seen on Earth, it could have been any used bookstore anywhere on Earth.

The gnome woman came scurrying out from the back. "Come on, do you think I can keep dark arts books just sitting about?" She threw her hands in the air and stomped back behind a curtain.

"Dark books? What?" Jenna hissed. Carabella and Crell didn't say anything but both looked ready to fight.

"If it's a book like the others, she probably can't open it. Some people think that's dark arts." Ghortin pushed the curtain away.

The gnome woman smiled as she blocked a pile of books. "Let me see the coins."

Ghortin poured a pile of small gold coins into his hand, closing his fingers over them when she got too close. "The book?"

"Fine." She turned around, dug under a massive pile of books, and held out a small, black book. That it was dark arts was given away by what looked like dried blood on the edges of the pages.

"That's—" Jenna started to speak but was cut off.

"Just what I was looking for. Thank you, Falcon, I believe?" Linton entered the back area with his sword at Carabella's back. "I wasn't certain how I could make contact with you as I figured once you saw me, you'd burn the shop down."

Jenna thought he'd been speaking to Ghortin but his eyes were fixed on the bookseller.

Falcon snarled and held her hand up with a spell crackling inside her fingers. "Lich. Death mongerer. You can't have this. Never."

"And if you let loose that spell, the royal empress' guards will be on you in moments. I will kill everyone in this town if you don't hand the book over." His smile was horrible. "And then I can raise them to do my bidding. Even you. I will have that book."

Jenna tried to take a step back to get more room if she did have to use a spell, but Linton pressed his sword into Carabella's back. "It's much harder to raise the dead with holes in vital organs, but with my new book, I can do it. Don't make me start with this one."

Ghortin slowly turned around. "I didn't know that Qhazborh was bringing in liches to do his bidding. They must be desperate."

"I am not a lich; I am a necromancer. My Powers came from the gods and goddesses themselves. That book was written for us, did you know that? I was told to come here and find it from a higher power."

Jenna shivered. Necromancer or lich, Linton was basically the walking dead. Not a zombie, he looked normal, but with the right books, he could do some damage. Ghortin had told her of them during her early training. Because of the issues with their brains, they couldn't remember spells and could only do magic with books. She looked at the one still in Falcon's hand.

There was no way Linton was getting that book. Even

with Ghortin's magic dampeners on her, she felt the evil-ness in it.

She was getting ready to blast him apart and deal with the impact of using her magic when Ghortin beat her to the punch.

The words he spoke were fast and slippery, not ones that lingered even in Jenna's ear. He held out his left hand and Linton was blasted through the wall.

Falcon swore. "You are mages; you're going to bring down the patrol on all of us." She tried to run past Car-abella.

Carabella grabbed her. "I don't think so. I can't use magic, but I have other ways to stop you." She twisted Falcon's hand. It didn't look like much, but Falcon's face contorted and she dropped the book. Carabella stood back as Falcon broke free. She nodded to a dust rag on a table. "I can't touch it, and you shouldn't touch it. Grab that rag before you get the book, this thing needs to be destroyed."

Ghortin nodded then ran out after Linton. Linton was limping but he still ran off.

Crell helped Carabella wrap the book in layers of blan-kets. Jenna went to help them but was lifted off her feet and landed near a pile of books.

"*I am sorry. The book is here. You must get it.*" Typhonel had appeared again and was now able to fling her body around. She'd be more upset but she saw a familiar look-ing gray spine in the pile of books he threw her into. She grabbed it and felt a purr come from it. That this was one of the three books of the cuari—five, she cor-rected herself—was clear even without opening it. But of course, she had to. The pages looked like the other two. She quickly shut it. Falcon might have had the wrong buyer, but she had the right book after all.

"I can't destroy this thing without magic. I need you or Ghortin." Carabella shook her head. "That won't work either, we need to get far from here to destroy this."

"Too bad we're a thousand miles from the volcano chain." Crell had checked down the alley to see where Ghortin and Linton went but came back.

"You are brilliant!" Carabella's face brightened and she rolled back her sleeves.

"No!" Jenna had just finished securing the cuari book in the bottom of her pack and looked over. "You can't use magic." She'd tackle Carabella if needed.

"Pish, I know. I have portals rigged to a few choice locations. A few hundred years ago I was studying volcanism. The portal is small on this one, but I don't need much room." She opened a small box-shaped portal. A blast of heat filled the room. The book wasn't large but it still took some work to fit it and its blankets inside.

With a burst of flame, the hole closed a moment later.

"That was rude. The empress is serious about not allowing magic. My portal was shut down by someone other than me." By the way Carabella narrowed her eyes, Jenna was glad she wasn't the empress.

Jenna pulled out some coins and left them near where the book was. She looked up to see Crell and Carabella watching her. "I don't like stealing—unless absolutely needed. Falcon did lose two books today. How are we going to find Ghortin?"

"Judging by the direction they took off, I'd guess they went toward the woods. Linton wouldn't want anyone else recognizing him—clearly, Falcon knew who and what he was." Crell led as they left the bookstore and got their horses. Jenna tied Ghortin's behind her own. "He should have waited until I could help."

"That's my son, never waits for anyone." Carabella glanced up and down the street then raised the hood on her cape.

Jenna did the same but couldn't tell anyone, even herself, why. It felt like something was watching them.

The trail in the woods was wider than it looked from the outside. At first, Jenna couldn't figure out why as nothing was out here, then she saw the odd building. It looked as if someone had started with a church, then introduced off-colors and angles. It almost looked normal, but subtle tones of color and edges that were just a few degrees off left an unsettling result. Before seeing this, Jenna would say it would be impossible for architectural design to make someone physically sick. This one managed to do that. She looked away quickly.

Carabella stopped her horse and started shaking. "Those things were all destroyed." Her voice was barely a whisper.

Jenna rode alongside her but had to touch her arm to get her to look her way. "What is it? Carabella? What is that thing?"

Crell rode forward but had her bow ready. "That's a Qhazborh temple, isn't it? Damn, my great-great-great grandmere told me how they destroyed them all. That thing doesn't look new either."

"Ghortin is in there. He went in there. I know he did." Carabella's voice was stronger but she still hadn't moved forward.

"Then we go in." Jenna started her horse forward, then thought better of it. Whatever that temple was, the horses were as agitated as Carabella. "Second thought, let's leave the horses here. I don't want to tie them, but could you ask them not to leave?" Both Carabella and Crell had shown the ability to speak to horses. Jenna patted her mare and asked her nicely, but she wasn't sure she understood.

The temple had been silent when they approached and it stayed that way as they went to the door. Jenna got there first and opened the door a crack.

Ghortin was there. Unconscious and chained to a bloody wall, but he was there. Linton was nowhere to be seen, but a tall, blond human was securing Ghortin's feet into cuffs.

Ravenhearst turned with a flat smile. "Thank you. I didn't want to have to hunt you all down. Linton isn't the brightest minion." He laughed as the door locked behind them.

CHAPTER FIFTY-EIGHT

"TALIA?" THE MAN started to get out of the chair, but Talia stepped away from him and raised her sword.

"What did you do to my brother? Was he one of the bodies you dumped in the channel and we missed him? Talk, demonspawn, or I'll see how long I can keep you alive with limbs cut off."

"It's *me*. They grabbed me on the ship, like everyone else. Hon? Flini? What are any of you doing here? Tell her it's me." He raised hands with bloody knuckles, but both were caked with red blood not green.

Hon and Flini looked less certain than Talia, but they too drew their swords.

Keanin stepped forward, pausing next to Talia, at her nod he turned to the man. "You don't know me, but I am a friend of Talia's and I know what you are. Answer her questions." He raised the man, chair and all, into the air.

"It's me! Gods! It is me." He finally looked down at his tunic. "This isn't my blood. I fought that creature off after I saw what they did to the pirates they took. Look." He lifted his tunic. A crude bandage made out of another shirt was wrapped around his torso. He pulled it back and showed a nasty gash across his skin. "It's red, I bleed red. It's me."

Talia turned to Keanin and put her hand on his arm. "It's him. I know it."

Keanin held him aloft for a few more seconds, and then lowered the man.

Talia ran forward and hugged him as tight as she could

without pulling his wound open. "Damn you, Diath, you're alive." She was laughing and crying.

Storm stayed back but Edgar moved closer.

"How did you survive against a demonspawn? That's what you fought if it bleeds green."

"I guess I need a new tunic," Diath said as he plucked at it. He finally looked up. "I didn't. There were two of the demonspawn and they'd cornered one of the remaining pirates and myself. We fought and were losing badly when the pirate gets this look in his eyes and starts chanting some spell. Guess he was a magic user but hadn't wanted to use it in front of them." He paled. "They did some awful things to another magic user they found, and it took a long time for him to die. But this guy realized he was about to die anyway, so he spells both of the creatures." Diath leaned forward. "They changed. Right there. Massively long arms, scaly skin, backward legs.... it was awful."

"And?" Talia had been trying to wipe the blood off him but all of their supplies were back on the boat.

"And then they killed the pirate. Tore him apart actually." He paused, then shook his head. "They were coming for me when both started choking and grabbing their throats. I ran forward, stabbed them as many times as I could, and jumped off the ship."

"They choked? But they breathe fine when they've taken over other forms." Storm wanted to believe him, but they'd run across too many demonspawn for that to be the case.

"They did. I don't know what the spell was that he said. I'm not a magic user. But I could tell you the words, they'll be in my mind for the rest of my life. Maybe whatever spell he used poisoned them?"

"What were the spell words?" Keanin asked.

Diath shrugged. "Lieniath. Colopsia. Duinth."

Keanin's eyes went wide. "That's not a strong spell, but

it's used to uncover the truth, it wouldn't poison them. There were no other words?"

"Nope. Only those. That pirate saved me from them, even though he couldn't save himself."

Edgar nodded. "How long between when he spoke the spell, when they changed, and when they collapsed?"

"Not long. Maybe three seconds for them to change? Could have been faster, it was right after the final word was said. It didn't take them more than a few seconds to kill him, maybe ten seconds in all? They looked like they were dying when they went down, but I couldn't take the chance. That's when I stabbed them and ran."

"Then what poisoned them?" Storm asked.

"Maybe it's just being here that did it. This isn't their world, right?" Hon still kept his distance from Diath, but he'd put away his sword.

Storm shook his head. "They transformed when we first fought them in the ballroom back in Lithunane. They were fighting that way."

"They'd changed by their own choice that time," Edgar said. "And they didn't last long after that rogue mage took the king and Ghortin. You were already gone, called back to Irundail by the family beacon. I was there. They all collapsed not long after you left. Franklin claimed he'd cast a spell but no one could prove it. And honestly, no one believed it. We know Franklin was working for Ravenhearst and lied all the time. Maybe he was covering their weakness?"

Keanin started smiling. "If we can get enough of the demonspawn together, I can spell them. Then we wait for them to die."

Diath winced as Talia continued to try and clean his wound. "Except they still killed the pirate before they started having problems. They'd take out anyone near them."

"Unless we get them in a situation where they can't get

to anyone." Edgar smiled. "What if a medium-level spell user chanted the reveal spell while Keanin got them into the air? You've gotten quite good at that by the way."

Keanin frowned. "I wouldn't be able to hold them long, especially if there are a lot of them."

"From what Diath said, it might be enough." Storm preferred fighting directly, but against demonspawn, that wasn't a great option. "We need to see if this works. We don't have much of a chance to get out of this country anyway, and wouldn't you like to take some of those creatures down?"

"And those women who went into the castle." Talia looked to Keanin.

He paled. "They have to be stopped. I've no idea why they're creating what they're creating, but it can't go on. We need to do this."

"They're trying to find a way around their inability to live long on our world." Edgar shook his head. "Damn it. If they can breed creatures with their strength, who aren't threatened by having to take another's form...they'll be unstoppable." He grimaced. "More so than they already are."

Talia turned to her brother. "You mentioned that they tortured a magic user? Could you tell why?"

"They wanted to see the level of his magic. He wasn't strong enough, I guess, so they eventually killed him."

"Has anyone ever seen them use magic?" Talia asked.

Keanin started to answer, then paused. "There was magic being used on me when I was attacked...but I don't think it was from the demonspawn. There were kelar and human mages there." He shook his head. "I don't know how I never noticed. But no magic from them." He turned to Storm and Edgar. "In Lithunane, they didn't use magic, that rogue mage did. In the Mark-are, the fake king had magic users with him. And he was pulling magic from me to hold all of you in place. Talia, you're brilliant!'"

"And that could be another benefit of making hybrids with the species from this world. If they mix with strong magic users…" Edgar stopped. "We have to stop them. I'm going to pass this information to Ghortin and Rachael. We need to go after the demonspawn now. Even if we don't survive."

Storm followed him to the corner of the room while the others talked with Diath. "I'd like to speak to Jenna if you get through. I'll keep it short."

"I'll hand it over after I tell Ghortin." Edgar's hand tightened on his shoulder. He knew what Storm needed to tell Jenna.

Edgar held the wand but kept it close to his ear as he quickly told Ghortin what they'd discovered. "Storm needs to speak to Jenna. Then I'm contacting Rachael, this information needs to be shared." He handed the wand over and stepped back. "I can't go far, but I'm not listening."

Storm took the wand. "Hi, Jenna. I just wanted to let you know that we're about to do something dangerous and possibly fatal. Ghortin can fill you in. But I want you to know how much I care about you. I love you. No matter what happens that won't change."

"You're scaring me. Not the I love you part, I love you too. What are you three doing?" Her voice rose a few octaves.

"Trying to save the world, same as you. I can't talk, we have to kill a bunch of demonspawn—if we can. Take care of yourselves. I love you." He ended the call before she could say more. He'd said what he needed to say, and more would just tear the hole in both of their hearts larger. She knew his feelings, that was what was important.

Edgar took the wand back and leaned forward. "You have some dust in your eye."

Storm wiped the tear away. "Thanks."

Rachael's call was more detailed as Edgar had to share the spell words with her—Ghortin already knew them.

Afterward, they walked back to the others and Diath watched them. "So, the seven of us are going to destroy a bunch of demonspawn, in a secure castle with hundreds of guards and hotshots gathering for the tourney?"

Edgar gave a lopsided grin. "More has been won with less. Unless you have somewhere to be?"

"Nope. I've already lived longer than I thought I would. What's the plan?"

The plan was alarmingly simple, but probably the only one that had a slim chance of success. They sorted it out, then snuck out of the cabin. Waiting until nightfall had been strongly encouraged by Edgar, but Storm didn't think they had that long.

Hon knew of a back way into the castle. He'd spent his teenage years in Khelaran with a traveling father. Teenagers always found a way to get where they weren't supposed to be.

The entrance was a level above the dungeon and probably part of the original castle design but forgotten over the centuries. They hacked their way to the doorway, the overgrowth was massive, then they couldn't get the door open.

"It's been a while since I was here." Hon tugged on the door some more.

They'd agreed to limit their magic usage until the time to attack as they didn't want to risk giving themselves away. Even so, after ten minutes of all of them fussing with the door, Keanin looked ready to blast it.

Edgar grabbed his arm. "Hold on, I think I have one of those preset spell bombs Ghortin gave me." He'd used most of them at Shettler's Point, but after some slapping of various pockets, he pulled out a small round object. "This shouldn't give us away the same way your magic would. The explosion might be more than we'd like, but hopefully, this isn't a regularly used part of the castle."

Keanin stepped back with a bow. "And if anyone does come down here and sense magic, they'll think it was Ghortin—if they can trace anything. For this plan to work, the demonspawn can't know I'm here until it's too late."

The spell bomb gave a pop and the lock loosened. It still took both Hon and Storm to pull it open and even then only a little. It was enough to get in, however.

The corridor was empty and filthy, both good signs. Storm followed closely behind Hon as he led them to some equally abandoned stairs. They were only a flight up when the screams started below them.

"They are torturing people down there." Storm froze then turned as he heard a child yelling, "*Leave him alone.*" "The people of the poor area—they grabbed the kids too. You go on. I need to stop this." He started back down the stairs.

"By yourself? Seriously, if we do make it out, I'm telling Jenna you have some extremely bad tendencies." Keanin turned to follow and so did the rest.

"I can get them out. You go on with the plan." Storm needed to do this, but they also had to stop the atrocities that the demonspawn were doing.

"No. And what's the point if we're going to let innocent people die? Isn't that what we're trying to stop?" Edgar asked.

Storm started to argue then shook his head. "Let's free them." He stopped at the door they'd come in at. "Can two of you work on getting that door open wider? They'll need a way out and won't have much time."

Hon and Flini nodded and went down toward the door.

"He's confident, I'll give him that. Where'd you find these people anyway?" Diath nodded toward Storm. He had a pair of daggers ready, one from Flini and one of

Edgar's extras.

"I needed some help finding you, and they were available." Talia patted his shoulder.

The sounds came from the only cell with people in it, a large one, but there wasn't room for the fifty or so men, women, and children who were crammed inside. Three guards were pulling the adults out one at a time and beating them. They weren't even asking questions.

And they were cocky enough to have left the cell door open.

Storm pushed the door open wider. "Doesn't seem like a fair fight. Maybe you'd like to step back." All the frustration at not having been able to protect Keanin, Jenna, or anyone else he loved came out as he attacked the closest guard without waiting for a response. Talia dove in as well, with Edgar taking the third. Keanin and Diath herded the terrified people out of the cell.

Which was harder than expected as the people they were rescuing seemed frozen in place. Storm saw a little boy watching him. "You need to get these people out. Safety is waiting." He got the words out as he blocked a blow from the guard he fought.

The little boy nodded and started pushing people. "Out! We get out!" Soon all of them were following Keanin up the stairs with Diath bringing the rear.

Storm waited until they were gone, then ran his sword through the guard and let him drop.

Talia and Edgar finished theirs off as well.

"Not sure how smart that was, but we had to do it." Storm shook his shoulders out. He'd feel better if there had been a few more to fight. He wasn't a violent person, but pent-up frustration was getting to him.

"We did. Let's go find the others." Edgar ran up the steps with the other two close behind.

The townspeople from the cell were gone and Hon, Flini, Keanin, and Diath were pulling to close the door to the outside.

"They made it, but there's no way they'll not draw attention. We won't be going out that way," Diath said.

That had been the plan, but Edgar didn't look worried. "We'll get out somehow. But we need to move fast, too many things are going to make them notice us."

Chapter Fifty-Nine

JENNA DREW HER sword. She hadn't liked Raven-hearst the second she met him. He'd only increased that feeling in the past year. Hopefully, she could get rid of the problem for good.

"You'd think Qhazborh would supply you with better help." Carabella had recovered from her original shock at finding this place and crept forward. She also had her sword out but her hand was shaped as if she was going to let loose a spell.

Crell moved a few steps over, aimed, and fired an arrow at Ravenhearst.

He batted it aside easily. "My god will enjoy having so many sacrifices. As for you, cuari, please cast a spell. It would be nice to get you with the others of your kind." He waved his hand, and a dark cloud, not unlike what Jenna had seen in the ruins as they were leaving, appeared behind him. A dozen warriors made of bone and shadow stepped forward.

Jenna had no idea what they were, aside from hor-ribly creepy, but Carabella gave an inarticulate yell and charged for Ravenhearst.

He laughed and flung her back against the far wall. She slumped to the ground, unconscious. "They can take you awake or not. Makes no difference to them." Three of the creatures moved toward Ghortin, their jaws opening impossibly wide as if they were going to eat him.

Crell continued to fire arrows but they had no effect. Jenna yelled and ran forward. In mid run, a force took her over. "No. You cannot do this. Let your gods and goddesses know, we will not stand for it." Typhonel was back and had either found friends or was now referring to himself in the royal 'we'.

Jenna didn't care, as words she didn't know and would never remember flowed from her. The things going after Ghortin screamed, charged toward her, and slowly vanished halfway to her. Even Ravenhearst paled.

"You can't take action here. The gods can't take action." He scrambled backward but was trapped against the wall.

Jenna ran to him. "Your deities crossed the wrong line. Go back to the abyss and join them."

She had no idea what Typhonel was planning on doing, she was pretty much along for the ride. But she felt his hatred of Ravenhearst. And she strongly agreed with it. Typhonel put his fear of what could come into Jenna's hands, then her hand went to Ravenhearst's head and his existence ceased to be.

Jenna felt an odd popping sound as everything that Ravenhearst had been vanished. Then Typhonel fled her mind and she crumpled to the floor.

Crell patted her cheek and pulled on her arm. "I don't think we want to stay here. Whatever you just did really pissed off the owners of this place." As she spoke rumbling came from the floor.

"I could use some help." Carabella had recovered and was working on the chains on Ghortin. "He's still not conscious and we don't want to be in here."

Jenna scrambled to her feet. She felt a bit lopsided, and off-balance, but was able to help free Ghortin. He started to awaken as they crossed out of the doorway.

"It's going to take this part of the woods with it," Crell yelled as she ran for the horses. The land around them was shaking and caving in as a sinkhole formed around the building. There was no way to tell how far it would go, but the building and a few massive trees were already lost from sight. "Get up, Ghortin, can you ride?" The look on her face said if he couldn't, she was going to toss him over the saddle. Jenna forgot that derawri were small in stature but massively strong for any size.

Ghortin wasn't running but he nodded and climbed atop his horse. "What happened? I was chasing Linton, now I'm here."

Carabella raced out with the rest following. Jenna stayed alongside Ghortin; he didn't look great. "Ravenhearst. Linton brought you to him. He's dead now."

"Linton?"

"Ravenhearst. My friend took care of him."

"Talk later, run now!" Carabella called back.

They made it to the town and the shops. Falcon came running out. "There you are! You have to hide; the magic searchers are looking for you."

Ghortin swore. "They'll keep searching until they find a magic user. Fine." He to a murder of crows in the trees behind them and waved his hand. "You all now have a magic signature, my friends. Go fly far and wide."

"Not sure what you did, but let's hide this way. My shop is too well known." They tied up their horses then Falcon led them to a storage room. It was open but so dark it would be hard for anyone to see in. "I also sell fabric, but not under my name. Stay here."

Jenna took her arm as she started to leave. "Thank you isn't enough. Why are you doing this?"

"Things have been wrong here for a while. I think I want to be on the side that fixes them. Not to mention, you paid me well." She smiled and vanished.

Ghortin was just sitting down when his vest started buzzing. He frowned almost the moment he answered it and kept his words low. Then he handed it to Jenna.

There was only one purpose for that call, Storm didn't plan on surviving.

CHAPTER SIXTY

HON CONTINUED TO lead and they went back up the stairs they'd started on before. They couldn't save everyone involved, but they'd managed to get that group out. Hopefully, that counted for something.

The stairwells grew less dusty as they got to the more utilized part of the castle, but they hadn't met anyone. Yet.

The wailing at the next floor stopped them.

"There aren't dungeons here," Hon whispered and turned to go up the next flight.

The wailing turned to screams of terror. "That doesn't mean they don't have victims here." Storm ran down the corridor.

Diath ran along with the others. "He's not afraid of anything. Does he think he's an avenging prince or something?"

"Yes, actually." Edgar ran faster to catch Storm.

The room they ran into had once been a large meeting hall but hadn't been used for a while. It was now a bower of women—some pregnant. Mikasa spun as Storm ran in.

"Oh, my beloved fiancé, I am so glad I get to be the one to take your life. I will make it as slow and painful as possible."

Keanin and Edgar stopped behind Storm, and Keanin started forward when he saw the pregnant women.

Edgar grabbed his arm. "Spells."

Storm held back from attacking Mikasa even though she pulled out a nasty short blade.

But even he was shocked when Edgar muttered the disclosure spell and every woman in the room changed.

Except for the pregnant ones. There were five of them and they all shook sharply—they were fighting it—but kept their non-demonspawn forms as they ran toward the back of the room.

The Mikasa demonspawn charged for Storm, her claws glimmering sickly. Keanin got all of them in the air before she could get him but she swung at him anyway. The screeching changed as the demonspawns' air supply faded. Once none of them were moving or yelling, Keanin dropped them.

Diath and Talia ran forward and cut off their heads. After a moment Hon and Flini followed, making sure that none were missed.

"Damn it!" Keanin ran across the room to an open secret door. "They escaped. The pregnant ones escaped." He started to follow when a rumble shook the stairway and Edgar barely pulled him back in time as the entire ceiling collapsed and the hidden stairway was buried in the rubble.

"They had an escape plan and either one of them can do magic, or someone set up a spell to protect them." Edgar didn't let go of Keanin's arm. "Either situation, there's no way they wouldn't have heard that collapse in the rest of the castle. We have to get to the throne room before the king and his courtiers are turned. If they aren't already."

Keanin looked ready to climb through the debris but shook it off. "We will stop them. We will."

They made it out of the room and up the stairs when they heard boots coming down the hall below them.

Storm looked to Keanin who was paler than before but staying upright. "Are you going to be able to do that spell again? We've no idea how many demonspawn are in the throne room."

"I have to be. Just remember, don't let them take me." The strength he used to grab Storm's arm was a good sign.

"I'll kill you myself if it comes to that."

Keanin smiled. "Thank you. Let's finish this."

The stairway Hon led them up was in far better shape than the others. He stopped in front of a heavy door. "This is the throne room. A side entrance only, but once we commit, this is it."

"Shall we?" Storm took a deep breath and they shoved open the door.

The throne room wasn't as full as he'd feared, but full enough to make this a very short fight. Edgar and Keanin ran in, with Edgar chanting the disclosure spell as he ran.

Storm almost threw up as at least a hundred courtiers and nobles changed into demonspawn. The king didn't and luckily for him, none of the guards around him did. They closed ranks and pushed the king behind them.

Keanin spelled the demonspawn but it was clearly harder this time. He repeated the spell twice before they all rose high enough to be unable to lash out at anyone near them, but they'd already struck down a few people. Keanin shook as he tried to keep them up, finally dropping to one knee. The demonspawn were starting to choke but were still active when Keanin collapsed and they landed. Weakened, but still deadly, the exposed demonspawn sprinted for the king.

Knights came rushing in to fight back against the demonspawn.

Storm ran back to Keanin. He was breathing but his eyes had rolled back in his head.

Ignored by the knights fighting the dying demonspawn, Hon stood at a nearby window. He came back swearing. "Those pregnant women-who-aren't-women just left in a carriage heading for the docks."

Keanin fluttered at that and the others helped pick him up. "We can't let them leave."

"Agreed." Storm looked around and spotted the public

access stairway—which right now was empty. "This way."

Keanin leaned on Talia but he was recovering as they ran down the stairs.

Edgar kept going once they got outside and came back with a string of horses. "No time for saddles. Those demonspawn have a lead on us and a ship waiting."

"Damn it, they're going for the *Golden Harpy*." Diath jumped on an unsaddled horse and took off.

Keanin waved aside help. "I'll collapse after we've destroyed them." He didn't do it gracefully, but he got on a horse as well as the rest of them and they raced down the road.

The carriage the women had been in was dumped at the entrance to the dock, blocking it, so they got off their horses and ran. To see the *Golden Harpy* cutting lines and sailing directly out to sea.

"Don't they need to take the channel?" Storm swore as the ship took off. They must have had a crew standing by. One with enough magic for them to sail against the wind.

"Never seen someone do that." An old fisherman coiling his lines shook his head as he looked over. "You all supposed to be on that ship? It's suicide to go out the way they're going. Be glad you missed it." He nodded and went back to his work.

Keanin was stunned as he watched the ship. "No. They can't get away." He started to collapse as the adrenaline he'd been running on finally gave out. Storm and Talia caught him before he fell.

"I don't want to rush things," Diath said as he looked behind them. "But we might want to leave. Folks are taking notice and once they finish with those demonspawn in the castle, we're going to be brought in."

Talia nodded and shifted Keanin to Storm. "I think our ship should still be here. Hopefully." She led them down the dock to the smaller one where the *Reef Dancer* was docked.

"*Our* ship?" Diath laughed and jumped on board. "Looks sound."

The rest got on board and got Keanin into a cot.

"And we have friends coming our way." Diath had cast off the lines and was moving them out but this wasn't the time for the channel. They'd have to go out on the open ocean too. The knights coming their way pointed out they didn't have time to sort things out.

"Go. Just take off. We can figure things out later. The guards might have finished off the demonspawn, but I don't think we want to be around answering questions." Edgar was watching the knights, but he had Keanin's bow and quiver near his feet.

"I can help." Keanin was whiter than the sails and barely standing, but he was on deck. The sails filled and Diath headed them out to sea. "I don't care where we go, as long as it's not here."

Storm helped Keanin stand as they looked out over the ocean.

CHAPTER SIXTY-ONE

"WE HAVEN'T WON, not by a longshot," Ghortin said. And we'll have to make sure all magic users know the spell to disclose the demonspawn. It's an old one and not common."

Jenna rocked back. She'd pushed aside her terror at whatever was happening to Storm and the others while they were fighting to save Ghortin. It all came slamming back now. And clearly showed on her face even though she said nothing.

Carabella dropped an arm around Jenna's shoulders. "Don't give up on him. Storm is a lot tougher than even he knows. They'll survive. I know they will."

Jenna couldn't say anything but leaned into Carabella. They had to have survived.

They hid as the guards marched by, but there was no indication that any of them picked up on their magic signatures. Ghortin's trick had worked and judging by the way the guards were heading out into the woods, the crows were giving them a good run.

"That is a very tricky spell." Carabella made herself comfortable on a pile of fabric next to Jenna. "I'll expect you to show me how it's done when we've solved my little magic issue."

Ghortin nodded and then jumped and grabbed the taran wand from his vest. His smile was huge as he listened. "I am so glad to hear your voice, even if you are running. Let me get her." He handed the wand to Jenna.

"Can't talk, running for ship, but we're still alive. Will see you in a week or so back in Lithunane." Storm's voice was breathy but Jenna had never been so happy to hear someone in her life. "We're going back on the water, so might be out of touch for a bit."

"Stay safe, all of you." She wanted to say more but the wand cut off. "I think he got on the boat." She wiped away her tears. "I'm so glad they're okay."

Carabella beamed as if it was all her doing. "I told you."

Ghortin had just put the wand back when it started up again. "What now? Maybe more good news, we could use it." He held the wand up. "Yes? Things are great here—well, not great, but we saved the Strann empire. How are you?"

Jenna shook her head. Yes, they stopped the attack and got Ravenhearst out of the picture for now. But she wasn't convinced he was dead. No body, no proof. She knew a lot of people who would like to dance on his body when it happened.

The voice on the other end was faint and Ghortin had to hold the wand close to his ear. He was no longer laughing and had gone pale. "You've done what you can. Thank the deities that the rest of the family was still in Irundail. Safe travels. I'll make sure Crell warns her rangers. Do Storm and the others know? Understood, tell them, and then get out of there." His hands shook as he ended the call.

"What's happened?" Jenna felt sick to her stomach at the sense of foreboding that hit her.

"Lithunane has fallen." Ghortin's voice cracked and he couldn't look at any of them.

"What? How?" Jenna was stunned and only half heard Ghortin's next words.

"Resstlin and most of his advisors were murdered last night. Their bodies were found behind locked and bolted doors. At least half of the guards were also killed before anyone knew they were under attack. Garlan, Tor Ranshal, and Rachael survived but the fighting is bad. No one is certain who is behind it, the attacks have been sudden and brutal. They and the rest of the survivors are heading north to Irundail." He looked lost as he tucked the wand away. Irundail was a few weeks' travel by wagon from Lithunane. Those would be hard weeks if the attackers hounded them.

Crell immediately pulled her wand out and called Tigen to warn the derawri people. She also asked that the deathsworn go south to help the survivors of Lithunane. Then she contacted one of her rangers to pass on the warning and call for assistance to them. Her words were sharp and terse as she ordered the rangers to flee north to Irundail and help others doing the same. There were several small villages close to Lithunane that needed to be cleared out as well.

"We saved Strann from whatever hell Ravenhearst and Linton had planned. Storm, Keanin, and Edgar saved Khelaran from the demonspawn—and we've lost our own kingdom?" Jenna watched as the people of Strann went about their daily business in the market. Most had no idea how close they came to falling under the control of the followers of Qhazborh, let alone that just to the south of them another kingdom was not so lucky.

"The kingdom isn't lost yet, but losing Resstlin and Lithunane are horrific blows," Ghortin said.

"So we're going to war." Jenna thought of Meith's warning. This was the path above all others they needed to avoid. And it was already before them.

THE END

DEAR READER,

Thank you for joining me on another adventure with Jenna, Storm, and the rest. As always, I appreciate you for coming along on the newest escapade. The next book in this series will be out in 2022.

If you want to keep up on the further adventures of any of my characters, make sure to visit my website and sign up for my mailing list.

http://marieandreas.com/index.html

You can also sign up on Amazon to follow me and they will keep you updated.

https://geni.us/NZ6jX0o

If you enjoyed this book, please spread the word! Positive reviews are like emotional gold to any writer. And mean more than you know.

Thank you again—and keep reading!

ABOUT THE AUTHOR

MARIE IS A multi-award-winning fantasy and science fiction author with a serious reading addiction. If she wasn't writing about all the people in her head, she'd be lurking about coffee shops annoying total strangers with her stories. So really, writing is a way of saving the masses. She lives in Southern California and is owned by two very faery-minded cats. She is also a proud member of SFWA (Science Fiction and Fantasy Writers of America).

When not saving the masses from coffee shop shenanigans, Marie likes to visit the UK and keeps hoping someone will give her a nice summer home in the Forest of Dean or Conwy, Wales.

CPSIA information can be obtained
at www.ICGtesting.com
Printed in the USA
FSHW010703150921
84704FS

9 781951 506148